INHERITANCE

AN AGRIPUNK THRILLER

THE MARTINIERE LEGACY BOOK ONE

JOYCE REYNOLDS-WARD

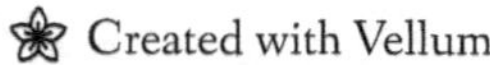 Created with Vellum

CHAPTER 1

Ruby Barkley hadn't worn this much makeup for a long time. She felt like scrunching her facial muscles to see if they could still move as she walked down the hallway from Makeup to the Green Room, but resisted the temptation. Not that the cosmetic job would as much as crack. She knew better, from wearing makeup like this during her years in the rodeo queen world, though not this heavy. The right formulation would hold up to anything, including blizzards and driving rain. But it had been a long time since she'd done the rodeo queen thing.

Too many years wearing just moisturizer and mineral powder.

Ranch work didn't require much else, if even that. But getting reaccustomed to wearing heavy makeup was just another unpleasant necessity for recording the presentation of the 2059 AgInnovator Superhero Contest finalists.

Three point seven five million dollars at stake, she reminded herself.

Ruby touched the silver locket at her neck. She'd polished it this morning until it shone, a pre-competition task that went back over forty years to her earliest junior rodeo days. When she hadn't worn it, things had gone wrong.

A door opened and an androgynous dark-haired, almost fishbelly-pale figure wearing the dark green and blue uniform of an AgI indentured worker careened through it, crashing into Ruby. The chain holding the locket snapped and it fell to the floor before Ruby could grab it, popping open. The small picture inside fell out.

"Oh! I'm sorry!" The indentured person's voice was flat, almost mechanically so. They knelt and picked up the locket and chain, handing it to Ruby. As their dark brown eyes met hers, they cringed away, turning their gaze to the floor. "Oh no. Ms. Barkley, I'm so sorry. I didn't mean to do it."

"It's all right," Ruby said. "But can you get the picture for me, please?"

"Oh. Yes. I'm sorry, so very sorry," the indentured whimpered as they gathered the picture between index finger and thumb and held it out to Ruby with a shaking hand. Ruby gently took it, half-smiling at the old, faded picture of Gramps and Granma Ryder.

Need to reglue it when I get back to the ranch.

She fit the picture back inside the locket, and it stayed in place as she checked it, then examined the chain. Ruby sighed with relief as she saw that the jump ring holding the clasp had loosened. She could repair it when she got back to her room tonight.

"It will be all right," she said to the indentured as she slipped locket and chain into the pocket of the fringed white buckskin jacket that had been part of her Pendleton Round-Up Princess wear.

"Please don't complain. Please," the indentured begged.

"Why would I? It was an accident, and it's fixable."

The indentured bowed low, almost touching their head to

their knees before straightening up. "I thank you, Ms. Barkley. Thank you, thank you, thank you!" They backed away from Ruby until they reached the next door, and ducked inside.

Ruby frowned.

Now what was that all about?

Some companies were harsh with their indentured workers, but she hadn't thought that the AgInnovator, AgI, would be one of them. Then, on the other hand, she was seeing a lot more indentured here than there had been three years ago, when she'd won a one-year Innovator award.

Maybe it's about the pressure from it being the twenty-fifth anniversary of the AgI. Or because I'm a Superhero finalist.

She shrugged. Nothing she could do about it now. All the same, she rubbed her fingers over the locket tucked away in her right pocket as she continued down the hallway toward the Green Room. A lot had changed over the past twenty-five years, and not just the weather.

Ruby stopped at the door, taking a deep breath and giving the locket one last squeeze. She patted the crown of her good luck silver belly Stetson hat that was part of this ensemble. Her hat—and hair—stayed firmly in place. At least she'd won the battle of the hair. The stylist had wanted to curl Ruby's silver-streaked, long red hair and create an up-do that wouldn't go with her hat. Ruby had insisted, and now her hair swung free with just a hint of hairspray. Except for the silver in her hair and the lines on her face, the image that looked back at her from the mirror once the cosmetician and hair stylist were done was almost exactly like that of Ruby the Round-Up princess.

She slipped into the Green Room and paused before diving into the crowd of competitors, Innovator staff, and AgI indentured around the prepackaged snacks and drinks, her stomach churning with high-key anticipation of *showtime* like it used to do before every run-in at the beginning of a rodeo performance.

Only then she'd had Sunshine with her, the palomino mare quivering eagerly, just waiting for the gate to swing wide so she could explode into a gallop as the announcer bellowed *"And here's Queen Ruby Barkley, from Thunder County Days!"* Or *"Princess Ruby Barkley from the Pendleton Round-Up!"* Or *"Your Miss Rodeo Oregon, Ruby Barkley!"*

Buck up, girl, it's just another Innovator announcement, she told herself. *Everyone else here is just as nervous as you are and they're just as desperate to win the Innovator money, no matter what level they're at. We're all broke farmers and ranchers, here to entertain the big-city world.*

Ruby walked further into the room and clicked up the cam bot provided her by AgI for social media postings during the Superhero competition. It darted out from its docking station on her wrist and hovered in front of her. She smiled widely as it took her picture, the same rodeo queen smile she'd perfected years ago.

Getting ready to go into the Green Room for the AgInnovator Finalist announcements. Wish me luck! she dictated subvocally.

A hologram hovered in front of Ruby, and she checked picture and sound before clicking *send*, not only to her personal channels but to the official AgInnovator site. The *Approved* chime from the AgI site dinged in her earpiece. Good. Ruby clicked the bot back to its dock and strode toward the food and drink. She didn't have Sunshine but she did have the familiar swirl of her old Round-Up chinks around her legs. Part of the costume and role-play for this competition. At least this formal Round-Up outfit still fit.

Here I go. It's just another Innovator. Let the games begin.

And yet it wasn't *just another Innovator.* The final stages of the RubyBot's development and licensing depended on this competition. Twenty-five years of hard work distilled down to one month of social media campaigning, product launch, and close scrutiny by the AgI inspection teams to assess her project for viability. So close to completion...but so far away, if she couldn't get the bucks from the Superhero Innovator. $3,750,000 a year for five years, and unlike the Superstar, no need to show progress toward a reported goal.

But only one of us five can win. And it's got to be me.

"Excuse me," she said to the flannel-clad back of a burly man chatting with a sharp-faced blonde woman, right in front of the food and drink. Ruby's lips tightened until she got a clear view of the woman's face. Not Mariah. Good.

"Sorry," Flannel Man said, turning toward Ruby. His eyes widened as he recognized her. "Um, really sorry, Ms. Barkley!" He backed away from the table, edging out the blonde.

Ruby widened her smile at him. "No need to apologize—and call me Ruby." She recognized him as one of the lesser finalists, up for one of the first level Innovator prizes, a one-year $50,000 grant. "Don Lane from Tillamook, right? Dairy farmer?"

Lane nodded, his long dark beard wagging. "Really sorry, Ruby," he repeated.

She waved it off. "It's a crowd in here. To be expected." She deftly ducked into the opening Lane had given her and grabbed a can of green tea. "But I do thank you for the opening to grab some tea." It was too damned congested in here for her comfort, even with fresh C-19 and G9 vaccinations required before the recording.

"You're welcome. And—good luck."

"Same to you." She eyed the food and decided she didn't want any just yet, even though it looked like real food and not synth. Not the way her gut was churning. "But I suspect you're in good shape to pick up an Innovator. Not everyone shows up for every recording at that competition level, and appearances count in this game. The more you promote and cooperate with the appearance schedule, the better your chances are."

Lane grimaced. "I know. I lost the Superstar in my third year because I couldn't get away from the farm for the final report, and my stats were borderline. Windstorm played havoc with the main feeding barn and, well…non-appearance plus borderline stats got me cut."

"Yeah. I know that dance far too well myself." She dipped her head in acknowledgment. "I've been there. Good luck." She turned away from Lane to survey the rest of the room, tensing slightly. Both Mariah and Gabe were finalists for the Superhero Innovator, and for a moment she'd thought the blonde was Mariah.

"Mom." Her son Brandon, one of the Innovator producers, made his way through the crowd to join her, suave in his tailored navy-blue suit and neatly trimmed black beard against brown skin that reminded Ruby of his father Gabe at that age. "You're ready to go?"

"Been through makeup and all."

He surveyed her, frowning slightly. "Your Round-Up outfit and not Thunder County Queen?"

"I prefer this one. Fits the older me better—gotta lose more weight for the Thunder County outfits. I was a skinny teen way back when. Plus, most people know the Round-Up better than the Days."

"Gotcha." Brandon took her arm. "We're staging the Super-heroes over here." He gestured to a corner and rolled his eyes. "I'm trying to sort everyone out as they come out of Makeup. Tight schedule with the addition of the Superheroes this year."

"Understood." Maybe she'd be able to make nice with the two Superhero nominees who *weren't* Gabe and Mariah, a pork rancher from the Midwest and a rice farmer from the South.

"Mariah is still in Makeup," Brandon said. He rolled his eyes. "Running late, or so she told Markey. Did you see her?"

"Why am I not surprised? And no, I didn't see Mariah. Not that I'd acknowledge her anyway."

Brandon snorted as he guided Ruby toward the corner. "So far it's just Dad here for your group. The other two are running late as well. But Swait had a legitimate traffic issue and Cho apparently needed to deal with a sick kid before leaving the hotel. Mariah was in the building and just dawdled her way in —not to worry, Ma, you still beat her hands down when it comes to looking good for your age."

But my looks weren't enough to keep your father, Ruby thought bitterly as they approached the corner. She saw Gabe in one of the overstuffed chairs in the corner, hand resting on a cane, and startled.

He looks old.

Even so, spotting him still made her heart jump momentarily, just like it had when she first saw him swinging a leg over a saddle bronc. Then anger quickly tightened her gut as she remembered other incidents.

No time for that.

She hadn't seen Gabe for seven years—no, eight—since Brandon had turned eighteen, and their shared custody had ended. His dark hair was clipped close to his head, more gray than black, and his goatee was mostly gray and white with a few black streaks. His normally brown skin had gone pale. He struggled to his feet, leaning heavily on the cane, and stretched out his right hand.

"Ruby, dear. It's good to see you." He'd clearly lost a lot of weight.

She moved her tea to her other hand and clasped his. *Presumptuous of him to assume I want any physical contact. But now was not a good time to object.*

What?

She fought back her startle at the touch, her hand lingering in his for more than the barest of formalities. Gabe's hand was dry. Warm. Soft. When had Gabe gone soft? This was *not* what she expected to feel in Gabe's hand.

He's really gone downhill.

"Good to see you, too," she said mechanically, still off-kilter and surprised.

He sighed, letting his fingers trail along her palm before thumping back down into his seat. "I'm sorry to be rude and sit back down, but I'm still in rehab."

Ruby winced. "I didn't realize."

He gestured at the chair next to him. "Go ahead and sit here if you'd like. Recovering from the G9 virus is no walk in the park. You're lucky to have avoided it."

G9 virus. That explains a lot.

She hadn't been at risk because of Thunder County's swift quarantine measures. But the reports she heard about G9 were horrific. Hallucinations. Body aches. Seizures. High fevers. Post-G9 syndrome that mimicked polio and other nasty viruses in long-term effects, especially cardiac. Not something she would wish on anyone, even Gabe. And now that she thought about it, Brandon *had* told her when Gabe contracted G9.

As Ruby sat, she noticed that the other chairs were grouped further away from Gabe's seat. From the faint smile Brandon gave them, she suspected the arrangement was deliberate on his part. Brandon snapped his fingers and a cam buzzed to him.

"Lean in close for a picture," he said.

"*Really*, Brandon," Ruby growled.

"It's good social media," Gabe said quietly.

"Yeah. After all, the two of you were winners in the first Superstar competition," Brandon said. "And now you're separately up for the Ag Superhero. Talk about history! Twenty-five years after the Innovator show started, and three of the original competitors have made it to the finalist stage."

"Big difference. This year we're competing in February, not October," Gabe said. "That's a change."

Brandon's lips tightened. "Too many other shows in the fall." Then he forced a smile. "The only thing that would be better media is if the two of you got back together during the competition."

"Yeah, no, that's not going to happen," Ruby said through her teeth as the bot snapped several shots. She didn't add *and what about Mariah? Wouldn't the showrunners love it if we replayed that drama? No, I don't want to go there.*

Gabe took her hand and leaned closer as Brandon beamed. "Stranger things have happened."

"You gonna support the RubyBot if we do get together for the show's sake?"

Now it was his turn to mutter through his teeth. "My microbials are a better option."

"And just how close to a distribution license have you gotten with them?"

"I'm getting there. Another couple of years."

"The RubyBot's in final trials."

"Well, congratulations," Gabe muttered in a tone that did not sound congratulatory at all. He started to release Ruby's hand, but then clamped down as he glared at someone on the other side of the room.

A hologram popped up in front of Brandon as he summoned the picture view, flicking through several shots before finding one where they were holding hands and both of them were smiling.

"You want copies?" Brandon spun the holo so they could see it clearly.

"Not really," Ruby said.

"Sure," Gabe said, his attention still focused elsewhere.

"I'll send one to both of you. But this one is upload worthy." He snapped his fingers and Ruby heard the faint chime as the picture landed in her inbox. Another snap and the drone whizzed away, apparently taking pictures of the gathering. Brandon typed something, then grinned.

"I've got to go, Mom, Dad," he said. "You be nice now!"

Ruby snorted. "I won't bite if he doesn't."

Gabe forced a chuckle. "Same old Ruby." He winced and leaned back in his chair, still clinging to Ruby's hand as if he'd forgotten he still held it. "God, this is tiring me more than I anticipated." His thumb started tracing a shape on her palm. A barrel-racing pattern? No. A trefoil.

"I didn't realize the G9 bug was so bad," she said. "Brandon told me it killed Rachel. I was sorry to hear that, Gabe. She made you happy. He didn't say anything about how severely you got it."

"The G9 came on fast," Gabe said, lips tightening. "Even as near as we are to Pendleton, though, it wasn't close enough. Rachel died during the medevac. They say my work with the microbials gave me some protection. She—she didn't get that."

"I'm sorry," Ruby repeated. The G9 hadn't made it to Thunder County. After the early reports, the County had blockaded the high mountain valley's entrances, with inspection and quarantine stations at the two roads that provided access to the Thunder Valley. County medical services had learned over the years to react quickly to fast-moving pandemics. High-mortality illnesses that left survivors crippled overloaded the County's limited medical services, and the G9 had been classified as one of those. After the mutated flu that nearly killed Brandon as a kid, things had changed.

"Yeah."

An uncomfortable silence fell between them. Gabe chewed

on his lip, eying Ruby as he still held her hand. Then he tensed, once again glowering as Philip Martiniere, head of the large Martiniere Group that had investments in assorted ag-related technologies as well as indentured labor pools, specialized body modifications, and more, walked in their direction.

"What the hell is he doing here?" Gabe growled.

Ruby shrugged. "I guess he's one of Georgy Batineau's investors." Batineau had been the owner of AgI until it had gone public ten years ago as other game show financing endeavors became popular. Now almost any major debt that could result in indenture had some sort of fundraising game show for a handful of lucky contestants. Medical debt. College debt. Gambling debt. And assorted small businesses and towns.

"He can buzz right off if he thinks I'm kissing his ass," Gabe said. His gaze didn't move from Philip Martiniere and his thumb retraced the trefoil on Ruby's palm as Martiniere matched Gabe stare for angry stare.

The Martiniere Group trefoil is what Gabe's tracing on my hand, she realized. *What on earth?* She knew there was some connection between Gabe and the Martinieres...when they first got together, he'd been on the run from their indentured bounty hunters. But she thought that had been taken care of years ago. Why would Philip Martiniere be interested in Gabe now?

Then *she* scowled as a slender, sharp-faced blonde woman in a shiny silver A-line sleeveless dress with matching stiletto heels joined Martiniere. Mariah Meyers.

"And there's Mariah," she said sourly, as Martiniere turned his back to them.

Gabe eased his grip slightly but didn't let go of Ruby's hand until Martiniere moved off, Mariah in tow.

"So. It sounds like you're still flogging the RubyBot." Traces of his angry growl still hung in his voice. Was his anger aimed at her or at Martiniere? She wasn't sure.

"And you're still pushing microbials," she countered.

Gabe shook his head. "Ruby, Ruby, Ruby. The RubyBot's tech is just too complicated to sustain in the field. You keep trying to put too much into it. That's what screwed us over the first time."

"What screwed us over the first time was your distraction with Mariah and not paying attention to the growbox while Brandon was sick!" Ruby snapped.

"Ruby. That's unfair."

"Is it? And speak of the devil...." Ruby's voice trailed off as Mariah left Philip Martiniere and walked toward them.

"Well, well, well, if it isn't the old gang," Mariah drawled. "Did they go out of their way to recruit the first Superstar winners or what?"

"Just the three of us," Gabe snapped. He remained seated. "Temira and Jeff weren't there."

"Hog poop and dryland rice." Mariah rolled her eyes.

"Any better than GMO corn?" Ruby shot back.

"It's RNAi manipulation," Mariah said, an exasperated tone in her voice. "Gene switching is *not* genetic manipulation. Just turning on switches already there in the RNA. And I don't do GMOs, I do blockchain trackers."

"And how easily can they be altered to fit your record needs?" Ruby bit back a grin as Mariah scowled. *Got you.*

"Ruby—" she began.

"Attention! Attention!" Brandon clapped his hands in the center of the room, interrupting Mariah's response. "It's showtime, folks. I'll see you out there. Markey will herd you out by group." He pointed to Markey, a tall Black woman with neatly cornrowed hair, then strode out of the room.

"She's not using any hotshots, is she?" one of the other ranchers joked.

"No, but I've got rattlers and flags," Markey answered,

laughing. She brandished her pad. "All right! Innovators on deck. I'll call the rest of you as we're ready. Let's line up by group next to the door—got you." She glanced down at her pad, frowning. "Aren't we short a few?"

"One way to weed them out," the blonde who had been talking to Don Lane giggled. Ruby flinched as she spotted a green and blue diamond-shaped tattoo on the webbing between thumb and index finger of the woman's left hand. *Another AgI indentured.* She half-wondered what this one's role was—attractive, perhaps an entertainer?

Ruby exhaled and sipped on her tea. A heavy-set Black man and a stocky, muscular Asian woman followed one of the indentureds to their cluster.

"Temira Cho," the woman said, smiling politely. "I'm the hog poop girl." From the sharpness of her tone and the glance she gave Mariah, it was clear she'd heard Mariah's comments. "I guess we sit and wait until they call us."

"And Jeff Swait, rice."

"Ruby Barkley, various grains and cattle," Ruby said.

"Gabriel Ramirez, same products as Ruby, but you can call me Gabe."

"Mariah Meyers, futures and farm-to-table tracking software."

More uncomfortable silence after their introductions.

"So, what Innovators have you won?" Ruby asked politely when the silence grew too heavy.

"Star Innovator, 2043," Temira said as she sat in the next closest chair to Gabe. She sighed. "Made it for three years, washed out in my fourth."

"Oh, that was close," Ruby said.

"Not as close as you two were."

"Close is close," Gabe said tightly. "And the Star with only one year's failure allowed is tough."

"But Ruby, you've won a Star since your Superstar, right?" Jeff said. "Completing the Star is an accomplishment in itself."

"Well—yes," Ruby said.

Mariah sniffed. "*Completing* the Superstar is better than any Star."

"Only if you don't get indicted for fraudulent organic grain sales." Ruby took advantage of that opening. She didn't get many opportunities around Mariah.

"I was *acquitted*," Mariah growled. "And you know it."

Silence again.

Jeff cleared his throat. "I've won a couple of Innovators, but nothing big, just the yearly prizes." He looked at Gabe and Ruby. "I watched your progress in the original Superstar, decided that maybe I needed to stick with the small stuff until I knew more about how my adaptations worked. I'm working on improving drought resistance in dryland rice strains."

"Microbials?" Gabe asked.

Jeff shook his head. "Some RNA manipulation, some biobots. I had to play around with drought resistance before I found the right mix that I could put in one product. But I wanted to make sure things worked before I applied for the Superstar and when the Superhero came up..." he shrugged. "How could I not go for it instead? I've got good tech and good support, and the symbiotic combination of Swaitrice and Swaitbot really works."

Ruby nodded. She'd been following the releases about Jeff's bots, nervous that the tech was too close to her RubyBot. But the Swaitbot lacked the feedback reporting mechanisms she'd wrestled for years to stick into the Ruby, and was tied to only one crop.

"I'm finishing up a closed loop application, not just with generating my own energy but developing a produce line for regional markets," Temira said. "Dealing with the poop is a big part of it, along with swine fever resistance." She grimaced. "Synthpork is really popular but there's enough high-end demand for the real thing. I'm trying to add organic vegetable production in order to use—" she rolled her eyes, "—*hog poop*, but it's tough to establish with microclimate weather changes. I also have my own butcher shop and offer custom services. I'm not offering a singular device like the rest of you but an entire system."

"Superhero contenders!" Markey called. "It's your turn! Line up over here."

Ruby paused to click up her camera bot again.

Going into the show now, she dictated. She noticed the others doing the same with their cams.

As she sent the shot to the AgI site, she saw the caption Brandon had added to the picture he'd uploaded of her and Gabe. FORMER SUPERSTARS GETTING TOGETHER AGAIN AFTER THEIR DIVORCE? STAY TUNED TO AGINNOVATORS FOR THE LATEST EXCITEMENT!

Goddamn it, Brandon! she thought. But there was no time to say anything as Markey herded them past Brandon and backstage.

I am so going to chew him out later, she decided, left hand tapping against the white leather of her chinks while she practiced her rodeo queen wave with the right, waiting for her cue. Just before she stepped on the stage, she took a quick moment to stuff her hand in her pocket and rub the locket.

RUBY'S STOMACH ROILED AND GRUMBLED BY THE TIME SHE reached the off-site afterparty held in the penthouse offices of one of the major AgI principals. Of course, there had been pictures after the recording. *And* the mandatory short interviews with AgI investors and screeners for a future show. *And* politely brushing off paparazzi excited by Brandon's presumptuous suggestion about getting back together with Gabe. *And* scheduling the weeks when she'd be audited by the AgI inspectors—essentially, someone from AgI would be on the Double R every week during the next month. All tedious, but necessary as part of the pathway to victory. She could have put all that off until morning, but she wanted to leave Los Angeles as quickly as possible after the formal breakfast tomorrow.

Brandon was right about the appeal of me and Gabe getting back together.

It seemed like the official media wanted to talk to both her and Gabe, enough that they were the last contenders to reach the party.

"Sorry there's not much food left," one of the indentureds said as they rushed to Ruby's side. "We got shorted on our orders. But I can offer you some slurry."

Ruby wrinkled her nose. "If it's all you've got...." At least she had real food back at her hotel room. Slurry would hold her appetite until then. And this indentured didn't have the brittle nervousness of the blonde in the Green Room or the servility of the indentured that had crashed into her in the hallway.

"I'm afraid so. Red, green, or yellow?"

"Make it green, and add a shot of whisky to it." She eyed the crowd. Still too many people for her comfort level. "Make that a double shot." Green slurry was the closest one to real food, the whisky would make it palatable, and she'd need the fortification to handle anything that might pop up in connection with Gabe or Mariah.

"Will do."

Ruby sighed. She looked around again. The number of indenture-branded people present set her teeth on edge. AgI hadn't struck her as a company that would bind that many to its service due to debt. Or was this the fate of failed contestants?

Don't think about that, she told herself for the umpteenth time. *Remember that there's been a bad recession and the fact you're still ranching is a win. You're not a climate refugee and your lands are still producing.*

Some of that was due to sheer luck, but a lot to the good practices that the Ryders had practiced in Northeastern Oregon since the Depression.

All the same it haunted her. Too many nightmares over the years about being forced into the ranks of the indentured, if not her then Brandon. Too many late nights doing other peoples' books to see how easily falling into indenture could happen. And now to see indenture shoved into her face so blatantly....

Stop it.

She made herself look for her opponents. Gabe had gotten here before her. He now sat in a chair, surrounded by a crowd. As always. But was that a plate of real food in his lap? She growled to herself, annoyed. *Of course* Gabe had managed to find food, or persuaded someone to hold him a plate. Where were Jeff and Temira? Or Brandon? She spotted Brandon talking to a couple she didn't recognize, and marched toward him. The indentured server intercepted her with the glass of green slurry.

"Thank you." She took a sip. It was hard to decide if it was decent slurry or if the sharp bite of the synthwhisky made it better. The alcohol should have cut down on any bacterial contamination, not that green slurry held that many issues. It was the blandest-tasting of the slurries, but also the safest. She still didn't like it. Another sip, and she continued on her way to her son.

"Brandon. We need to talk."

"Just a minute." He turned back to the others.

"Brandon." She used her sharpest *Mother is unhappy* horse trainer voice, crossing her arms as best as she could with her slurry and tapping her right boot toe. He winced.

"Excuse me, but I need to talk to my mother," he said. He backed away from the couple and joined Ruby. "Now what, Mom?"

She jerked her head toward the balcony. At least the Los Angeles air was breathable tonight. "Private."

He sighed as he followed her. "Is this about the upload? I *told* you it would make for good media."

Ruby coughed. Even though the air was allegedly breathable, there was still enough stuff in it to irritate her nose and lungs that were more accustomed to clean, fresh, mountain air.

"*Yes,* it's about the upload," she growled, taking a bigger gulp of her slurry. "You had no right. Especially since it's never going to happen."

"Mom, you're going to have to do something above and beyond the normal Innovator competition to win this one."

"I've managed to complete a Star and win a couple of Innovators."

"I know. And I know what it took from you to do it. I was there when you did all that, remember?"

"You don't think I can win without that sort of game-playing."

Brandon sighed. "Mom. I'm trying as best as I am able to give you an edge within the limitations given that I'm now a producer of the show. Winning these things isn't just about the quality of your innovation. It's also about your public appeal. The viewing audience needs more than plain old stats. They need drama. A story. What happens if you lose the Superhero? I know from the quarterly ranch reports that you're struggling financially."

"I'll get another loan."

"With what? Look. You're not getting any younger."

"We're so close with the RubyBot. Last stage of the licensing."

"And how many years have I heard that refrain? Come on, I still have a twenty-five percent share in the ranch. I know what your financial status is." Brandon ran his fingers through his hair, a nervous tic he shared with Gabe. "Listen. If you combine efforts with Dad, you've got a better chance of winning. Of getting everything paid off, settled with creditors, and some boosts to finalize the RubyBot over the next five years. Then maybe you can retire and won't have to work so hard."

"Hard work doesn't hurt anyone. Not like sitting on your ass."

"Mom. We almost lost Dad last year to the G9. All it takes is one bad illness and you'd be in the same position that he is, if not worse, and not *able* to work as hard as you want. Meanwhile, AgI can use your vision. Your skills. Your ability to assess new tech. I'd like to bring you both into the company."

Ruby gulped down the rest of the green slurry/whisky mix. "Is hiring us for the company what this is all about? How we both ended up in the finals?"

"No. Well—partially yes. Part of it is scripting out a story."

"And if I play along with the story, then I've a better chance of winning?"

"*Both* of you together have a better chance of winning."

"Then the voting is skewed, and the only reason I made to the finals is so you could set us up with a romantic storyline to fulfill your childhood dreams of reuniting us. I should have known." She turned to go back inside.

"Mom. No. It's not like that." He swallowed hard. "I'm just doing show production. I have no control over the voting. I'm firewalled from that because of you and Dad. But I will tell you that the team's run some probable outcomes, and—the story of you and Dad getting back together because of the Superhero is a really high vote-getter. The audience doubles if you do, with high approval ratings. It's not just me wanting to see you two together again. The top execs think it would be really good for the show."

"Well, if they think it's so good, why don't they just say so? Or turn it into a romance show?"

Of course they have to jazz it up. Too much competition for clicks these days.

"Mom."

Ruby sighed. "I'm not happy about this, Brandon. And I want to see what you send out about us in the future first."

"Prior approval isn't in your contract."

She rolled her eyes. "All I'm asking for is simple human decency. I'm going to have to deal with the issue in my own social media. I'd like to know about any bombshells before they land, okay? I'm not asking for veto authority. Obviously, I can't."

Though I'm gonna have Remy look at my contract again, just in case.

"Will you cooperate with the storyline?"

"I guess I have to, don't I? Within reason, I'll cooperate."

His face softened. "Thanks, Mom. Now I really have to get back to those folks. They're doing some innovative work in tropical bioremediation. AgI—" he looked around cautiously and lowered his voice. "We're looking into expansion into bioremediation, and they work with the leading company. No names. It's on the hush right now, okay? But if I can land them for a future Superstar or even just a special report, that's a big gain for me. And if we can get them to market through AgI— even better. But I've gotta negotiate it."

"All right. Go schmooze."

He kissed her on the cheek and hurried off. Ruby sighed. What had her little boy grown into? Once she had hoped he would follow her footsteps and take over the Double R. It didn't seem possible now.

She rejoined the party, fatigue and the noise around her making the crush unbearable. At last she decided to leave. Tomorrow was going to be a long day.

Mariah intercepted her on the way to the door. "Ruby. Got a moment?"

"Depends on the subject." Ruby tensed. What sort of scam was Mariah planning now? And yet—sometimes Mariah's plots worked out. It made sense to at least hear her pitch, if only to know what she was planning. She nodded. "Sure. I've got a moment. But not for very long. Tomorrow's a travel day. I need to get back to the ranch."

"Come on." Mariah jerked her head toward a closed door. She tapped a code into the lock and they entered an office paneled in a dark red wood—or stained? Ruby couldn't decide which. She wondered how Mariah had managed access to such an opulently-furnished office. Then again, the woman did have connections everywhere, business and romantic alike.

Mariah walked over to a sidebar with a half-full decanter. "Drink?"

"Might as well." She'd need it for whatever Mariah was going to bring up.

Mariah poured both of them generous straight shots. "Straight up, no ice, if I remember correctly."

"You do." Ruby sipped the whisky, savoring the smoky flavor. Not synthwhisky but a good quality authentic Scotch, probably older than the AgInnovator since production of genuine Scotch single malts had faded in the last twenty years due to resource limitations in Scotland. Her lab manager Martin was experimenting with the distilling process back home at the ranch. But that was purely small batch artisan production, a break from the lab work on the RubyBot using excess from their grain crops.

"A toast to innovation." Mariah raised her glass.

"To innovation." Ruby sipped her drink as Mariah gulped hers down. "What do you want, Mariah?"

Mariah laughed. "Never one for the social maneuvering, eh, Ruby?" She drank the rest of her whisky. "So here it is. Once the competition is over next month, I'll make you an offer on the Double R. Ranch, production facilities, everything. You retain patents and intellectual property rights on the RubyBot. But the rest of it? I'll give you a good number, based on how things turn out in the competition."

"And the royalty income?"

"You'll get a share of it."

"Why would I want to sell to you? I'm going to win."

Mariah snorted. "You keep telling yourself that, girl. Look. I know you're in financial trouble."

"That's the definition of a good farmer or rancher."

"I'm trying to be nice here." Mariah's lips pursed for a moment, then relaxed. "I know what the AgI is trying to do with you and Gabe. I saw the post from Brandon. I also know that there's no chance in hell that you're going to get back together with him. Will you win if you don't? I don't think so. And if you don't accept now, my offer will be lower then."

"Easy to talk without throwing out dollar figures." Ruby savored another rich, smoky sip.

"Ten million, then, give or take a few hundred thousand. Only if you commit now. Otherwise it goes down by two million every time I ask."

Ruby choked on her sip. "That's all? The Ruby's worth more than that once it's in full production."

"Ah, but you're got to get it there," Mariah said. "How

many years have you been fiddling with it? Ever since the first Innovator? You'd think after twenty-five years you'd have *something* on the market."

"And how many times have you gone through indictments in that twenty-five years?"

Mariah's face hardened. "You're not going to get a better deal than this, Ruby. Especially if you let it drag until you can't leverage your debt any further without going into indenture."

Ruby tossed back the rest of her drink and set the glass down firmly on the desk, not caring if it left marks on the polished surface.

"And here's my answer, Mariah. Not just no, but *hell no*. I'll see the Double R trashed and destroyed before I let you and whomever you're fronting for get your claws into it. I grew up on that land. My family sacrificed a lot through many hard times to make it a going concern. You're the last person I want to see with that place. And I seriously doubt you can come up with that much money."

"Not right away, no," Mariah said. "But in the next month? You bet. I can come up with that money, faster and better than you can."

"I still don't believe it."

"Is that your final answer?"

"You'd better believe *that*." Ruby whirled and marched out of the door. Somehow, she managed to extract herself from the party and catch a rideshare back to her hotel. By then, she'd calmed down enough to post a final smiling picture in the rideshare with the caption *A nice time in the city and with the folks at AgI. But tomorrow I have to get back to work. Keep your eyes open for the next blast from Ruby Barkley and the Double R!*

Back at the hotel room, she took off the hat, washed and moisturized her makeup-stiffened skin, and carefully packed away her Round-Up outfit. Then she delicately reassembled the locket and placed it on the nightstand so she could put it back on in the morning. She poured herself a final drink from Martin's whisky and prepared herself a light dinner from ranch beef summer sausage, crackers, and the last, carefully hoarded dried carrots from the previous season's scant harvest to go with it. She dropped into a chair by the window and stared out at the bright glare of the city lights against the brownish-gray smog while she ate.

Here we go into the spotlight again, Ruby girl.

And it was going to be worse than before, especially with Mariah gunning for the ranch. Why?

Such an interest didn't fit anything that Ruby knew about that bitch Mariah Meyers.

Unless it's personal and she wants to screw me over one last time.

Ruby tossed down the last of her drink.

This time I'll win.

No man at stake for her now. The odds were in her favor.

CHAPTER 2

A RESTLESS NIGHT'S SLEEP AND A MILD HANGOVER contributed to fuzzy brain as Ruby entered the banquet room for—thankfully—the last event of *this* go-round at the Innovators. One of the indentured intercepted her as she wandered amongst the tables, looking for Temira and Jeff.

"The Superhero table is over here," the person said. Ruby noticed all the workers were sufficiently androgynous and alike in form that she half-wondered if AgI had developed either clones or lifelike androids.

Not likely.

More possible was that these were indentured with body-altering tech.

Hotel indentured?

No, they wore AgI-labeled polo shirts and brown slacks. But they all had similar facial structures despite their different skin color so that they looked disconcertingly alike. Ruby stifled a shudder. Thank God she and Gabe had managed to keep Brandon from falling into indenture, even with divorce, student loans, and the crash of the initial RubyBot.

Though what sort of hooks does AgI have into him?

Some employment contracts were little better than indentures if the company really wanted to control an employee.

She followed the indentured to a round table near the podium. Temira and Jeff were already there, looking uncomfortable, separated by an empty seat. The person guided Ruby to an empty chair across the table from them, between placards with Gabe and Brandon's names on them.

A man with silver and gray hair stopped three tables away, staring at the placards. Something about him looked familiar. A celebrity of some sort. Ruby bit her lip as she tried to place him, then realized who it was. *Philip Martiniere.* He scowled at her and turned away, heading for the main table.

"Thanks, but I'm moving." Ruby picked up her card and went to the empty seat between Jeff and Temira. Mariah's placard marked the place. Ruby handed the placard to the person. "You can put that one next to Gabe." Might as well get a feel for her new opponents.

"But Ms. Barkley...." Their objection trailed off at Ruby's glare.

"I really prefer to sit here. Please move this seat assignment."

The person sighed and placed Mariah next to Gabe. Ruby sat, noting that both Jeff and Temira relaxed.

"I hope you don't mind," she said as she reached for the carafe, hoping that since this was a high-end hotel there would be real coffee.

Jeff heaved a relieved sigh. "Not minding at all."

"I wasn't looking forward to sitting by Mariah. She was a bit over the top last night," Temira admitted. "Wanted to talk about buying my property once the Innovator is done."

Ruby stifled her startle at Temira's words by stirring powdered creamer and sweetener into her coffee. She took a tentative sip. Real coffee, but far from the best variety. But better than anything she could get in her hometown of Lakeside except for special occasions.

Not just me, then. What the hell?

"It sounds like Mariah's making multiple offers," Ruby said. "She also pitched me."

"And me," Jeff said. He shook his head. "I don't know how many times I told her *no*. I've got family I can hire that want to work on the land. What the hell would happen to them if I sold out? Not taking the chance of them becoming like *them*." He jerked his head toward a passing AgI minion.

"I'm hoping my kids will want to stay on the farm," Temira confessed. "But they're barely out of diapers."

"Do you still have a 4H program in your county?"

Temira shook her head. "Just Future Farmers of America at the high school."

Before they could say more, the minions set small plates of grapes, melon chunks, and fake cheeze on the table. Ruby helped herself generously to the grapes, and took a small piece of cheeze. Fake cheeze was so variable in quality. She broke off a smaller piece of her cheeze to sample it. One of the better versions of fake cheeze, she decided, a rich, buttery flavor that almost had the right mouth feel. She took a second chunk.

Mariah arrived at the table shortly after the fruit and cheeze, scowling at Ruby as she dropped into her chair. "I'll have a mimosa," she snarled at the server. She made a face at the plate of fruit and cheeze and nibbled at the grapes. "So, Ruby, I see you're already wheeling and dealing."

"Just like you were at the party last night, my dear," Ruby kept her voice steady as Mariah's glower deepened.

"I do have the best tracking systems," Mariah said. "Proven and reliable."

Ruby snorted. "And easily altered to show what you think the algorithm needs to reveal." Now she was *certain* that Mariah's role in the competition script was to add a further level of conflict between them.

Am I cynical or not? No, just too many years competing for the Innovator awards. Of course, they're going to script the conflicts between the finalists. That's why we were selected, not just because of the quality of our inventions. It's a game, Ruby, and you've got to play it, too, if you want the three point seven five million dollars for five years, she reminded herself. Striving to become the Round-Up Queen or Miss Rodeo America didn't have this much at stake. *And fewer knives in the back.*

"My Know-It algorithms are more reliable than your Ruby-Bot," Mariah countered. She took a big gulp from her mimosa as the server handed it to her, and grimaced. "The orange flavor is off in this substitute and the pulp is clearly a fake." She handed it back to the server.

"I'm sorry, Ms. Meyers. Supplier issues," the server said.

"Oh, I know. It's in all the market reports." Mariah waved her left hand airily. "But I had hopes that *this place* would have access to a better-quality juice product."

"Not in adequate quantities for everyone at this big an event, I am afraid, Ms. Meyers."

Mariah raised her brows. "But if I slipped you a fifty, what would that get me?"

"That—would be a different story, Ms. Meyers."

As Mariah continued to negotiate with the server for the higher quality mimosa, Gabe hobbled over and collapsed into his seat, giving Ruby a wistful smile.

She ignored him and returned to her conversation with Temira and Jeff. Brandon and Markey joined them, Brandon sitting next to Gabe and Markey by Mariah. Brandon frowned at Ruby. She shook her head at him and summoned up her camera bot to take a picture of herself, Temira, and Jeff that she could send out once they left the breakfast. At this point she was confident that the RubyBot could beat their programs. Though Jeff—his strategy was a good one, and if she wasn't in competition with him, she'd give him the edge over Temira.

He should have aimed for the Superstar instead.

A small twinge of guilt throbbed through her. Young competitors like these two were really the ones who the Superhero should be featuring, not old has-beens like her, Gabe, and Mariah.

On the other hand, they've got their lives ahead of them. For us this is the culmination of a life's work.

As the main course of a palm-sized omelet, synthbacon, and a small sugary pastry was handed out and the assorted dignitaries from AgI started speaking, Ruby tuned them out, running down a mental checklist of what she had to do both here in LA before she left and then in Portland before hitting the road.

She hoped breakfast didn't run too late. As it were, with everything she had to do, it'd be midnight before she reached the Double R. If she were lucky. It was a good thing she had done her interviews last night instead of leaving them for the morning.

* * *

WEATHER DELAYS PUT RUBY IN PORTLAND AT 4 PM. SHE messaged Rick Keysing at the AgSupply labs as she worked her way through baggage claim and out to the economy lot.

Please let the chargers be working, she wished as the shuttle drifted through the lot. She rubbed her locket as they stopped next to her truck. She shoved luggage and the supplies she'd picked up in LA into the back, tipped the shuttle guide, disconnected the slow charger, and climbed into the cab, holding her breath as she pressed the truck's start button.

Everything lit up and the charge indicator was full green. Ruby heaved a relieved sigh. The truck was just old enough to not always work well with the new version of chargers here at the airport. It was one thing that would be replaced if—*no when* —she won the Superhero. She selected AgSupply's location from the autodrive software and settled back to read the messages that had accumulated while she'd been on the damn shuttle flight.

Lots of generic media inquiries that she shunted off to her look-at-later, low-priority file. A few specific questions and interview requests that she'd deal with on the ride home. Nothing untoward in her updates from Charlie, the ranch manager at the Double R.

She clicked off her messages and settled back into her seat as the truck drove through Beaverton-Hillsboro to the labs near Forest Grove. Once it left the highway, Ruby had to take over driving. She muttered and cursed at the heavy stop-and-go traffic as the rain grew heavier near dusk. But even the heavy rain wasn't enough to wash out the industrial stink that hung around the metro area and wafted into the cab despite her filters.

Need to clean them before the next Portland trip, she told herself.

It was a relief to get away from traffic when she parked by the old cement-walled warehouse that held the AgSupply labs, even if it was only for a short time. Rick glowered at a holo over his desk as she entered the office.

"Beck's gonna have my head if you keep me too late," he grumbled.

Ruby handed him the bag she'd picked up in LA just for Rick and his partner Beck O'Toole. "Maybe this will make her happier?" she suggested.

Rick peeked in. "Oh—are those real avocados?"

"Supposed to be certified," Ruby confirmed. "I ran them through the tester. Tracker confirms local backyard origin— unless it's one of Mariah's fakes."

"Those damn things," Rick muttered. He poked in the bag. "Chocolate or cacao?"

"Cacao, I'm afraid. But look below it."

"Wait—is that real bacon?"

Ruby grinned. "A gift from a competitor, some of the samples she was handing out at AgI. Shelf-stabilized precooked, organic bacon from her own facility. Temira Cho's Happy Food Farms. Provenance—she gave this directly to me."

"Beck will forgive me a lot for avocados and real bacon," Rick said. "Even if the avocados aren't the best." He pushed his lanky form up and hobbled toward the warehouse. "You're gonna need to get these stems into a growbox pretty darn fast. No later than tomorrow morning."

Ruby grimaced. "Weather report has heavy snow over the Blues. But I should make it. Timing is such that I'll miss the worst of the storm."

"I can drop some nutrient solution into the sets you choose, to give you twelve more hours. But after that, they've gotta be boxed," Rick said. He stopped by a set of containers. "Ready for you to check."

Ruby pulled her scanner out of a knee pocket on her cargo pants and carefully reviewed each of the ten lots she had ordered to be cultivated before leaving for AgI. The first two checked out with their provenance solid, clear lines of origin tracing back to the original cell cultivation. These stems, when inoculated with Ruby's line of nanobots, created a biological bot capable not only of communication about soil and plant conditions but also able to slow-release tiny doses of nutrients or biologic weed and pest controls as needed until programming told it to die near harvest.

A broken provenance line showed up in the third lot. Ruby shook her head and marked that one as refused. Two more bad lots that hadn't developed quite right, then two good ones. Two more bad, and one good.

"Fifty percent acceptance," she said finally. Disappointing. Rick and Beck usually had more solid stem cell lines.

"You sure about that?" Rick pointed to Lot Five. "That's a minor hiccup in the grow line. You've accepted them before."

Ruby shook her head. "Can't take any risks with the Superhero lot. Gotta have everything above reproach."

"But Five is workable, as is Nine."

"Rick, if I didn't have three point seven five million riding on these stems, it'd be different. I'd take them because you're right, they're workable—but I've got too much at stake. I can't risk it right now."

Rick sighed. "I understand. Just be aware that it's getting tougher to grow clear lines here, with the background air pollution and the fluctuations in water quality. Filter costs are playing havoc with our bottom line. Beck and I are talking about moving everything to the coast. Someplace where we have more control over the water, better air, and—less crime." He hesitated. "We were broken into at the condo two days ago. Cams showed they were armed, and the cops tell us it's a gang that just loves to torture anyone they find in their break-ins. It was a damn good thing that we were both working in the lab and not at home. We lost personal devices and she's fighting with the credit bureaus right now because the thieves have been spinning off fake identities. At least we got our accounts locked down. Still, she's packing everything and we're putting the condo up for sale. Gonna move into the office here until we find a new place, and hope we don't get attacked."

"You're both safe. That's what counts. As for the move— you do what you have to do. I'm sorry, Rick. But with the

Superhero at stake, I've got to be picky about the lots I take. This makes things tight for me because I don't have any margin for error."

"I get it. We have an investment in your success. If you win the Superhero, then that's a win for us too as one of your suppliers. It's just—" he shrugged. "Filters. Crime. Plus local clients are falling off right now with the latest surge in urban development. Normally I could sell your rejects but these? Gonna have to recycle them."

"If you can just hold on for a bit longer, maybe put them in stasis, I might be able to find a market for you," Ruby said. "I'd take these, but I don't dare deal with the consequences of a mix-up right now. The RubyBot is just too finicky at the moment." *Compromising on the stems was one thing that went wrong twenty-one years ago.* "And you keep my deposit on those lots."

"Thanks for the help, Ruby," Rick said. "It's getting tough. Sorry to sound so negative, but after the break-in, we're both feeling pretty down."

"I get it, Rick. Boy do I understand. But hey. Let's get some publicity going for AgSupply. Take advantage of the Superhero connection." She clucked up the cam. Rick plastered a smile on as they shook hands, both looking directly at the bot. Ruby captioned the best pic, *Buying African clawed frog stem cells at the best supply company ever, Rick Keysing and Beck O'Toole at AgSupply Systems in Hillsboro, Oregon! You want good biobot stems, go to Rick and Beck. I endorse their products! Tell them Ruby sent you.*

She uploaded it to the AgI site. "There. That'll put you on the radar. Maybe you can sell the rejects before they go bad or you have to put them in stasis."

"Maybe." Rick handed Ruby the pad with the invoice. She studied it, then added an extra five thousand for the failed lots and transferred the funds. Worth it to help Rick and Beck, and she'd still come in under budget.

Rick raised his brows as he saw the payment. "You didn't have to do that, Ruby!"

"Call it an appeal to good karma," she said. "You and Beck have done right by me over the years and I feel bad about those rejects. Besides, I need you to stay in business, whether it's here or on the coast."

"Well, thanks." Rick turned away. "Lemme get that nutrient into these lots. We'll keep in touch. Good luck."

After Rick loaded the new nutrient medium into Ruby's selected lots, he fired up the forklift and put them into the back of Ruby's truck. She secured each box and checked to make sure they wouldn't slide around.

"At least the cold weather will help keep them viable for longer," he muttered, his lips tightening.

"The advantage of living in Thunder County." She paused. "You know, if you're looking for a clean place to relocate...."

"Have to convince Beck, because it's so dry and farther away from things." Rick shrugged. "And supply lines. You're way the fuck out there."

"Just keep it in mind," Ruby said.

If she won the Superhero, maybe she could even manage to set up a facility for Rick and Beck at the Double R. If she won.

Winning has to happen first.

And then she'd be in a better position to give people like Beck and Rick a helping hand. Just like others had helped her.

CHAPTER 3

After she was clear of the Portland metro traffic, Ruby switched on the autodrive and pulled up her messages, occasionally checking the stats on the stems in the truck bed. She relaxed as the truck settled into the flow of the I-84 program.

Three of the messages were simple interviews that required only a written response. She put those aside for the straight stretches once she had passed The Dalles. Given the curves and the heavy rain, she still needed to be aware of what was happening on the road in case she needed to override the autodrive. A fourth required recordings. Another one for the straight stretch. She decided to take a look at her set-asides, but as she had thought, none of them were particularly useful.

That done, she settled in for checks on the ranch data from the permanent recorders staked in each field. Yeah, Charlie was there, and on top of both livestock and field conditions, but all the same, it was Ruby's job to be aware of what was happening.

The time passed quickly, the rain fading away as the truck whispered along the freeway and they left the wetter west side of the Cascades. Ruby occasionally glanced out into the dark when she wanted to take a break from the blue glow of her screen. Clear night, with occasional sighting of stars. Ground fog near the John Day River. Then clear again as the truck glided up onto the Columbia Plateau and away from the river, though the distant glow of truck stop lights were dulled, a sign of more fog to come.

Ruby turned off the freeway at the first truck stop to recharge, right at the edge of a heavy fog bank. Technically, she had enough charge to make it home, but any delays over the Blues could suck her charge down to nothing, and the chargers here were better than in Grande City. Besides, it was time for her to walk around a little bit to keep from getting too cramped up—a consideration that became more important with aging.

As she pulled up to the bank of chargers, next to another big farm truck, the fog blew in around them, dimming the light.

Good thing I know how to do this by feel.

She plugged the truck in, sighing with relief as the charger dinged to confirm a good connection.

"Ruby? Is that you? Damn chargers!" Gabe's voice. Of course, he'd be on the road home at the same time. She straightened up to see him fumbling to unplug his truck, wrestling with connector and cane. Despite her misgivings—*is he going to take this as a sign that I'll go along with the AgI script?*—she went to help him. It *was* the humane thing to do.

"Let me get this."

"Thanks." Gabe scrabbled to gather his fallen cane, then used the grill to pull himself upright as she disconnected the plug and reseated it at the charger.

Another old truck like mine that requires manual connect and disconnect.

So he wasn't doing that much better financially than she was. It did match the impression she'd gotten from Brandon, but for some reason seeing Gabe like this just felt—wrong. Just like his soft hands. This wasn't the Gabe she had known.

We're both getting old.

"There," she said, standing there, unsure of what else to say. Had he already been sick before the G9? Not active? She couldn't conceive of Gabe being inactive.

He flexed his hands. "Thank you," he repeated. "These fogs sink into my bones so that my hands won't work right. Doesn't matter if it's here or on the West Side. If it's foggy, they hurt and I can't get a good grip. It was a real fight just to get plugged in." He sighed. "If I can get the Superhero, that might just be enough cash for me to get things in good enough shape that I can afford to sell out and relocate."

"Mariah hasn't made you an offer yet?"

He snorted. "The only offer she's made me is for my share of the Double R." He coughed. "Unlike the rest of the Superhero finalists, or so I've heard."

It was a cliché to say that her blood ran cold, but all the same, Ruby shivered, staring at Gabe as the acrid-smelling fog blew around them.

Just the chill from the fog. Just the chill from the fog, she told herself.

Not from a threat she hadn't anticipated.

But. She held forty percent of the ranch's LLC. Charlie and Martin held twenty-five percent, and they were unlikely to ever sell out to anyone but Ruby. However...Gabe's ten percent and Brandon's twenty-five percent could cause her problems if Mariah bought their shares. Thirty-five percent together. If Mariah wanted to make Ruby's progress difficult, she could buy out Gabe and Brandon. Not enough to stop any action, but enough to drag argument out past seasonal timelines for implementing the RubyBot, and delay the licensing that would mean Ruby could sell it on the open market.

"I'll match or beat any price she gives you," Ruby said. "No questions asked."

Gabe laughed. "With what? I see your financials, Ruby."

"I'll find a way." And that was another reason Mariah didn't need to own shares of the Double R. She'd learn too much about what was going on.

"You're getting old, too. Maybe you need to be thinking about retirement."

She pressed her lips together, ignoring the hint, just like she did when Brandon tried that argument. "If I recall the settlement agreement correctly, you have to give me first purchase option. I want to exercise it, and I'll do whatever it takes, Gabe."

I didn't put first purchase on Brandon's shares, damn it.

Or had her lawyer Remy Trask inserted it at the last minute? She hadn't thought it was possible for him to consider other possibilities.

Talk to Remy tomorrow morning.

"Ruby, Ruby, Ruby," Gabe sighed. "We need to talk."

"Yes. But not here."

"I'll be in touch. Right now, I just want to get off the road. Let me know if things are too bad over the Blues...I'd be happy to let you stay at my place."

I bet you would. And wouldn't the AgI showrunners just eat it up. No. "I'll be all right."

"It's an option." Gabe struggled into the truck's cab and rolled down the window. "Thanks for your help. And keep the offer in mind."

"Talk to me before you sell to Mariah." She needed to talk to Remy, have her review the legal agreements again, damn it, along with the AgI contract.

"All right." He started the truck and backed out. Ruby mechanically checked her stem lots, then locked everything down. Now she was running paranoid. Dare she leave the truck? What if

Mariah had hired someone to sabotage her stems? She hadn't thought about that possibility, but this charging station and truck stop would be a perfect place to break the locks on the canopy and tamper with the stems, especially with the fog drifting in.

Ruby paced around the truck, stomping her feet to stay warm in the near-freezing temperatures, checking road conditions via her comm as she circled. Still, she wasn't so distracted to keep from pulling her scanner out to check the fog's acid levels and look at the long-range forecast. While spring in the Thunder Valley trailed behind the Plateau, this felt like a possible early spring. Barely enough time to get these bots grown and ready to release, if past weather patterns held true. She shivered.

Too much like that last season of Superstar twenty-one years ago.

Another blustery, early spring, with snow and ice one day, sunshine and short sleeves the next.

But at least this time she wasn't dealing with a cheating husband. That was an improvement.

At last she climbed back into the cab, thankful that she had the tiny portable toilet installed in a walled off section of the back seat—mandatory these days with the limited resources available at charging stations. Then she stared out at the deepening fog.

What was Mariah's game?

The truck finally beeped to advise her of a full charge. Ruby disconnected it and checked the stems again. All fine. She winced at the charging bill that popped up on the readout. A surcharge for not using the inside facilities. A big surcharge. Normally she wasn't worried about her cargo, but...well, perhaps that needed to change. She started up the truck and slowly felt her way back onto the freeway through the murk, grateful when the software clicked in and she could turn on the autodrive.

Before long, the fog cleared. The stars twinkled in the sky above, the lights from various center pivot sprinklers and the occasional house mirroring them below. Fewer house lights than there had been twenty years ago, more pivots and windmills. And then the drop into Pendleton and thicker, choking fog that made Ruby glad she wasn't driving through it live. She checked the road program for updates, in case she had to take the wheel herself through the Blues. All clear. And she was tired, so she put away her screen and settled back in her seat, setting all the warning alarms so she could take a nap before leaving the freeway at Grande City and switching to live driving.

She couldn't sleep. Her mind kept spinning, thinking about what Gabe had told her. His ranch was just a short distance from the freeway near the small town of Blue Bucket, in the foothills of the Blues. Was he already home? Too bad the storm over the mountains had spent itself so that she didn't need to find a place to wait it out. Diverting to Gabe's place to spend the night would definitely be an addition to the show script, and add some tensions.

She needed to think further about this when she wasn't so tired. She needed to talk to Gabe, but not over a comm, even if she used the most secure algorithms to lock it down. *Might be something in Pendleton that could be private...*and then memory rose to choke her throat.

It all happened at once. They had finished setting up the growboxes for the latest version of the RubyBot, the one that was going to save their butts for the Superstar judging this year. Charlie programmed the bot creator to start automatically in sixteen hours. Gabe was concocting the nutrient mix with Martin. Ruby was slow-moving as she got Brandon ready for the day, already feeling this second pregnancy. Then Branny vomited, followed by a hard cough, cheeks bright red, eyes sunken. She took his temperature. 101.9 degrees.

"Mama, I don' feel good," Brandon whimpered.

"It's okay, honey." Ruby gulped and called the doctor, dread filling her as she recognized the symptoms from the warnings about the new flu.

Gabe called from the lab, voice impatient and abrupt, like it had been over the past six weeks. "Not enough growth medium. Gotta go to Pendleton to get more. Why aren't you here to monitor the grow? I thought you were on your way with Branny."

Ruby paused the conversation with the doctor. "Branny's bad sick, Gabe. I've got to take him to the hospital. I think it's that new flu. I called, and Doctor Sheri says don't mess with the office, take him to the ER. I can't do the growboxes. Can you pause things?"

A hesitation. "I can." There had been a time when he didn't sound so grumpy. When had that changed? This last pregnancy.

"You'll be back in time to restart before the stems go bad?"

"Yeah, yeah, I should be back if you aren't." More sharpness, more anger.

"I don't know, Gabe." She brushed back a strand of curly dark hair sweat-glued to Brandon's forehead. "Kiddo's in tough shape. I'm scared."

Gabe softened. "He'll be okay, darlin'. Trust Doctor Sheri. She'll pull him through. I'll be back in time. Or you will."

Only he hadn't been back in time. And she'd been at Brandon's side in the hospital, quarantined as she also succumbed to the new flu virus within an hour of bringing him to the ER. Later her friend and rodeo queen mentor Vickie, a nurse at Thunder County Memorial, told Ruby that even though she had collapsed, she'd revived enough to crawl toward Brandon's bed. After several *attempts, the harried hospital staff gave up and put her bed next to Brandon's. But she remembered none of that. Memory was a blur between feeling dizzy next to Brandon's bed and waking to Charlie's stricken expression. Gabe was nowhere to be found.*

The expensive stems died. There was no time to cultivate another batch of the full RubyBots before planting, and that test run failed—second year in a row, which dropped Ruby and Gabe out of the Superstar competition.

Even worse, the nosy AgI bots had gotten pictures of Mariah and Gabe meeting in Pendleton. Dinners. Hotels. Sneakshots of the two of them having sex. All forwarded by someone at AgI after Gabe and Ruby had been eliminated and Mariah had succeeded in that year's AgI season.

Not that it mattered. By then Gabe had left the Double R, leaving Ruby to manage Brandon and the ranch on her own as they recovered from the flu. Charlie and his husband Martin had helped Ruby keep the ranch afloat after Gabe's departure, and in return Ruby had given them a twenty-five percent share in the ranch since there was no way she could pay them for what their support meant to her.

As things turned out, that choice to give them the share instead of scraping up all the cash she could afford to throw at them had saved her butt in the divorce. She kept a forty percent share for herself, and assigned another twenty-five to Brandon—which allowed her to grant Gabe ten percent as part of the divorce settlement.

No. Pendleton would not be an option. Not with those memories.

Gabe could come to Grande City. They could make a big deal of the meeting for AgI...and then figure out someplace quiet to work out their roles in private.

Another unpleasant thought occurred to her.

What if Brandon's future with AgI depends on him selling his share of the Double R to Mariah? On me and Gabe getting together during the show?

Ruby groaned and leaned her head on the wheel, careful not to disconnect the autodrive. What if her only option *was* to go along with the Superhero script?

I'll think about it tomorrow, when I'm on the land. I can't think straight about this right now.

IT WAS ONE AM BY THE TIME RUBY DROVE INTO THE Double R's brightly lit barnyard. Lights still showed in the main house, Charlie and Martin's smaller cottage, and the bunkhouse where their assistants Terri and Julie slept. Porch lights switched on for all three buildings as she turned off the truck, sending much-needed cheer through Ruby's thoughts. Charlie and Martin's heelers, Rusty and Crimson, raced to meet the truck, stub tails wagging their rears as they recognized the familiar vehicle, barking happily.

I'm not alone.

As solitary a creature as she had become in the past few years, it was still reassuring to know that she had people here.

Ice crunched under Ruby's feet as she crawled out of the cab, her every muscle tight and tense. Too much time on the road without a break. She hadn't paused for her usual stop to stretch in Grande City, worried now about security and timing for her precious stems. She stretched and yawned, then bent over to pet the ecstatic heelers before she hobbled back to unlock the cargo area. Charlie, Martin, Terri, and Julie joined her.

"You looked good on the show," Julie said. "I've been

rebroadcasting select links and the RubyBot intro sales video all evening. Your numbers are rising."

"That's good news." Ruby popped open the back, pushing the button that raised the canopy high enough for her to stand, and checked the lots again. To her relief, the numbers showed no losses. "We need to get these lots loaded into the growboxes ASAP. Delays. Rick loaded more nutrient before I left, but...it was slow going over the Blues and then between here and Grande City, I had to really throttle speed down once I had to go manual. More ice than snow from this last storm."

Charlie climbed into the back. Ruby jumped out as Martin and Terri went for the two ranch forklifts.

"Only five lots? I thought you ordered ten," he said.

"I did. Rejected the other five."

He straightened up, frowning. "We couldn't recover them? Five is cutting it awfully close, especially with the Superhero judging coming up. Not like you to reject mildly flawed lots. Or are Rick and Beck slipping?"

"No, they're not slipping. Rick was saying that air and water quality issues are causing them to spend a lot more on filters. If it wasn't for the need to have everything as clear as possible—I just didn't want to take a chance on them getting mixed in with the competition batches."

"Understandable. That's going to be a problem with the air and water quality issues in the long run. Does Rick have a plan to deal with them?"

"He's talking about moving to the coast to get away from air and water quality issues. But that's not all. He and Beck had a break-in at their condo the other day, and he sounds pretty rattled. Said the cops told them that the guys were a known violent gang."

"Shit! Are they okay?"

"No one was home. They were lucky, but they lost stuff

and I'm sure some money before they locked down their accounts."

"Not good." Charlie shook his head as Julie climbed into the truck bed.

"Yeah." She suddenly wondered if that break-in was a coincidence. It was no secret that Rick and Beck supplied her stem cells. What if someone wanted to sabotage her efforts? So far they had avoided the attention of activist groups like We Love Animals and Nature, who had targeted other stem cell cultivators on the grounds that they promoted unnatural solutions to agriculture issues.

Now you're just being paranoid, she chided herself.

"Ruby. Hey Ruby. You with us or zoning out?" Charlie said gently.

"Just thinking. Got a lot to think about. Stuff going on and it's not all what it seems on the surface."

"Like you and Gabe getting back together?" Charlie and Julie eased the first lot to where Martin's forklift easily lifted it, then did the same for Terri and the second lot.

Ruby spluttered. "Where did *that* come from?"

"It's all over the Innovator press," Julie said, straightening up and pressing her hands against her back to stretch before helping Charlie move the third lot. "Lots of speculation going on in social media about you two right now."

Damn good thing I didn't stop at Gabe's tonight, then. At least not before we've talked and I've had time to think about it.

"I'm—not sure." Ruby hesitated. How much did she want to disclose around Terri and Julie?

If you don't trust Julie and Terri, you'd better fire them. They need to know what's up.

"Not sure?" Charlie squatted next to the fourth box.

"There's a lot going on with the Innovator and I don't understand all the undercurrents. Brandon blindsided me with the Gabe and me getting back together promos. Plus, Mariah's made an offer to buy the Double R. She's also talked to Gabe about his shares, and I'm betting Brandon as well. And—" she hesitated. "I don't know what to think about Rick and Beck's break-in. What if they're targeted because they're my supplier? So far they've been under WLAN's radar, but this is likely to change."

"Well, let's start with Mariah," Charlie said. "She called us tonight with all sweetness and light in her voice."

"What did she say?"

"Didn't talk to her. She left a message for us to call her. But we could guess."

"Yeah." Ruby scuffed a toe in the snow, looking down. She took a deep breath and met Charlie's eyes. "And as for Gabe, well, AgI is putting a lot of pressure on me to make things up with Gabe. Good for the show numbers. Good for...." Her voice trailed off.

"Good for one or the other of you winning?" Charlie finished, a cynical tone in his voice.

"Yeah," Ruby repeated. "I don't know what to think. I'm starting to feel like a prize broodmare. Sure hasn't been like this with the Innovator before." She paused, wondering if she should say something more about the increased number of indentureds at AgI.

No. It's probably not important.

Martin and Terri returned for the third and fourth lots.

"Well, isn't that what the Innovators is all about?" Charlie said after they left. "Sometimes selling yourself requires going out of your comfort zone."

Ruby leaned against the back of the truck, finally letting herself relax. "I know. But it just seems more intense."

"It's gonna be more intense. We're talking a big one-shot.

And it's been a few years since you won the Star," Charlie reminded her. "A lot has happened since then."

"There's more," Ruby said. "Mariah has made offers to buy out every Superhero finalist *but* Gabe—she only talked to him about his share in the Double R."

"What's her game?"

"She's fronting for someone. Just wish I could figure out who it is, so I know who we're fighting."

"I wouldn't waste your time worrying about that," Charlie said. "Focus on the Ruby and winning the Superhero. Don't chase your tail worrying about motives. We don't have time for that crap."

Ruby exhaled slowly and grinned at him. "Thanks for the reality check, Charlie. I was getting myself worked up on the drive home."

He shrugged. "It's nothing."

Julie climbed out of the truck. "I'll get pix of Terri prepping the lab and starting the boxes," she said. "We should be posting step-by-step process pix to the Innovator."

"Agreed. I'll be in there in a minute. You probably want me in those pix as well." Ruby winced. The last thing she wanted to do right now was another photo op. Bed sounded really, really good instead. "Gotta keep the social media going," she said, as much to encourage herself as anything else. Get it done and over with.

"Absolutely. But you don't need to be there for the setup process. I'll get pix of you inspecting." Julie trudged off, ice crunching under her feet.

Ruby waited until the lab door slammed shut behind Julie.

"I'm spooked. Mariah. Rick and Beck," she confessed to Charlie, pushing herself up on the tailgate next to him as he loaded his pipe. He lit it, inhaled deeply, and passed it to her.

"Don't let Mariah get into your head," he said. "Remember

that she runs a big bluff. Always has. And as for Rick and Beck...if you start going down that trail without further information, you're just going to get yourself all paranoid. You don't need to do that. Get more data before you get too worried."

"I know." Ruby inhaled and let the smoke trickle slowly out of her nose. She handed the pipe back to Charlie and rolled her shoulders, waiting for the welcome warmth from the marijuana to start easing the tension.

Charlie lit the pipe again. "I'll let Sheriff Wilhite know about this stuff in the morning. She called while you were in LA and told me to let her know if we needed more patrols, because of the Superhero. Terri's been tweaking our patrol drones and amped up the boundary bots, especially around the test fields."

"Thank you." Ruby heaved a relieved sigh. "I started getting jumpy on the way home. Paranoid about WLAN."

Charlie exhaled a thin cloud of smoke and handed the pipe back to Ruby. "I don't think we have much to worry about from WLAN. Maybe if the RubyBot had more to do with animal ag that would be an issue."

Ruby shrugged. "You just never know with those folks. And now that I'm an announced Superhero finalist, who knows what's going to crawl out of the woodwork?"

"True that. So what are you going to do about Gabe?"

"I need a break. I need to win the Superhero." She shook her head. "I just keep getting the feedback that to do it, I'm going to have to sell myself. I guess the question is that of price and when, not if, I'm going to do it."

Charlie handed her the pipe again. She inhaled, then tapped the ashes in the bowl with her forefinger. Dead. She knocked the ashes onto the ice and handed the pipe back to Charlie. Already she could feel tension ebbing out of her shoulders.

Charlie tucked the pipe into his coat pocket.

"Just don't sell out for a pittance," he said. "Remember what you're worth. The RubyBot. The Double R. Don't sell yourself for cheap." He clapped her on the shoulder, then headed for the lab.

Ruby pushed off of the tailgate and closed the back before climbing into the cab and driving the truck into the carport to hook into the charger. She took deep breaths of the fresh, clean, cold mountain air as she trudged to the lab for the last photo-op of a very long day.

Charlie's right. I can't sell myself for cheap.

But what price could she tolerate?

CHAPTER 4

Morning brought swirls of fog over half-melting snow and ice on the ridges around the home place, but the mountains still stood out above the fog. Ruby soaked in the familiar, beloved views while sitting at the kitchen table and choking back a piece of toast and sipping a cup of fake coffee —*at least it has caffeine!* Home. The craziness of the Innovator seemed to be very far away from her cozy kitchen with the view of mountains. Ruby lingered at the table for just a few more moments, treasuring the temporary peacefulness. Another long day ahead but at least she'd eventually get on horseback and out on the land. *Her* land.

Then she took a deep breath, refilled her cup, and went into the office. Ruby tapped up Remy Trask's law office, not knowing if she was relieved or worried that her call immediately got put through without Remy's wife and assistant Shannon answering.

The projection screen flickered into life over Ruby's desk. Remy peered at Ruby over half-frame black reading glasses, her short dark hair askew. She leaned her elbows on her desk and clasped her hands together.

"Let me guess. You have concerns about the Superhero contract with AgI," Remy said, before Ruby could speak.

"I can't imagine why you would think so," Ruby said wryly.

"I can speculate, after watching social media all day yesterday. Shannon's got you flagged, and boy was your name bouncing around. I anticipated you might have some concerns, so I reviewed the contract. I would have called you this afternoon if you hadn't gotten in touch first." Remy leaned back in her chair and took her glasses off, chewing on the earpiece of one temple. "And here's your answer to that question I expected. You signed away prior approval of anything officially posted by an AgI employee using your picture, unless you can make a case for it going against AgI's interests or personal defamation. Which I'm guessing doesn't fit in this situation."

"Not even if it's your own son who posted it?"

Remy burst out laughing. "Why that little stinker. So it *was* Brandon who posted that pic." She grinned and leaned forward. "Hey Shannon! I win the bet! You owe me lunch."

Ruby rolled her eyes. "You were taking bets on who started all this? You *scum*."

Remy smirked. "And who has not only been your ranch and divorce lawyer but was Thunder County Days Princess with you, girl? I was guessing that Brandon would have the guts to do that. Looks like I was right. You got anything else?"

"This one is more serious." Ruby took a deep breath. "I need you to look at the share agreements for the Double R. I need to know if it's only Gabe who has to give me the right of first refusal when it comes to selling their interest in the ranch. I've forgotten—and something has come up."

The mirth faded from Remy's face and she turned to the side, pulling up her files to project over the side desk. "Problems arising because of the Superhero?" She slid on her glasses and leaned forward, scrutinizing the screen, reaching up to flick through clauses and highlighting certain phrases, keeping some sections while discarding others.

"In a nutshell, yes."

"I'm pretty sure you're covered. I can't imagine I would do it just for Gabe and not the others." Remy chewed her lip. "Yep. Got all three share agreements up here. You're covered. Brandon, Charlie and Martin, and Gabe. All have a clause which requires them to offer you their shares in the Double R before selling them to any other interested parties." She sat back in her chair and spun to face Ruby. "Who's the problem?"

"Mariah Meyers. She's approached me, Gabe, and Charlie."

"Well, the RubyBot is close to final licensure, and you've got a potentially huge payoff coming once that happens. She's probably just the first of what will be many potential investors who want a piece of it once the word gets out—and it *will* get out, thanks to the Superhero." Remy pulled her glasses off. "And there's another issue I wanted to bring up with you. You have to create an addendum to this agreement covering income from the RubyBot. That's the part which isn't covered. While you were away at the Superhero, latest court decision changed the rules, and there's no grandfathering in so I'm up to my neck covering clients left in the lurch. You're one of them. Right now the RubyBot's considered to be ranch property, but there's some gray area about who the royalty rights really belong to— you alone, or a mix of you, Charlie and Martin, and Gabe, because of the work records. I'm still looking at the decision to see how it specifically affects you. The work history is the problematic part because it does not match up with share allotments."

"But Brandon isn't a part of the work on the RubyBot."

"No, he's not, but he has other interests that could argue for him getting a share of the income. Charlie, Martin, and Gabe could all argue that they have a significant interest in the RubyBot because of the way you've written those agreements and their documented work on it. As a result, the RubyBot income claims would not match the ranch LLC division of interest. That's what we have to fix, ASAP, so they're aligned with the ranch LLC payouts."

"What about Julie and Terri? Julie's been working in the lab with Martin."

"Do either one of them have ranch shares? Have you any agreements with them above and beyond standard employment contracts? Performance bonuses don't count."

"No."

"Then they're fine." Remy sighed and rolled her eyes. "It's frustrating as hell because of the way that decision was written. Everything was all right until then. At least you're not my only client caught in this mess."

"Shit. I guess I'd better have you fix this before the final RubyBot licensure filing, then."

"Yep. Think you're going to have problems getting them to sign off on an amended agreement?" Remy peered at the screen again.

"Not with Charlie and Martin. They're working on it now. Brandon shouldn't be an issue either. I'll talk to him when he's up with the AgI crew later this week. Gabe—I don't know. He hasn't shown an interest in the RubyBot since he left me, and—" Ruby paused. Did she really want to get into the details? *Yeah. You'd better.* "He still believes his microbials are the better route. It was—part of the discussion about whether we play along with the AgI reunification storyline."

Remy frowned. "Well, I guess you'd better figure out how that lies for sure, then, shouldn't you? *If* Gabe's still that disinterested in the Ruby, and *if* it doesn't impact the AgI script, you might just be able to get him to cooperate. But that's two big ifs. You need to nail him down about his interest in the RubyBot."

"I'm hoping that he'll be cooperative. But geez, Remy, I can also see a legitimate reason for him to want the income. He's in bad shape. I think he wants to sell out so that he can retire, so I can't predict what he's going to do. The G9 hit him *bad*."

"He didn't look that good on the show," Remy said. "I was wondering if he was having health problems."

"He looks awful in person. He needs a cane to get around, and when I saw him at the truck stop last night, he was having problems disconnecting his truck from the charger. He said the arthritis in his hands was giving him problems."

"Okay, girl." Remy dropped her glasses on the desk. "Here's another issue. As your friend and attorney, let me give you this piece of advice. Do *not* let yourself get suckered into feeling sorry for him and getting back together for any other purpose than advancing your campaign for the Superhero. He put you through too damn much hell and he's still a man, with the little brain that sometimes outmaneuvers the big brain. And you are far too inclined to take in strays."

"Brandon's pushing for it, too."

"Brandon's a big boy who should keep his nose out of his parents' business. What happened to that Rachel woman Gabe married—no, wait, I saw it in the AgI coverage. She died of the G9. I am really, really surprised that AgI isn't pushing him the story of him being a widower due to the G9 because it's about as hot as the two of you getting together. Might even amplify the getting together again story."

"Oh great, something more to look forward to in social media." Ruby sighed. "I don't know what to do about Gabe yet, Remy. We've got too many difficult questions to deal with before I could seriously consider getting together with him again—ever. Even faking it. It's not just the RubyBot."

"What does your gut tell you?"

"I'm not sure."

"Well. Protect yourself. Because this is a prime scenario where he hooks up with you because he needs a caregiver. That is not your style, and it's just going to end up with you getting tied down and hurt."

"Thanks, Remy." The relief flooding through her was a sign that she was on the right track. "Believe me, if we do agree to work together in whatever capacity, even if it's just for the show, you'll be the first I'll tell. I wouldn't do this without an agreement. Both of us have too many independent interests at stake."

"Good for you. I'll draft up an addendum to those agreements covering the RubyBot—should have done it sooner in the licensing process, I'm slipping—and get back to you when it's ready."

"Thanks, Remy."

"You take care—and watch out for Gabe!"

Ruby signed off. She sipped the rest of her coffee, then gathered up what she would need to ride out. Time to get centered after all the chaos of the Innovator and take a break with a good horse underneath her. Besides, those test fields needed inspection before they released the new version of the RubyBot in the next week or so—depending on the condition of the current grow.

Her first stop was at the lab. Ruby shed her mud boots at the door and went into the vestibule to pull on protective suit, hood, and booties. Biosecurity was now more important than ever. Once she was garbed, she prowled along the line of grow-boxes, checking the readouts. It was tempting to peek into the boxes but she resisted, knowing from past experience that there would be nothing to see yet.

The stats on the growboxes looked good, the preliminary

growth before the stem cell organisms went through the joining process with the mechanical nanobots proceeding at a normal pace. Martin and Julie waved to her from the clean workroom, where they were setting up for the next step in the RubyBot production process. Martin put his tools down to come talk to her outside of the clean room, switching outfits before joining Ruby.

"Grow stats look good," Ruby said as he met her by the boxes.

"They're looking great. Doesn't look like we're going to lose any, either. We can start integrating the bots with the stems tomorrow, then start loading the final algorithms. Should be ready to spread them in the fields by the end of the week, depending on the weather. Forecast looks promising so far, but you know how the weather can be."

"Timing should work for the first visit by AgI, then."

"Really?"

"Have to hear confirmation, but yes. We're going to have them on site at least once a week for the next month."

Martin scowled. "I'd better put Julie on biosecurity monitoring duty, then. What a pain. Just when I need her to focus on the RubyBot specs."

"Can we hire Scott back to manage those details? Has he been reliable—if not, can we bring someone else on, preferably someone we've had here before? I hate to take Julie away from lab work just to wrangle the AgI people."

"Scott would work," Martin said thoughtfully. "It's just whether the high school will sign off on him spending as much time working here as we'll need since it's his senior year."

"I'll talk to him today to see if he's interested. It would make a good senior project—if he's on board, I'll write up a proposal and send it in."

"Okay. And if not, he might know another kid. I just hate

bringing someone new in who doesn't know the biosecurity protocols. That means someone has to take time to train them."

"Hmm." Ruby chewed her lower lip thoughtfully as a glimmer of an idea came to her. "You know, if we bring on several kids and train them, I could add that piece to my Superhero coverage—training the next generation. And it could deal with the time issue."

"Who's going to do the teaching, though?"

"I'll manage it. Let me talk to the agtech teacher. I'm thinking collaboration with a biosecurity unit—which probably means it's my job, especially if I add it to what I'm doing for the Superhero."

Martin frowned thoughtfully, nodding slowly. "That's an interesting prospect. They'll have to be responsible kids."

"Probably juniors and seniors, preferably seniors. Shoot—if the RubyBot takes off, we're going to need to think about long-term hiring. Why not train potential workers?" God. Why hadn't she thought about this before? Until now, licensing and production of the RubyBot had seemed a far-off goal. Suddenly, the prospect of doing something besides research and development was all very real—with a lot more implications than she had been considering until now.

Gabe was the one who did all this long-range thinking. If— no, when—I win the Superhero, my orientation has to change. No longer R and D but production.

She'd been so locked into the creation side of the Ruby that she hadn't thought very far into the future. Marketing. Planning. She needed a marketing guru if she was going to avoid the clutches of someone like Mariah.

"You know, training interns is a good idea," Martin said. "You'll take care of the proposal?"

"After I ride out and check the fields," Ruby said.

"You don't have to do either task today if you've got too

much to do—tomorrow should be soon enough. The stems aren't growing that fast, and Charlie and Terri have been keeping an eye on the field temps and snowmelt."

"I want to eyeball the fields myself. It's more than just checking on the test fields. I need the time on the land after all the craziness down in LA. Got a lot to think through, and sometimes the best way to do that is on horseback. At least for me."

"Got it—and I don't blame you one bit." Martin stretched. "If we were further along in coding the nanobot structures, I'd come with you. But we're not."

"That's okay. We're all going to be out there on release day."

"Yeah."

"I'll check in with Charlie—surprised he didn't message me with the morning updates. I suppose something came up?"

"He's in the cow barn. Difficult calving—two of them."

"Crud." Not that the success or failure of the cattle line would affect her Superhero status...these were the leftovers from Brandon's 4H and FFA breeding operation, and she'd continued with the cattle because they were a relatively rare bloodline. Plus she had just enough boutique beef clients from Brandon's show years to make the sales pencil out.

She went back to the vestibule and put her lab suit into the decontamination box. Then she left that chamber and changed back to barn boots to walk between the buildings. She changed her boots and washed her hands at the cow barn's entrance. More biosecurity, especially during calving season. There were just too many problems out there any more.

One black cow was in the first medical pen. She glared at Ruby through the panel gate as a spraddle-legged white-faced black bull calf tried to balance on his feet while he rooted at her udder. Ruby paused to check out mother and son. The little bull was dry, his face that pristine newborn white that range babies lost within a few days of being out on pasture. As she watched, he finally latched onto a teat and nursed eagerly. Ruby pulled out her scanner to check the chip implanted in the cow's ear. This cow's third calf and first bull. Rated as an excellent range mother, a good milker with a strong protective instinct. With any luck, he was one of the two that Martin had mentioned—a good resolution. She moved on to the next pen. Charlie and Terri were with this cow, Terri rubbing the heifer calf dry while Charlie ran a calcium infusion line into the cow.

"You missed all the excitement," he said. "Two breech presentations. The Witch over there is doing fine, had no problems once we got everything straightened out. But this girlie—" he rubbed the cow's neck, "—started showing signs of milk fever. Good mother and milker, like the Witch over there, but Sweetcakes is a lot more chill about people. Thank God. The Witch can be difficult."

"You got things under control?"

Charlie nodded. "Got a lot of stuff left to do in the day, though."

"What's your plan? Anything I can do to help?"

"Well, I'm going to finish up with these girls, then check on the others in the calving pen. Gotta go to the co-op to pick up some new fence panels and pipe for the waterers. We've got a leak—fortunately just at the frost-free faucet so I don't have to dig too far—but I'm thinking I'd better run a scan on all those lines."

"Is it in the house corner pasture?"

Charlie nodded. "All older pipe that we put in fifteen years ago."

Ruby sighed. "I was afraid that stuff was going to go out one of these winters." For a moment she thought about staying and helping Charlie.

No. That's one reason I hired Terri and Julie, to help Charlie and Martin. More time to work on the RubyBot. More time to ride horses.

Charlie shrugged. "From everything I'm seeing on the monitors it's just going to be one location. But...when one goes out...."

"They all start going out," Ruby finished. "I'm going for a ride and check the fields. Anything else I should be doing while I'm out there besides the usual?"

"Hey, will you take a look at the boundary fences?" Terri asked, looking up from the calf. "I started getting some weird readings from the sensors last night. But it was after dark, and then we had this going on, so I haven't had the chance to investigate it. Tried to send out a drone this morning, but it got all futzed up."

"That doesn't sound good."

Terri rose as the calf flopped around in her first attempt to stand up. "Sometimes drones get cranky. But I figured we'd better check on the boundaries today, especially with amping up our security. If you can do that as part of your ride, Ruby, that'll get me ahead of things."

"So it means a longer ride. Be still my beating heart—it's right what I need to do. What horses need work?"

"I rode Pard yesterday," Charlie said. "Casey's gimping around, I think she's trying to cook an abscess. She's in the barn. I was going to soak that hoof after I get done here—but could you do it for me before you ride out?"

Ruby pursed her lips, thinking over the remaining horses. "I can do that. How feisty has Legacy been over the past few days?" Sunshine's great-granddaughter was four years old, and the young palomino mare was high-energy and inclined to take any excuse she could as a reason to run. She'd come back from the trainer last fall with a tendency to buck that Ruby thought she could eventually school out of the golden mare.

"She could stand a good long ride, if you're looking for a horse that needs some wet saddle blankets."

"I'll take Legacy then."

"Have fun."

"I will." Ruby scratched Sweetcakes's head, eyed the Witch and her son, then went back to the entrance, washed her hands, and changed back into her other boots. The horse barn was at the end of the row of lab, feed barn, cow barn, and then horse barn with small attached indoor arena opposite the machine shed. As she opened the barn door, Casey, Legacy's dam, whickered at her.

"Looking for treats, girl? Give me a moment." Ruby trudged down the aisle, turning on the main overhead lights instead of the low-level daytime lights. Casey nickered again, her tone more urgent as Ruby walked past her to the feed room. She grabbed several cookies from the treat bin and a hoof pick from the tack room. As she returned to Casey's stall, the chestnut mare added a couple of kicks to the door.

"Quit!" Ruby snapped as she untied the green nylon web halter and its matching lead rope from the stall door. Casey stopped banging but she pressed close to the front of the stall, pushing forward through the opening as Ruby slid the door open.

"Get back there," Ruby murmured, clucking as a signal to send Casey back. The chestnut mare reluctantly hobbled a few steps away from the door, barely touching the toe of her right forefoot to the deeply-bedded straw. "Looks like an abscess all right, huh, ol' lady?" Ruby kept her voice low and soothing as she haltered Casey, then fed her a cookie.

The chestnut mare still tried to hurry out of the stall, even on three legs. Ruby didn't take her any further than the first set of crossties in the barn alley. She ran her hand down Casey's right foreleg—no heat, no swelling, no dangerous digital pulse indicating possible laminitis—yep, probably an abscess. She lifted Casey's hoof and picked out the manure, then probed the sole. A section by the mare's inside heel felt soft and spongy... yeah, an abscess getting ready to burst.

Ruby eased Casey's hoof down and fed the mare another cookie, rubbing the big diamond-shaped star on her forehead. "Looks like it's time for some hoof soaking, girl," she said. Casey's ears pricked forward as Ruby went to the tack room to get the Epsom salts and soaking boot. After filling the boot with warm water from the sink in the feed room, then adding the salt, she carried it back to Casey and carefully eased her hoof into the boot, tightening the strap at the top to secure it.

That done, she clicked to her comm to set a timer for fifteen minutes. Couldn't leave Casey alone for this because it *was* possible for an agile horse like her to slip out of the boot. Ruby fed Casey another cookie, patted her pocket to make sure she had enough cookies to keep the mare settled, then got a chair and set it up nearby. That done, she pulled out her scanner and called up the link to the boundary trackers. Casey's ears flicked forward and back as a property map shimmered into being between them. She snorted, then flicked her ears forward again as Ruby enlarged the map, looking along the edges for any anomalies, the lines and lights catching her attention.

Ah. There was the problem Terri had talked about, a flashing bright red segment. Located in that corner near Vickie and Mike Chandler's property, in the Lone Pine pasture. The farthest corner of the Double R from the ranch buildings, the summer horse pasture. Ruby scratched her chin thoughtfully. Should she check the fields first or head straight for the anomalies, figuring that whatever repairs she would have to do would take time? Or should she just scout it out?

Eh, better head straight out to fix that problem.

It could be as easy as a sensor in the network gone bad. And if it were something worse, she'd need the time to either fix it or figure out what needed to be done. Ruby typed in a diagnostic and let it run, getting up and moving around the projection to feed Casey another cookie.

She groaned as the diagnostic came back with inconclusive results. Okay, she'd need to stop by the mechanic shed to pick up replacement sensors, just in case. Hopefully it wasn't the whole line gone bad. Just what she really needed to deal with right now, when they wanted to increase their security. But it had to be fixed today, if it could.

On the other hand, she might as well program a new algorithm into that whole line. Yeah, that corner of the property was isolated and she couldn't have better neighbors than Vickie and Mike, plus Jim and Carol Reed on either side of that field. But it was a potential security hole, for anyone determined enough to sneak around on private property to snoop on what Ruby was doing. And there would be more of that now that she was known as a Superhero finalist. She wouldn't put it past WLAN to give that a try.

The timer chimed. Casey recognized the signal and raised her right hoof, shifting her weight impatiently and stomping, sloshing some water over the rim of the soaking boot.

"Hold on, girl, just hold on." Ruby switched off her scanner before she went to Casey and slipped the boot off. A small hole oozed pus from the suspicious soft area at her heel.

Good.

She picked up the boot and dumped its contents into the feed room sink, rinsing it out. Then she hung the boot on a dowel to dry and gathered up another, smaller boot, drawing salve, and gauze. She dropped these items in her chair and got a small bucket, filling it with hot water. After cleaning Casey's hoof in the bucket, she squirted a bit of the drawing salve on the gauze, pressing it against the sole before slipping on the protective boot over the hoof. She fastened the straps tight, then led Casey forward. The mare walked normally, except for lifting her hoof high the first two steps because of the boot. But she was putting weight on it again.

Ruby fed Casey another cookie before putting her back in the stall. Then she put away the chair and the other tools she'd used, gathering a saddle with saddlebags that she hung on a saddle rack in the alleyway. She picked up a saddle blanket and snaffle bridle with long rope reins from the tack room and put them on the saddle. Then she marched out of the barn to gather up the sensor repair materials she would need, along with the necessary tools and put them by the saddle. That done, she gathered more cookies and a rope halter, finally, *finally* able to catch Legacy after all the prep.

The horse herd wintered in a fifty-acre field behind the main ranch house, ten geldings and mares ranging in age from Casey's yearling son to old Sunshine herself, now approaching thirty-five years old. The horses raised their heads from picking at the remnants of the previous evening's hay feed, watching Ruby as she slipped through the big panel gate. Sunshine was the first to start walking toward her. Legacy and her brother Dancer snorted, then took off at a run. Pard picked up a gallop next, which spread through the herd until they all galloped toward Ruby.

The horses stopped twenty feet away from her. Old Sunshine pinned her ears and tossed her head at the others, marching forward to get her cookie first. Even though her face was almost white with age and her spine prominent, she still ruled the herd, with the Paint mare Crystal as her second. Ruby stood with Sunshine a moment after giving her the cookie, taking the time to scratch her poll and ears as the golden mare nuzzled her. Then she patted the old mare on the shoulder and walked away from her. Sunshine headed for the heated automatic water fountain. Now that the herd leader had moved on, the other horses surrounded Ruby. She handed out cookies.

"Legacy. Come on, girl," she said softly. Legacy pricked her ears forward, then pranced toward Ruby, at one point snaking her head to snap at Dancer to keep him from crowding Ruby for treats. Ruby quickly tied the halter on Legacy's head and eased her through the gate. The mare snorted at a flapping tarp by the machine shed and jumped sideways as Charlie came out of the cow barn. A growl from Ruby made Legacy settle but she was still energetic, ears flicking back and forth, head high, and generally just full of herself.

"She's full of beans today!" Charlie called as he walked to the machine shed.

"Just like great-grandma!" Ruby yelled back, grinning, remembering the early training days with Sunshine. Legacy didn't just *look* like Sunshine, there were days when she *acted* like Sunshine. For caution's sake, after she saddled Legacy, she took the mare into the small indoor arena that was part of the horse barn to start out. Last fall's trainer had used harsher methods than Ruby realized. More often than not, now, Legacy bucked hard before wanting to gallop her usual six circuits of the arena before settling.

After two big leaps and her six hard loops at the gallop, Legacy slowed and was willing to walk on a loose rein. Ruby dismounted and loaded the saddlebags. Then she took Legacy through the alleyway and outside, remounting the golden mare in the barnyard. She settled the mare into the big, ground-covering walk that most of Sunshine's descendants had, riding through the bottomlands instead of uphill, deciding to go to the Lone Pine Pasture by way of one group of the test fields after all. *Look it over quickly, come back and test later,* she told herself.

Slowly, Ruby relaxed into the presence of the land around her. Last night's snow was mostly melted, though the skies were gray and threatened rain at some point. A raw damp wind gust roared by, flicking Legacy's mud-stained white mane around and making Ruby grab the brim of her hat to settle it more firmly. Legacy's hooves squished in the bottomland mud, but her stride remained steady despite the occasional slip of one hoof or another.

They passed a strip of old Ponderosa pines clinging to the side of a ridge. Ruby drew a deep breath, savoring the rich earthy scent of early spring and the faint roar of the breeze in the treetops. Such a contrast from yesterday...she was in the crowded airport shuttle at about this time, she thought. Then it had been the flight, and the trip home...but now she had Legacy striding along underneath her, ears flicking back and forth, occasionally mouthing the bit softly as she played with the contact between it and Ruby's hands.

Home. Where I belong.

Thoughts of Gabe intruded, and she brushed them away. Not yet. Not until she was ready to consider such things. She needed more time on the land first.

The draw divided and she turned Legacy to go up the left side on the route to the Lone Pine horse pasture, past the first test field. They crossed a small bridge over a seasonal creek. Legacy arched her head and eyed the snowy wooden planks suspiciously, but obeyed when Ruby pressed her calves against her sides. They followed a narrow track along the east side of the field. The creek ran on the west side, its path marked by old cottonwood trees.

Ruby halted Legacy about halfway up, studying the field. Patches of snow still remained amongst the stubble of last year's crop, but where the snow was clear she could see the faint green of winter wheat seedlings. She blinked up the time—

well, she could scan this field at least, and then the next one. No time to backtrack and look at the fields up the right-hand draw, at least not today. She pulled out her scanner, activated the drone module and programmed the parameters of the survey she wanted, then flicked it out to hover over the field.

The buzzing as the scanner glided over the field caught Legacy's attention. Her head shot up and she stared at the whirring *thing* as it traversed the field. Ruby felt the mare's back muscles tighten up underneath her and took a shorter grip on the reins to forestall a buck or spook. The scanner finished its route and whizzed back toward them. Legacy snorted and backed two steps before turning to whirl away. Ruby guided her around into a spin which left them facing the scanner. Legacy crowhopped as it got closer.

Ruby sighed and clucked the hold signal to the scanner. She dismounted, grabbing the halter rope off the saddle horn and leaving her reins crossed over Legacy's neck. She walked the length of the lead rope to the hovering scanner, and snapped her fingers to have it follow her hand. Then she moved carefully toward Legacy, keeping the lead tight.

"About time you learned how to deal with these devices, little mare," she said quietly. Legacy raised her head high, blowing a long nervous roller snort through her nostrils. "Not gonna kill you. You've seen them working the fields. Got to learn how to tolerate them up close. You're going to have a lot of exposure to these things over the next few years, if everything works out."

It took a few minutes, but at last Ruby stood next to Legacy with the scanner buzzing softly in drone mode, still hovering over her hand. The palomino mare finally blew on the scanner, then dared to touch it with a nostril, jerking back at the vibration. Ruby waited, continuing to talk softly as Legacy touched it again. A few more minutes and several more touches, and then the mare blew a relaxed snort, shaking her head. Ruby deactivated the drone mode and tucked the scanner back into a knee pocket. She grunted with the effort as she climbed back onto Legacy.

Getting stiff. Getting old.

Still, Legacy was tense enough that Ruby urged her into a long trot along the track to use that energy productively, heading for the next field. They dropped into a walk to cross another bridge, which also earned the suspicious study from Legacy, before riding up the west side of this field.

This time Legacy was alert and watchful, but allowed Ruby to pause the scanner and then ride up to it so she could retrieve the scanner from horseback.

"Good girl." Ruby patted Legacy's neck, adding a short scratch in an itchy spot along her mane.

Learns quickly, just like Sunshine.

They followed the track away from the field and started to climb toward the top of the ridge. Up here the ground still had a skiff of dry snow, and wasn't so muddy. Ruby urged Legacy into a lope through the trees. The track stopped at the top of the ridge. Ruby halted Legacy to let the golden mare catch her breath. Then she turned the mare north, toward the Lone Pine pasture.

Now Ruby let herself think about Gabe. What did she really want from him after all these years? Another relationship? Remy *was* right. Gabe as a spouse had required caretaking, and that had been when he was young and healthy. She doubted that things would be much different these days, especially since he now had health problems. So. One point against getting back together with Gabe, at least in a personal relationship. Maybe if they had remained married, she would feel differently about it, but now? No.

And that was another thing. Ruby *liked* having her own

life. Her own bed to herself, not needing to compromise or check in with anyone about her personal life. Professionally, yes, she was accountable, had been accountable to Charlie and Martin for years as their boss and partner. But personally....

Would she want to give some or all of that up to have Gabe back? True, he was still a damn attractive man...not that Ruby burned to take him to bed again.

Plus letting herself trust Gabe again...ah, there was the catch. The big piece. Trusting him not to break her heart was risky. That more than anything else made Ruby hesitate. She could ignore or work with the other two points. But trust was the breaking point.

A professional collaboration might have some possibilities, and she wouldn't be risking heartbreak. Gabe had always been a better long-range planner, and generous with his skills. The two of them together had been a great professional team—one reason why they had earned that first Superstar. But the personal screwed everything up. So maybe that was what she needed to focus on, pretending a personal connection while collaborating professionally. Gabe could probably make use of her skills, too.

Her thoughts about Gabe broke off as they approached the gate to the Lone Pine pasture. It was a wire gate, so Ruby had to dismount to open it. She untied the halter rope again, then tied the reins loosely to the saddle horn so Legacy wouldn't step on them, planning to walk from here. After wrestling the gate closed, she pulled out the scanner to help her locate the problem sensor. This close, she should be able to get more details than she had before. She'd have to find a good place to tie Legacy as well.

Annoyingly, the sensor data was still muddled and incomplete. Ruby growled wordlessly and tucked it away. This did not look good. She angled toward the nearest boundary fence.

The cross-fence between pastures looked all right, but they hadn't put sensors on those posts, only the boundaries.

They reached the corner and Ruby trudged uphill along the boundary fence, Legacy following her. She stopped to check a sensor on top of one of the rockjack posts, anchored by a wooden tripod and box that held a pile of rocks. The self-test flashed green. Nothing was wrong with it. Ruby frowned, and pulled her scanner out. No signal. That shouldn't be happening if the self-test said nothing was wrong...unless the signal had been hijacked somehow.

What the heck?

She checked several more sensors, some on rockjacks, others on braces and the stouter posts. More of the same. Then, as they reached the crossbrace midway through the fenceline, she groaned. On the west side of the brace, the fence held strong and tight. On the east side, all four wires sagged loose and the fence was flat on the ground, half of the posts pushed over.

Elk? she wondered. No, the herd normally jumped the fence, they wouldn't break all four wires right at the brace, and they sure wouldn't knock the posts down.

Human action. We Love Animals and Nature at work?

Ruby pressed her lips tightly together. She checked her comm, hoping that maybe enough connectivity remained on the nearby boundary fence for her to reach the ranch. Nothing.

She hesitated, then went to the saddlebags to pull out the snub-nosed .38 in its holster. Sabotage. Had to be. For what reason she wasn't sure yet, unless it was WLAN (and they usually chose more visual and dramatic actions), but she wasn't going to take any chances. She slid the holster onto her belt. Normally she didn't wear the pistol because...memories. But she always carried it with her when riding out alone, just in case. Not wearing the pistol was a choice Gabe had scolded her for in the past—*no, now is not the time to think about Gabe. Distraction.*

Then she followed the fence line further, down a short slope and back up. All along the way, the fence was flattened, and wires cut on each side of the steadying rockjacks. Ruby sighed. She tied Legacy to one of the rockjacks. How far did this fence cutting go and why hadn't the sensors warned of it? They should have gone off.

At least it was easy to pull the downed fence away from the rockjack where she'd tied Legacy. But this level of fence repair wasn't going to be a simple one where she could just splice the break. Not with half the posts knocked down. Even the occasional metal t-post had been pulled up. She'd have to replace fenceposts as well as sensors, and reestablish the network. And that would be expensive.

And then there was the wire. They'd have to string new wire. For how far? She'd better call Ron Campbell when she got back to the ranch, see if he could come up tomorrow to give her a quote. But at least she could get some of the pieces gathered up before any creature got tangled. Ruby pulled heavy gloves out of her saddlebags and started rolling up and dragging the downed fence and posts to make a pile.

As Ruby worked, she studied the land around the posts. No tracks of human, vehicle, or horse, and it was muddy enough that she should have seen *something*. The fence-cutting must have happened when there was enough snow that whoever did this hadn't sunk into the dirt. Why hadn't the sensors issued a warning earlier? This was exactly the sort of thing they had been set up for. But that would mean the cutting—and the hijacking of the sensors—had happened some time ago. The snow had been off of these ridges for at least a week, even though it lingered in the sheltered stubblefields at a lower elevation. Why hadn't the sensors alerted until now?

She should take at least two sensors for examination and maybe more. Ruby detached one. Gathered a few, then put them in Legacy's saddlebags. Maybe Martin and Julie could figure out what had gone wrong. She reached for another sensor. It suddenly flared bright red. Ruby backed away from it. *Now* it was working. Why?

Cr-aa-ck! Gunfire, from nearby and behind her as something stung her cheek—*on my own land!* Ruby dove for the ground, pulling her pistol free, outrage and fear pulsing through her. Another shot—*where the hell is it coming from?* She snapped off a shot toward where she thought the shooter was. Not that she could reach them...sounded like a rifle...but at least they'd know she was armed.

Legacy reared high and pulled against the rope as a third shot rang out, right after Ruby's. The main post of the rockjack that she was tied to broke and the golden mare bolted, head pulled at a slant as she dragged the chunk of wood, frantically running as it bounced along beside her.

Damn it damn it damn it!

Ruby desperately eyed the ridges around her. Where could that shot have come from? She'd think she could see anyone shooting at her from that angle. Unless they were fleeing.... She snapped off a second shot in that direction. Maybe that would send them running if they weren't already.

She waited, but there were no more shots. After what seemed to be an eternity, she waved her hat. Nothing. Ruby cautiously straightened up. Still nothing. She patted her stinging cheek. Felt like just a scratch. The bullet must have hit a nearby rock and spalled off a small chip. Lucky. She walked over to the rockjack. Legacy shouldn't have broken it that easily. Ruby inhaled sharply as she saw that the rockjack's main post had been sawed three-quarters of the way through. She knelt to study it closer. The outside edges of the saw marks had been carefully obscured so that a casual observation wouldn't reveal the cut.

Ruby pressed her lips tightly together. *Sabotage. For sure.* WLAN? This looked like something they would do. Legacy was likely to hurt herself if she ran very far with that post chunk flailing around at the end of her lead rope...unless it managed to slip loose. She sighed.

Legacy was headed for Vickie's place, away from the noise that had spooked her, not back toward the ranch. With any luck Vickie's gates would be closed so Ruby could easily catch up with Legacy, see how bad things were, and hopefully get a trailer ride back to the home place from Vickie. Otherwise they faced a long walk home.

At least the ground was soggy enough now that she could easily follow Legacy's tracks in the mud. To her relief, she found the broken post on the ground fairly quickly, and didn't see any sign of horsehair or blood on it. Maybe, with the chunk gone, Legacy would slow down and let her catch up.

She whistled and called. Nothing.

Ruby traipsed along, occasionally stopping to call and whistle before checking her comm status. Still no signal, so she couldn't call the ranch, or Vickie, for that matter.

Closer back to the land than I really wanted.

Ruby chuckled for a moment in spite of the situation. Wasn't it always something like this when ranching? Oh well, she wasn't hurt and hopefully Legacy was all right as well. She inhaled deeply, hoping to eliminate the last traces of polluted urban air from her lungs. At least it was a nice day and not snowy or rainy.

Trudge, trudge, trudge. Would she reach Vickie's before noon? Or perhaps find Legacy? At last someone answered her whistle and call. Ruby couldn't hear what the person was hollering, but it *was* another person.

"I'm over here!" she yelled.

"Ruby!" Vickie's voice, from a distance.

"I'm over here!" Ruby repeated.

And then two heelers topped the ridge line and started barking at Ruby.

"Tippy! Boots! Come here!" she called. The heelers galloped toward her, still barking, until they skidded to a stop by Ruby. "Good dogs, good dogs," she said, scratching their heads as they squirmed around her legs, vying for attention from a known friend. And then Vickie came over the ridge, riding her black Dolly mare and leading Legacy. Vickie picked up a trot and to Ruby's relief it appeared that Legacy was trotting fine with no bobbles. The dogs charged back toward Dolly and Legacy. The golden mare startled, her eyes wide, showing the white sclera around them.

Vickie halted Dolly and spoke softly to Legacy. Ruby strode over to them.

"Thanks, Vickie," she said. "I was afraid I was going to have a real long walk."

"Took some work to catch her," Vickie said. "She's real skittery right now."

"Someone took a shot at us." Ruby took Legacy's lead. "Rifle, sounded like. Something big." At least it didn't look like Legacy had been hit. Just frightened.

"What?" Vickie's jaw dropped. "You okay?" She leaned over to look at Ruby's cheek. "That doesn't look deep but it's long."

"Yeah. Think one bullet hit a rock and knocked off a chip."

"Damn lucky. Bullet could have hit you or knocked that chip into your eye."

"No kidding." Ruby blew hard, shaking her head. "Someone cut fence for at least a quarter mile along our boundary. Knocked all the posts down, even the t-posts. I'd tied

Legacy to a rockjack, only to find out that it had been partially cut through, then masked so that I couldn't see it was damaged until she broke it."

Vickie whistled. "So *that's* what happened. I was riding out because the sensors said there was a problem. Then I saw Legacy running the fence by the gate."

"Same here. Sensors out, and then I found the problem." Ruby scratched Legacy's neck, then examined her chest and legs, visual at first, then gently rubbing her hands up and down Legacy's forelegs. "Fence looks like it was cut before the snow went off." Her legs were fine. Legacy flinched when Ruby poked at her chest and neck—a little soreness, to be expected.

Put her in the barn and give her some painkiller tonight. She found a fresh fingertip cut on Legacy's left haunch. *So she got hit by a chip too.* That would have added to the reasons for the golden mare to spook like that.

"That's not right. Those sensors should show when that happened."

"Exactly." Ruby sent Legacy out to the end of the lead rope and clucked to her until she trotted. She watched the mare move until satisfied that Legacy wasn't hurt bad, just mildly sore. "Whoa, Legacy." The mare eagerly came to her and Ruby scratched her forehead and poll. Legacy sighed and relaxed. "I ran the self-test on the sensors. Nothing wrong with them...but I can't pick up the network at all. The signal's been hijacked."

"What the hell is going on?"

"Sabotage is what I'm thinking." Ruby grabbed the saddle horn. She shook it and Legacy jumped. Ruby sent her back out on the lead to trot until she calmed. "Looks like Legacy got off lucky. I was afraid that damn post might have broken one of her legs, or that she'd gotten hung up."

Vickie whistled. "Damn. That *was* lucky. Could have hurt her bad."

"Yeah. And now I wonder what else is wrong with that damn fence."

"Did you get a look at whoever took a shot at you?"

Ruby shook her head. "They hightailed it and I never got an eye on them."

"You'd think they'd have kicked off one of your other boundary sensors. No way they'd go by the ranch headquarters."

"Unless they snuck off toward the Reed place. And now I'm not sure just how much I trust any of my sensors. Damn it, I so did not need this extra chaos. Not with the Superhero expenses breathing down my neck." Ruby stopped Legacy. This time the golden mare stood quietly when Ruby shook the saddle horn. She checked the cinch, tightened it, untied the reins from the saddle horn, and swung back up onto Legacy's back.

"Thanks for catching her, Vickie. I was worried."

"She came right to Dolly once I called the dogs off. At first I thought she'd dumped you, but then thought no, not with the reins tied to the horn and the lead rope dragging—especially with a loop in the lead. Then I wasn't sure just what had happened. Glad you're all right. Want company on the ride back to your place? It's about as far for you as it is for me from here, and I'd like to see what is going on with that fence line."

"I'd sure appreciate it. Whoever shot at us had a rifle."

"Got mine right here," Vickie said, slapping the scabbard underneath her leg. "And I think we should take turns holding each other's horses while we look at it. If they cut one rockjack, they probably cut more."

"That's what I figured. Thanks, Vickie. I'll trailer you two back."

"Eh, I'll ride Dolly on the road. Won't take that long, and she needs a good long work, anyway." Vickie patted the black mare's neck. "She's getting fat this winter. I've not been getting out as much as I should." She frowned. "This aging stuff isn't for sissies."

"Yeah. Gabe looks like shit. He got the G9 last year, along with his wife. She died but he didn't—he thinks his microbial work might have somehow helped him along."

"More likely that he's too cussed for the G9 to haul him off."

"Yeah. He's gone soft, though. Using a cane and all." Ruby tightened her lips and focused on Legacy's mane. "Makes me wonder. I'm six years younger."

"So are you getting back together with him? Lots of PR coming out of AgI hinting that it might be a possibility."

Ruby snorted and rolled her eyes. "How much of that is Brandon's agitating to get us together? I got pitched to reunite by both him and the upper execs. They say it's a good storyline that will lead to many views."

"Oh God, the almighty clicks. But are you leaning that way?"

"Are you kidding? It's all about the clicks—all part of how the AgI works now with all the game show financing competition. And the Superhero stuff seems to be even more about storylines and clicks than the Superstar was. I suppose it makes sense that they want a greater entertainment value. More money at stake and it being a one-off thing." Ruby exhaled through her teeth, popping her tongue against the roof of her mouth. Legacy perked up. Ruby encouraged her to move into a jog. "Now I wonder if I shouldn't do something with all this coming down. The fence cutting. The shots. The tampering with the sensors. That would give 'em some drama."

"You sure you want to give whoever did this that much publicity?" Vickie encouraged Dolly to catch up with Legacy.

"It might backfire on you if you do it wrong. Especially if it's activists like WLAN."

Ruby shrugged. "It's drama. And drama is a big part of this whole production. The more clicks I get, the more people want to follow my story, and the better chance I have to win the Superhero."

"Makes the queen business seem straightforward."

Ruby laughed. "Yeah, between speeches, beauty pageant, horsemanship, and ticket sales, sure does." They rode silently for a few minutes. "Unfortunately, no one's running a queen competition to fund ag projects. If they did, I'd have it locked up solid. So the Superhero is what I've gotta do if I'm going to get the RubyBot off the ground—and I have to do that, Vickie. I get the Superhero, then I can launch the RubyBot and pay off a lot of bills."

"And if you don't win?"

"I'll figure something out. Always have." Ruby chewed her lip. "Maybe this fence-cutting drama will outweigh the push from AgI about cooperating with the Gabe storyline."

"You seriously considering it?"

"For real? Come on."

"Stay firm in your convictions," Vickie said. "What he did to you and Brandon was unacceptable. Taking up with that Mariah—and just how the hell did she end up being a finalist on the show with her history?"

"Wouldn't I like to know that myself."

"More drama?"

"Yeah. But there's more to it. She's been buzzing around, offered to buy out the two newbies in the Superhero. Plus—she contacted Gabe and Charlie about buying their shares in the Double R. And she wanted to buy me out."

"What the—what kind of game is she playing?"

"I wish I knew," Ruby said.

Vickie sighed. "I've got a further complication for you. Was going to come over after I checked the fence. We've had some rogue killbots showing up on our fields, found them yesterday. Haven't run an analysis because I wanted your people's input on what they could be. I've got samples."

"Huh. That throws some additional problems into the mix. Shit." Ruby frowned. "I wonder if the fence cutting is tied to that. Maybe I should talk about the rogue killbots along with the fence cutting."

"I wouldn't. Not until you've got more solid information. But yeah, it does sound suspicious."

"I'd better talk to Jim Reed. If he has killbots spreading on his land too, then it might explain what's going on with the fence. I only took samples on two of my fields—god, I wonder if I've got those rogue killbots too."

"Still leaves the question of just how someone was able to access our lands."

"Yeah. Hey. I'll go ahead and give you two a ride back to your place. I want to pick up those samples."

Vickie chuckled. "I've got a few in my saddlebags. No need to have you rush around just to haul us back. Won't take us that long, and Dolly needs the work. I imagine you've got a lot on your plate already, and this mess just adds to it."

"That's sure the truth," Ruby conceded. It *was* going to be a long day. She wanted to get started on recruiting interns at some point during the day as well. But first she had to call Ron about the damn fence.

"Or I tell you what. Let me talk to the Reeds, and we'll meet at your place tonight, and he can bring you his samples, too. This affects all of us, not just you."

"Gotta agree with that. Thanks, Vickie."

Vickie shrugged. "Mike and I would much rather have you manage to stay on the Double R than deal with whomever it is that Mariah Meyers is fronting for. Jim and Carol probably feel the same way. I'm sure you're gonna have your hands full, no matter what. So if we can help you, I know for sure I'll do it."

"What would I do without neighbors like you?" Ruby grinned at Vickie. "You've done a lot for me over the years. Thanks, Vickie."

Vickie shrugged, blushing, and clucked at Dolly to trot. Ruby did the same for Legacy. She felt better now that she wasn't out here alone.

Looks like no more solo rides until I'm done with this damn Superhero competition.

Oh well. It was only a month, after all, and well worth the sacrifice.

CHAPTER 5

THE COMM BUZZ IN HER EAR STARTLED RUBY. THE projection flashed *Brandon Ramirez* in bright red letters over the spreadsheet she was working on. She sighed, and glanced up from her work to see the last flecks of magenta and red sunset clouds before answering. How had it gotten so late? She had managed to get back to the house by one pm, in spite of all the craziness with Legacy and the fence cutting.

It's been a long day for sure.

"What the hell is going on, Mom?" Brandon shouted over the connection before she could say anything, almost before the projection settled, waving his hands frantically, just like Gabe would when he was excited or upset. "Fence cutting—sensor tampering—someone taking a shot at you and Legacy—fence posts sawed off! What is going on? Are you all right?"

"So you've seen the clip I uploaded about today's events."

That was fast.

Vickie had helped Ruby shoot a good half-hour's worth of documentation of the fence cutting, the broken posts, and the lack of any tracks in the mud. But the sensor that had flashed at Ruby was shattered into bits—from what? The rifle shot? Possible. Ruby had edited that footage out of the clip she'd given to

AgInnovator. That had been a chore, editing down thirty minutes to five minutes of very quick montages about the destruction plus Legacy's skittishness and chest soreness.

"Seen? Hell, Mom, I just got out of a meeting about it. Now we're wondering if this is an attack on you specifically or all our Superhero candidates. No one else in the Innovator is reporting problems, and WLAN isn't making any proclamations."

"Not reporting so far, you mean. Figuring out the extent of the problem that we have to deal with is what we are looking at right now," Ruby said, deliberately pitching her voice to be low and calm. She leaned back in her chair. "But as you can see for yourself, I'm all right except for this scratch on my cheek."

She flinched as she brushed fingers across it. Vickie had cleaned it out when they got to the Double R. It was still touchy. Right on her cheekbone. A little higher and the chip *would* have hit her eye.

"You've reported this to the authorities, I hope?" The tension eased slightly from his face.

"Yep. Vickie has as well since it involves our boundary fence—we both talked to the sheriff. But I'm still going to be responsible for fixing it. Jim Reed is checking his fences—I'll know if he has issues, too, later on this evening. I wouldn't be surprised to find out that he's had fence cut as well. It has all of the hallmarks of a WLAN action."

"Except they're not claiming responsibility, which is weird. I don't mind telling you there's quite the uproar going on here," Brandon continued in a calmer tone, running his fingers through his hair. "Was it really that bad?"

"There's a lot more going on that I didn't put into that video clip. I've got thirty minutes of footage, plus there's things going on that I left out of the clip that may or may not be related to the sabotage."

Brandon flinched. "More going on? Ma, what the hell?"

"There's rogue killbots, on both the Chandler and Reed properties. Martin thinks, from scans I did today, that we have them on our test fields, too. We're meeting tonight to talk about the killbots as well as the fences. Martin and Julie are doing research on some samples of those killbots right now, and yes, before you ask, Terri's videoing their lab work. I'm keeping as complete a record as possible." Ruby paused. "This could be a local thing, but if so, why the three of us? I'll know more later on, after I talk with the Chandlers and Reeds. They're checking their own situations in further detail."

"God. Ma. That's still—" Brandon shook his head. "Things like this aren't supposed to happen in Thunder County!"

Ruby masked a quick grin with her hand so that Brandon wouldn't see it. "Oh honey, at one time this was the Wild West. That's why I'm getting together with Jim, Carol, Mike, and Vicki tonight. Neighbors take care of each other."

"This situation plays all hell with the story line," Brandon muttered. "Though so far your votes seem to be trending, ever since you posted that clip. It has gotten you more support."

"There you go. More drama, more eyeballs and clicks. Much more interesting than your dad and I getting back together, hmm?"

"Mom, if you set this up just to avoid us going down that storyline...."

Ruby sat up. "I hope to hell you didn't think I *made* this happen! Not only is it a distraction, but it's expensive to deal with. I'm going to need to replace that whole line of sensors—maybe all of my boundary sensors, as well as repair a good quarter-mile of fencing. That's before we start dealing with the rogue killbot issue and cleaning up everyone's fields. And I have to wonder if contending for the Superhero is a factor in this whole mess."

"That's—our concern as well," Brandon sighed. "Despite

the lack of claims, we've not ruled out activist groups. Just because WLAN is silent doesn't mean other organizations might not be involved."

"It sure ups the stakes for me, because I need to win in order to pay off the expense of replacing fences and sensors. I'm not going to ask the Reeds and Chandlers for financial help unless it's clear that all three of us are the targets. Otherwise, I'm assuming that they're affected only because they're my neighbors."

"Please keep us posted, and for heaven's sake, will you *please call one of us* before you upload something as important as this again? Legal is freaking out about the implications."

"Gee, I didn't think this would be that big a deal," Ruby said sarcastically. "Brandon, sooner or later AgI is going to have to deal with sabotage. I'm surprised there hasn't been more of it during past competitions besides low-level stuff. This—this is more than I would anticipate. And if it's found out that the Superhero is a motivation for this—AgI's got problems."

Brandon swallowed hard, looking down. Ruby stared at him, suspicion rising.

"Brandon, *have* there been other incidents?"

He looked up, the sheepish expression on his face a dead giveaway.

"There have been," she said flatly. "I know your expressions too well, kiddo. What's going on? My Innovator and Star awards had a couple of minor incidents. Nothing like this."

"If this ends up being tied to the Superhero, it *will* be the biggest sabotage the competition's ever had. But. It's not without precedent." Brandon slumped back in his chair. "Nothing in this year's competition until now. Minor interferences last year that we could tie to WLAN. But three years ago —yes, there were some big problems with the Superstar. Collusion between two competitors to sabotage the other four finalists, no activist groups involved at all. We kept a lid on it, came up with a face-saving reason to dismiss the saboteurs, but... some of it leaked. That's why the storyline with you and Dad getting back together seemed to be such a natural. A positive element. Both of you have immaculate records, not just with AgI but in your business dealings."

"If the cleanliness of our past business history is a concern, then why the hell was Mariah allowed to enter, much less serve as a finalist?"

Brandon winced. "She has—special circumstances. Georgy himself pushed to have her in it." Georgy Batineau, the president of AgI, had been one of Mariah's consorts for many years.

"Well, she's one of my sabotage suspects. You know she's been approaching everyone about buying them out except for your dad—and she only wanted to buy his share of the Double R."

"I know," he snapped. "She's approached me as well. But it's all scripted out, Ma! And I'm behind a firewall so I can't affect the voting."

"Wait. Mariah's approaches are part of a script?"

"She suggested it to Georgy, Mom, and he'll do whatever she suggests. The original plan was only for four finalists. Just like it was planned to have both of you on the show to offset any influence I might have. Fortunately, you both have strong offerings." Brandon held up a hand. "Wait. Before you say anything, it's agreed that she is not going to win. She has a contract stating that." He frowned. "Please don't share this with *anyone*, Mom. I'll get in trouble if it's found out I told you."

"Of course. But still—*she's not really a competitor?*"

"She's getting compensation in return for playing her role," Brandon said tiredly. "Her offers to buy everyone else out are supposed to add drama to the finalist competition. You'll see bigger and more dramatic offers as the month goes on and we start weeding out competition."

"Lovely," Ruby grumbled. "I suppose future offers will be recorded, if they haven't been already?"

"Her interviews at the party were recorded," Brandon said. "They'll be edited into later episodes."

Ruby shook her head, then rested her forehead in her hands. She couldn't really object to this. Not with the way the contract was written. But still...wait. They wanted drama. If the fence cutting was drawing eyeballs, maybe she could get some compensation from AgI for the fence. She sat back up.

"This fence thing is really problematic, Brandon. Especially coupled with rogue killbots and the extent of the destruction. Those sensors and the timing of the cutting...why didn't they show up until today, when I've returned from recording the finalist announcement? I'd say that argues for a connection with the show since it's pretty clear it has happened at least a week or two ago."

"Yeah, that's one thing that Legal was concerned about," Brandon said. "And besides checking in to make sure you were all right for myself, I do have some good news for you from the show. We'll pick up the tab for fence and sensor repair especially since—well, doesn't look to me like makeup is going to cover that injury so people will wonder. Send a report when you know how extensive the problem is."

"Well." She was momentarily speechless. This wasn't an action that she had expected AgI to take. *Clicks must really have been good,* she thought cynically. Then again, Legal was concerned. And neither the Reeds nor the Chandlers had signed agreements not to sue the show, either. "Thank you, and pass the thanks along," she said finally. "That's a big help."

"AgI will also be posting a reward for catching whoever it was," Brandon said. "Last thing we want is for something like this to become a regular state of affairs with our competitors. But once things escalate to this point, we need to squelch sabotage, whether it comes from your competition or another source. Our investigators will be on site tomorrow, by the way. They should have already talked to Vickie and James about permissions, and they'll be working with the Thunder County Sheriff's Department. We're scripting out a show focusing on this incident, as part of a wider focus on farm and ranch crop and livestock crime problems, such as crop thefts, vandalism, livestock thefts and so on."

"Thanks," Ruby repeated. "And the rogue killbots?"

"Get more information and a source before we do anything more with it," Brandon said. "That—that's something I know for sure that our people don't want to publicize." He frowned. "Eight years ago two competitors deliberately released pheromone modifiers on each other's fields to interfere with pollination. I was one of the staff working on it, during my internship." He grimaced. "That was a delightful *welcome to your new job* moment."

"I didn't hear about *that*." Ruby frowned. "I got an Innovator that year—I would have thought I'd hear some rumors."

Brandon shook his head. "No. That's the kind of thing we shut down fast. Not good for the show. Same goes for the rogue killbots. We need to know the origins before we get too public about them. But the fence cutting and someone taking a shot at you—that's something we need to publicize and draw a line. Just—next time—hopefully there won't be a next time—don't post but check in first. Okay?"

"So you can craft the spin." Now she just felt tired.

"It affects scripting." He half-smiled. "Though there are several writers who are singing your praises right now. They're happy to have the overtime due to this new development."

"All right." Ruby sighed. "I'll let you know what James says about his fences."

"Actually—" Brandon hesitated. "If you could tape the meeting and upload it tomorrow? I should be able to get you some edit points by morning to fit the narrative we're creating. Don't include the killbots but do record your talk about the fences."

"Get releases?"

"Got 'em." Brandon smiled but it looked world-weary, not the expression of the little boy who had once loved to ride out on the Double R with her. "And Ma?"

"Yes."

"Be careful until you've figured out what's going on with this fence and shooting stuff, okay? Please. It might be an activist group like WLAN, or...something else."

"I will. And you take care of yourself. You're looking tired."

Brandon shrugged. "It's a busy month. Love you, Ma. I'll come stay at the Double R after we finish filming, how's that? I need to get up there and spend time with you and Dad."

"You're always welcome here," Ruby said. "And as for your father—well, that's something you'll have to take up with him."

"Ma." Brandon grimaced, hesitated, then shook his head. "You two are stubborn as hell. As you insist. All the same, I love you."

"Love you too."

He signed off. Ruby stretched and went over to the window. She crossed her arms, chewing on her lip as she studied the snow-covered mountains as dusk fell.

Well, if AgI picks up the tab for fixing the fences, that'll be a big relief.

All the same, she wasn't going to count on that likelihood until she actually saw the cash in her account.

AgI gives, and AgI can take away.

And then there was the revelation about Mariah. Ruby didn't know what to think about that—yet.

THE MEETING THAT EVENING WAS AS MUCH A SOCIAL occasion as a war council. Vickie and Mike brought an apple-raspberry crisp while Jim and Carol brought buffalo jerky, cheese, and crackers to add to the dried fruit, popcorn, chips and homemade salsa made by Martin. Then there was much whispering in the kitchen as Charlie wandered into the big living room, holding something behind his back. Several cams hovered behind him, then darted to preset recording sites, humming softly.

"All clear," he called into the kitchen.

"What's going on?" Ruby asked, even as Charlie grinned and showed the bottle of champagne. "Oh no, you guys didn't... you shouldn't have...." Her voice trailed off as Julie carried a tiny cake into the living room and set it on the big oak table under the picture window to join the crisp and other nibbles. Martin and Terri followed with another bottle and glasses for all.

Well, this'll make for a good scene for AgI.

"Thought that before we talk about these problems, we need to celebrate you making the Finalist round," Vickie said. "We'd already talked about doing something like this, and, well —good before the bad."

"You shouldn't have," Ruby said. But she couldn't deny the warm feelings that washed over her as she studied the cake. CONGRATULATIONS RUBY was carefully iced in bright red over the chocolate frosting—and she hoped the cake was chocolate, too.

After they ate the cake and crisp, as well as a glass of champagne and other nibbles, they settled into couches and chairs.

Ruby sighed. "Fun time's over. But I do have some good news. AgI has offered to foot the bill for all of our fence and sensor repairs. I got written confirmation from Brandon just an hour ago."

"That's a good thing," Jim said. "Carol and I rode out after your call—Carol went with the deputies while I checked the fences. Besides sensor malfunctions, we've also got fences cut. Just along the boundary with your property—no, wait. Also a smaller cut on the Forest Service boundary. Near as they could tell, that was how whoever it was got access."

"Did they find any sign of either the fence cutters or the shooter?"

Carol frowned. "They got excited about a couple of things but were pretty closed-mouth about it. Said they'd keep looking around. They said that AgI's own investigators are coming tomorrow?"

"That's what Brandon told me." So AgI *had* been in touch with the sheriff. Good.

"No sign of the fence cutters right up to the Forest Service boundary—snow's gone off. But they were going to go up that way and see what sign they could find," Carol finished.

"Well, that's something. I really am sorry that you're getting drug into this mess because of me," Ruby said.

Carol tightened her lips and shook her head. "It's not right that it's happening to you, Ruby."

"How extensive is the damage?"

"Two sections of about a quarter mile each," Jim said. "No response from the sensors along that whole line."

"The signal got hijacked," Terri said. She ran her fingers through her tightly curled black hair, frowning. "Multiple alternative routing to several different sites. I turned that information over to the deputies—my tracking came to dead ends. I suspect portable sites that shut down after you rode out there, Ruby, set to switch off once someone came to investigate. It looks really suspicious to me."

"It wasn't a cheap operation," Julie added. "Whoever did this came through and slapped diverters onto each sensor within those areas where they cut fence. By hand."

"Any clues about who it might have been?"

"Nothing," Martin said. "So far. But odds are, given the weather we've had this winter, they probably cut fence and tampered with the sensors on the same trip. They'd have to silence the sensors first, then cut the wire."

"Either a long day for one person or else they brought multiple people, hmm?" Vickie said.

"It'd take several days for one person to cut all that wire and saw posts the way they did as well as mess with the sensors," Martin said. "Even two people—and each additional person added to their group just adds to the risk of someone noticing what's going on. Especially in winter. And coming in from the Forest Service land, someone would be likely to see their vehicles."

"Or someone camped out nearby, worked a little bit every day, and arranged to be picked up when they were done," Ruby said. "But there's a limited window of time when they could be there—I doubt there would be much interest before I made it into the Superhero finals."

"Say about two weeks ago." Charlie frowned. "Any earlier and I would have seen sign on the last ride I did up that way. And the snow's been off a week. So...sometime during that week."

"They would have to plan things awfully fast, given that I was announced as a finalist three weeks ago," Ruby said.

"And how much interference are other AgI competitors getting?" Mike asked.

"Brandon said there's been some sabotage," Ruby said. "But —I don't know how much he can tell me. I got the feeling he might be holding some information back."

"Probably is," Vickie said. "You know how these competitions are."

"Nonetheless, it's a big relief to hear that AgI is willing to finance the fence replacement," Jim said.

"Yeah," Ruby said slowly. "So if you can get me the data on how much fence you lost on that Forest Service boundary, I'll get the repair estimates to AgI. Also, I'm going to ask for funding for you to have sensors on all your boundary fences, not just the ones we share. I think that's a really good idea."

"I'm not going to turn it down, that's for sure," Jim said.

Silence fell over them. Ruby eyed Julie. "What's our recording status?"

"It's time to turn them off?"

Ruby nodded.

Julie clucked to the cams and they obediently buzzed to her. Ruby waited for Julie to give her a thumbs up to ensure they were all shut off before continuing.

"Now we need to talk about the rogue killbots. Not going to record this because Brandon's pretty squishy on this subject. But I also have to apologize for this particular problem, because I don't think you'd have it if I wasn't going for the Superhero." She grimaced. "I'm sorry. It seems things are a lot more complicated in this competition than they were twenty-five years ago."

"Lot more money at stake," Vickie said. "And when there's money in play, you're gonna run into people who are going to push the limits."

Jim leaned forward in his chair, his gnarled hands clasped together. "You've been pretty good about dealing with situations all the years I've known you, Ruby. Fair and straight-shooting. Bot overflow from your experimental fields hasn't been a problem until now, which makes me think that this is someone targeting you. And maybe this fence cutting is part and parcel of this other crap going on as well. Sure seems possible to me."

"Well," Martin sighed. "I've had a chance to look at the profile of your bots as well as the ones from Vickie's land and the scans Ruby got on two of our fields today. We've got them too—and they're all the same."

"The good news is that I've devised a counterbot that we can release in a couple of days to clear the fields," Julie said. "It won't take long to grow it. But—the reason we can do that is because the foundation of the killbots were designed by someone with connections to our records."

Ruby tightened her lips. Now they were at the hard part. She'd already seen the ties—at least this one wasn't a surprise. She had insisted that it was her job to tell the others.

"Key parts of the rogue killbots match some of Gabe's designs," she said. "Old, so it's not a definite link to him—but it came from someone who had access to his work at some point during the last twenty-some years."

"Gabe!" Vickie snapped. "Figures that it'd be based on some of his crap."

"Why would he want to mess with your program?" Jim frowned. "I never figured him to be that—petty."

"Three point seven-five million dollars for five years," Ruby said. "That's enough to encourage a lot of sneaky behavior, even though the sanctions are pretty nasty."

"But the flip side is that it wouldn't have to be Gabe who contributed to these bots. Those designs are readily available and working out the kill piece focusing on other tech in the field isn't hard," Martin said. "Gabe's programming structures are the foundation for those killbots that keep new biobots from spreading beyond selected fields normally—the solution for drift and overspray issues. Killbots that survive past the programmed border of influence and time parameters not only are new, but now that someone's figured it out, they're going to be a huge problem in the future. Because if it can happen here, to us...it's going to start happening elsewhere."

"Is it just us so far?" Vickie asked.

Martin nodded. "At least, if it's happening elsewhere, no one is talking about it. Yet. I've been scanning product reports and no one is claiming problems."

"Well, maybe this is something you can add on to your programming. Beef up the RubyBot further," Jim said.

"I'm afraid to push the programming any more than I am already without more research," Ruby said. "Too many variables and you increase the likelihood of complete systems failure without the opportunity to figure out what caused it. Anyway. Once we get this counterbot grown, we'll push it out to the two of you as well as spread it on our fields." *Good thing Rick still had those reject stems on hand.* "Rick and Beck are hauling the stems for the counterbots out tomorrow. Themselves. And it's a simpler grow than the RubyBot."

"That sounds good," Jim said. "Thanks, Ruby."

"That's all I have," Ruby said.

"It's a lot," Jim said. "But at least we know where we're going with this.

Yeah, Ruby thought. *And I'm going to have a little chat with Gabe. Face-to-face. He wants to talk? Well, I'm going to find out just how much he knows about this damn rogue killbot based on his tech—and the fence cutting.*

She sure hoped that Rick and Beck got here early tomorrow.

THE LINGERING GLOW FROM THE TREATS AND THE champagne still lingered as Ruby prepared for bed, showering and slipping into flannel pajamas before padding downstairs to the living room. She poured herself a neat shot of Martin's brew before returning to her bedroom. Her rocking chair sat by the window, an old Duncan Phyfe side table next to it, with coasters, a water bottle, and a book from her grandfather's collection of Craig Johnson mysteries on top of it. Ruby settled in the chair and reached for the book. She half-smiled as she looked at the cover. Gramps hadn't cared for the Netflix series, preferring the book sequence to the TV version. But she knew them both, since Granma's choice had been opposite.

She let the book rest in her lap. Today's adventures could have fit right into one of Craig Johnson's Longmire stories. Ruby leaned her head against the back of the chair and rocked, taking slow, deep, breaths and closing her eyes, only now realizing how jangled she still was. She was home. Where she had grown up. Where she'd raised Brandon. Her refuge, after home had fallen apart when she was still little and Granma and Gramps had taken her in, got her away from the fights and the drinking/drugging and the drama that led to her parents' deaths.

Ruby opened her eyes. She sipped the whisky and eyed the silver-framed photos on the wall. Gramps and Granma standing next to Ruby in her Thunder County Days Rodeo Queen regalia, a big smile on her face as Sunshine looked at the camera, ears forward. It had been taken before the final performance on Saturday night. The photo of Gramps and Granma in her locket came from that photo shoot.

What would they think if they could see me now?

Granma had been proud of her achievements as a rodeo

queen. *Following in my footsteps,* she had bragged when Ruby won the queenship for Thunder County Days. She'd been in poor shape when Ruby was crowned as Miss Rodeo Oregon, but had still managed to attend her coronation.

Gramps had boasted of her achievements as a rancher and farmer.

Her comm buzzed from where she'd left it on the vanity after brushing her hair. One of the numbers that didn't go to automessage, she noted. But not on the select list of callers that automatically got put through.

"Caller?" she queried.

"*Gabriel Ramirez,*" the comm answered.

Ruby sighed. "I'll take it. Camera on." Why was Gabe calling so late? *I hope Brandon's all right.*

"Hey Ruby." Gabe's projection shimmered into a life-size replica in front of the vanity. Like her, he sat in a rocking chair, still wearing jeans and a snap-button shirt. She noted that he looked better than he had the night before, also sipping on a glass of what she assumed was also whisky. He peered at her with a concerned expression. "I just saw your upload today. You all right? I can see the scratch. You're damn lucky it didn't take out an eye." Concern edged his voice. Real or feigned? With Gabe it was sometimes hard to tell.

"A little shook up, nothing more." What was his game? Was he really that concerned about her?

"Would have called Brandon, but I wanted to set up a meeting with you, so I figured—why not just call directly?" He smiled. Once, that slow, big grin that spread across his face from the corners of his mouth to his dark brown eyes would have made her heart flip.

Now her feelings were mixed, though she had to admit that dark sideways gaze still gave her a momentary thrill. And if this rogue killbot *was* one of his designs...she had to wonder what further implications that would have.

"Meeting?"

"About—the reunion storyline." The smile lingered on his lips, right corner turning up even more roguishly.

"Oh. That." She sighed. "I've had a lot of other things to think about today."

"I understand. Sounds like you've had a rough time." The smile faded slightly. "All the same, whether we get back together for real or not, I think we should talk about how we're going to make this work for the show, so that it creates an effective storyline."

"I'd be interested in talking about doing it for the duration of the competition." Ruby sipped on her whisky. She wanted to gulp it but no—not until after Gabe hung up.

"Maybe we could meet for lunch tomorrow, say in Grande City?"

Ruby drew a deep breath. "I've got a lot going on during the day because of what's happened."

"How about dinner, instead? A *nice* dinner."

"Nice? In Grande City?" Despite herself Ruby laughed. "Good grief, Gabe, have you forgotten about the dining options there?"

"There is the Southfork House," Gabe said, a persuasive note in his voice.

The Southfork House was located ten miles east of Grande City, in the foothills. Once it had been their favorite getaway. And...it had been the site of their last, disastrous dinner together before their divorce had been finalized.

"I don't know, Gabe," she said slowly. "We might want something with a better personal history."

"Hey, so our last time there wasn't so good." The smile

grew again. "Don't you think it's time we created new memories for Southfork?"

"I'd—sooner not. There's a lot of complicated history and I'd much rather not deal with those memories just now." She thought about the options in Grande City. Neither of the Mexican places would hold up to Gabe's standards and she didn't feel like listening to his complaints about them. "How about the Chinese place?"

His face fell slightly, but then the smile gracefully reappeared. "The Happy Flower it is. What time?"

"Mmm. Not too late. I still need to drive back through the canyon—unlike you I have to be on manual the whole way." She tapped her fingers on the chair arms, thinking. An hour and a half drive after another day likely to have its own problems. When could she reasonably get away? "How about six?"

"Six it is. And Ruby—please be careful."

"I always am."

He snorted before signing off. "Yeah. Right. Says the woman who snuck herself into a saddle bronc competition. Okay, see you tomorrow at six at the Happy Flower."

"The Happy Flower it is."

Ruby barely waited for Gabe's image to fade before she tossed down the rest of her drink, then went to the living room to pour herself another one. She paused to look out the windows before going back upstairs. It was unlikely that she'd spot any intruders, but better safe than sorry.

The graceful forms of a couple of whitetail deer nibbling on scattered bits of hay near the cow barn were the only movements that Ruby saw. She heaved a sigh. Perhaps she should think about getting another dog for herself. But she'd figured that Martin and Charlie's dogs, along with the two that Julie and Terri had brought with them, were more than plenty to have on the ranch. She'd wanted to be solitary for a long time and the death of Brandon's old Curly a couple of years after he left the ranch hadn't moved her toward replacing the old Australian Shepherd. Not that she disliked dogs. She just didn't care for their mess in her house.

But after a day like this it would be nice to have a dog around. Another presence, something to warn her about intruders and keep her company.

If Gabe wasn't so damn untrustworthy when it came to her heart...dared she trust again?

Ruby thought again about the closeness of the rogue killbot's schematics to Gabe's designs. No. Best not to trust Gabe.

CHAPTER 6

Be at your place in half an hour. Ruby raised her brows at the text from Beck as she finished washing her breakfast dishes. She clicked up the time, frowning. 7 am. Rick and Beck must have left Portland early, around 1 am to get here that soon—but why? She appreciated the early arrival of the counterbot stems, which would let them get the grow started earlier...but again, why were they here so early?

Must be planning to turn around and drive back today, she decided. That made sense. They could have slept on the way out while the rig drove with only one charging stop, then switched to manual at Grande City.

But still, something didn't sit right about this early arrival. It wasn't typical for Beck and Rick to head out in the middle of the night. She'd been planning for them to get here around noon. Ruby checked the refrigerator. Did she have enough food on hand to offer them breakfast? It was the least she could do since they were clearly bending over backwards to help her.

At least I hope that is what's going on, and not that they're trying to get away from further problems.

The break-in at their condo would make them nervous. Something else...no, they were probably just being helpful. But meanwhile, she needed to make sure she had something to feed them, and in any case, she'd eaten her reserves down before leaving for the AgInnovator recording. As good a time as any to take inventory.

Barely enough hash browns in the freezer...she'd planned to do grocery shopping in Grande City after dinner with Gabe. Plenty of synthbacon. Dried pepper chunks and dried onions from last summer's garden. It would be a stretch but she could fix a decent breakfast if they needed it. Ruby prepped the coffee pot with coffee substitute and programmed it to start brewing in twenty-five minutes, then mixed the peppers and onions with the hash browns. Five minutes in the air fryer and breakfast would be ready when Rick and Beck wanted it. And if they didn't, well, she had her own breakfast ready for the next few days.

Ruby finished up in the house and headed out to the barns for her share of morning chores, stopping by the lab to tell Martin that the counterbot stems would be there soon. Then she hurried to the horse barn. Charlie was already there, soaking Casey's hoof while Legacy watched, hanging her head over the stall door. She whickered when Ruby came in.

"I'd say she's ready to go back to pasture," Charlie said, nodding toward Legacy. "Moving around the stall okay, eating all right, fussing a little because she wants out. Heck, Casey's ready as long as we put a boot on that foot. Get Legacy out of here. I'll turn Casey loose when we're done."

"Sounds good. Beck sent me a text fifteen minutes ago—they should be here soon."

Charlie raised his brows. "That's fast service. I'm surprised —didn't think they'd be here until noon. They aren't early risers."

"Yeah, that was my thought as well. Then again, they might have decided to drive through the night instead." As Ruby led

Legacy out, Charlie's comment confirmed that uneasy sensation in her gut. Had Beck and Rick experienced further break-ins?

Stop worrying. You'll know what's going on soon enough.

Charlie unsnapped one side of the crossties and held Casey's halter as Ruby took Legacy past her, then retied Casey. Ruby and Legacy went back to the main pasture. The other horses raised their heads from nibbling hay remnants. After Ruby untied her halter, Legacy bolted toward the herd, running smoothly. Ruby sighed with relief. No harm done from yesterday's excursions. It could have gone so wrong so quickly.

But it didn't, she told herself. This time, anyway.

Rick and Beck's big van rolled into the barnyard as Ruby walked back from the pasture. Rick pulled up in front of the lab. As he and Beck climbed out, Ruby's heart sank. Something *was* wrong. They both appeared to be tired, dark circles under their eyes, hair disheveled. Her faint uneasiness grew. This didn't look like leaving early to provide service. This looked like leaving early because something bad had happened.

"Didn't expect you two this soon," she said, trying to keep her tone light as she walked toward them.

"Yeah, well, shit happened," Rick said, exhaling slowly. "It's a damn good thing we loaded the van with your stems early yesterday evening."

Ruby stopped hard. "What happened?" Her gut tightened even more at this confirmation of her suspicions.

Beck ran a shaking hand through her black-rooted blond hair. "Someone firebombed the lab last night, threw it into the office. We'd been staying there after the break-in at the condo." Her voice wobbled. "I—I couldn't go back to the condo. It was like being violated and I kept hearing things when I was there alone. We thought we would be safer staying at the lab—moved our stuff into the van, parked it in the warehouse. If we hadn't been in the back, in the lab proper, securing the next grow and packing up your stems so we could leave early today—we wouldn't have made it out. Barely got the van out of the warehouse in time, threw what we could into it from the lab before getting it out of there."

"Shit."

"We lost everything, except what was in the van. Saved some stem seeds but I haven't the damnedest idea yet if they're viable," Rick said.

"Oh no," Ruby groaned. That was a huge loss for Rick and Beck. "What are you going to do? Insurance?"

"If the stem seeds survived, we've got something," Rick said.

"Insurance won't pay shit these days," Beck added. "I spent the drive hassling with them."

"And the cops?"

"Useless. There's been a run on attacks on stem growers like us of late, is all they could tell us," Rick said. "They think it's some religious crazies instead of WLAN, but...." his voice trailed off. "Our condo was attacked again at the same time, another firebomb. Threats on social media."

"There's just too much going on right now," Beck said. "And the cops seemed scared themselves. They advised us not to return to the lab or the condo because of those threats and thought we needed to drop out of sight, get out of the metro area. They'll keep in touch as they find things out. Whoever did it knew that we were sleeping in the office. That showed up on social media." She shivered. "Some of the stuff on social media is...toxic."

"I'm sorry to hear that."

Martin drove out a forklift as Rick opened the back door of the van.

"Your stems are in the back," Rick sighed. "I'll point out

what is yours. I don't know how long we can keep the stem seeds viable—if they are viable now. I think the refrigeration chambers maintained enough power on our way out here, but there's no guarantee. First priority for our power generators had to be your stems, Ruby. I had to short the seeds."

"They're probably okay," Martin said. "You've got good freezer chambers. They'll hold for longer than you think."

"Where are you planning to go?" Ruby asked, helping Rick load the first lot onto the forklift.

Rick shrugged. "Need someplace where I can preserve those seeds."

Ruby chewed her lower lip. "I think we might have room in the lab to store your seeds, and I've got extra rooms in the main house for you to stay."

"You sure you want the hassle, Ruby?" Beck said, voice rough. "You've got a lot going on, and this was the second attack on us...do you really want to bring the crazies down on you?"

"You're as safe here as you would be anywhere." Even so, Ruby made a note to herself to contact the sheriff so that the checkpoint could be alerted. That might slow any crazies coming in. *If they aren't already here.* "Have you been checking the Innovator feed?"

Beck shook her head. "We were hustling to get the stems you ordered repackaged and loaded, then getting the next batch going. Damn, we lost those! No room on the van and with the heat exposure, who knows how well they'd grow anyway?"

Ruby sighed. "Then you missed my news. You're not the only one having problems. Someone took a shot at me when I was checking fences and fields yesterday. I have boundary fences cut and the sensors have been hacked. I'm not too worried about you staying here, even if you might be targeted by crazies. I've got issues of my own."

Rick paused as he guided the second box to the back of the van. "What the hell? Someone shot at you?"

Ruby tapped her cheek. "That's where this came from. We think it was a rock chip. I was checking out that boundary fence that had been cut when I got shot at. Along with that, there's those rogue killbots I wanted these other stems for. It's affecting not just me but my neighbors now. So if someone's after you two for growing stems—who knows? It could just as easily be your connection to me and not anything you did."

"Wow." Rick shook his head as Martin returned with the forklift. Ruby helped him with the next box.

"Martin, how much spare room do we have in the lab?" she asked before he pulled away.

"Some, depends on how much space is needed and how biosecure it needs to be."

"The freezer units for Rick and Beck's seed stems? Take a look at what's in the van besides our stems. Beck and Rick got firebombed last night, and this is what's left of their stuff."

"What the hell—I wondered why Rick was hauling the freezer chambers." Martin climbed off of the forklift and came to the van, sticking his head inside. "What were you able to save, Rick?"

"Seeds for the AH749W, primarily, maybe a couple of smaller lines. We lost everything else."

"Well, if there was any seed line to save, the AH is the best one." Martin scratched his chin. "Let's get these stems unloaded and into the growboxes, and then we'll see what we can do for the seeds. We've been rushing a lot of stuff out for RubyBot production so we've got some room. Just decontaminated a whole storage section yesterday after starting the next group of RubyBots. Talk about timing. It's almost as if I knew that we needed the space. Normally I don't get the lab cleaned up that fast, but with the AgI inspectors due to show up soon, I wanted to get that out of the way."

Rick perked up slightly. "That sounds like the best damn news I've had for a couple of days. After our condo got broken into—and now this—we've got nothing."

"Glad to provide some cheer."

"While they get the lab put to rights, let's get your personal stuff into the house," Ruby said to Beck.

Beck's face scrunched up. "We weren't able to save a lot. Maybe a couple of clothing changes. Computer cubes. Rick damn near got killed grabbing the records we hadn't already stashed in the van—we were going to ask you to store some things already. Thank God we don't have meds to deal with, because we lost all of our personal hygiene stuff."

"Well at least you have the cubes. And we can get you more clothing and personal items. I've got clothes in storage, and if you give me a list—I'm going to Grande City this evening."

"We shouldn't be putting you out...."

"It's an old three story ranch house meant for a big family and remodeled to handle tourist stays. Right now, it's just me living here. You guys can stay at the ranch until you've figured out what to do."

Or until I can talk you into setting up shop here and we expand the lab.

Beck's face crumpled. "I've just been going over and over what we're gonna do between arguments with insurers, especially since the cops think we should go into hiding." She gulped, blinking hard, tears starting to run down her cheeks. "Oh God, Ruby, I thought I was going to lose Rick. He fought with the firefighters when they wouldn't let him go back in to pull out that last deep freeze core. And where we're going to start over again, I don't know...."

"Let's see what the future brings." If she won the Superhero, she could set them up locally if they didn't want to work at the ranch.

Beck buried her head in her hands, shaking with tears. "We just knew we had to get those stems to you, at least get a start with some funding from your payment because God only knows how long it would take for the insurance to pay us out, especially since it now looks like it was a political job. But we didn't have any idea of what we were going to do after this delivery. Where are we going to set up another lab? Where is it safe?"

"For now, you're welcome to stay here."

"But the Superhero—isn't this going to mess with your competition?"

"I'd be an idiot to ignore the needs of my friends in the name of the Superhero," Ruby said firmly. "No. You two are welcome to stay here as long as you need to. We'll figure something out."

And besides, she thought cynically as Beck sobbed on her shoulder, *it'll add more human interest to the Superhero.*

Though she could stand to have a bit less excitement and a bit more calm. *One more month,* she told herself.

"Come on," she said. "Have you two had any breakfast? Coffee's ready. Fake, not the good stuff, but at least it's caffeine."

Beck shook her head. "Didn't want to stop any longer than we had to—ran the charge down to almost nothing, hoped we could bum a charge off of you before we headed out again. Too scared to stop."

"Well, I can offer hash browns and synthbacon. Sorry I can't do more. I've gotta go shopping and stock up."

"I was figuring we'd make do with ration bars," Beck sniffled. "Oh God, Ruby. Thank you so much. I—I—our personal items are in the front." She went to the van.

"Hey Rick," Ruby called as she followed Beck and took a couple of bags from the pile behind the passenger seat. "When you're done, come up to the main house for breakfast. Martin, you too. Let's work out a plan to get Beck and Rick back up and running with their stems. We've got the room to do more than store their seeds, don't we?"

"It'll be a tight squeeze, but we should be able to set up appropriate isolation grow spaces. And once we get those counterbots grown and released, then we'll have more space to spare. We'll have to be flexible, but yeah. Should be doable."

"Thanks!" Rick's voice shook slightly. "But you sure? Someone's sure got it in for us."

"Beck and I have already talked about it. I'm targeted too. Might as well have all of us keeping an eye on each other." Ruby turned toward the house, thinking about where she could put Rick and Beck. Not Brandon's old room—she preferred to keep that for him. But the ground floor room that had been hers and Gabe's while Gramps was alive—yeah, that one would work. And it was next to the downstairs bathroom. Beck and Rick could have some privacy, and she could have hers.

Guess that's an end to the solitary life for now. It's a good thing that Gramps updated the place and put in two more bathrooms back in the Oughts.

There had been times when she'd cussed about the difficulties of keeping a big five-bedroom, three bath house functioning once Brandon had left and it was clear he wasn't moving back to Thunder County to live. Times when she had thought about inviting Julie and Terri to move into the big house instead of keeping the bunkhouse for themselves, even though they insisted they preferred its privacy and didn't want to intrude on hers.

But now she was glad to have the space. And, to be honest, the company.

LINGERING DAYLIGHT HUNG OVER THE MOUNTAIN RIDGE just west of Grande City as Ruby strode down the block toward the Happy Flower, fatigue pulling at her. She had almost cancelled on Gabe, figuring that she'd had enough to do that day already between the AgI inspection team, getting Beck and Rick settled, letting the sheriff know about the newest complication, talking to the school about potential interns, and dealing with AgI about the issues related to the attack on Rick and Beck.

The lab was crammed full with the RubyBot and the counterbot production lines, and storage for Rick and Beck's stems. At least the AgI inspectors had signed off on Beck and Rick's relocating their lab to the Double R, based on Martin's quick creation of flexible biosecurity lab design. She'd tweaked the recording of last night's meeting and uploaded it, then, after consulting with Brandon, had recorded an interview with Rick and Beck about the firebombing and the refuge she was providing to their stem cultivation services. Then she'd sent the video directly to Brandon so that he could fine-tune it.

But God, she could just imagine what her bottom line looked like right now. Her first task for tomorrow was going to be reviewing spreadsheets and projecting potential expenses tied in with fence/sensor/security fixes. And a separate spreadsheet for what it would cost to set Rick and Beck up at the Double R long-term. Even if locating them at the ranch was a temporary stopgap—she needed to expand her facilities. Once the RubyBot was licensed, she'd have to do it to handle production.

If she didn't win something from the Innovator she'd be screwed...and after finding out about Mariah, she was determined to wrest some sort of financial concession from AgI if she did lose. This sort of physical sabotage, not just aimed at her but at her neighbors and suppliers, had gone beyond the norm. The inspection team had already signed off on fence replacement, including the sensors. Now she'd need to ask about support for Beck and Rick—or maybe she should wait until the competition was done. Surely this additional complication would have earned enough clicks to bring in more funding and justify compensation.

If AgI could finance Mariah, then they can damn well finance me, even if I don't win.

All the same, she needed to create a fallback plan, and fast, for additional funding.

Remember, she told herself. *AgI gives and AgI takes.* They hadn't cut her any slack when the early RubyBot failed twenty-one years ago and Gabe had left her. She had managed to pull herself out of that black hole then, with help from Vickie, Charlie, and Martin. If she failed this time...*this time I had better plan on finding some sort of backup funding before everything goes into the hole. Can't trust AgI, either.*

Her whirling thoughts slowed as she saw Gabe standing outside the Happy Flower. He'd dressed up for the occasion, wearing a dark blue suit and matching trilby that emphasized his light brown skin, making him look healthier than he had looked at the announcement taping.

He should have worn this suit for that show instead. It doesn't make him look sickly and pale like that gray did.

Then Ruby shook her head. She wasn't his dresser any more! Granted, Rachel had probably served that function for him. But it was distressing that she found it so easy to fall back into old habits.

And he was just dressed up enough that she felt uneasy and underdressed.

Should have put more thought into this.

With getting Rick and Beck settled plus all the other things she'd had to do, she only had time to duck into the shower and throw on clean jeans and snap-button shirt before leaving. At least she'd remembered to grab her faux sheepskin coat, the good one for town, along with the nicer black felt Stetson. She looked like what she was, a busy rancher. But perhaps for the purposes of augmenting the AgI romance storyline she should have dressed up, made it look more like they were having a date.

No. Not playing that game until we have our talk—and I find out what piece he has to play with the rogue killbots.

Gabe spotted her and perked up. He said something to his comm and his camera zoomed out of its dock on his wrist and turned to record her approach.

Damn. I didn't think about the possibility of recording this for AgI. Must get into that mindset. Well, maybe I can make this fit into what's happened.

She snapped on her camera. Two could play this game.

"Hey, lady," he said, his voice deep and cheerful as she approached. "If you aren't a sight to see."

"If you like the older sights," she retorted, trying to keep her voice flat and failing as it slid into a playful snark, just like she couldn't squelch a grin. *Falling back into old patterns.* "I feel underdressed looking at you."

Why did she feel warm and glowy?

Oh crap, I still love the asshole after all. Father of my child. There's just something about him.

Gabe laughed. He offered his arm. "I had a presentation to attend in Pendleton before I came over here. Otherwise I'd be less dressed up, too. Trust me, I don't wear suits every day."

"Presentation?" She took his arm. The door slid open and they waited for the waitbot to seat them. She overheard some whispers that grew louder.

"Hey! That's Ruby and Gabe from the Superhero!"
"Wow! So maybe they are getting back together after all?"
"That's Ruby and Gabe."
"Ruby and Gabe. Ruby and Gabe."

"Yes. Water management conference." He grimaced. "I've been in negotiations with the tribe, the city, and the county to turn over part of my land to their management. Too many five-hundred and thousand-year flooding events happening over the past ten years. I'm located in a good place to route the high water from flash flooding into swales. We're talking about those details because I want to keep some control of the land and get compensation should I lose a crop."

Other cams started to hover around Ruby and Gabe as a waitbot approached them, a rectangular two foot by four foot gray bioplastic device with the capability to extend appendages as needed to carry out food, project menus, disinfect tables and seats between customers, even expel rowdy customers if required. The faint hum of the propellers that kept it aloft had a *click-click-click* that sounded to Ruby as if one were malfunctioning.

"Reservations?" it intoned before Ruby could say anything to Gabe.

"Gabriel Ramirez, for two."

"Follow me."

The whispers tagged along behind Ruby and Gabe as they obeyed the waitbot's instructions, still walking arm-in-arm. Ruby was self-consciously aware of the cameras tagging along behind and all of the attention on them, noticing that even more cams popped up to record them.

Okay, this is going to add to the social media buzz.

She hoped she hadn't picked up any mud on the back of her pant legs after getting out of the rig. Another thing that she probably should have cleaned up, but it would have taken even more time to wash the truck.

The waitbot seated them in a booth. It wasn't exactly private, but then again, it had the best light for the camera, and it *was* away from most of the other customers. Gabe hung his hat on a hook at the end of his seat. Ruby put hers on the table, choosing to hang her coat on the matching hook on her side. She debated about asking for a privacy screen. Maybe eating in public had not been the wisest choice, especially this close to Thunder County. She'd forgotten that one of her biggest clusters of supporters lived in the area. It was probably the same for Gabe. Still lots of farmers here, people eager to cheer on a local winner. Having *two* local finalists made the AgInnovator of even greater interest to local viewers.

No. If they raised a privacy screen, it'd just make people even more convinced that they were seriously getting back together. She'd just have to be careful about raising the issue of the rogue killbots.

Gabe leaned over, starting to reach for her before dropping his hand on the table.

"That scratch looks bad."

"Just a scratch. So are you getting some compensation for the restricted use of the land that you're turning over?" she asked as she reviewed the selections projected from the waitbot's electronic menu. A lot of her favorites were marked as not available, out of season, or had an outrageously high market price (justified by the time of year and limited storage, of course). Ruby settled for a stir-fry with synthpork, bok choy, and rice. She marked the *Separate Tickets* box at the bottom of the menu.

"A mix of tax write-off donation and in-kind contributions," Gabe said. "We're still working on the details. I'm serious when I say I'm downsizing. The long-term aftereffects from the G9 are pretty significant, possibly crippling, and—" he shrugged. "I don't know how much longer I'll be able to keep working. Right now my focus has to be on the microbial adaptations I'm working on. I don't need all that land for my test sites, and if I can help stabilize the local hydrology while getting a crop off of those fields when they aren't needed for flood management, that's all for the good."

"I—see." This was new. Gabe had always been thinking about the bottom line in the past. But she supposed that having a serious illness like the G9 would help focus concerns. Should she say anything? *Why not? It's something you need to bring up if we're going to play along with the AgI storyline.* "That's somewhat of a change in how you do things. What's the bottom line? Didn't that used to be your favorite saying?"

Gabe chuckled. "It's a realistic financial choice when you look at the long-range projections. Both for me and for the region. And let's face it, Brandon isn't going to come back to the land, so I don't feel an urge to preserve my holdings for the next generation. He's not coming back to your Double R, not to my Moondance."

"It appears to be that way." Ruby heaved a heavy sigh.

"You given much thought about what happens to the Double R when you can't work it yourself any more?"

"Honestly? I've been too focused on turning out the RubyBot to worry too much about what happens. The family...." She let her voice trail away. Were any of them still alive? It had been years since she'd talked to them. No one was left of the Ryders except her and Brandon, and as for her father's people, the Barkleys—both Aunt Grace and her daughter Jeannie were dead. It was a relief not to deal with begging Barkleys any more.

"The RubyBot," Gabe sighed, almost as heavy as her sigh had been. "You're still obsessed with that project."

"Just like you are with the microbials," she countered.

He raised his hands. "Okay, okay, I get it. We still have our favorite solutions to farming in the face of climate change."

"It is something we need to discuss if we're going to—" Ruby glanced at both of their cameras, jerking her head toward them. She twirled a finger around to remind Gabe that it wasn't just their cameras recording. At least the others were at a discreet distance—not as secure as a privacy shield would be. But they were at the standard public recording distance, no close ups.

So amateurs, not anyone from the media.

Media recorders would be in their faces, flashing their privacy bypass passes from AgI.

"I agree," Gabe said. "For now, we need to concede that we have our separate foci. You okay with that? I am, for the sake of cooperating with this storyline. It furthers both of us."

"For now, yes." The food came, along with water. Ruby pulled her metal chopsticks out of her purse and poked at her stir-fry. She made a face at her first bite of synthpork. Bitter. Even worse, it crumbled in her mouth and released even more sour taste as the crumbled pieces mixed with the sauce. Not the better stuff, definitely a lesser quality than what she tended to buy. She picked the pieces out and tasted the bok choy. Better than the synthpork, and the sauce at least overpowered the remnants of the sour synthpork flavor.

They ate quietly, Gabe also sorting out pieces from his food. Ruby noticed that the other cams started to drift away as it appeared that all they were doing was nothing more exciting than eating. At last he put his chopsticks down.

"I did see you've had some excitement above and beyond the Superhero," he said, gesturing toward her cheek.

Ruby pushed her food aside, grateful to be done with it. The Happy Flower's cooking had gone down in quality since the last time she'd eaten here a month ago, on her way back from the Superhero prelims. It was probably due to late-season end-of-storage supplies. They'd be better in a couple of months as fresh produce started coming on the market again.

"Which incident are you talking about?" she said. "The fence-cutting? Someone taking a shot at me? Rick and Beck moving in because their lab's been firebombed and their condo broken into?"

Gabe raised his eyebrows. "I hadn't heard about Rick and Beck. I knew about the fence cutting and your being shot at."

"It's a nasty situation." Ruby sipped her water. "They've received social media threats, and the cops have told them to get out of Portland. I got video of the two of them talking about what they're going through, and me offering them shelter. Sent it to Brandon but I don't know when he's releasing it."

"What?" He frowned, looking confused.

Ruby pursed her lips. Was his hearing failing as well? "I took video of Rick and Beck talking about what they've been going through. I don't know when Brandon's releasing it."

"I got that part. But they're staying with you? Why you?"

Ruby nodded. "Yes, I'm giving them shelter. Right now what's left of their lab is at the Double R. Rick and Beck are staying in Gramps's old room, and I've offered them a space to rebuild their operation. AgI has approved the additional presence."

"But—but—but why are they staying with you? Ruby, are you crazy? Don't tell me you're off on one of your paranoid moments again." For a moment distress flickered across his face. It didn't match his tone and it set her on alert, dousing her pleasant glow as thoroughly as a pan of icy water poured over her head would have.

"The cops suggested they get out of town. I figured my place was the best and safest option, and god only knows I've got lots of space in the house. Tight squeeze in the lab for now, but that can be worked with. Besides, they've saved my butt many times over the years. I owe them." Ruby eyed Gabe carefully. She had expected him to be concerned about what had happened to Rick and Beck, but something about his behavior raised a red flag.

I've seen this from him before—but where?

When he was having an affair with Mariah.

Bitterness at that memory flooded through her.

So why didn't he like the idea of Rick and Beck being at the ranch? Why did he want to hide what would otherwise be a logical concern?

Gabe stared at her, his face now a studied blank. He knew *something* about the Beck and Rick situation, she realized, a sick feeling in her gut. And coupled with the rogue killbots, that meant he was involved in something not-quite-right.

God damn it, Gabe. I had hopes that maybe, just maybe, things had changed.

"But why you, Ruby?" he said finally. "And wow. Just wow. Why would anyone attack Rick and Beck? They're only the best stem cell growers in the Northwest."

"Gabe, the cops are concerned about this too."

"And you *know* that Rick always runs a wee bit paranoid. Don't make this into another batch of conspiracy theories!"

Ruby bit back her initial, angry response. *Think.* Was his reaction just a little bit *too* smooth and schooled? Ruby couldn't decide. One quarter of her wanted to accept his reaction as real. Damn it, she didn't *like* feeling like this, especially when Gabe was being so friendly. If it hadn't been for something he'd done, or said, or tone...she might have thought he was being sincere.

But remember what happened when Brandon got sick. Gabe bugged out on you then, and those versions of the RubyBot failed because there was no one there to help Charlie and Martin save the grow. Gabe lost you the Superstar payout because he was too busy chasing Mariah's tail while you were down sick.

If it hadn't been for Charlie and Martin, the first expensive prototypes of the RubyBot that had been funded by the Superstar Innovator would have failed completely. But enough of the prototypes failed, and because it was the second year in a row where they didn't perform to spec, the remaining six years of Superstar payouts to Ruby and Gabe had been cancelled.

And then there was that awful night after they were cut from the Superstar.

She'd wanted to drink heavily because Gabe's reaction had been horrible afterward. They had a long argument about whose fault it had been. She had splurged on a direct flight back to Pendleton instead of Portland, had taken a hotel room planning to drown her sorrows that night before renting a vehicle in the morning and picking Brandon up from Vickie's. Then she came down to the bar...and found Gabe and Mariah drinking together, Mariah in Gabe's lap, kissing, hands all over each other as the mediacams rolled....

The look on his face now.

That's where she had seen it before. It was the same expression he had worn throughout the humiliation of going through an extremely public divorce because their Superstar win made them temporary celebrities. And that brought up memories of scrimping and scrounging to pay off her part of the marital settlement while supporting Brandon.

Why was I such a fool to think even the slightest of reconciliations could be possible?

"Think about it," she growled. Gabe tensed. A faint hum arose around them as cams started drifting in their direction, attracted by their raised voices.

"Think about what?" he said defensively. "You're just being paranoid."

That defensiveness was not good. Not good at all. It fit his divorce behavior, and it confirmed her earlier suspicions.

He knows something. He's not innocent.

Her heart sank and the lump in her stomach grew heavier. She had hoped things could be different.

"I've been shot at. Both the Reeds and the Chandlers have had fence cut, and the sensor array system is down. And now there's been multiple attacks on Rick and Beck. My suspicion is that they were attacked because they're my stem source. Gabe, I'm not making things up."

"But why would anyone want to do any of that to you? Ruby, that just doesn't make sense. Yes, you'll get some harassment because of the higher visibility due to your Superhero status. That's all it is."

"Why would anyone want to introduce rogue killbots to Vickie, James, and my properties at this stage of the competition? You tell me. That seems to go beyond simple harassment."

Gabe straightened up, frowning. "Rogue killbots?"

Ruby nodded slowly, watching Gabe's reactions. "Rogue killbots that don't have any parameters for location or time, and no shutoff switches." She flicked up a partial privacy screen. It didn't exclude their cams, but it'd keep out everything else, short of a certified mediacam.

"That—that doesn't sound right." He seemed genuinely shaken by that idea. *Not part of whatever it is he knows, then. That's something. Maybe.* "That's damn stupid design. Why would someone do that to you, now of all times?"

"Three point seven five million dollars is at stake, Gabe. And Mariah's sniffing around wanting to buy up shares of the Double R. You tell me what that adds up to, especially given the past history between her and me. You know what she's like." Would Brandon have told his father about Mariah's true status? "What she's capable of."

"No. No. Not Mariah." That denial rang true. So what the hell was he connected to with all this crap? No. He couldn't be linked to the attacks on Rick and Beck, no, that wasn't a Gabe thing. But if it wasn't the attacks on Beck and Rick, if it wasn't Mariah, then just what was it? "It doesn't make sense, Ruby. Perhaps after you got the RubyBot licensed—"

"Or maybe someone doesn't want me to get the RubyBot licensed," she said.

"That's crazy." No, there was that tone in his voice that she hated again, that hinted he was hiding something from her. Licensing. That had to be the issue. And the rogue killbots would be just the thing to interfere with the licensing process, screw her up not just with the Superhero, but with marketing the RubyBot afterward.

Just takes a little interference to gain a bad reputation. And —make me dependent on someone sliding in to rescue me. Is that what this is about? Gabe forcing me into a position where he's my only option out, so that he'll have me as a caregiver?

Ruby tightened her lips. God. She couldn't believe this of Gabe—could she?

"You think? It's my area of greatest vulnerability."

Gabe kept shaking his head. "Killbots without range or time limitations. Damn it, Ruby, I *know* those fucking killbot algorithms. It can't be done. At least not with anything that's based on my designs." He scowled at her. "Because that's what you're hinting at, isn't it? Mariah and I are conspiring to take you out using rogue killbots to interfere with the RubyBot's performance. That's damn stupid. What the hell do you think I am?"

"Take a look at the schematics and decide for yourself."

Ruby took a deep breath and summoned up the specs for

the rogue killbots. She strengthened the limited privacy screen. Why share this information with any of the cams, especially now that more of them hovered *just outside* the privacy limits? No need to give anyone any further ideas.

Gabe fumbled in his pocket and pulled out a pair of reading glasses. He leaned over the table, studying the schematics. Ruby tapped her fingers on the table as Gabe fingered through the details, layer by layer, waiting for him to discover what was at the foundation of the killbot.

Gabe's eyes widened. He shook his head, pulled off his glasses, rubbed his eyes, then replaced his glasses and enlarged the schematic. His lips formed the word *no* as his face paled while he scrutinized the details.

Then he snapped the projection closed and tucked away his glasses.

"So," he said, voice suddenly devoid of all emotion.

"So," she said, her voice matching his for flatness. "Recognize the design?"

Gabe snapped off his camera. He stared at her. "Ruby, I *didn't do it*."

"You've lied to me before, and you sounded just like you do now," she said, just as the waitbot cruised by. She signaled and it handed her the pad with her check. She paid her bill.

"God damn it, Ruby!" His voice rose. "This isn't twenty-one years ago! I thought we'd grown past that!"

She slammed her hands down on the table, rising to her feet, barely noticing when the privacy screen fell as a result and too angry to care any more. "Stop gaslighting me! You betrayed me then and you've not given me a reason to trust you now! You're lying to me about something. Is it Mariah? Or are you just begging to get me back so that I'll take care of you in your weakness? Is bankrupting me through destroying my chances at the Superhero your twisted way of making me dependent on you? I can think of a lot of legitimate reasons for me to be worried. My suspicions weren't paranoid then and they sure as hell aren't paranoid now!"

More cams buzzed around them, including—*damn it, here comes the mediacams!* She had to get out of here, *fast.*

"I'm not lying, Ruby! And no, that's not what is going on at all."

"Don't give me more of that mansplaining bullshit!" She reached for her hat and jammed it on her head, yanking on her coat, anger overcoming discretion, even though she saw cams, both private and media, buzzing close, too close. "I know when you're not telling me the complete truth. You've screwed me over too damn many times in the past. You tell me just what I'm supposed to think when I see this level of baloney going on. I know what I'm seeing. That's your work at the foundation of those—" She choked back the word *killbot* just in time. "—devices."

The waitbot whizzed over to them. "Is everything all right here? Please lower your voices, you're disturbing the other patrons."

"Ruby, *it's not me.*" Gabe's voice lowered. "I swear, *it's not me.*"

"Tell that to your damned girlfriend who's trying to buy me out. Tell that to our son who still has pipe dreams about Mommy and Daddy getting back together!"

"Ruby—"

"I'm done." She pivoted and marched out of the Happy Flower, batting at a cam that wouldn't get out of her way fast enough.

God damn them. God damn them all.

"Ruby—" Gabe's voice wobbled. She fought the temptation to look back at him and stomped out of the restaurant instead.

It wasn't until she reached her truck and had programmed in the short drive to the supermarket that she let herself cry.

Why did I even think that it was possible for things to be different between us?

When the truck stopped in a parking space, she realized her camera was still rolling. For a moment she contemplated deleting the footage.

No, she decided. Enough of the event had been recorded by other sources that their fight was going to be splashed all over the Innovator channels.

But she did send her footage to Brandon.

She just barely avoided adding any text to the video. Let him judge for himself what had happened.

Then she sank back in her seat. Pulled up the shopping guide and placed an order to be brought to the truck, grimacing at the size of the service fee before confirming the order. She couldn't afford this. Not with Beck and Rick on her dime, not with everything else going on.

But right now she couldn't face the buzz of mediacams that would be likely to descend on her if she tried to do her shopping in person.

She let more tears come while waiting for her order to arrive.

Until now, she hadn't realized how much she had been hoping that maybe, just maybe, things could have been different between them. Or how much Gabe's original betrayals still hurt, even after twenty-one years.

Four more weeks of life under the microscope.

If she didn't need that three point seven five million dollars, she'd walk away from the Superhero right now. It would be worth it to avoid this heartbreak all over again.

CHAPTER 7

The next morning Ruby was deep in her spreadsheets, calculating what it would take to accommodate Rick and Beck's operation at the Double R, when her comm buzzed.

Remy Trask flashed in bright blue and purple letters.

"Accept," Ruby said. She hadn't expected to hear back from Remy quite this soon—but it was a welcome break from the numbers and the headache from last night's poor sleep.

And damn, I need her to create a lease agreement for Rick and Beck to use the labs. I talked about it with them but we need to make it formal. Too many things to deal with all at once!

"Girl, you can't just avoid the media drama, can you?" Remy's tone was half-approving, half-sigh.

"Yeah. I saw that last night's dinner at the Happy Flower got spread all over the internet, not just on AgInnovator."

"And your issues with the fence cutting, and the sensors, and taking in Rick and Beck...girl, you've been busy over the last twenty-four—no, make it *seventy-two*—hours. I think that just about anything that has *Ruby Barkley* tagged on it is going to go viral now. You gaming the Innovator or what?"

"I wish it was as simple as that." Ruby sighed and sagged

back in her chair. "There's stuff that hasn't been released. Except maybe from those recordings of our fight—I haven't screened them."

"What would be—oh no. The killbot issues are real? That video just popped up on the AgI official feed this morning."

Ruby nodded. "Did the video show anything about those designs being based on Gabe's old work?"

"Fuck no. Is that what the argument was about?"

"Pretty much."

"Well, shit. This makes things complicated." Remy chewed her lip. "I've got the RubyBot interest assignments drawn up. But are you going to be able to talk reasonably to him?"

"Either he wants more of the RubyBot or he doesn't care at all."

"Or he has his own design ready to roll should the RubyBot fail."

"It's not something that he's disclosing," Ruby said. "Everything he's been doing for AgI is based on refining his initial microbial research. He'd have to be working with someone like Beck and Rick to develop his own bot designs, and he isn't. If he is, he's either burying those ties pretty damn deep, or else he's not working with anyone credible."

"Maybe he wants to crash the RubyBot, buy out your interest, and develop it from there along his own lines," Remy said.

Ruby paused, cutting off the denial she wanted to make. *Could* Gabe do that? She hadn't thought about that possibility, but yes...it was a likelihood.

"Maybe he could do that if he won the Superhero," she said finally. "I'm running numbers now. He'd have to grab everything from me, and even then he'd have one hell of a startup investment. I just don't think he has the financing to pull it off. I *have* to win to make this work, but I'm not going to cheat to do it, either."

"Unless he hired you and your people to continue your work."

Ruby sighed. "I don't think even Gabe is that mercenary."

At least I hope so.

"Mariah could be. And there's some weird activity going on around her current organizing and financial activity," Remy said. "I've had Shannon researching Mariah's activities since we talked yesterday. That lady's up to something."

Ruby rolled her eyes. "She's always up to something. It'll come out soon enough, and I just don't have the time to worry about her at the moment. You've got the revisions to the RubyBot income agreements?"

"Sending them to you now. The faster you get them signed and back to me, the better, considering how things are going."

"Well, Brandon's supposed to be here today, setting up cams and scouting out the prep for filming interviews. I can check with him then. I've already talked about it with Charlie and Martin—no issues there. Gabe—I think I'd better give him a day or so before I go back to him with this."

"Get Brandon and Charlie secured. Then that only leaves Gabe's ten percent for you to be concerned about."

"I will. And there's more. I'll send you notes, but we've worked out a tentative lease agreement for Rick and Beck to use the labs at the Double R to resume their business."

"Oh really?"

"It's going to be quite an investment, and I need to find independent funding. I can barely swing it to get the initial setup started. But if the RubyBot goes into serious production, I'll need the expansion whether they stay or not. I'm hoping they stay because I'm factoring it into my planning, and it would be nice to have stem seeds generated in-house."

"You sure you're not biting off too much? If you don't win the Superhero—"

"At this point if I don't win, I'm screwed anyway," Ruby said. "Unless I get some concessions from AgI. Given what Brandon told me about Mariah's status—she's not a real competitor, she's in the mix solely to provide dramatic tension, and they're paying her compensation for that role. I have no idea how much she's getting—but she's getting compensated."

"Oooh. Now *that* is an interesting bit of news."

"And highly confidential. I don't even know if Gabe knows. Not that it matters—but Brandon told me this was absolutely secret."

"Understood. Now. About this contract with Rick and Beck. You say you've worked out a rough version already?"

"Sending the notes to you now. Sat down with them and Martin, and I think we've covered every contingency." Ruby paused. "The kids want to give me a continuing interest in their business in repayment for the space. I'm not sure I want to do that. From what they've said, their Metro facility in Hillsboro is a total loss, along with their condo. All they have is one solid stem line with possible fragments of others. It's going to take them a lot more time and money to rebuild than they think if they strike out on their own. I'm looking at the numbers now."

"Giving you a share might be the only means they have for paying you right away, if things are that bad. I'd take their suggestion. How much of an interest in the business are they offering?"

"Forty percent. Which would give me a controlling interest if they split up. I don't want to be in that position."

"Twenty-five percent might be a better choice in that case, and you can give them the option of buying out your interest once their sales rise to a certain level. Have you looked at their books?"

"That's part of the data I'm crunching this morning," Ruby said. "From what I see, it's going to take them a couple of years to rebuild back to their previous strength, unless they get a big infusion of cash. I can't give them that unless I win the Innovator. Mariah might be able to finance Beck and Rick, but stem cell production is not part of her core business. Their other customers are reliable but small—however, there's one farmer in the Palouse who might end up being their solid biggest customer simply because they'd be closer and it would be easier for him than it has been. Fortunately his growline is one of those that survived sufficiently intact. It won't take them long to fulfill what he needs—if I prioritize giving them the space to do it."

"Sounds promising. So why haven't they expanded before now, if their prospects are so good?"

"Location costs in the metro area. Rick was already talking about moving to the coast for cleaner air and water. He didn't say it but I'm thinking that finding a bigger space is also another part of the whole mix. It ain't cheap in Portland metro. Plus they would need funding to take that next big speculative jump, and doing that overwhelms them. I'm seeing it in their books. They're lab rats, Remy, not business managers."

Remy snorted. "As if you are."

Ruby laughed with her. "I'm better than I was after all those years bookkeeping as a side hustle to keep the ranch going. And really, this does fold in with the plans for the Ruby-Bot. I just need to find side funding to bring them fully on line, because I don't dare build out *too* much in hopes I win the AgI. But it is going to stretch my credit lines to the max."

"Is this something that could provide ranch income if you run into licensing delays with the Ruby, or if you don't win the Superhero?"

"It will take a couple of years at the most optimistic projection, four to six years worst case—but yes."

"Sounds good. Are they all right with you sending me their financials?"

"Yes. They understand that it's part of the lease agreement and their offer to give me a share of the business. I have copies of everything relevant."

"All right." Remy sighed. "I'll get back to you tomorrow."

A text from Martin flashed across Remy's projection. *The AgI team is here, and Brandon is snorting around like Gabe used to do. You need to get out here and talk to him.*

"I've gotta go, Remy. Situation developing. AgI is here."

"I'll get back to you."

"Thanks."

Remy's image faded. Ruby took a deep breath. What the hell could Brandon be angry about? Yesterday's fight with Gabe? But what did he expect?

She texted Martin. *Go ahead and send Brandon in. Probably better that I talk to him in the office and get him out of your hair.*

Thanks, he answered. *He's on his way.*

She sent Remy the files she needed, then closed and secured the records she had been working on, and glanced around the room. Nothing untoward was in sight—good. Not that she *should* mistrust her own son, but there were some things he'd be better off not knowing.

Brandon stomped into the kitchen and she sighed. He was in a mood, no mistaking that. Just like his father. She reclined in her chair, steepleing her fingertips and fixing a steady, calm gaze on the door. Just like she used to do when he was a teenager and had the occasional angry outburst—most often after he returned from visitations with Gabe.

"Mother!" He marched into the office, scowling, still wearing his biosecurity boots but not the suit. He must have rushed right over from the lab. "What the hell is going on?"

"Sit down," she said, keeping her voice quiet, the same voice she used on Legacy when she started bouncing around.

"I want an explanation, damn it."

"Sit. Down. *Now.*" She escalated her voice to corrective horse trainer mode.

"Do you realize how many problems that revealing the killbot issue is creating? I'm having to put out media fires all over the place and the speculation is horrific. Dad is downright *pissed* right now, says you've accused him and Mariah of conspiring against you—"

"Brandon. *Quit.*" She punched the *quit* hard, her sharpest horse trainer vocal correction, omitting the *damn it* which usually followed when she used it on a horse.

Brandon flinched. *Good. It still works.* Not that she wanted to use the technique often, whether on horse or human. But *that voice* stopped his word flow, and he dropped into the chair, shaking his head before dropping it into his hands.

"Oh God. I've got a lot riding on the Superhero success," he said in a quieter tone, not looking up at her. "And this sort of blowup is not what I need."

"I'm sorry. But you need to talk to your father because I'm not the only player. You saw my version of the video."

He raised his head. "Yeah, and I saw Dad's too, along with his yelling and ranting at me afterward because of your claims."

"I'm sorry," Ruby repeated. "But did he tell you that those damn rogue killbots we found are based on his version?"

"Um—no." Chagrin tightened Brandon's face and he shook his head again. "He didn't say one word about the sourcing."

"So take a look for yourself." Ruby pulled up the schematic for Brandon.

He slid his chair closer and began his review. When he was finished, he sighed and slumped back in his chair.

"God damn it, this looks bad for Dad. He didn't bother to

tell me about this little piece of the puzzle. You're right, that's his foundation. How bad is the infestation?"

"So far, just me, the Reeds, and the Chandlers. Vickie and Jim were going to talk to other locals, just in case."

"What are you going to do?"

"That's why Beck and Rick are here—originally to deliver the stems I need to grow the counterbots, but now because they don't have anyplace else to go."

Brandon sighed. "And then there's the issues raised by their lab being firebombed. At least it doesn't appear to have WLAN ties."

"One thing to be grateful for. We're focusing on stopping those rogue bots. Martin and Julie have whipped out a design which should work, and we are on track to release it in the affected fields tomorrow. We'll know how effective it is within a week—lucky that Vickie and Jim caught it when they did. Otherwise I'd be delayed in releasing the RubyBot, and that—"

"Would compromise your chances in the Superhero," Brandon finished for her. "Yeah. Suspicious timing. I understand your concerns, Mom. But now—what's the story with Beck and Rick staying here? I know the basics from the video you sent. But staying here? What's next? Is this a temporary thing while they get the counterbots going, or what? From what I saw in the labs, it looks like a permanent setup. At least from what I remember of your lab layout."

"I'm hoping they'll stay after we get the counterbots going. We've got a tentative lease agreement going, and I'm looking at what it will cost me to expand the labs to accommodate them without depending on the Superhero money."

"That's a huge investment." Brandon winced. "Quite the gamble."

"I think it's worth it, especially after looking at their books. Their problems have been no time to think about long-term management and the inability to expand as rapidly as they needed because their work requires both of them to focus on the lab. I'm working on a proposal to get them student interns from the high school—well, for me, too, with the Ruby."

"Student interns?" Brandon perked up. "Which teacher are you talking to?"

"Scotta Stuart. Which reminds me, they wanted to tell you congrats on landing this position with AgI."

"Good old Mx. Stuart." A faint grin flitted across Brandon's face and for a quick moment Ruby saw the teenaged Brandon who had loved his agronomy tech coursework enough that she had hoped the RubyBot would keep him on the ranch. "So they're back at Thunder County High? Last I had heard, their cancer was pretty bad."

"They're in remission right now."

"Please tell them thank you for me. The interns should make a nice side storyline."

"And it allows me to set up a pipeline of lab workers, which we'll need with expanded labs and the Ruby getting licensed. Which reminds me. Remy sent me modifications of our share agreement, focused on the potential RubyBot licensing income. Legal changes and all. I need you to sign off on the modified agreement for your share of the Double R."

"The RubyBot's part of that?"

"It's one of the ranch assets."

"What does the modified agreement do?"

"You get a share of any income from the RubyBot based on the percentage interest you hold in the Double R."

Brandon shook his head. "Can we channel that income back into the ranch, or else to a trust? If I get money from the RubyBot anytime soon, it ends up dancing awfully close to conflict of interest, and I'd sooner not deal with AgI's lawyers on that subject. But I could end up needing the income myself at some point. Take care of that issue and I'll sign, no problem."

"I'll message Remy. The income from Rick and Beck's business may end up being a part of the ranch income, too. Once they get established and all, that is."

"That piece should be okay," Brandon said slowly. "I'll talk to AgI's lawyers and get back to you quickly." He straightened up. "And God. Dad. I'll talk to him. I suppose this shoots to pieces any hope of you two cooperating on a reconciliation storyline."

"Branny, he's lying to me about something. Just like he did when he left us. And it's tied to all this crap I'm going through. I won't—I *can't*—collaborate with him on something like AgI's romance storyline until he comes clean with me. If they want us to dance to that line, he's got to fess up."

"I'll see what I can do," Brandon said. "Because that storyline *is* a big draw for followers. Boy, if you saw the reaction your fight drew last night! Any sort of make up meeting is going to add to the draw."

"It's in your dad's court right now."

"I'll do what I can. I'd staked a lot on being able to pull off your storyline. If I can't—I've got to find another big story draw like that. Or I'm in big trouble."

"Then tell him. He's got to be straight with me. No more bullshit, understand?" Ruby eyed Brandon. Should she press him further about AgI?

"I'll do what I can, Ma."

"And you be straight with him about what it's going to cost you." She paused. Time to push harder? "That said, I'm not entirely sure what's at stake here for you. I thought your job was solid at AgI."

Brandon looked down at his feet and grimaced. "Crud.

Now I need to get myself cleaned again. But I was just so frustrated and angry, and from the way Dad phrased it—"

Ruby raised her right hand. "You don't need to say any more on that subject, Bran. We've been through crap like this before with him."

"I just thought it would be over when I was an adult." Brandon sighed and stood up.

Still avoiding telling me why he's so worried. What's happened?

"Some things never change," Ruby said sadly. "And Bran. What *is* at stake for *you* in the Superhero?"

"Mom, I—" Brandon threw up his hands in frustration and went over to the window, looking out and not at her.

Ruby waited. It was a pattern she recognized from his teen years that went along with the quick anger, followed by contrition and then explanation. If she waited it out while Brandon thought through what he wanted to say, instead of pressing for an immediate response, then she would learn more and he would be less defensive. A technique that had worked better with Brandon than it ever had for Gabe.

At last he sighed and turned to face her.

"I've gambled everything on the Superhero pulling down big clicks. I pitched the Superhero to Georgy Batineau himself. The Big Boss." Brandon drew a deep breath. "It's a mess, Ma."

"I didn't know you were working at that level," Ruby said. "We both met him during the first AgSuperstar." When they'd met Batineau, his behavior had triggered a defensive reaction from Gabe. *I'm not leaving you alone with that asshole,* he had said. *The way he looks at you when he thinks I'm not paying attention...don't trust him, Ruby.*

Toward the end, though, Gabe's protectiveness had faded. Why had it changed? Mariah, other women, or something else?

He had been spending a lot of money and she had never been able to figure out on what. Or had the time and resources to investigate further once it was clear he was done with their marriage. She had just wanted to get out without dragging it out in a long court battle that would suck up time and money. Drugs? Gambling? Other women, not just Mariah? She had no idea what was happening.

Brandon nodded. "He remembers you well. It was '*oh, your mother was a rodeo queen,*' over and over during my final interview at AgI. That stuck in his mind almost as much as the RubyBot. Those memories got me in the door more than anything else when it came to pitch time for the Superhero." He hesitated. "Oh hell. I might as well tell you everything. The fact is, the AgI show numbers have been declining over the past three years because of all the competition from other shows like it. Georgy is ready to end it because it's bringing the rest of the company down and isn't driving as many clients to AgI's consulting services as it did for around twenty years. It costs a lot to produce. Not so much the payouts to the winners. Even adding in five years of the Superhero keeps things workable, especially since the completion numbers on the Superstar are —dismal."

"It's a pretty stiff bar to pass—must document growth and development according to ten-year plans created in accord with AgI staff," Ruby recited, almost without thinking. "Know the criteria for completing the Superstar by heart."

"Over twenty-five years only ten finalists have completed the full ten years of the Superstar," Brandon said. "And there are whispers of further issues—" he shook his head, staring at his feet. "Bribery. Collusion. Worse."

"How?"

"Back to the Superstar. It's been gamed for years."

Ruby rolled her eyes. "Brandon. Those rumors were circulating even when your dad and I were competing in the first

Superstar. How valid are they? Georgy's slimy at times, but that's been a big cash cow for AgI."

He looked back up. "I—Ma, I went to work for AgI because while you and Dad lost the Superstar, I saw what winning the Innovator for a year and the Star for five did for both of you on your own. I thought it was a good idea, and those programs are sustainable. But over the last five years, fewer and fewer competitors are showing interest in the Superstar. We have to guarantee consideration for the Star and the Innovator awards if the competitor fails—those levels get weeded out pretty aggressively too, but we can move some of the Superstars to Star and Innovators, and the Stars to the Innovators."

"So the Superstars are declining because the word's gone out that it's hard to complete." She wanted to be bitter. If the option had been available to revert to the lower Star account-ability levels twenty-one years ago when they failed the third year of the Superstar, maybe she wouldn't be in the financial mess she was in now.

Brandon nodded. "The way it works now, the Superstar winners are internally known from the finalist period on if not sooner. It's the finalist that our projections suggest will bring the most value to AgI once the year's contest is done. Promotion of AgI, visibility, and—" he hesitated. "Kickbacks to AgI from the income of their startup projects. It's not a huge percentage and it's different with different groups. I just found out about the kickbacks to AgI."

Ruby froze.

Remy didn't say anything about this in the AgI Superhero contract.

"I don't believe I've signed any such agreement," she said finally. "Remy would have been screaming if it was in that contract. And I don't remember such an agreement with the Star or the Innovator."

"It's because I fought for the integrity of the Superhero," Brandon said. "It's not in anything but the Superstar contracts."

"Branny, why are you staying with AgI? There's enough other sources of ag startup financing out there—I've been thinking about those."

"The Innovator is the most visible program," Brandon said almost too quickly.

"But bribery, fixing the contest, collusion, kickbacks...." Ruby spread her hands wide. "Do you really *want* to be connected to all this? Surely you could take your expertise to another independent startup funder? Another game show?"

"Once I could. But I can't now." He turned back to the window, hands clenching and unclenching. Then he wheeled to face her. "Ma, I can't afford to leave AgI now no matter what they do. Not only did they buy up my student loans—a share of what I make goes to them now—but...." He bit his lip. "I owe them a lot more money than that. Triple the loan amount, in fact."

"Branny! What the hell?" Her blood ran cold as she studied her son, the pleading, shamed expression on his face. "Why didn't you come to me for help if the student loans were too much?"

"Ma, you're leveraged beyond leveraged. I already know that from your quarterlies. And it's not just the student loans. I did something stupid, because Dad was sick and Rachel's family wouldn't lift a finger to help him after she died. I took on his debt. The collectors threatened to get me fired from AgI if I didn't give them something. I—I started betting on games. Football, basketball, baseball. I've always had an eye for those performances, and it was supposed to be safe. A better return than going through the casinos."

Ruby shook her head, suddenly realizing. "You went through illegal bookmakers."

"It worked until I bet on a game I didn't know was fixed because my sources failed," Brandon said. "It was stupid of me. I didn't see the indenture clause when I signed off on the bet."

"Branny. No. Oh no."

He nodded. "They showed up at work to drag me off. Mariah slid in and distracted them, and word went to HR. AgI bought out the indenture."

"Oh Branny. How much?" And it had been *Mariah* who had saved him. That rankled more than anything.

He wouldn't look at her. "Three point five million dollars. Twenty indenture years. So when I pitched the Superhero—I offered them lifetime indenture to pay off all my debt if it didn't reach a certain level of eyeballs by the end of the show. I promised I would select attractive competitors not just for the Superhero level but the Superstar and the Star this year." He exhaled heavily. "I offered to find the best candidates that would provide the most exciting storylines. I guaranteed an insane number of clicks."

"And if you succeeded?"

"No indenture. Forgiveness of the gambling debt, Dad's debts, and the student loans."

"Bran. Oh Branny," Ruby repeated. She rested her elbows on the desk and leaned her forehead on the palm of her hands, shaking her head, doing her best to keep her whole body from trembling at the sick feeling in her gut. "Why didn't you talk to me before doing all this?"

"I was trying to bail out Dad. Would you have listened to me?"

"But medical debt...those collectors are in violation of the law...you could have fought...he could have fought...."

"At what cost? It takes money to fight those claims," Brandon said. "Dad is leveraged as bad as you are, Ma. Worse, because I learned the gambling trade from him, and...Dad's got more in play than I do," Brandon said, voice distant. Ruby raised her head to stare at Brandon as he continued. "Where do you think I learned all the gambling tricks from, where I developed the connections? Dad's good at hiding it, and was always able to cover his bills until—until he got sick with the G9."

"*Both* of you?" she whispered.

That's how he paid off the indenture bounty hunters. Gambling. But got himself into a bigger hole.

Was that a factor in their divorce?

Brandon nodded. "They won't put him through indenture, he won't last long enough to pay them off. He's gambling everything he's got on winning the Superhero. I—I also took on his gambling debts too, as well as his medical, though I don't think he realizes how much of it I've done. That's why the dollar figures are so high for my debt."

"And if you don't make the clicks?" she whispered.

"You don't want to know," Brandon said. "Full indenture at AgI is not...pleasant."

Ruby shuddered. She could imagine, remembering the dull-eyed indentureds at the finalist recording. "How much does your dad know about this?"

"Not how deep I'm leveraged. Not about the indenture. Ma, I was trying to spare both of you." Brandon's voice broke. "I really was. I know how tough it is. I see not just your accounts but Dad's because I have a forty percent share of Moondance—and you're both getting older. Dad's health is compromised and I—I worry about something like the G9 happening to you. I was just trying to help."

Ruby stared at her hands. Now it was her turn to consider a response, because the first things that came to mind weren't useful. *How could you be so stupid* and *why didn't you talk to both of us about your plans* weren't going to make things better, and at the moment she was at a loss to come up with any other reaction.

And Gabe. God. She'd have to make it up with Gabe for Brandon's sake. Even if Gabe was behind the rogue killbots—it was entirely likely given this information that he hadn't done it willingly but had been forced to cooperate. She'd gone into that meeting with him pissed off and on the prod, but she should have realized that he really had been surprised by the details.

Was gambling debt why he left me and Brandon so many years ago? What kind of lock does Mariah have on him—or whoever has a lock on her?

She sighed and pushed her chair back, walking to the window. Stared out at the barnyard. The Double R was in her blood. It had been her refuge, ever since her grandparents had taken her in as a little girl when her parents followed the siren song of meth and opioid addiction. The Ryders had managed to keep the Double R through economic crashes. Commodity crashes. Drought. Storms. Yeah, Brandon didn't want to continue the ranching tradition, but she wasn't ready to give the place up. Was she?

At the same time, she couldn't sacrifice her own flesh and blood. Her son who had sold himself to protect both her and his father. Just to keep the ranch for what was likely to be the last generation living on it. Was the Double R worth more to her than Brandon? If he went into full indenture—no, she couldn't let that happen to her son.

Ruby's fists clenched tight. If she sold the Double R to Mariah then that—plus additional money for the RubyBot— would save Brandon. And, most likely, Gabe as well. Whatever she thought about Gabe, he *was* Brandon's father. If she had to bail him out in order to avert the doom descending upon Brandon, so be it.

And yet—part of her rebelled against just giving up. *The*

Ryders fight until they're dead, Gramps had told her. *You don't give up even when it looks bad.* Her first horsemanship trials for the Thunder County Days Rodeo royalty had been a disaster and she'd barely slid in as princess. It had taken hours of schooling difficult horses over the winter, acing her speeches, and busting her butt selling tickets to earn the title of Queen. Even though Granma was sicker than hell that winter, Gramps had supported Ruby and given her time to compete, had been pushing her to keep fighting, keep trying. Her hand slipped up to her locket and she clenched it tightly, deriving some comfort from it. Gramps would understand if she had no other choice—but he'd be after her to keep fighting until the very end.

Mariah is a last resort. But god damn it, I'm going to win the Superhero or die trying. And if that means I have to make nice with Gabe and play the game that AgI wants us to pay—then so be it. I'll sell myself to save what I love.

She exhaled slowly and turned to face Brandon.

"I need you to talk to your father," she said quietly. "I need you to tell him everything, like you just did with me. *Everything*. Not just what's going on with the Superhero, but how this affects you. What the stakes really are. Taking on his loans and the threat of you going into full indenture. You own enough of our ranches that AgI could lay claim to his microbials and the RubyBot while still keeping you in full indenture."

Brandon's shocked expression told her that he hadn't thought about that possibility.

Ruby nodded. "Yeah. We're all at risk now."

"Ma, I'm sorry."

"You did what you thought was right, Bran. But in order to fix it, your father and I need to talk. I need you to tell him I want to talk to him. Here. At the ranch. Away from all cams. At the safe place. He'll know what I mean."

"Does that mean you'll cooperate with the storyline?" Glimmerings of hope softened the tight muscles of Brandon's face.

Ruby smiled. She walked over to her son, staring straight into his eyes, projecting every ounce of determination and hope that she could summon up.

"I may have lost Miss Rodeo America but I sure as hell won Miss Rodeo Oregon against the chick who beat me out for Round-Up Queen. I will cooperate so hard with that damn storyline that the clicks will blow away their teensy little minds at AgI. Now you just have to get your father in line."

"Thank you, Ma." Brandon hugged her. "Gotta get back to my peeps now." He paused. "It may take a couple of days before I can get to Dad. This stuff—" he pulled away with a sigh. "I don't want to talk about it over electronics."

"No. You don't. Just remember this. You come from tough people, Ryders and Ramirezes both. Not so much the Barkleys." *Though, damn it, this is a stunt more worthy of the Barkleys than the Ryders. Damn it, Gabe.* She was going to chew his ass hard on this one. Gambling? Really? Even to pay off the indenture hawks? "We'll overcome this," she continued. "We'll win—all three of us."

"Thanks again, Ma." Brandon kissed her forehead. "I—I don't know what to say."

"Just get back to work and kick butt like you learned to do."

"I will, Ma. I'll give you a list of safe places here where I didn't put cams before I go."

"That would be helpful."

"I'm sorry I put you in this mess."

"We'll do what we can to fix it. One way or another."

Brandon hugged her again, then left.

Ruby went back to her chair. But she didn't pull up the

spreadsheets again. She wrapped her hand around the locket, taking comfort from it as she thought.

This was going to take a hard-core campaign to pull off. Who could she trust to manage the details, help her choreograph what she and Gabe would need to do to win the most clicks? Gabe would have useful additions to any plan—after all, social media was one of his strengths, and he'd have some insights about long-term developments, but they needed an outsider to manage the plan while they implemented it. Vickie —Vickie knew how to put the polish on appearances. Not hiring her to help them with the Superstar had been one of their mistakes.

Ruby released the locket and tapped the fingertips of her right hand on the chair arm as she thought. At last, she opened a desk drawer and pulled out an old legal pad and a handful of pens, scribbling on the paper until she found a pen that worked.

Paper and pen might be old-fashioned, but at least it wouldn't be able to transmit a plan to any outsiders.

CHAPTER 8

"Here you go, Ma," Brandon said softly in her ear. He shoved a piece of paper in her right hand.

"Thanks, Bran." She slipped the paper in her jeans pocket without looking at it. "When do the interviews start?"

"Let me pull up the schedule." He clucked and a set of columns popped up in front of him, details shielded from her by a red filter. "We got some good material with Mx. Stuart and the intern kids today. Gotta love it when impromptu stuff like that comes up. But I'm definitely going to have a team here on Friday for their first day. If that works for your plans. And then the Friday after will be in LA for the first elimination."

First elimination.

The thought was like a hard rock in her gut. No. She—and Gabe—were going to make it through this first one. She'd gamble on the script wanting both of them to go all of the way to the finals.

Two cuts and then the two of us against each other.

Wait. Wasn't there a collaboration clause? She'd have to check the contract again.

"What did Martin and Beck say?"

"Both thought it was good."

"All right, then. Friday." Three days from now. She could handle that.

"The lab team is going to be here day after tomorrow, though. It's not a whole day, though—just a review."

"Thursday and Friday. I'll put that on the ranch calendar." She clicked it up and made the additions.

"Okay, Ma. Later." He sprinted for the lead vehicle in the AgI flotilla of white vans.

Charlie joined her as she watched the convoy of four vans leave. "And so it begins," he said wryly. "I saw the calendar additions."

"Yeah." She waited until the last van was clear of the property and driving down the road before she pulled the paper Brandon had given her out of her pocket.

Safe Places To Talk:

Horse barn tack room (feed room wired and will pick up loud convos)

Horse pasture, face away from house

House bedrooms—all on third story

Cow pasture and calving pen, face away from house and barn

Outer pastures though there will be links added as your fence and sensors are fixed

Charlie and Martin's house

Bunkhouse

"What's that?" Charlie asked.

She showed him the paper.

"What the—"

"Shh. Let's go to the horse pasture and check on Legacy and Casey." Ruby tucked the paper back in her pocket and checked her jacket pocket to make sure she had enough treats to share out with the herd.

Charlie raised his brows but walked with her to the pasture after doing the same check of his pockets.

As always, old Sunshine led the herd to join them. After each horse got a treat, Ruby checked Legacy's legs and chest while Charlie looked at Casey's hoof. At least Casey still had the protective boot on.

Charlie straightened up and brushed the mud off of his gloved hands. "All right, Ruby. What the hell is going on? What's so hush-hush that Brandon's telling you about safe places to talk?"

Ruby sighed. "I have to cooperate with the Gabe reconciliation storyline for the Superhero."

"What the hell? Ruby, what on earth did Brandon do to sweet talk you into that bullshit?"

"Brandon's in trouble, Charlie." She swallowed hard, fighting to keep her voice flat. "The only way for me to help him is by winning the Superhero in the biggest, flashiest, most over-the-top means possible."

Sunshine pinned her ears to drive Legacy away and pushed in close to Ruby, as if she sensed Ruby's emotions. She buried her head in Sunshine's neck. The golden mare curled her head and neck to enfold Ruby. She inhaled deeply, for a moment wishing herself back twenty-eight years, when her biggest concern was winning Miss Rodeo Oregon and worrying about Gramps and Granma's health, not the Superstar, the Superhero, or any of that crap. When Gabriel Ramirez was just her bronc-riding lover with sardonic quips, a darkly handsome gaze, a fascination for a spunky smart redhead who could ride a horse better than he could, and not the man she had married.

"Oh hell. What's Gabe done now?"

Ruby shivered and raised her head. "Not entirely his fault. Rachel's family cut Gabe loose after she died. Brandon stepped in to help him with medical bills because Gabe was so sick. He started gambling to help raise funds to help Gabe, went to illegal bookmakers. Gambled on a game he didn't know was fixed, and didn't see the indenture clause attached to the loss if he couldn't pay it back. They tried to grab him at AgI. AgI bought the indenture—but in order to get his way free, Bran's got to get the most clicks possible, and he already owes them for his student loan debt. He gambled a stunning success for the Superhero against full indenture for the total he owes AgI." She left the rest of it out about Gabe's gambling debts. Charlie didn't need to know.

"Oh, *fuck*." Charlie paled.

"Yeah."

"How much does Gabe know about this?"

"Not as much as me—yet. Brandon's going to talk to him, but it has to be face-to-face."

"I get it. So that's why the list of safe places to talk."

Ruby nodded. "And I've got to have it out with Gabe in a safe place because we *don't* have an option but to cooperate with the AgI storyline now."

"How much does Bran owe?"

"Three point five million."

"Oh *fuck*," Charlie repeated. "And that will eat up most of your first year winnings."

She shook her head. "If he gets the clicks and the eyeballs, the debt is wiped out. Completely."

"Well hell. That explains a lot of what's going on. If you're crippled so that you can't perform well enough to win the Superhero, then you can't help Brandon, right?"

"Not unless the implosion is sufficiently spectacular that Brandon gets the promised viewership as part of the process. I'd much rather not see that happen, which means—Gabe."

"Fuuuck," Charlie groaned. He threw his hands high and started to turn away.

"*Don't* face the house," Ruby snapped.

Charlie turned around. "Sorry. Forgot. What happens now?"

"Not a lot of other options. I do have an offer on the table from Mariah. So do you. Worst case, I'll sell the Double R rather than see Branny indentured for life."

"Yeah. I can see your reasoning for going with Gabe instead." Charlie sighed.

"I'm wondering now what kind of pressure has been put on him. That might explain what happened with the rogue killbots."

"Could be. But three point five million. How the hell?"

"He also picked up Gabe's medical debts. And Gabe's gambling."

Charlie sighed. "I knew about the gambling with Gabe—I thought you did."

Ruby shook her head. "Not a clue. Literally. I thought it was all other women. If you knew, why didn't you tell me?"

"I didn't know until a few years ago, when Martin and I went to Vegas for the National Finals and saw Gabe. Didn't talk to him, ducked out of sight, but it was clear he's a high roller from all the good treatment he and his wife got. At that point we agreed it really wasn't anything that affected us." Charlie scratched Casey's neck. "And now it's Bran as well. God, Ruby. What can we do to help?"

"Just keep things together," Ruby said. "Don't rip Gabe a new one when he shows up. I told Bran that I wanted to talk to Gabe in a safe place. Here. Tell Martin so he doesn't freak out. I don't know how close we're going to be working with Gabe yet, but I'm going to take it as far as I have to in order to win. It's going to be like campaigning for Miss Rodeo Oregon." She started finger-combing the tangles in Sunshine's mane. Maybe she'd bring the old mare into the barn and give her a good grooming for old times' sake.

No. She had to talk to Vickie next. Ruby patted Sunshine in apology.

"You going to manage all this on your own? How are you gonna keep Gabe from running over you? You know he can be like a freight train when he grabs hold of an idea."

"That was the old me—but still. I've been thinking about that. I'm going to hire Vickie to manage us. Gabe can get someone else if he wants, but she did well enough for me before when I was queening. Should have hired her for the Superstar twenty-five years ago."

"Yes, you should have. Think she'll hold up for it?"

"She's not that much older than me, Charlie!"

"Fifteen years starts to be a big difference. She's what—in her seventies now?"

"Something like that." Ruby said. "Maybe I'll give Vickie a call and ride Legacy over."

"No," Charlie said firmly. "Remember what we agreed to? None of us rides away from the home place alone, whether it's on a horse or in a crawler. You drive your truck to Vickie's with full shielding, and you call when you get there."

"It's along the road," Ruby protested feebly. But she knew what he meant, and besides...dark was coming. Even if she jogged Legacy both ways, she'd be up against the early spring sunset. She patted Sunshine's neck again and turned back to the house. "Either way, I'd better get going. Still got a lot to get through before the day's finished."

Charlie fell in beside her. "We're behind you all the way, Ruby."

"Thanks," she said.

"Well," Vickie said as they sat at the old white drop-leaf table in her bright yellow kitchen, sipping slowly from their coffee cups. "You know what I'm going to tell you, right, Ruby?"

Ruby grimaced and took a larger swallow of her spiked coffee. She eyed the whisky bottle sitting between them as she set the cup down—more of Martin's distilling—and dribbled a little more into her cup. "Do I have to?"

Vickie fixed her with a stern, steady gaze. "You hired me to do this."

"Yes, but—"

"Ten things. Every day. Only this time instead of ten things to remember about the future of agriculture in a world of rapid climate change, it's ten positive things about Gabe. It can be small things. You can even repeat them. But every day. You think of ten positive things about Gabe, until you can fake what you need to do to put on a convincing enough reunion performance for social media."

Ruby swallowed hard. "All right. It's not like we have much of a choice, do we?"

"No. And Gabe needs to see me as soon as possible."

"I don't know how soon I'll be able to talk to him. It can't be in public or electronic."

"Good," Vickie said. "That will give you some time to get your head pulled together and have a few days of *ten things I like about Gabe* under your belt to shape your thinking so you don't blow up at him, because another explosion like the one that hit the screens from yesterday isn't going to help the image you're trying to create. Try a few now."

"Um—he's Brandon's father?" Ruby tapped her fingers on the table.

"Weak. But it works. Another."

"He used to be able to ride a horse pretty well." Ruby took a deep breath as Vickie nodded encouragingly. "He's still good looking, despite being sick, and he's taking care of himself and not letting himself fall apart. Despite being sick."

"More."

"Dang it, Vickie!" Ruby took another deep drink from her cup. She eyed the whisky and decided she'd had enough. "Okay. He's got a good mind for long-term management planning."

"Excellent."

"He understands the bottom line—but damn it, then why did he get sucked into gambling?"

"Don't go down that road just yet," Vickie advised. "Save that one for talking to him. Think about his financial management apart from gambling."

"He's not afraid to take risks." Ruby winced. Too close to the gambling issue for her comfort. She stared down into the dregs of her cup. "But this is all stuff I already know and acknowledge about Gabe. If I'm gonna play true to that reunion storyline, it needs to be personal. Not professional."

Vickie reached over and rested her hand on Ruby's. "That's all right. Work on this part first. You respect him as a professional. Take it from there. This is just a start, okay."

"Okay." Ruby glanced out the window. "Thanks, Vickie. Thanks for listening, and helping, and—just everything."

Vickie laughed. "We'll see how you feel in a month."

"If it means the difference between winning the Superhero or selling the ranch to Mariah to keep Brandon safe—then it's worth it, no matter what."

Vickie's hand tightened even more on Ruby's before she released it. "Keep on telling yourself that, girl. Now. Tomorrow I'll come over and we'll do a wardrobe review. Can't believe you haven't thought about this. I taught you better than that."

"I know. I've just been on the run trying to get the RubyBot licensure going." Ruby pushed herself up. "And speaking of that—I'd better get along home."

"Let's see." Vickie stood, clicking up her own schedule. "Tomorrow's clear. Then you have filming on Thursday and Friday?"

"Lab review on Thursday, not supposed to be the full day. No filming planned."

"But it will be filmed, no doubt about it." Vickie scanned Ruby from head to toe appraisingly. "Any idea when you'll talk to Gabe?"

"Oh God no. Hopefully not before Saturday."

"Good. That gives me time to do some work on your hair. And girl, we've *got* to do something about your nails and makeup if we're going to make a reunion storyline credible."

Ruby rolled her eyes but she smiled at the same time.

I should have brought Vickie on board even before I knew about AgI's storyline.

She'd forgotten a lot about fashion and looking good. Some of it was coming back now, but...it was something she hadn't thought about in a long time. It was a relief to hand over her beauty regime and social calendar to Vickie.

"And let me think. We need to put a look together for you so all you need to do is grab the appropriate outfit without thinking about it. Keep it simple but glam," Vickie said as they walked out to Ruby's truck.

Ruby opened the door. On an instinct she hugged the older woman. "Thank you, Vickie. Thank you for everything. Ever since...." She swallowed hard.

"I know," Vickie said, patting Ruby's back. "I know."

By the time she'd finished chores and worked some more on the computer, Ruby was exhausted. She almost felt like dropping straight into bed—no. The habits of a lifetime pushed her to the bathroom, to a quick shower to clean off the dust and muck from the day of ranch work. She frowned as she took the socks off her cold and clammy feet. Her toes were red and stuck together.

Suddenly a memory from the first years with Gabe flowed back over her. She was exhausted and awkward, toward the end of the second trimester of her pregnancy with Brandon. No—the end of the first trimester of the baby she'd lost when Brandon got sick. Actually, he'd done this during both pregnancies. He peeled her socks off carefully, rubbing them gently with a soft cloth before she went into the shower. Afterward, he would massage her aching feet, rubbing in skin cream before easing dry socks on for her to wear to bed, slipping in gentle kisses.

She smiled at the memory. Then sadness crashed over her.

When had things changed?

A month before Brandon got sick, she realized. Then she had thought it was Mariah and other women who had caused him to withdraw from her.

Now she wondered what had really happened.

You'll get a chance to talk to him and work it out soon, she told herself.

All the same, it was a sweet memory that she had forgotten.

Hmm. Maybe thinking ten nice things a day about Gabe would actually work.

"OH MY GOD," VICKIE GROANED AS THEY STUDIED THE pile of outfits on Ruby's bed late the next afternoon. "How did you let your wardrobe slip this far?"

Ruby shrugged. "No one to dress for, I guess. Money. Time."

"Let me see what I can do with this mess." She studied Ruby. "At least you're close to your old weight."

"Too heavy for the Thunder County Days outfits still."

"But you can't wear rodeo outfits to public dates with Gabe."

"I dunno. Remember he's an old saddle bronc rider with an eye for a cute princess."

Vickie snickered. "You're both older than that now. All the same, you need some softer looks."

"And the rodeo queen look plays well for the Innovator."

"Got it. But you still need some professional-looking ensembles, not just for recording sessions but for being out in the public." Vickie chewed on her lower lip. "Couple of skirts, a formal dress, light sweaters for spring. I think I have some workable items at home if I can't salvage what I need from your stuff here. I think you need a bit more formal look for lab shoots and travel. Good God, girl, you've still got a body that a lot of women your age would kill for. Use it."

Her comm chimed before she could answer Vickie.

"*Message from Mariah Meyers.*" it said in her ear.

Well, shit. She'd better see what this was about. It was probably the escalated offers that Brandon had been talking about.

"I've got to return a call, Vickie. Innovator-related."

"Gonna be recorded?"

"Most likely. It's Mariah Meyers."

"Oh shit, girl, you are NOT answering her call looking like this! It's time to glam you up as fast as we can." Vickie dug through the pile until she found a shimmery blue top and tossed it to Ruby. "Put that on." She went over to the dresser and rummaged through Ruby's jewelry as Ruby swapped out the snap-button shirt she was wearing for the sweater. She came up with a pair of freshwater pearl earrings. "And these."

Ruby hesitated. "Gabe gave me those for our first anniversary but I don't think Mariah knows that."

"You have something else he gave you that she'd know? And will match your shirt?" Vickie raised her brows.

Ruby fumbled through the jewelry box until she found the dangly blue topazes. "These. Gabe gave them to me when we won the Superstar. He made a big production of it at the after party. She can't miss them."

"Good." Vickie smirked. She ducked into the bathroom and came back with a makeup kit. "Geez, woman, we have got to do something about your makeup! At least your hair is presentable." She expertly applied lipstick and a brush of powder on each cheek. "*Now* you can go talk to Mariah. I'll stay here and put some ensembles together."

"Thanks, Vickie." Ruby hurried downstairs to her office.

Mariah's message was simple. *Call me.*

She wondered even as she placed the call if Mariah would pick up or if she was going to play the phone tag game. *Record,* she ordered the comm. She'd replay the conversation for Vickie once they were done.

"Ruby." Mariah's visage shimmered into being, apparently from an office very similar to the one that they'd spoken in after the finalist announcement. "Glad you got back to me so quickly." Her brows raised. "Doesn't look like I caught you out on the ranch."

"Paperwork is always waiting," Ruby said, eying Mariah's sleek black and white block-patterned top. She fingered one of her earrings, noticing how Mariah's face tightened. *Yeah. She remembers this.* "Especially when I'm in the throes of getting the RubyBot certified for distribution. Still working on licensing."

"I see." Mariah tightened her lips even more. "Have you been thinking about my offer?"

"Honestly? I've had a lot going on lately, Mariah."

Mariah rolled her eyes. "That's what I've been hearing. It sounds like the regular Wild West out there."

Ruby shrugged. "All in a day's work."

"I'm sure you're tired of being shot at."

"It's probably not as frequent as what you experience in LA or any other big city," Ruby said, waving one hand dismissively. "So no, I've not had a lot of time to think about your offer. I've a ranch to manage."

"I see. Well. Circumstances have changed somewhat from my last offer. I'm now prepared to sweeten the pot by another two million. If you sell to me today."

"Oh really? And what circumstances would those be?"

A tinny, artificial laugh from Mariah. "You haven't been watching your stats rise on the Innovator? You're the clear leader right now." She picked up a glass of water.

"In that case I think two million is chump change. Wouldn't you agree that doubling the offer is a bit more realistic?"

Mariah choked on her water. "Whaaat? We haven't even made it to the first cut and you think you're worth that much? Now who's being unrealistic?"

Ruby shrugged. "I've got more stuff coming that will jerk up my stats higher. I think once we figure out who's sabotaging me and my neighbors, especially if it's We Love Animals and Nature, my stock is going to shoot up even higher. In fact, I'd gamble on it."

Mariah winced. "So that's what you're basing this unrealistic counteroffer on? Ruby, talk about pipe dreams." But worry seemed to tighten her brow. "After all, WLAN does have its share of supporters."

"And it has even more opponents. But you have to admit, being under their gun is going to attract attention."

"Can you sustain it for a month? Especially since it's now clear that the Ruby and Gabe reconciliation story isn't going to fly." Mariah took another sip of water. "Twelve million if you accept today. That's my offer."

"And who says that the Ruby and Gabe reconciliation story isn't going to fly?" Ruby fiddled with her earring again. "After all, that is a known quantity of our past relationship. We fought. Dramatically. And the makeups were—oooh, they never got shown, but they were equally dramatic." She smirked at Mariah. "Don't you think the fight the other day added to the dramatic tension? We are good at that, as you should know. Just imagine what the makeup session after that fight is going to be."

Mariah's face locked down into a blank. "Twelve million. Today."

"How about I pay you that amount for your company instead? It looks like I might be able to pull off my big dream for a consolidated operation. I could use a side business of blockchain trackers."

"You—you—wouldn't *dare.*" Mariah's face flushed bright red.

"Try me," Ruby said softly, glaring hard at Mariah. "I have no doubt I could raise the money to take you out of business. Maybe I'll talk to Philip Martiniere. Even if the Martiniere Group won't fund me, I'll bet he'd be interested."

"You wouldn't dare," Mariah repeated. And then her image vanished.

Ruby ended her recording. Only then did she allow herself

to laugh. Then she pushed herself out of the chair to go back upstairs and share the video with Vickie.

She had to wonder just how much of it would end up being uploaded.

As it turned out, their entire conversation was featured in that night's upload. Once Ruby told Charlie about the call, he suggested they watch that night's Innovator after dinner just to see for themselves. Mariah's calls to Temira and Jeff led off the segment. Both were clearly uncomfortable as Mariah pressed them for a commitment, but both said no.

Then Georgy Batineau himself came on the screen, lanky and androgynous, glowering through his greasy dark forelock at the crowd.

"You think those were good?" he said to the audience. Loud cheers. "Then just watch what our rodeo queen Ruby Barkley did—how many of you want to see Ruby and Gabe back together?"

More loud whooping and cheers.

"How many were sad about yesterday's fight?"

Groans and boos.

"Well, have some hope here, folks! Watch this recording and tell us what you think!"

The clip rolled. Ruby had to admit she looked pretty darn good in that top, and the blue topazes were more striking even against fading red and gray hair than she had expected.

"That's telling her!" Rick yelled after Ruby made her speech about dramatic tension.

Her comm buzzed. *Gabriel Ramirez*, it whispered into her ear.

"One moment." She stood. "I've got to take a call. But go

ahead and keep watching." She grinned at the three couples, Martin and Charlie sitting upright next to each other, Julie and Terri leaning on each other, and Rick coiled protectively around Beck on the couch. A family, of sorts. *Her* family. "Let me know if there's anything good while I'm talking."

"No problem," Charlie said laconically. "Who's calling?"

"Gabe."

Hoots and hollers followed Ruby as she left. She hurried to the office, glad she was still wearing that top and the earrings. "Clear now," she said, standing in the middle of the room with her arms crossed.

Gabe's projection popped up a few feet away. "God damn, Ruby, that was great to see." He sighed. "It's been the high point of my day. I was scared shitless that they'd show my talk with Mariah. I told her to go to hell, that I was tired of dancing to her tune. It wasn't a good look. Rachel would have chewed my ass for being that rude." He rubbed his face and she noticed that he had dark circles under his eyes coupled with a worried expression. "But dear God, do *not* get yourself in with Philip Martiniere. Even to buy out Mariah. Please. I—know too much about the man."

"He can't be *that* bad." No. She would *not* react to that mention of his late wife—a woman he had loved, from all reports. *He was faithful to her,* she thought bitterly.

"He is." Gabe sighed. "But that's not what I called about."

"You talked to Bran?"

He nodded. "I agree. We've got to talk privately. A lot's going on." He sighed. "It's been a godawful day. I have my own mess to deal with now, and after talking to Bran...." He shook his head. "Yeah. But I've other reasons to come to the ranch. I need to consult with your people. I've got big trouble."

"Gabe, what's wrong?"

He tightened his lips. "That little problem you and your neighbors are dealing with? I have it, too."

She stared at him, shocked. "No. You're—kidding." She snapped up a privacy filter. It might not be enough to completely screen out any recordings but at least it would garble them.

"I wish I were. My ranch manager Tim brought the first samples in this morning. Almost identical to what you showed me."

"I see. We've got counterbots. Can you send me a schematic to pass on to my people, so they can tweak it a little for different conditions?"

He nodded, hope rising in his face. "Does this mean you have extras?"

"We're doing our first release on Friday and starting a new grow right away."

"I can't pay a lot right now."

"Understood."

He rubbed his brow. "Where are these damn things coming from?"

"I wish I knew. WLAN or someone else?"

"My money's on WLAN," he said. "But until I can make it over there, I'm going to do what I can. There may be a microbial counter to it but it's not going to completely stop those killbots. Mariah called me away from that work which is one reason why I ripped her a new one. Look. I can't get away from here until Wednesday. Just gives me Thursday to spread your counters before we have to leave for the next cut recording, and I hope I can hold it off with my microbial counters. But my first runs aren't looking promising."

"We can have your counterbots ready to go by then."

He smiled. "That's the second piece of good news that I've heard today. Watching you kick butt on Mariah was priceless."

His grin spread wider. "She clearly remembered where you got those earrings."

"You do too."

He chuckled. "How could I not?" He slumped back, sighing. "Ah, Ruby. I fucked you up big time and I'm sorry. We can talk about it in more detail later, but I just wanted you to know that."

"Thank you." She didn't know what to say next. One part of her was flattered while another wondered if his reaction was based more on his need for her counterbots.

He hesitated, clearly waiting for her to say more. "Okay, then. I'll see you on Wednesday. Do you think we might go for a ride?"

"Crawler or horseback?"

"The sensible thing would be crawler, but—" A wistful look softened his expression. "It would be great to ride. I had to get rid of the horses a couple of years ago. I've missed riding."

"I'm sorry to hear that, Gabe."

"It was probably all for the best. Rachel didn't ride and I didn't have the time or the people to keep the horses up like they should be."

"I don't have anything like your old Ranger horse."

"He was one of a kind, wasn't he? Just like old Sunshine."

"She's still going strong."

"You're kidding. That would make her—thirty-four?"

"Thirty-five," Ruby confirmed. "But we've got some steady rides here, if that's what you want."

Gabe half-laughed. "Steady isn't particularly what either of us would want, Ruby-girl. But, given my condition, I'll take a steady horse over a crawler. If you'll spare me one."

"I think I can do that." She let herself smile. "But we both need to carry long guns. If someone takes a shot at me again, I want a chance of hitting them."

"Now you're being smart," Gabe said. "I'll bring my saddle rifle. Still have that."

"Sounds good." She swallowed hard. Gabe's old saddle rifle was a match for hers, a pair they had bought right after getting married. "I still have mine."

"Think we ought to bring it up for any recordings?"

"We'll mortify the townsfolk with our matched rifles," she said.

He laughed. "See you on Wednesday, Ruby."

"See you on Wednesday."

She took a deep breath after Gabe's image disappeared. Her mail pinged with a big attachment. She took a quick glance to see the schematic there and forwarded it to Martin and Julie with a note, then rejoined the others.

"Well?" Charlie asked.

"Gabe's coming on Wednesday," she said. "Hey, maybe we should check on the calving pen."

Charlie raised his brows but didn't say anything. They went through the kitchen to the mud room and pulled on coats, boots, and headlamps before going out in the blustery evening. Ruby kept quiet until they were moving around the cows in the calving pen. So far none of them appeared to be in labor. Most were lying down and chewing their cud. They made their way to the far fence and stood there, staring into the dark cow pasture.

"What's going on with Gabe?" Charlie asked.

"He has a rogue killbot infestation too," Ruby said. "Sent me the schematic just now. I didn't look at it too closely, but it's a match for what we've got from what I saw. Did they show his and Mariah's conversation?"

"No. That was an interesting omission."

"Gabe said he told her to go to hell. She pulled him out of

the lab. He's working on a microbial stopgap, but he doesn't think it's going to work."

"Yeah, where he is at a lower elevation, he's more under the gun than we are for timing. That's gotta hurt. Think it's gonna eliminate him?"

"I don't think they're going to cut Gabe this go-round. Not if we give AgI hope of breathing life into their damn reunion storyline. They'll find some reason to overlook this."

"Shit," Charlie growled. "To think that ranching's come to this, at least for small ops. Well, you just revived that storyline tonight."

"Yeah." A gust of wind pushed her around a little bit. "It does make me wonder just who is behind all of this. Is it a separate AgI operation to juice up the stories or is someone actually interfering with us?"

"I don't know. I'd leave that kind of speculation to those involved in investigation. It's too easy to get distracted and right now we need to be focused on winning the Superhero with the RubyBot."

Ruby laughed and turned away from the fence. "Right as ever, Charlie."

CHAPTER 9

Friday morning dawned bright and clear, with just a touch of blustery spring south wind blowing. Ruby stood at the kitchen window, sipping her coffee as she appraised the weather in light of the day's events. A good warm day coming up, that would clear the last traces of snow off of the fields that they planned to do the releases on. Too bad, in some respect, because releasing the counterbots would be more visually effective if there was a skiff of snow on the ground. Entirely possible this time of year, but she had the sense that snow was done for the year at this elevation. She clicked up her weather calendar and noted the time, temperature, and conditions. Then she allowed herself to check the stats. Warmer earlier this year. That meant a hot and dry summer ahead.

Water optimization algorithms should be a priority.

Ruby finished her coffee and set it in the sink. Beck entered the kitchen, still looking sleepy-eyed though she was fully dressed in jeans and heavy sweater with her bleached hair pulled and pinned back tight against her head in full lab configuration. She poured herself a big cup of coffee as Ruby gathered breakfast dishes.

"I'll get those," she said. "My turn."

"Eh, get yourself fed first. It's going to be a big day," Ruby said.

"I'm good." Beck said. "Rick brought me up a protein bar."

"You know, we've got real food to spare. I've got enough to cover all of us. You don't need to scrimp."

"Not scrimping." Beck deftly eased Ruby aside to fill the sink with soap and water. "Just not letting myself get out of the indenture habits. Safer that way."

"Why?"

Beck paused from washing out the second sink. "Body mods that affect how many calories I can process."

"I thought the law said that all body mods were supposed to be pulled once you fulfilled indenture."

"Ha!" Beck rinsed a dish and placed it in the rack. "That's what they tell you. Maybe it's true for the guys and here in North America. Rick doesn't seem to have any leftovers. But I sure as hell have leftover hormonal tags. Most former women indentureds do at least until menopause. Both here and in Europe."

"Really?"

Beck nodded as she chugged the last of her coffee and then washed her cup. "There's a whole online community of us, Ruby. We compare notes. It's pretty damn obvious, especially when some of us get dragged back into indenture to bear a rich someone's baby. And it's illegal to pull them."

Ruby inhaled sharply. "So the rumors are true."

"Far as I know, yes. At least it's happening in Europe. Not gonna be me if I can avoid it, but the apparatus is still there. If I start bleeding again, that's the sign that someone's got plans for my body that doesn't include what I want." Beck dumped the wash water into the graywater holding tank.

"How are you going to stop them?" God, that was an awful thing to be facing.

"Rick and I were saving to have my ladyparts yanked. Uterus, ovaries, the whole shooting match. We were on track to do that until this crap happened. I'm still on the waiting list in Portland but god only knows how soon that will come through. If it comes through."

"Who held your indenture—if I can ask?"

"Biosystems AG," Beck said. "That's where I learned my lab skills and met Rick. We were both supposed to be life-time indentures, but BAG cut us loose as a bonus after we created their trademark line and set it up so that anyone with half a brain could create those seeds and grow a good strong line."

"That makes sense." And it explained a lot. "Were you two working here or in Europe?" Ruby eyed Beck curiously. Most of BAG's ops were in Europe and while release terms could be generous, it wasn't usual for former indentureds to be able to scrape together enough cash to leave the continent. Especially under current trade strictures.

"Europe," Beck said. "We got lucky because GrowInc wanted our skills and were willing to pay the relocation fees to bring us to North America as employees, not indentured transfers. Lots of money exchanged hands over us, and we were happy to get the hell out." She pulled up one sleeve and showed Ruby a tattoo on one forearm—the BAG logo with a red slash over it. "Couldn't do that over there. You can't even mark yourself as a former indentured." She dropped the sleeve and drew a deep, ragged breath. "I'll die before I become an indentured again. Bad enough to know my ladyparts can still be put under obligation."

Ruby shook her head. "God. Beck, I don't know what to say."

"You don't have to say a damn thing. You already did what was needed," Beck said. "We owe you big time for taking us in like this, Ruby, and trust me, Rick and I will go to the wall to help you succeed. No matter what it takes."

Interns here, Charlie texted Ruby, her comm speaking it into her ear.

"Guess I'd better get going," she said to Beck. "The interns have arrived."

"I'll be out there in a sec," Beck said.

Ruby grabbed the coat that Vickie had designated as *recording work coat* from its peg on the coat rack in the mud room. Today's garb was a slightly nicer pair of work jeans, another shimmery turtleneck in black that hopefully wouldn't show much muck or dirt, and the freshwater pearl earrings that Vickie had picked out the other night. One of Ruby's *ten things good about Gabe* moments had included going through her jewelry collection to sort out the jewelry he had given her so that she could wear it as a reminder. There was a silver pair of earrings that matched her good-luck locket, several sets of turquoise earrings and bracelets, and a couple of pairs of malachite earrings. There had been more there than she had remembered.

Gabe did like to give me jewelry.

Now she wondered how much of it had come from gambling wins.

No, not something to think about now.

Nor was it a good idea to think about Beck's revelations. She jammed her flat-brimmed brown working hat with stampede strings to hold it tight on her head against the wind—nicer than the black one she had been wearing, which had been banished by Vickie until after the Superhero was decided. Then she pulled on her boots and went out.

Chaos ruled in the barnyard, directed by Charlie and Terri. It wasn't just the interns, it was the vans of Innovator film crew, media crews, and assorted vehicles along with the short white school bus that had brought the interns from the school. Ruby had invited as many local politicians as would show up to observe the initial orientation of the students and their first job, which would be doing the support work for releasing the counterbots.

She was pleased to see that Sheriff Wilhite was amongst the politicians, and that a couple of her deputies moved amongst the rigs, monitoring things.

"Ruby! Over here!" Charlie waved. The students clustered around him, with the local politicians in a wider circle with reporters and video setups on the furthest ring out.

"Howdy," she said as she joined them. Scott grinned at her. "Glad to have you folks on the team. I'm going to make some remarks, and then I'd like to have each of you introduce yourselves." She waved at the cams and the reporters pressing in around them. "Ignore all this stuff. It's important but it doesn't affect you. Okay?" She met the eyes of each of the five students waiting, pleased when they nodded back.

She took a deep breath and faced the larger group. "All right, everybody. Welcome to the Double R. I'm Ruby Barkley, as most of you already know, and today is a blue-ribbon day in a lot of ways for us. We're on the brink of launching an exciting new biobot, the RubyBot, which not only monitors soil and plant conditions on the nano level, but has the capability to assist seedlings to access soil nutrients, release fertilizer, pesticides, and herbicides as needed in a pinpoint capacity, help plants conserve resources when faced with temperature extremes, and utilize irrigation effectively. These actions are transmitted to field-based sensor arrays which, again, provides the farmer with nano-level data about what is happening in each field at the individual plant level."

"STOP NATURE ABUSE!" One of the reporters charged toward Ruby, gesturing to two other men who followed her.

"You're contributing to the destruction of our ecosystems with this technology!"

Ruby's jaw dropped as she recognized the indentured who had crashed into her at the finalist recording last week. Or was she just imagining that? She stepped forward as the person grabbed at one of the students, shoving that person away from the kid. The person whirled to take a swing at her. No. Not the same person, but uncannily similar.

Sheriff Wilhite and her deputies grabbed the three protesters. They kept screaming as they were dragged away. "NO MORE ECOSYSTEM DESTRUCTION! SAVE ANIMALS AND NATURE! RUBY BARKLEY IS A NATURE ABUSER!"

The shouting stopped as the protesters were shoved into the sheriff's van.

Ruby took a deep breath.

"Thank you, Sheriff Wilhite and your deputies!" she called out. Wilhite waved an acknowledgement as she returned, flanked by the deputies as the van pulled out. Ruby noticed there was another sheriff's van parked at the end of her driveway.

Good.

"Sorry for the interruption," she said. "So. What's happening today is that we're going to put a pre-release bot on our fields." *And those of the neighbors,* but she didn't add that. She had sat down with Vickie and Julie last night to script out this presentation, referring to the counterbots as *pre-release bots* in any media. "One of the challenges in using a biobot like the RubyBot is that we want to ensure that there are no other bots of any other type left active on the field which could interfere with our new release. While our tech is good, it's better to be safe than sorry, especially in these early days. What you are going to learn today is the basic introduction process which we will then use in a few days to release the actual RubyBot. Understood?"

Nods from the students.

"Ms. Barkley!" one of the reporters called.

Ruby shook her head. "No questions, please. So. What happens next is I'm going to ask these five students to introduce themselves and say a couple of words about what they hope to learn from working in the Double R labs. These students are seniors in the Thunder County High School agronomy track. While they're going to be learning about biosecurity, we're also going to be teaching them the fundamentals they will need to know in order to get jobs at the Double R once the RubyBot is launched and we're in full production."

She gestured to the kids. Scott stepped forward.

"Well done," Charlie said quietly into her ear. "Didn't expect that."

"I'm glad Sharon was on the ball with her deputies," she whispered back, watching as Jolene Penth, the second student to speak, spoke about her desire to work in bot grow labs.

"Networking with AgI, I think. Wonder if those are our saboteurs?"

"Oh, if only that would be true and that they don't have other buddies out there," she said.

"Definitely WLAN."

Ruby nodded, clapping as Jolene stepped back and Kenny Weston took his turn to speak. When the students were done, she stepped forward again.

"This is the face of our agricultural future," she said, gesturing toward the students. "I'm hoping that with production from the RubyBot and other projects I have in development, that this will be an ongoing cooperative endeavor which will provide employment for local students who don't want to leave Thunder County to find opportunities. At least that is my long-term goal, and if I win the Superhero award, I plan to use those funds not just to promote my own projects but to make life in Thunder County better for all of us who live here."

She grinned at the cams as applause rose. There were a few questions but not many. Then she stepped back to let the head of the county commission and other politicians speak, fixing a smile on her face and thinking about the release process as they nattered on.

Out here, on this sunny early spring-like day, it was easy enough to believe that anything was possible.

THE CROWDS FADED AWAY AFTER THEY LOADED UP THE crawlers with the boxes of bots to be released. A handful of the AgI film crew remained. Ruby climbed onto the lead crawler, Jolene with her to open gates. They motored out slowly, the faint whine of the electric engines under a load the only indicator of the weight of the boxes being pulled on the carts.

"Just open the gate and hop back on," she told Jolene as they approached the first gate. "Last one through closes it."

"Got it!" Jolene popped off the crawler as they stopped at the first gate. Ruby waited until Jolene was back on the crawler behind her before starting up, retracing the steps she'd followed not that many days before on Legacy. No sign of snow remained, and the faint hint of green against brown that had been present then was stronger now. She wondered what early wildflowers might be starting to unfold in the little folds of the ridges.

Might have time to look when I'm out here with Gabe.

Hmm. Maybe they could call their meeting "wildflower hunting." Her mouth quirked in secret amusement. Gabe would appreciate that joke. They'd used it around Gramps to mask romantic encounters.

The procession split up where the two draws forked. Ruby led Martin, Beck, and two crawlers of AgI film crew up the left hand draw while Charlie, Terri, and Rick turned right. Julie had stayed back at the lab to keep an eye on things and start preparing the second grow of counterbots for Gabe.

The tracks of the crawler and cart clattered across the first bridge. Ruby halted at the foot of the first field.

"I want you to keep the film crew happy," she said to Jolene. "Ask where they want to film, but keep them away from us while we're working. They need to be ten feet back from the boxes, and they can't send their cams over the field until I say it's clear. We don't want to risk any interference from their transmissions until the bots are oriented to the field. Okay?"

Jolene nodded. "What if they give me any problems?"

"Then call for me. But I don't think they will be. This is an experienced AgI film crew. They know not to mess with a tech release. And I'll reinforce that expectation. Let's go talk to them now."

She walked over to the AgI team.

"Hey Ruby. What's the protocol today?" Maggie, the video crew head, stepped away from the AgI crew clustered around their crawlers.

Ruby gestured to Jolene. "Jolene is going to be your minder while we work. Jolene, this is Maggie. She's a pro at this."

The two bowed formally to each other.

"Parameters?" Maggie asked.

"I've told Jolene. Ten feet back, no cams over the field until I give approval because we need the pre-release bots to get oriented first. Transmission interference risk. Keep that ten-foot elevation while filming the field." Ruby winced, reluctant to reveal that weakness. "It's something we're still working on."

"Got it."

"Anything else you need, talk to Jolene. She knows where the food is, can tell you about the area, all sorts of good stuff. I'm leaving you in her hands."

"We'll be good," Maggie said.

Ruby left them and went to the box where Martin, Beck, and Scott waited for her.

"Ready?" Martin asked.

"Let's do it," Ruby said.

"We'll start with the first half here, go partway up the track, then release the rest of this box."

Ruby nodded. The four of them each picked up a corner of the growbox and carried it to the field's edge. Martin raised the bottom door as the other three carefully tipped the box to encourage the bots to leave their nursery. Ruby couldn't keep her smile hidden as the blue-green tiny beetle-like bots scurried out of the box. At first the release looked like a wave of blue-green carapaces about three feet long and a foot wide. But the line thinned until she couldn't see it any more.

Martin focused on the box readout, lips moving silently as he studied it.

"That's all of that batch," he said finally. They eased the box back to a level position and carried it back to the cart. Martin returned to the edge of the field, studying his scanner. Ruby joined him, looking over his shoulder at the activation readouts. At first, nothing. Then little red dots where the counterbots encountered killbots. The dots soon became a steady flow of red.

"It's working." Martin sighed with relief. "Let's get the next round unloaded."

They drove partway up the field and released the second batch.

"Okay to film over the field yet?" Jolene called as Martin

and Ruby repeated the wait for the counterbots to start working.

"Gimme a couple more minutes," Ruby yelled back. "And then they can also come film this." She pointed to Martin's display.

Once the red dots started merging the second time on the scanner, Ruby nodded.

"All clear for filming!" she said.

Maggie and Jolene came over to her. "What's happening here?" She pointed at the scanner readout.

"All that red? Those pre-release bots are oriented and working. We needed you to stay clear so that they could focus on the bots already in the field and not be diverted to your cams."

"What happens if they get diverted, besides not doing their job?"

"There's enough of them that they could take down your cams," Martin said abruptly. "These bots do have flight capacity."

"Oh. I'll tell my crew that for sure." Maggie and Jolene left.

Jolene stayed with the film crew as they headed for the next field. That release was also uneventful. At last they reached the final field, Homestead, the one that Ruby *hadn't* been to the other day when riding out. This one was the highest elevation test field, and the closest to the Reed place.

The other two fields had been more protected and the wind hadn't been blowing down there. Up here, there was enough of a breeze to make Martin frown.

"Let me do a check," he said as they stood by the boxes. "We may need to approach the release from the other side."

"I'll let Maggie and Jolene know," Ruby said.

Martin nodded, his dark face tightened with worry. "Tell them to double the distances. This could be enough of a breeze to make things challenging with their cams. I'm not sure yet how quickly these bots are going to settle."

Ruby nodded and went back to the AgI crew. "Martin's looking at a different approach. This wind can make dispersal complicated. We need to double your safe distances when we do give film approval—and I might not approve it for this plot. Just saying."

"We got pretty good footage of the other fields anyway," Maggie said. "Though this one has the prettiest views. It'd be great for some framing shots."

Ruby glanced around at the snow-covered mountains to the east and south. "It is, isn't it? Well, while Martin and Beck are checking things out, I can talk about the location a little bit." She went on to tell a story from Gramps's days about this field and how it always seemed to be the one that ate machine parts. She pointed out the remnants of the original homestead that had once been here that gave the field its name.

"What caused them to leave?" Maggie asked.

"Weather," Ruby said. "Up here on the ridges it gets pretty darn severe in wintertime. Even with our warmer temperatures these days, this field can drop to minus twenty Fahrenheit during a blizzard. Back in the old days, temps of sixty below were not unheard of. Now imagine going through that in a wooden shack without modern heating and insulation. And hard winds blowing snow in through cracks. Lots of drifts out here thanks to the winds."

Maggie shivered. "This is enough of a breeze to make me cold."

Ruby and Jolene exchanged quick grins.

"That's life in Thunder County. The Indians thought the whites were nuts to stay up here year-round and not go to the nice warm river canyons in the winter." Ruby shrugged. "They were right. This field is one of my marginal ones, and if I win the Superhero, my next priority will be to try to restore the original grassland in this field."

"That's doable?"

Ruby nodded. "We restored the Lone Pine pasture back to grassland. It's an even higher elevation than this one."

"But you're not running stock up here."

"Too early. Grass hasn't come in yet. But when it does, it's some of the best feed ever."

"Ruby!" Martin called. "I've got the points figured. We're gonna need to move."

"And that's my working orders." Ruby sprinted back to Martin.

"We're gonna release from the north side," Martin said to her. Ruby nodded and hopped onto her crawler. They circled the big field and stopped.

This time the initial release wave was more scattered as the wind picked up. Some of the bots took wing, landing further in the field than the previous drops had.

"Not liking this," Martin growled. "These bots like to fly more than I want to see for a counter—erm, *pre-release* bot. But I had to program in a certain amount of flight capacity, just to make sure they get all the strays. That needs to be the next tweak."

"Yeah," Ruby said. They watched the scanner data. It took longer, but soon red spread across this half of the field.

"Glad I saved the largest batch for this field," Martin muttered. "Ruby, there's interference coming from somewhere nearby."

Ruby's skin prickled. "Enough to pull this field from the RubyBot release?"

"Eh, Homestead provides some of our most challenging test conditions. I'd hate to do it. But I'm going to allocate more of the RubyBot to this field than the other two to compensate. Let's see what happens with the counters."

They returned to the crawlers and to the second release location. From here Ruby could look over to the next ridge, which was the Reed ranch. The boundary was down in the draw that separated the two ridges. She wondered what the status was of the sensors on *that* fence. They were going to be replacing them all anyway, but still....

The release on this side of the field was also slow, with more bots flying and circling aimlessly until they settled on the ground. Martin muttered at the scanner as they watched.

"What the hell—" Maggie yelled. An AgI cam rose from the collection on the cart. "What idiot set that one off?"

The cam buzzed across the field, swooping low. Maggie cursed and yelled, wrestling with the virtual cam controls as the cam dove lower and lower.

"I can't control it!" Maggie screamed. "Programming autodestruct now!"

"Don't bother!" Martin yelled back as a swarm of blue-green bots rose from the field. As the cam dropped further, the bots covered it and it crashed in the field. Ruby stared, fascinated, as its shape flared bright red on the scanner.

Maggie ran over to them. "Damn it, Ruby, I'm sorry. None of my people admit to setting it off. I don't know what's going on. We had all our cams switched off, or so I thought."

"There's interference of some sort going on up here," Martin growled. But he pointed to the scanner. "Your cam is gone now." The bright red patch where the cam had been faded.

"They did—what?" Maggie spread her hands wide.

"Consumed it."

"Is it going to be a problem for our bots?" Ruby asked.

Martin bit his lower lip as he focused on his scanner readout. "Got good data from that absorption. The good news is that no, I think it provided them with some more energy so they're going to be stronger bots and better at their job. Good news for this field." He turned off the scanner. "But now you understand why I didn't want you getting too close."

"I'll say so," Maggie sighed. "Live and learn. Just wish I could have gotten some footage of that process."

"I'm just as glad you didn't," Ruby said. She walked back with Maggie to the AgI crew. "Look. Until we have a chance to analyze the data, is there any possibility of you keeping this incident under wraps? I'll tell Brandon what happened, of course. It's part of my reporting. But I'd just as soon this information not get out to the public—just yet. Proprietary design and all that."

"Understood," Maggie said. One of her crew cleared his throat and she glared at him. "*Understood,* John?"

He nodded.

Ruby hiked back to her crawler. She paused by Martin. "Was this something you expected?"

"Not—quite like this," he said. "But it does give me some peace of mind. Julie's going to be thrilled to see this data. She's the one who was concerned the most about potential interferences." He hesitated. "There's some prospects for development here, as well. That algorithm might just work on our replacement boundary sensors. And to see that the counters can take on something as big as a cam—she's going to be dancing because that was her design."

"That would be a relief," Ruby said. She continued on to her crawler, with a lot to think about on her way back to the main part of the ranch.

CHAPTER 10

"I'm really sorry about your cam," Ruby said to Brandon when he called that night.

Brandon shrugged. "I've talked to Maggie. John was careless and didn't shut it down completely when he should have. You won't see him again." He rubbed his forehead. "It does make things more complicated. I've issued a directive to our staff to be more careful in the field."

"All the same, I'm hoping you're not reporting on it."

"We didn't get any video, so as far as my people are concerned...what happened to the cam would be as if one of the local eagles decided to attack it. It does happen, Ma. Sometimes a cam takes a dive because of tech interference or something else. The year we had a commercial fish farm competitor, we were losing cams to ospreys and orcas."

"Really?"

"Oh heck yeah."

"Thanks. But I thought I'd better let you know for certain."

"Oh, no kidding. I appreciate it." He cleared his throat. "Have you heard anything further about your protesters from this morning?"

"WLAN," Ruby said flatly. "That's all Sheriff Wilhite

would tell me." She hesitated, wondering if she should bring up the similarities between the indentured and the one protestor.

Brandon shifted uncomfortably. "There's one complication. One of the protestors is a former AgI indentured. The one you had contact with."

So I didn't imagine it.

"I had—noticed a resemblance. Aren't body mods supposed to be removed once indenture is over?"

"Not always," Brandon said. "It takes an agreement between the parties for the former indentured to retain their mods. I'm not sure what happened here, but that person was not supposed to retain their mods. I had to do a lot of editing on that segment between it and you. The footage was just too good to let go but we didn't want the protestor to be identified as one of our former indentured. Don't be too surprised at what you see in the next episode, okay?"

"I won't. I guess. It does bother me to see a connection between AgI and WLAN, no matter how tenuous."

"You're—not the only one," Brandon said slowly. Then he scowled. "I've gotta go, Ma. You take care of yourself, and I'll see you in a few days."

Ruby stretched once his image faded. It had been a good day overall. But she was still wired from the excitement, and wanted to talk to someone. She hesitated as Gabe came to mind. Should she?

She went to the bathroom and checked herself in the mirror. She looked like she would after a day's work on the ranch, and her hair was crushed down. Her top had a faint mud stain on one sleeve.

Not like this you won't.

Even if they kept this call entirely private, maybe she wanted to practice looking good for—for someone. For the cams, at the very least.

Still, it made her giggle as she showered, slipped into her pajamas, and picked out her nicer robe. It still looked worn and faded, but at least there weren't any holes in it. Instead of opting for Martin's whisky, she made herself a cup of herbal tea. Then she retreated back to her bedroom. Even with Rick and Beck in the house, it was still quiet. They tended to go straight to their room at night and were so soft and discreet about making noise that it was easy to forget they were there.

Now that she was settled in her rocking chair, she called Gabe.

"Ruby. What a surprise!" He smiled at her from his office chair, face softening from a tight, strained expression. "What's the occasion?"

"Oh, I don't know. It's been a busy day here with the counterbot releases—oh wait, I'm supposed to call them *pre-release bots*."

Gabe laughed with her. "The things we do for this damn show. And it still feels weird to be doing it in February instead of October."

"Yeah. Anyway, I'm still wound up." She sipped on her tea. "And in light of things, I thought it might be a good idea to give you a call."

"Well, I'm sure glad you did." He snapped away the computer projection over his desk. "I've been pounding my head against...my little issue here...and agonizing over it some more tonight isn't going to make one bit of difference. The release went well?"

"There were some interesting moments." She thought about what she should share on this line, and decided to save the counterbot-cam encounter for when they could talk face-to-face. "Overall, the releases are doing what they're supposed to do. We had some wind and—other things happening in the Homestead field. But it all worked out. I'm happy."

"I'm looking forward to seeing them in action," Gabe said. "I'm glad it went well."

"I did have some protestors here for the big announcement."

His brows shot up. "Oh? Who?"

"WLAN. Calling me a nature destroyer."

He grimaced. "I'm concerned about that here as well. There really seems to be a whole bunch of that crowd wandering around the area. Tim found signs on the edge of my property that looks like someone was setting up camp. Had the sheriff clear them out, one of the participants was a low-level protestor. The weird thing is, from the shots the sheriff showed me, there was one who looked like some of those indentureds at AgI."

Ruby shivered. "That's—interesting. One of my protestors was a former AgI indentured. Brandon told me about that."

Gabe gave her a sharp sideways look. "What the hell is going on with these people?"

"I don't know."

"Take care of yourself, Ruby. That doesn't sound good."

"Sounds like you need to be doing the same."

He nodded, but the worried expression didn't leave his face. "I'll pass the word on to Tim. Other than that, how's things going?"

"Busy. Spring's coming. Nice day today, but we'll see what tomorrow brings. Spring in the high country. You know how it is. Maybe when you're here we ought to go looking for wild-flowers."

As she expected, Gabe chuckled at their old code for slipping out alone. "That sounds promising and a nice break for both of us. I'm looking forward to that. Oh yeah. I was able to work some fields today. Nothing for the Innovator yet, got to get those items to prepare the field first."

"It does make sense to clear the fields of any potential active bots. I'm thinking that was a piece that was missing from before. We should have been thinking about that back then."

Gabe pursed his lips thoughtfully. "You know, I agree. I think it's a piece I've been missing with my projects as well. But you know how it is. You just get busy and start relying on scans alone. Then you miss something lurking in the field that causes you a problem."

Ruby nodded. "Given what's been happening, I think it's an avenue that we're going to start integrating into our processes."

"I thank you for the idea. I'm going to approach my preparations from that angle as well." Gabe stroked his chin thoughtfully.

Ruby yawned, suddenly realizing that she was tired. "I'm sorry, Gabe, but all of a sudden I'm feeling wiped out."

"I'm feeling like I could crash myself," Gabe said. He smiled. "Thanks for the call, Ruby. It was what I needed tonight. Looking forward to seeing you in a few days."

"Me too. Bye." She shut off the connection and headed for bed.

THE NEXT FEW DAYS SETTLED INTO AN UNEXPECTED pattern of quiet. Ruby, Charlie, and Martin took turns riding out to check on the counterbot releases with either Julie or Terri joining them. The fence repair crew showed up and started working on the boundary fence between the Double R and Vickie's place. Ron Campbell assured Ruby that all his workers had been checked. She wasn't too worried as she knew all of them—local workers with good reputations.

She kept working on the *ten good things about Gabe*

process. But she didn't call him, and he didn't call her. The weather switched back and forth from day to day, one day bright and sunny, the next overcast, cool, and rainy. Typical spring, if early.

Gabe called her finally, on Tuesday night, when she had finished everything for the day and was reading in her rocking chair. Ever since the other night Ruby had taken to wearing her better robe over her pajamas when doing her bedtime reading. Just in case.

"Hey," he said, also in pajamas and robe. "Everything on track for tomorrow? Been wondering how your work's been going."

"We're good for tomorrow," she said. "You'll be able to take a nice batch of pre-release bots home with you."

"Well, that's good news." He smiled. "I think I'm on track with a microbial complement. Can your pre-release bots take on an additional mode?"

"Adding in microbial elements—that would be a payload, right?"

"Yes."

Ruby pursed her lips thoughtfully. "There's enough space on that bot that as long as it isn't too complex, it should be doable."

"That would be good. I started thinking about adding an element that could cancel out any microbial leftovers I might have on my fields."

"Sounds like a good idea. You have it ready?"

"Yes. Already mixed up."

"Then you might want to bring it so that Martin can load it into the mix and record those stats. I'll check with him about developmental stages but if we load the microbials when you get here, then they'll be integrated in time for release tomorrow. Keep data on how that goes, okay?"

"Of course."

"There is one thing that's happening." She chewed her lip, thinking about the best way to bring this up. "The Homestead field has some interesting results. I can give you more details tomorrow. But it appears that having a little bit of interference doesn't appear to be a problem for these pre-release bots."

"That's good news."

"Still want to go for a wildflower hunt and ride after the Ruby gets released? I need to charge extra crawlers if you aren't up for a ride."

"I'm still up for a ride," Gabe said. "I've been looking forward to it." He shifted in his recliner. "Like I said, I've missed having horses around, but just no time for them. Any idea which horse you're going to stick me on?"

"Probably Red while I ride Pard." Red was a former roping horse. Charlie had won a few competitions on him. "He singlefoots."

"That sounds good. I'm really looking forward to this, Ruby."

"So am I."

And to her surprise, she found that she really meant it.

TRUE TO HIS WORD, GABE ARRIVED EARLY ON WEDNESDAY morning. Ruby had already decided that the release of the RubyBot was going to lack the fanfare of the pre-release bots, with only the AgI film crew on site. She didn't want to deal with yet another WLAN appearance, and while AgI would have fun with her riding off with Gabe, it wasn't going to be a big promotional thing just yet, not until they set their parameters.

She frowned as a second vehicle pulled in behind Gabe's

truck. Then she saw the Moondance logo on the front door. He'd brought an escort, apparently. She grabbed coat and hat and rushed out.

Gabe and another man stood by his rig. "Hi Ruby. This is my ranch manager, Tim Vanhorn—my version of Charlie. I thought it would make more sense for Tim to head back right away with the pre-release bots rather than have them sit around here all day. And instead of routing everything through me, he can talk directly to your people."

"Glad to meet you, Tim." They bowed to each other. Ruby turned toward the lab. "Did you bring your microbial inoculates? Martin has the bots set up for loading."

"Yes," Tim said. "We figured I'd add them under his supervision, then I'd load up and go. Unless transport right away is not a good idea."

"I don't know why it would be particularly problematic." They reached the lab and pulled on the preventative wear. Martin was fussing over the boxes of RubyBots when they came in. Ruby introduced Tim to him and the two of them went off to the sector where the pre-release bots for Gabe had been isolated.

Gabe whistled as he surveyed the lab. "Wow. This is quite the change from twenty-one years ago."

"It is, isn't it? I've been adding on a little bit at a time, as I find money to do it. I've been wanting to expand the lab even further and I'm hoping that the Superhero will give me what I need to make it work."

Gabe nodded. "It's bigger than my own lab. But then, with the different steps that you need for the bots, it would have to be."

"Different stages for sure."

He peered at one of the growboxes. "Sure has come a long way. You've done well, Ruby."

"Thanks."

Rick left the section that had been walled off for the AgSystems seed grows.

"Rick, this is Gabe Ramirez, Gabe, Rick Keysing, one of the best damn stem cell seed growers we've got."

"I've heard a lot about you," Gabe said. They exchanged bows. "It's an honor to meet you in person at last. With any luck I'll be able to buy some of your product."

"Well, it's looking more and more like there will be product to buy," Rick said. "We revived a second growline, Ruby. It was touch and go—but that gives me two good seed lines to work with. A lot better than what I had anticipated even a couple of days ago." He grimaced. "Not sure about the other two lines we salvaged. But Beck's been working her magic. She seems to be able to bring struggling lines along better than anyone else."

"Doesn't hurt that she's willing to put in the long hours it takes," Ruby said.

"And it helps to be living this close to the lab." A rare grin crossed Rick's face. "Ruby, you're spoiling us. It's wonderful to be able to walk to the lab."

"It's all in my evil plan to get you to set up here," Ruby said as Martin and Tim rejoined them.

"It's working," Rick said. "A few more months of this and I won't be able to pry Beck away from the Double R."

"Hey, I can always use more people in the lab," Martin said.

"Sounds good. What's our transfer process?" Ruby asked.

"We're going to move Gabe's bots into the outside wall room to inoculate them," Martin said. "To save on decontam hassles, Tim and I will do the work. It's not a big job nor will it take long. We can go directly from inoculation to loading them up. Then we can shift priorities to the RubyBot."

"There's not going to be any transport problems?" Gabe asked.

Tim shook his head. "These are pretty robust bots, Gabe. I'm impressed with what I see."

Martin chuckled. "You got the updated algorithms." He eyed Ruby. "I told him about the Homestead incident."

"The Homestead incident?" Gabe's brows rose.

Ruby told him about it while Tim and Martin went to work.

"That—must have been fascinating to watch," Gabe said when she was done.

"And a bit scary," Ruby said.

"I do like those capabilities in a bot like that. Especially since there was some interference. We've been checking our boundary sensors ever Tim came across that encampment. It's good to know that there's that sort of aggressive response available."

"Yeah, but the overreaction can be a bear. I just hope we haven't created our own problems here. At least they seem to be dying back once they've finished the job, like they're supposed to do."

"Well, that's good."

They went back outside to watch the boxes being loaded onto Tim's rig.

"I'm going to get Jerry and Kathleen to help unload back at Moondance," Tim said. "It looks like we're on track to start our releases tomorrow morning first thing."

"I'll see you then," Gabe said.

Tim nodded. He climbed back into the cab of his truck and left.

"We'll get the RubyBot loaded now," Martin said. "You two still riding horses?"

Gabe grinned. "I'm planning on it."

"Well, let's go catch the horses," Ruby said. She wondered how Gabe's cane would do in the mud and how he planned to lead Red. But this was what he wanted to do, and if she had to help him—well, that was another reason for her to ride the quieter Pard today instead of Legacy.

She matched her stride to Gabe's slow walk as they went to the horse pasture. She had brought two halters out yesterday to hang on the fence just in case things were proceeding as planned.

Gabe grinned as Sunshine galloped in the lead as the herd came running. "That's the old lady herself, huh?"

"Yeah. The other palomino mare, the chestnut mare, and the chestnut colt are her descendants. The chestnut mare's the dam of the palomino and the colt."

"Beautiful," Gabe breathed. "That younger palomino was the one you were riding when you were shot at, right?"

"Yes. That's Legacy." Ruby gave him some treats so he could feed the herd while she caught first Red and then Pard. Sunshine headed directly for Gabe. He gave her an extra treat and a neck scratch. Ruby handed him Red's rope. "Here's Red."

Gabe tucked his cane under his left arm and took Red's rope. "Okay, fella. This old man is gonna need your support to the barn."

Ruby let him lead Red through the gate first before she brought Pard through and closed it. She noticed that Red matched his steps to Gabe's, and that after a few steps he moved his right hand from the lead to Red's neck for support as Red walked calmly. She hurried Pard to the barn and got him in the crossties, then pulled out grooming tools for Gabe to use as well as herself.

It took Gabe longer to groom Red. Ruby took the time to tack Pard and stick a blanket plus their lunch in her saddlebags, then fetched Red's saddle blanket and tossed the saddle on for Gabe. She handed him the bridle.

"Figured you could handle this yourself."

"If I can't I'm in worse shape than I thought," Gabe retorted.

Ruby looked around for Gabe's cane. "I don't see your cane."

Gabe finished buckling the bridle throatlatch and patted one of his two holsters. "Folds up into this." He tied Red's halter rope to the saddle horn. "I'm going to take him out and get my saddle rifle from the rig. I've already got it scabbarded."

"Good idea." She had set hers on the back porch.

Gabe and Red headed out slowly while Ruby bridled Pard, then led him to the house where she retrieved her rifle and slipped it into the scabbard. To her relief, by the time she joined the group of crawlers and carts, Gabe was up on Red and waiting. She swung up on Pard. Another reason for riding this pair was that they could be hobbled and would graze quietly while they talked.

She opened and closed the gates from horseback this time. The split was much as before, with Maggie's video team traveling with Ruby and Martin's group. She didn't bother with hobbling Pard when they stopped but just handed the lead rope to Gabe.

"No reason for you to get down," she said.

He grinned. "Honey, right now I don't *want* to get down. It's been too damn long since I've sat on a good horse. And a singlefooter to boot. Loving it."

She hurried back to help unload the first box of RubyBots. Martin finished his preliminary scan with a smile.

"The pre-release bots did their thing and they've switched off," he said. "We'll know more once the RubyBots activate and start feeding back data, but I'm betting they also have contributed a few nutrients to the mix as well. No detail scans, but levels sure seem to be higher than they were."

"That's good."

This time the bots spilling out of the chambers were a bright ruby red. That had been the reason for naming it the RubyBot in the first place—that, and Gabe's insistence it should be called after her. The red made it easier to visually track the spread of the bots into the field. Martin switched on his scanner, waiting for the wave to scatter. As each bot switched on, it formed a blue dot on the screen. until there was a swath of blue across the field.

Ruby heaved a relieved sigh. They were on their way. She returned to get Pard's lead from Gabe and swung up.

"Went well?"

"Yep. First of six releases."

The rest of this field and the next were uneventful. Ruby admitted to a bit of nerves as they climbed to the Homestead field. This time no wind blew and the sun shone. She thought she could spot a couple of white blooms off to one side—not her favorite ox-eye daisies yet.

Martin took his time measuring this field. Ruby didn't dismount until he finally nodded.

"Don't have the interference this time," he said.

"Ron's been working on this fence line," she said. "They don't have the sensors up yet, that's probably why you're not seeing anything."

"Could be."

The release was uneventful, and Maggie was able to get shots incorporating the mountains.

"The Ruby's awfully darn pretty to watch in a release," she said to Ruby. "I thought your other bots were pretty, but the RubyBots just sparkle. You didn't manage to do that just for the camera value now, did you?"

Ruby laughed. "Wish I could have thought of that. Nope, just an accident of how we grew them. They came out bright red that first time and they've stayed red ever since. That's how they got the name RubyBot—well, that, and Gabe punning on my name."

Maggie jerked her head toward Gabe. "Got something going there?"

"Yeah. We're going wildflower hunting."

"Sounds romantic."

"Probably sounds more romantic than it's going to be. We've gotta talk in private. Strictly private. There's a lot of things to work out."

Maggie grinned. "But it looks like you might have some fun as well. All clear to get a shot of you two riding off?"

Ruby rolled her eyes. "Hey, the bosses are gonna like that scene, so go for it."

"Maybe riding off while holding hands?"

Ruby guffawed. "We didn't even do that at our wedding! Granted, we were riding a pair of broncs and needed both hands on the reins. That's pushing it a bit too far."

"All right, all right. A girl's gotta try to get the best scene, right?"

"Right. Have a good trip back to the ranch. I guess we'll see you on Friday, right?"

"Yeah. Friday in LA." Maggie groaned. "Hope I get to come back out here for the next round of filming should you survive the cut. It's been a nice break to be up here in Thunder County."

"You'll be back," Ruby said. "See you."

She stopped by Martin before getting Pard. "We're going to drop down into Ladyslipper draw, go into the canyon a ways where we'll be out of contact. Gabe and I both have saddle guns, and he's packing a pistol. At least one. I've got my .38."

Martin nodded. "Yeah, I saw him scabbard his rifle. How soon before any of us should get worried?"

"If you hear shots or if the horses come back unhobbled, come looking, of course. Otherwise...we should be back before dusk. I don't know how long this is going to take."

Martin patted her shoulder. "Good luck."

"Thanks." She hoped she didn't need it.

She rejoined Gabe and the horses and heaved a sigh. "All right. There's that obligation taken care of."

"Now let's go *wildflower hunting*," Gabe chuckled.

She side-eyed him. "I'll have you know that the only blanket I packed is for sitting on."

Gabe snorted as he turned Red away from the others. "Not gonna be anything more happening, no matter how this goes."

"That's pretty confident." She eased Pard into a jog. Red struck into his singlefoot gait.

Gabe grinned. "He's pretty smooth."

"Yeah, Charlie's always liked his gait."

Pard quickened his steps to keep up with Red's faster gait.

"And as for the other," Gabe said. "Let's just get that little piece out of the way right now. I *can't* do anything, no matter how much I want to, Ruby. The G9 took that away from me too. A sexual relationship is right off the table as far as me fucking you or anyone, not for lack of interest but lack of ability."

Ruby raised her brows. "That sucks. I'm sorry."

"Oh well. Doesn't mean I couldn't get creative and give you or another partner pleasure. It just means, well..." he shrugged. "It's an intellectual entertainment for me these days. I wanted to get that clear right off the bat. Not that I thought you would be interested, but...now you know."

"I hadn't been thinking along those lines, really." All the same, she flushed.

"Didn't think you had. From all accounts you've been living a pretty celibate life. Not that I've been following or anything." Now it was his turn to flush slightly.

Ruby exhaled sharply. "Okay. Now that *that* little piece is settled. I thought we might want to talk down by Ladyslipper Spring."

"Interesting choice."

"It's probably the most private spot on the ranch."

"That would be good, yes." He reined Red back as the trail down the side of the ridge narrowed. Ruby rode ahead. The spring was where she secretly thought that Brandon and perhaps the pregnancy she had lost to a hydatidiform mole had been conceived. It was private, and was also pretty. There were old downed logs that could provide a place for them to sit without having to wrestle creaky joints to get back up. The horses could graze as well—she figured there'd be a little bit of early grass to keep them occupied. Though all the same she planned to hobble both geldings.

Once they arrived, she went over to steady the right stirrup as Gabe dismounted. He lost his balance for a moment after swinging his leg over the saddle and grabbed the horn to keep from lurching off.

"Hips don't work like they used to," he growled.

Ruby undid the hobbles on Red's saddle and fastened them around his forelegs before unbridling him and hanging the bridle on the saddle horn. She went to Red's saddlebags and pulled out a thermos, handing it to Gabe. Then she dropped the lead and took care of Pard, extracting their lunch from one saddlebag and a folded blanket from another. Pard hopped over to graze next to Red.

"So which log do you want to sit on?" she asked Gabe as he leaned heavily on his cane.

"Probably the easiest one for me to get to," he said, irritation in his voice. "Not the closest one. That looks like it's rotting and will fall apart on us."

"The next Ponderosa?"

"Looks sturdier."

She went to that tree and spread the blanket on it, setting their lunch on top. Gabe struggled downhill, tight-lipped until she hurried back up to take the thermos and offer a free arm.

"I hate this," he growled as he leaned on her. "Hate it, hate it, hate it. Goddamn G9. It's made me old before my time. Riding Red was a nice break." He heaved a relieved sigh as she helped him sit and he leaned his cane against the tree. "But thanks for setting up the ride, Rubes. I appreciate it more than you can ever imagine."

"You're welcome." She reached into the sack. "Not a lot of choices, I'm afraid. Roast beef or...roast beef." She held the two beeswax paper-wrapped sandwiches out to Gabe, and he took one.

"Beats synthpork. From Bran's old herd?"

"The only reason I have beef to eat this time of year. I've enough customers to turn a small profit and have some beef for us."

"Yeah. I occasionally get lucky. One of my neighbors has a small custom chicken farm. If I'm lucky I get her old stewing hens. But her hens lay pretty well."

"Haven't had the space for chickens for years. Vickie keeps me in eggs." Ruby took a bite of her sandwich and focused on eating. Once she was done she slipped the wrappings back into the sack. Gabe handed her his. She'd wash them up tonight for reuse.

"Well," Gabe said finally, after taking a long drink. "How the hell are we going to handle this? I'm assuming that you're going along with the reunion storyline, from the way we've been talking lately."

Ruby raised her hands and dropped them on her thighs. "Do we have a choice? It's not just about us any more. If it ever was."

"Yeah." He tightened his lips. "God damn, Ruby. I did not realize he was in so fucking deep. And for so much of it to be my own stupid damn fault."

"You couldn't help the G9."

"But I could have done something about the gambling." He shook his head. "Three point five million between student loans, my medical debt, and *our* gambling debts. Jesus. Talk about a body blow. And—" he sighed heavily. "It was my damn fault that Bran got into gambling in the first place. I introduced him to the bloodsuckers and taught him the game."

"*Why?*" The cry almost wrenched out of Ruby's gut. "Why did you have to risk everything like this? God *damn* it, Gabe! Why was gambling so important?"

Gabe looked away from her and shook his head. "It was stupid. I agree. And yet—" he drew a ragged, deep breath. "It was the thrill. Knowing that I could get lucky and beat the system. I didn't notice when Bran was watching me do it while he was growing up. I didn't know he was gambling when he was in school. Not until he had a bad loss and came to me for help."

"Gabe. He was gambling when he was in school?"

He raised his hands. "I don't know what to say, Ruby! He said he was trying to keep from borrowing more money and hoped to pay off his loans."

"God." She shook her head. "I had no clue."

"I fucked up. I fucked a lot of things up. I like taking risks. You know that. I was always playing cards on the circuit. Was damn good at it, too. It wasn't until later that I started betting on games. I had an eye for it."

"That's what Bran said about himself."

Gabe winced. "God. My own words coming back to haunt me." He sighed. "So yeah. My stupidity has put us in this position. We can argue about my gambling all day and it's not going to change that fact one bit. I'm a fucking adrenaline addict and I'm trying—really trying—to get away from gambling above and beyond what we do every day in farming and ranching. Rachel knew about my gambling. Participated in it. She loved to go to Vegas as a high roller's wife, take in some shows, spend some time at the slots. I don't think she realized how deep into that world I was."

"Was?"

"Yeah. *Was.* I don't know. I lost so much of my old self to being sick that I just never felt like picking gambling back up when I got better, even when the bills got bigger. Bran told me that he was taking care of my medical bills. My—other bills that I couldn't keep up with when I was sick. I didn't ask. For a while I was just too tired to ask, and then—I didn't want to know."

"Shit."

"Go ahead, Ruby. Yell at me. I deserve it." He stared straight ahead and not at her.

"What about Mariah?"

"What about her? That bitch sucked me into that world. Things were tight when we failed that second year of the Superstar. She told me she had a system if only I'd trust her. Supposedly infallible. So I did, trying to raise some funds on the side, especially when we found out that you were pregnant again."

"Oh." That explained some of the cash flow she hadn't had time to figure out and had thought reflected some calculating mistakes she had made.

"Yeah. I thought she knew what the hell she was talking about but she didn't—and the price she demanded was my body. I thought that was an easy price to pay. Then." He shivered. "Later, she wanted me to come further on board with her little schemes after you and I split and it was tempting—oh God, was it ever tempting. But something, some instinct warned me to hold back and I didn't throw in with her."

Ruby shook her head. "I don't know what else to say, Gabe."

"Yeah." He rubbed his hands on his thighs. "So now. Knowing what you do. You still want to go ahead with this game, even pretending?"

"I don't know that we have a choice, for Branny's sake."

"Yeah. For Branny's sake." Now he looked at her. "Could there be more?"

"Gabe—I don't know. What happened between us hit me pretty deep and hard."

"Are we doing this for Bran's sake only?"

"I have enjoyed being friends again," she said faintly, now the one to look away. "We were friends before we were lovers, and that's what I've been pulling on to prep myself for this. I can do that for real. And for the rest, I can playact. A little bit. Until the last few days I didn't realize how much I'd missed being able to talk to you."

"Friends, then." He held out his hand and she took it.

"Friends. Colleagues. Allies."

They sat hand-in-hand silently for a few moments, listening to the woods around them and the horses' snorts as they nuzzled the ground looking for early green shoots.

"There is something hinky going on with AgI this time around," Gabe said finally. "AgI, WLAN, and I don't know what all else. The change in running the program from an October date to February. And then when Bran told me about his situation, it just added to my uneasiness about this whole damn mess."

"It's not the same company that it was when we won the Superstar," Ruby agreed. "I've been having the same feelings. That finalist announcement was downright creepy at times. Especially with Philip Martiniere lurking around."

"Yeah. Some of this stuff doesn't make sense." Gabe's hand tightened on hers. "God, Ruby, I'm grateful we've got each other's backs. At least until the final cut. And maybe even then. If I win, I'd still like to work together on combining the microbials with your RubyBot. Funding toward the next stage."

"I—I—thank you, Gabe. I think we can work something out if one of us wins."

"I'd like that." He released her hand and took off his hat, hanging it on his knee before running his hands through his hair. "I'm serious about getting out of ranching. Even with Tim and Kathleen holding down the fort, it's more than I'm going to be able to handle by myself in a couple of years." He chuckled. "I'm not sure whether I should be insulted or flattered that all Mariah wants from me is my share of the Double R and not the Moondance. Then again—" he was solemn again. "It's likely to end up with the tribe, at least the parts that I don't donate for watershed management. Probably the best long-term use for that place."

"What will you do in the long run?" she asked.

Gabe shrugged and put his hat back on. "I don't know yet. It depends on how much cash I have on hand once I get everything paid off. Bran thinks I should come on staff at AgI to work on my microbials, but—" he shook his head. "Any further work I do in that area is going to be limited. And you?"

Ruby stared straight ahead for a moment. "I can't imagine leaving the ranch," she said finally. "I'm so close to having the labs really start working the way I want them to. There's Charlie and Martin, and then Brandon, and I suppose I'll keep doing my best to bring new kids along in the field. That's kind of been my dream, anyway."

"You're a better person than I am, Ruby Barkley. And always have been."

Ruby coughed. "Yeah. Well. So how are we going to play this? We have another show to record day after tomorrow. One of us could be cut. Do we go in all lovey-dovey? Maggie did record us riding off, so we've got a good launch for the reunion storyline."

"I don't think they'll cut either of us, especially if we show signs of playing along with the romance storyline." Gabe grinned at her. "Wanna go down together and share a room? You know now that it'll be safe."

Ruby spluttered. "Wait a minute—moving *that* fast?"

Gabe's eyes twinkled at her. "You did tell Mariah that we had spectacular fights and spectacular makeups. It could be a fun game. We could really camp it up, and I think it would piss her off big time. I'm all for that."

"Well, if you put it *that* way...it does sound tempting." She grinned at him. "And besides, you always have been a good kisser."

"Wanna practice?" But she noticed he was shivering a little now that the sun had moved on.

"Let's save it for the real time," she said, getting up. "You look cold."

"Yeah," he said slowly. "Goddamn G9."

She helped Gabe to his feet and gathered up the blanket. The horses had wandered away so it took her a couple of minutes to catch them, then take off their hobbles before leading them over to Gabe. He stood on the hillside, staring at the ground, not looking up as she came up with the horses.

"Ruby. Look." He gestured with the cane. "I haven't seen one of those in years. I—I thought they had gone extinct."

She swallowed hard as she saw the bright magenta and white of a ladyslipper orchid.

"I haven't seen one of those for years, either," she said, her voice suddenly gone raw. "Not since we broke up."

"Maybe it's an omen."

"Maybe."

She helped Gabe up onto Red, then swung up on Pard, leading the way out of the draw.

CHAPTER 11

Their way back to the home place took them by the Homestead field.

"The RubyBot sure did turn out pretty, didn't it?" Gabe said as they rode by the field.

She grinned at him. "That was your doing."

Before he could respond two shots rang out. Gabe yelled and grabbed at his shoulder as Red staggered sideways. Ruby pulled her rifle out of the scabbard and whirled Pard around, eyes scanning the ridge next to them.

More gunshots. She fired in the direction she thought they'd come from. Pard flinched under her, but he'd been ridden in cowboy mounted shooting at one point during his career and she'd hunted off of him, so he didn't react further.

"Gabe!" she hollered. Was that movement on the far ridge —yes! She fired again.

No answer except an inarticulate yell. She turned her head to see Red bucking hard, reins free as Gabe clung to the saddle horn, a red stain on the left shoulder of his coat.

Shit!

She scabbarded her rifle and sent Pard after Red. The big

black gelding had been a rodeo pickup horse once—a jack-of-all-trades who'd seen several different uses. She just hoped he remembered his working rodeo days and didn't decide to join Red in bucking. At least he was faster than Red.

As they came up on Red he stopped bucking and started running. She saw that the left split rein was broken. Maybe if she grabbed the halter rope she could pony Gabe and Red back to the home place.

But no, Gabe was starting to slip in the saddle, leaning left. If he went down he'd be at risk from both horses' hooves if she tried for the halter rope. She didn't have time to slow Red's runaway.

Get him off Red now.

Risky. It had been ages since they'd done this. She shifted her weight to her outside stirrup and brought Pard close, reaching toward Gabe with her right arm.

"Got you!" she yelled.

Gabe nodded sharply. He let go of the horn and slid his left arm around her back. She grabbed him around the torso and pulled, turning Pard away from Red, struggling to lever Gabe onto the saddlebags behind her. Red took off running even harder as more shots rang out.

"I'm on I'm on I'm on," Gabe gasped in her ear, wrapping his left arm around her waist, slamming hard against her back. "Let's get the fuck out of here!"

Ruby nodded and urged Pard back into a gallop. He couldn't keep that pace up for long, not carrying two riders, but if he could just get them down below the skyline without any more incidents she could ease up. Gabe's labored breathing worried her. But at least if Red didn't stop that would bring someone out from the ranch to help them. And if he did stop— well, she'd ride him and lead Gabe and Pard.

"Easy, Pard, easy," she breathed once they were down in the draw. The black gelding stopped sharply and Gabe lurched against her back with an *oof*. She looked ahead. No sign of Red.

Still running, then.

"You okay?" she asked Gabe.

"My shoulder hurts like a son of a bitch, but I think it's just superficial," Gabe said through gritted teeth. "God *damn*, that horse can buck. Either that or I'm out of shape. Probably both."

"Maybe we should stop so I can take a look at you."

"Hell no. We're out here alone, and who knows how many of *them* there are. I heard at least two different shooters."

"I got several shots off at them." He was trembling slightly now. Shock?

"Well, maybe that's what I heard. All the same, Ruby, let's get back."

"You sure you don't want me to look at it?"

His shivering was getting worse. He must be going into shock.

"N-no. This is a G9 reaction to stress. If you can stop for a moment, I can dig a med out that'll help. But I need to get someplace where I can safely sit for a while, *fast*, after I take it." His teeth started chattering. "Oh God. This is a bad one."

"Maybe I should lead Pard or put you in front of me."

"It's not *that* bad!" he snapped as she stopped Pard. He fumbled in his left pocket. "Oh hell, I'm too shaky to get it."

She crossed the split reins on Pard's neck and half-turned in the saddle. Gabe's pallor shocked her. She slipped her right hand in his jacket pocket and found the container he'd been fumbling for.

"This it?" she asked, holding it up.

Gabe nodded. "One—no, two pills, please."

She shook two tiny white pills out into her palm and held it up to his lips. He picked up the pills with his teeth and dry-swallowed them.

"Water?"

He shook his head. She tucked the container into his jacket pocket and faced forward, picking up the reins in her right hand instead of her left, using her left to hang onto Gabe's arm to help steady him.

"Can you stick on if we jog?" she asked. "He's not as smooth as Red."

"Yeah, yeah, I'll be okay," he growled. He leaned his head against her shoulder. The quivering started to ease. She wanted to urge Pard into a long trot instead of this easy jog, but she didn't want to jostle Gabe any more than necessary.

Goddamn it, Red, why didn't you stop?

"I think Red got hit, too," Gabe said, and she realized that she had spoken out loud. "He staggered a little with that first shot. And then I got nailed with that second shot. Not his fault." He shuddered and pressed closer to her. "I think I can stick on if you want to long trot, Ruby. We've gotta hurry. That dose is going to make me pretty darn sleepy here soon."

"You sure about that? We can still swap so you're in front of me."

"I don't want to move until I have to. Just do what you can."

When she clucked at Pard, instead of extending the jog into a long trot, he eased into a slow lope. Gabe's arm tightened around her waist but he seemed steadier with the smoother but faster gait, even though he kept his head buried in her shoulder.

It was a relief when she finally saw Charlie roaring up the track in the big crawler, Martin next to him, grim-faced, a rifle in his arms. She eased Pard up carefully.

"Someone took a shot at us by the Homestead field," she said to them. "Gabe's been hit."

"Red got hit too," Charlie said abruptly as he climbed out of the crawler and came over to Pard. "Crease across his neck and another shot in his right hind. Somebody was getting cute and thought they could bring him down."

Ruby shivered. Creasing was an old trick that had once been used by mustang runners to knock down a horse. It killed as many horses as it knocked down.

"Bastards," Gabe growled. "Coulda killed that horse."

Charlie rested a hand on Gabe's leg. "You good like this or you need to get down?"

"Better get off for this horse's sake," Gabe said. "Not just that. I had to take some of my meds and I don't know how long it's gonna be that I can count on staying safely on."

"Then let's get you in the rig."

Martin and Charlie eased Gabe off of Pard and into the crawler. They turned around and sped off. Ruby urged Pard into a long trot. She wanted to start trembling herself—but not yet.

Not yet.

"You okay?" Beck asked as Ruby came into the kitchen after taking care of Pard and checking Red.

"I didn't get hit, if that's what you mean." Ruby held her hands out. They quivered slightly. "But I think I could use a stiff shot of something. How's Gabe?" She had noticed his rig was still here. "Did Charlie take him to the ER?"

Beck shook her head. "Stubborn son of a bitch won't go. Doc Sheri's been here and patched him up. Looks worse than it is. He had a go-bag in his rig. He's upstairs. Sheriff is talking to him now."

Ruby stifled a chuckle. So much like Gabe. "Then I'd better join them. Where is he?"

"Upstairs in the room next to yours."

"Thanks." She trudged up the stairs, following the voices. The door was open, and Gabe sat upright in bed, his left arm in a sling. The sheriff looked up from where she sat in a chair angled next to the bed, virtual keyboard and screen in front of her.

"Ruby. I need your version of what happened. We're just about done here."

"Give me a minute to clean up." She went into her own room and darted into the bathroom to wash her hands. She eyed the connecting door to the bedroom Gabe was in and unlocked it. Then she returned, dragging her rocking chair behind her. She was going to be *comfortable*, damn it, and since the only other option in that room was the bed…she'd bring her own chair.

Gabe leaned his head against the headboard, eyes half-closed, as Ruby repeated her version of what had happened. Sheriff Wilhite asked a few questions but otherwise just kept typing. At last she sighed and closed down her computer.

"I've got deputies out there on Reed's place looking at things," she said. "I'll get back to you two once we know more. So far there's been no sign that you hit anyone. My guess is whoever did the shooting knows what they're doing and had good long-range equipment. You gonna have AgI blow this one up too?"

"I'm not too thrilled about that notion," Ruby said. "Seems like the attacks are escalating. At the very least we've got to check in with AgI, but I'm concerned about revealing too much."

Gabe shook his head. "I'm with Ruby. Neither one of us

has talked to AgI about this yet, though we'll have to do that soon."

"We have been asked not to post about incidents but report them to AgI," Ruby said.

"All right, then." Sheriff Wilhite stood up. "I guess that's it for now. Keep me posted about anything else happening, all right?"

"You'll be the first to know." Ruby escorted the sheriff to the front door, then swung by the kitchen. She surveyed the food options, though she wasn't hungry, and ended up grabbing the jar of whisky and two glasses. She wanted a drink and Gabe probably did as well. Then she returned to Gabe's room. His eyes were closed but they flickered open as she came in.

"You up for company?" she asked, waggling the jar. "I can go back for food, if you're hungry."

Gabe shook his head. "Not hungry. Had a protein bar while Dr. Sheri was working me over. I could sure use a drink, though. I've had painkillers, but one drink isn't going to kill me. And I might even sleep better."

"Yeah." She poured them each a couple of fingers worth, then sat in the rocking chair. "What happens now?"

"Unless you want to call Tim and Kathleen to come fetch me, I guess I'm here for the night," Gabe sighed. "Between the meds and just plain being sore, I don't feel like moving."

"How bad is it?" She gestured to his arm.

"Looks worse than it is." He sipped on the whisky and made a face. "Whew. Strong stuff."

"Martin distills it from ranch grains."

"It's got a kick." He took a smaller sip. "But it grows on you. How are you doing?"

She held one hand out. It was trembling more than it had been when Beck asked. "Shaky now. The let-down is gonna be a bitch." But at least they were both safe. And it was over for the night.

He half-smiled. "You still got it in you, though, lady. That was some sweet pickup riding."

"You did a damn good job of sitting Red's buck. I guess I forgot that he had been a little broncy when he was a young horse."

"Well, guess that means that we're both in better shape than we thought." He grimaced. "This complicates things, though. I'm gonna have to hitch a ride with you to the Innovator tomorrow, no ifs, ands, or buts. I'm not going to be in any shape to handle my rig." He exhaled shakily. "We talked about sharing a room. I think that would be a very good idea. Now I'm worried about security in LA. If we're together we can watch each other's backs. Something about this whole thing does not smell right. Whoever was shooting at us was shooting at *me* this time. Or were they planning to take me down first, then you?"

"I don't know." It was worrisome. "But I do agree with you about watching each others' backs. This feels like more than WLAN."

"I don't *think* it's tied to the gambling," Gabe said. "That should have been settled when AgI bought out Branny's debts. So it's got to be tied to the Superhero—which takes us back to WLAN. But it doesn't fit their profile. Does it?"

"I haven't the faintest damn idea." She sipped on her whisky. "Or is it tied to the RubyBot? Or someone not wanting us to get together again?"

"There's no jealous women out there, if that's what you're asking. Hasn't been anyone else since Rachel."

She shook her head. "They shot at me before but didn't hit either of us. I think this is tied to the Superhero and the RubyBot."

"Someone's feeling threatened."

"I agree. But we're not gonna figure this out tonight. So. Which room should we cancel?" she said. "I've got a standard queen, that's what I usually get."

Gabe sipped more whisky and closed his eyes, which made him look thoroughly wrung out. "Let's stick with mine. I get a recliner brought in standard because it's the only way I can sleep these days. Aches and sinuses."

"Should I have the kids bring one up from the living room so you can sleep tonight?"

He shook his head. "This will work for one night. But I—"

"*Brandon Ramirez,*" her comm chimed.

Gabe's eyes opened. "I guess we'd better face the music. Looks like the sheriff called Brandon."

"Visual off?"

He shook his head. She switched it on.

"So what the hell—" Brandon began, then stopped. "Oh good. I've got both of you this time." He faced Gabe and gulped. "Are you all right, Dad?"

"I'll live," Gabe said tersely. "But I'm staying right here tonight. Bad G9 stress reaction and—" he moved his right arm, wincing. "I'm not going to be driving any time soon. Your mother and I are coming down together."

"All right."

"And we're staying in the same room," Ruby said.

Brandon turned to face her. "Does this mean that you two are cooperating with the reunion storyline?"

"Yes," she said.

Relief washed across his face. "Thank you. But I wish it hadn't taken something like this to make it happen."

"It didn't," Gabe said. "We'd already agreed to do this before the bullets started flying. This somewhat cemented our decision."

"What does the sheriff say? I know what she's said to us, but does she have any idea of what's going on?"

"Not the faintest clue," Ruby said. "I'm suspecting that since the shots came from Reed's land, whoever is doing this came through from the national forest. Hopefully they'll find something this time."

"I wonder how the shooter—or shooters—knew you were there," Brandon mused.

"The RubyBot release schedule has been up on the ranch website as well as the Innovator site," Ruby said. "We didn't publicize Gabe's being here, but if your people were uploading in real time, whoever's doing this would know that your dad is here."

"Lemme check posting times." Brandon pulled up a screen, frowning at it. "Maggie uploaded the bit about you and Dad riding off to go wildflower hunting about an hour before the shooting. The sheriff's office has that information."

"An insider, perhaps?" Gabe said.

Brandon winced. "I hope not, but...." His voice trailed off as he stared at his screen. "I see," he said thoughtfully, running his fingers through his hair. "Look. I'm glad to see that you're both all right. Be careful, and I'll see you tomorrow night. All right?"

"All right," Ruby said.

Brandon winked out without saying anything more. Ruby drained her glass.

"Want more?" she asked Gabe.

He finished his and shook his head. "One's the limit with these meds. Thank you."

"Do you need anything else?"

His drooping eyelids flickered back up. "Would you mind sitting with me for a while? No need to talk. Go ahead and bring your book. I'm just—" he swallowed hard. "Sometimes when the G9 hits me like this I'll have problems jerking awake if I'm alone in a room. Tim or Kathleen will sit in with me until I'm good and asleep. It's only an hour or so, and it's just you being present. Maybe saying my name if I start yelling. I'm sorry, it's stupid and weak, but...."

"Let me shower first," she said, getting up. "And I don't think it's stupid or weak. Stop being macho. Everyone's got vulnerabilities."

He snorted. "Thanks. I think."

It didn't take her that long to shower, pour herself a second drink, and grab her book. Gabe's eyelids flickered open when she came back in.

"Go ahead and leave the light on when you're done," he husked, sounding sleepy. "That's how I sleep these days."

"You need anything else?"

He shook his head. "Just someone in the room. It's amazing how soothing simple presence can be." His eyelids fluttered back down.

She opened her book and started to read. About fifteen minutes in, Gabe startled and gulped for air, eyes wide.

"Gabe, Gabe, you all right?"

He coughed and blinked. "Yeah. Yeah. Just normal. Thanks." His eyes closed again. She watched him for a few moments, then went back to her book.

Ten minutes later, it happened again. This time, she patted his hand. He smiled at her and took it. She held his hand until his grip slackened, then went back to reading.

There were no more incidents, and another hour's reading took her to the end of the book. Ruby tiptoed out of the room and back to her own. Once in bed, though, the day's events kept spilling through her thoughts. Why was someone shooting at them? And what had Brandon been contemplating?

At last she switched on her bed light and picked up the next book on her pile, another old favorite of her Gramps, this one an ancient cloth-bound Zane Grey that threatened to fall apart in her hands. Strangely enough, by the time she got to the scheming and the gun battles, she was ready to fall asleep.

Stories like this were entertaining when they happened to someone else.

CHAPTER 12

They both begged off from the dinner before the show, arriving at the studio just in time for makeup. Between travel time and being sore from yesterday's shenanigans, eating in while they rested sounded like a good idea.

Ruby guided Gabe to his chair in Makeup, then dropped into hers. At least she wasn't as sore as Gabe. She'd helped him get his shirt and jacket on in their hotel room, since his arm had stiffened up. They were both quiet as the cosmeticians buzzed around them, responding with grunts and monosyllables instead of speaking, both reserving their energy for the show. This time she didn't need to argue with the hair stylist. But Ruby was suddenly very aware that the cosmeticians and stylists all wore AgI indentured tattoos. What had seemed matter-of-fact before now felt threatening.

How many of these indentured had gone through situations like Bran's? She had accepted the creation of the corporate indenture class as a necessarily evil back in the late 20s, when the economy fell apart and it had seemed to be the only means by which to get debtors off of the streets. She hadn't liked the notion, but something had to be done.

All the same, the threat of indenture had been one factor in her choice to hire Julie and Terri. She had looked at the contracts when it became clear that Charlie and Martin needed help on the ranch and the labor pool had offered them. The dull look in their eyes when she picked them out of the labor catalog had struck her with a sense of wrongness.

It cost more, but she offset the higher pay rate for free workers by offering them housing and medical care as part of their compensation. Paying off their obligations for them so indenture no longer hung over Julie and Terri's heads was yet another claim on the Superhero money—if she won it.

At last they were done. Ruby offered Gabe her arm and he took it, using her as support instead of his cane.

"There are a fuck of a lot of indentureds working here," he breathed into her ear. "I hadn't noticed before."

"Yeah," she said back. "It's creepy."

"So. It's showtime. How shall we start?"

"I dunno. Wanna do a big kiss in the Green Room?"

His eyes twinkled. "Sounds like fun."

"Make sure we have their eyes. Then activate the cams and the big smooch."

"Another one during recording?"

"But of course."

It took five steps before the murmurs of *Gabe and Ruby, Ruby and Gabe* started. Ruby stopped, clucking up her cam. She waited until Gabe's cam was active, then pulled him close, trembling slightly. His lips brushed hers, then pressed harder as he tightened his good arm on her torso. The kiss deepened. Oh. My. She'd forgotten how good a kisser Gabe was. Her hat slid and she had to grab the crown to keep it from falling off.

Gabe pulled back from her with a grin as she straightened her hat.

"And that, folks, is how you kiss a rodeo queen," he

announced to the room. Ruby flushed. But she clicked up her pics and posted several to her account, without comment.

"Whew. After that I need to sit down," he said quietly to her. "Damn, woman. I'd forgotten how good a kisser you are."

"Likewise," she said. The crowd parted before them as they made their way to the chairs where they'd sat before. Mariah was already there, her face set tight and hard, glaring at them. Jeff and Temira grinned at them.

"So we're gonna have to compete with the lovebirds, eh?" Jeff said.

Ruby shrugged. "It just happened."

"Yeah. Right," Mariah spat. Her sharp glare at Ruby was almost enough to kill, if she had the ability.

Ruby smiled sweetly at her. "Some of us still have the old touch, Mariah."

Mariah rolled her eyes. "I need a drink." She flounced off.

Temira giggled as Mariah left. "You should have seen her expression when you two were kissing. If looks could kill you'd both be dead."

"Well, I'm really glad they don't kill." Gabe collapsed into the chair that Mariah had vacated with a heavy sigh.

"What happened?" Jeff asked, gesturing at Gabe's arm.

"Just an accident," Gabe said. His eyes met Ruby's. They had decided to keep downplaying this incident until Sheriff Wilhite told them more about probable suspects. Brandon and AgI seemed to be more than happy to keep it quiet.

As they talked with Jeff and Temira, Gabe suddenly stiffened, staring across the room.

"What's wrong?" she asked.

Gabe shook his head. "Nothing." He picked up Ruby's hand, once again tracing a trefoil on her palm. When she looked where he had been staring, she spotted Philip Martiniere glaring at them.

What is going on between him and Gabe? They clearly know each other. What the hell would the head of the Martiniere Group have to do with Gabe? That's definitely the Martiniere trefoil he's tracing on my palm. Why?

"Gabe?" she asked.

But before she could say more, Markey cruised by.

"It's time, people," she called. "Line up!"

And in the chaos of getting both of them sorted out, she didn't have time to ask Gabe why he'd reacted like that to Martiniere—and why Martiniere was glowering at them.

Before long they were herded out onto the stage. Georgy Batineau moved down the line of competitors just before they went live. He paused at Ruby and Gabe, shaking his head with a grin as they stood arm-in-arm.

"Ah, I'd had hopes that this might be my chance at last with the rodeo queen," he said, mock-scowling at Gabe. "But there you are—you stole her from me yet again!"

"Girls are always going to go for the saddle bronc cowboy, especially the classy rodeo queens," Gabe drawled. "Even the stove-up old man." But the lightness of his tone didn't match the glower he gave Georgy when Georgy took Ruby's free hand and kissed it.

"One of these days, fair lady, one of these days," Georgy said, patting her hand before moving on to Temira.

"Now I want to wash my hands," Ruby said out of the side of her mouth to Gabe.

"No kidding."

Georgy went through his opening patter. Three of the Innovator competitors were cut, and two Stars—one of whom was Don Lane, the Tillamook dairy farmer—were moved down to Innovator level. Gabe's grip on Ruby's arm grew tighter.

"Getting light-headed," he muttered. "Goddamn G9 side effects."

"Anything I can do?" she asked.

He shook his head. "I'll be all right, but no partying for me tonight."

"Works for me." Then they wouldn't have to deal with Mariah.

Two Superstars were cut completely, plus one moved to the Innovator, and one to the Star level. Then it was their turn to step forward.

"So who is going to be cut this round?" Georgy said. "Are we going to see yet another breakup of the renewed romance between our rodeo queen and her bronc riding prince?" He paced around Mariah. "Or will it be our Ice Queen?" He moved on to Jeff. "The King of Southern Rice?" He stopped by Temira. "Or our lovely young princess of closed loop hog farming systems? Let's see what our judges have to say about their accomplishments this week."

He went through the scoring mechanisms. Temira had suffered a setback when one of her methane digesters blew out. Jeff's Swaitbot had suffered from insufficient stem seeds to produce the estimated number of bots to put on his field. Mariah's numbers varied. Gabe's microbials had also taken a dip, though as of that morning their numbers were better. But Ruby had not only the pre-release bots but the early successful performance of the RubyBot.

"Our rodeo queen wins the judges' approval for this round!" Georgy proclaimed. "Second place goes to the Ice Queen. So my two queens are going to be duking it out to see who survives our next cut—or are they? Third place to the King of Southern Rice, and fourth to our saddle bronc prince. Be careful there, Gabe, you might end up losing next round. Last but not least is our princess of closed loop systems. But that's just what our judges say. What has our audience been saying?"

He waved a hand to bring up the social media stats. Ruby

and Gabe were tied for first place, followed by Jeff, Temira, and then Mariah.

The next set of stats combined their judges' ranking with the social media score to end up with Ruby, Jeff, Gabe, Mariah, and Temira.

"Oh," Georgy mock-sighed. "My dear Temira. Closed loop hog farm systems just do not appear to be the concern du jour for our audience. I am so sorry, but you are cut from the Superhero. But! Your scores are still high enough that you qualify for the Superstar! So sorry, but congratulations!"

"Now?" Gabe whispered into Ruby's ear.

"Wait until he asks me to comment," she breathed back.

"So, Ms. Ruby Barkley, former rodeo queen and Miss Rodeo Oregon, as the leader of this week's competition, what do you have to say to us?"

She turned to Gabe and they kissed again, with more intensity than they had in the Green Room. Whoops and hollers rose from the studio audience as her hat fell off. She took advantage of Gabe's arm on her back to lift up one foot to make it look more dramatic and bend back slightly, until his arm started trembling. Then she dropped it back down and straightened up. Gabe smirked at her as they moved apart and she winked at him. It *was* fun, especially since they were playing and not serious. She had forgotten how to play like this.

"Woo-ee!" Georgy whistled. "Now that is one heck of a comment!"

"Oh, I've got a few words as well." She waited until Gabe was steady before bending down to pick up her hat and clap it back on her head, leaving it a little askew. "I've had a few challenges to face this week, but it all came out all right in the end. I thank AgI for your support in helping me with some tough issues, and I'm looking forward to being the Superhero at the end!"

"Thank you, Ruby." Georgy went on but she tuned him out.

Mariah glared at them as the show wrapped up.

"You two had damn well better be watching your backs," she snarled, before marching past them and heading for the door.

"Is that a threat, Mariah?" Ruby challenged.

Mariah turned to face her, hands on her hips. Cams popped up around them.

"Take it whatever way you want. I'm going to beat your little ginger ass six ways from Sunday. Just you wait and see. You won't be able to keep this up, even playing your little games with Gabe."

"What makes you think it's a game and not for real?" Ruby said sweetly.

"You couldn't hold onto him before!" Mariah spluttered. "And now, he's—"

"Ladies, ladies, that's quite enough," Georgy said, sauntering over to Mariah. "Save your energy for later." He took Mariah's arm with a big wink at the cams and led her out. The cams followed them.

Ruby heaved a big sigh of relief. She didn't *like* this sort of thing.

"Let's head back to the room," Gabe said. "God damn her. And I don't know how long I can stay on my feet."

"She knows?" Ruby asked softly. "About you?"

"She tried to seduce me before this all started," he growled. "With predictable results, the little snake."

Brandon intercepted them before they left. "You going to be at the after party?"

"No," Ruby said. "We're going back to the room. After yesterday's excitement we both need our rest."

Brandon looked around furtively, then snapped up a quick

silence screen. "Listen. That's probably a good thing. I'll be in touch, but...whatever you do in the next week, be really, really careful. Okay?"

"Is there something we need to know?"

He shook his head. "Not here. Not now. Just be careful!"

They exchanged worried looks as Brandon rushed off.

The return trip to the hotel was uneventful. After taking turns changing in the bathroom, Gabe settled in his recliner while Ruby sat in the bed. They checked their messages in silence.

Gabe finally sighed and closed up his work. "Tim says that the counterbots are working well with the microbial load," he said. "Thank you, Rubes. It'd be me getting cut tonight if it hadn't been for your help."

"You're welcome." She dismissed her files, sighing as well. "The RubyBot has a couple of reporting glitches, but Martin's not worried. Things are chugging along just fine."

"One more cut show."

She rolled her eyes. "Yeah. Didja see our stats? We shot up big-time, both of us, after that stage kiss. And I gained more points over Mariah after that little spat afterwards. I didn't realize it was being broadcast."

Gabe chuckled. "Couldn't have happened to a better person." His eyes darted around the room. "And as for that very last thing...."

"Yeah. I've got to think about that." *Not here*, she mouthed.

He nodded. "I think I'm going to try to sleep now. We're rolling out early tomorrow. I took a pain pill so maybe, just maybe, I'll get some decent sleep."

"Agreed." She hesitated. "Same thing as last night?"

"If you don't mind staying awake for another hour. I'm sorry, Ruby. But that first hour trying to get to sleep is hell sometimes. Just hearing someone's voice when I first startle up really helps. I'm hoping it will be better tonight—and then tomorrow I'll be back home."

"Is it better there?"

"Sometimes. But we've got our routines. Part of the time I just crash in the living room while Tim and Kathleen are working." He yawned. "Means for early mornings."

"Nothing wrong with that."

"That's true." He reached for an eyeshade and pulled it on, then settled into his recliner.

Ruby went to her suitcase and pulled out a paperback. Another from Gramps's stash of old books, a collection of short stories and essays by H.L. Davis.

———

IT *WASN'T* BETTER THAN LAST NIGHT. GABE JERKED AND called for Rachel, twice. He apologized after each incident.

But it was the last one that got to her.

"Ruby. Ruby. Branny. No. No. You can't ask that—you already took everything dear to me—" he moaned. Then his eyes snapped open as he pushed up his eyeshade. "Ruby?"

"I'm here," she said, putting the book aside. "You okay?"

He gulped and took a drink of water. "Now *that* was a nasty dream." He shuddered and shook his head. "Third time's the charm."

"Want to talk about it?"

"No." His voice held no compromise. "It's nothing." Gabe pulled the eyeshade back down and turned his head away from her.

She wanted to push further, disturbed by his words, but something about the firm set of his jaw told her she wasn't going to get anywhere.

Besides, what did it matter? They were only friends, after all. And it had only been a bad dream.

———

THIS TIME THERE WERE NO DELAYS ARRIVING AT Portland and getting out of the city. They were able to clear the worst of the traffic by two. It would still be a drive partway in the dark, but that was all right.

"So," Gabe said, once she settled back in her seat and had set the autodrive. "What are we going to do next? How can we top this week?"

"Got any ideas—"

"*Sheriff Wilhite,*" her comm interrupted.

"Hello, Sheriff," she said. "I'm in my rig with Gabe, and we're on autodrive. What's the news?"

Only the sheriff's head projected on the screen between them. "Well, it's looking like a professional job on this last shooting for sure."

"This last one?" Ruby asked. "And not the first?"

"Last time we didn't have surveillance cams set up." Wilhite frowned. "Ron went ahead and mounted cams as part of the fence repairs over on Reed's place. We figured that if someone was going to come in to mess with your place, they wouldn't be coming in from the same angle, which they didn't. But we got solid pix and an ID. It's a pro."

"Connections to the mob?" Gabe asked tensely. Ruby shot him a questioning look. He raised his hand and shook his head at her. "I have had some problems with gambling debts in the past, Sheriff. But it was my understanding that they had been taken care of."

"No, she's not from that crowd. This one is corporate."

"What?" Ruby was shocked. "There's such a thing as corporate killers?"

"It's—not common, at least not in North America," Wilhite said. "But yes, it does happen. They tend to focus on problems with enforcement of indentured contracts."

"Oh." They exchanged glances again. Ruby continued. "Um, any idea *which* corporation this assassin is affiliated with?"

"She's freelance," Wilhite said. "But I'm talking to the big boys on this one. And all the same, I thought you both should be warned about this. Watch your backs."

"Are you telling AgI about this latest twist?" Gabe asked.

Wilhite hesitated. "Right now this is staying strictly within official government channels. Of course, you are free to share this information with them if you think it's warranted. But I would not recommend it."

"Thanks for the advice. We'll watch our backs," Ruby said. "And I'm in no hurry to tell AgI anything, if you'd prefer I didn't."

"It would be for the best right now, Ruby. Be careful." The sheriff signed off.

"Now what the hell is *that*?" Gabe said, shaking his head. "*Do* you want to keep AgI out of the loop?"

"I don't even think we should say something to Brandon about this."

"Oh, I'm not going to argue with you about that at all. This is turning weird." He ran his fingers through his hair and pulled on his beard. "I've got a really bad feeling about this, Rubes."

"So do I," she said.

"I'm kind of worried about you driving on by yourself."

"Yeah," she said slowly. "Can you authorize Charlie and Martin to drive your rig back to Moondance? Then they can come back with me."

"I think that's a really good idea. Give me their contact. I'll send them the autodrive code."

Ruby pulled up her comp and sent Charlie's email to Gabe. Then she called Charlie.

"We'll be at Moondance to pick you up," Charlie said grimly after she told him about the conversation with the sheriff. "Can you tell me more?"

"I—think this conversation should be held elsewhere. At Gabe's, perhaps."

"All right. We'll see you then."

"See you then."

"You're going to tell them," Gabe said once she had hung up.

"I've got to," she said. "They have my back. What about you?"

"I'd be stupid not to tell Tim and Kathleen." He frowned. "We're going to have to work some things out, because there's only the three of us on the place. But Kathleen knows people."

"That's good. How much are you going to tell them?"

Gabe inhaled through his teeth, tsk-tsking thoughtfully. "I don't know how much we should say about the atmosphere at AgI. You and I know what it was like, but without someone being there...I don't know. Maybe I'm just being skittish."

"Well, Charlie and Martin already know most of it. I was just going to repeat what the sheriff told us."

"Same is true for Tim and Kathleen. Maybe we should tell everyone together, and if the rest of it happens to come up in conversation...well, then we can say more. I've got a list of safe places to speak on site just in case."

"Brandon gave one to you, too?"

"Yes. And speaking of our son," he said. "In light of this warning from the sheriff. Do you think he knows something about the body modding and the corporate assassins? I've been wondering about his reaction last night in light of this. Sure, there weren't any good places to talk. But what the hell has gotten into him with this? It sure seems like there's a lot more going on than buying up gambling debt."

"This does cast a different light on what he said, doesn't it?" Ruby tapped her chin with her fingers. "God *damn* it, Gabe. I don't like how this is shaping up. I'd like to think that he's told us everything, but I'm just afraid he's in deeper than he's told us."

"I've been having the same thoughts too."

"Problem is, we can't walk. We're screwed if we don't play out the script with AgI, along with Bran."

"The solution is that one of us has got to win, and right now it sure looks like your stock is rising." Gabe tightened his lips. "But without going public about this last development, I don't know quite how we're going to keep interest growing."

"Perhaps we need to lay out a plan with Vickie. Be a bit more obvious about visiting each other. I should probably come to Moondance for a song-and-dance session where you can take me on a tour of everything you've got. And we can flirt a bit."

"I wouldn't mind a couple of lunch or dinner dates."

"Mmm. That might be good. Do we want to orchestrate another public fight and makeup?"

"I'm not sure I want to go that far," Gabe said. "Besides, it can get to be routine and boring and—we've done enough fighting in the past for five couples."

"Maybe we should see if the Round-Up will let us present a tour of their museum."

"Oh, that's a good idea. What else could we do?"

They spent the next hour brainstorming possible things to do as dusk fell outside. Ruby typed up their notes and sent them to Vickie. Gabe drowsed off. He looked much older when he was asleep.

This looks good, Vickie sent back as dusk began to fall around them. *When can the three of us meet?*

"Gabe," she said softly.

"Huh? What?" He startled awake and she felt a mild regret at rousing him after his poor sleep the night before.

"Sorry to wake you. But Vickie likes our suggestions and wants to know when we can get together."

"Lemme think." He tapped up his calendar, frowning at it. "I have a water management meeting at noon tomorrow, but I should be available about four. You think you could put up with me for tomorrow night, Ruby? I'm not going to want to drive back. Maybe I can have Tim bring me over and you can drive me back to Moondance. Or something." He scowled. "This watching our backs stuff is getting to be complicated."

"It's what we have to do. But tomorrow night works for me." She turned back to Vickie. "Did you hear that?"

"Loud and clear. I'll expect you by four." Vickie winked at them. "Don't do anything I wouldn't, kids."

"Vickie!" But Ruby laughed as she signed off and settled back in her seat. "That's set. And as for the bedroom, I can get a recliner moved upstairs by then."

Gabe smiled. "Thanks. I should get a room set up for you at Moondance. We could promote that as well. Lovebirds setting up rooms for each other. Think we should do short tour videos as part of the promotion?"

"You're enjoying this," she accused.

Gabe raised his hands. "Guilty as charged."

She glanced sideways at him. "Remember, just friends."

"I know. But it is fun to play without having to get serious about it." He sighed. "If only it wasn't the arm close to you that's mucked up."

"Can't do anything about that."

"No." He leaned his head back, yawning. "Sorry. Last night was a bad one."

"I noticed. You seemed to be having bad dreams."

"Sometimes I just get a run of them. It's not as bad after the first hour, but last night was hard. I hurt. I woke a lot. Damn, I'm out of shape. Feeling day before yesterday's ride." He eased his hat to cover his face and reclined his seat. "Sorry. I'm really tired."

Tired or just don't want to talk about it?

Ruby eyed Gabe, recognizing the pattern of evasion, but decided against pressing for more. That would take things beyond the category of *"just friends,"* and she didn't have the right to nag him. Nor, as she thought about it, did she *want* to pressure him. He was a grown adult, and didn't owe her any explanations, much as she wanted them. To ask more would be presumptuous.

She checked her charge levels, and decided not to stop. It wouldn't take long to charge up at Gabe's place, and perhaps stopping when it was just the two of them wasn't that good of an idea, given this latest news.

GABE ROUSED AS THEY DESCENDED INTO THE UMATILLA River valley.

"Take the second exit," he said, sitting up and readjusting the seat.

"Got it." Ruby took over from the autodrive. They headed south on the state highway. She noticed that the town had spread out this direction. "I didn't realize it was getting this developed out here."

"It's another reason I'm thinking about paying everything off and doing something different. I can't afford to retire, not fully. I have to do something for an income. Brandon keeps trying to talk me into working with AgI, but I'm not sure that's a route I want to take."

"The company sure doesn't look as good as it used to," she said.

"Eh, it was never that great an operation when you looked close," Gabe said. "Go ahead and take a left coming up."

She turned. Within a couple of miles the terrain changed from rolling hills to a steep climb. "Didn't realize your ranch was in the mountains. For some reason I visualized it being all flatland, especially with the water management stuff."

"Oh, I've got that as well. But the home place is on the point of a ridge, facing west. Gets nice breezes in the summer, but it can be nasty in the winter. However, the sunsets are glorious. Rachel—" he stopped, swallowing hard.

"I'm sorry," she said after a period of silence. "Don't feel like you're hurting me by talking about her. It's not—like it would be if it were Mariah."

He shook his head slowly. "She loved the place," he said softly. "She wasn't like you. Soft, not rock-hard, not fiercely independent like you. Not brittle like Mariah. She laughed, real laughs, and took a lot of joy in her life. Oh, that doesn't mean she wasn't strong. But she was a different kind of strong from either one of you, and after everything...." His voice trailed off again. "After everything she was the comfort I needed," he said finally.

"You loved her." Why did it hurt to say that?

Just friends, Ruby told herself fiercely. *And remember that both Vickie and Remy have cautioned you about getting sucked into this sort of thing with Gabe.*

"Not well enough," Gabe said. "Just like I was with you." He sighed. "I've been a selfish god damned son of a bitch, and I've paid the price for it. Had a lot of time to think about it when I was down flat with the G9 and couldn't do anything *but* think. I've made a big mess of things over the years."

She couldn't say anything to that. Ruby's fingers tightened on the wheel and she focused on driving. Gabe didn't look at her but stared straight ahead.

"It's a pretty place, I bet." she said finally, just to break the silence.

"Yeah. It's very pretty. The moon rises too late tonight for you to see why we named the ranch Moondance. But if you stay over in the next week or so, you'll be able to see it." He was quiet for a while. "It should make the place reasonably saleable." His voice turned bitter. "Probably will get bought up by some rich asshole for a second home. Though even Mariah doesn't want it. Unless she starts pitching me for the second round."

"Mariah probably has dozens of places. Besides I think she prefers the ocean."

"Yeah. Okay, take the next left again."

She turned onto a gravel road. They climbed to the top of a ridge, then followed the ridgeline to the tip.

"You can't see them in the dark but here's my high-elevation fields like the Homestead and Lone Pine," Gabe said. "Once we turned off the highway we were on my place."

"You own this ridge? Then where's the part that you're doing water management talks about?"

"Other side. There are stringers of timber on that side of the ridge, both sides of a draw that widens out fast. My property also spreads onto the other side of the highway. The tribe wants to ensure that the timber doesn't get logged off so quickly that the land can't hold water, especially in weather events. By the time all is said and done, really, the only part I'm going to be able to sell is this ridge top." He shrugged. "Soil's not right for wine grapes. I even looked at that. No such luck."

"They are picky." She'd done a viticulture survey on the Double R and come to a similar conclusion.

"And it's not big enough to run stock. Maybe I should just sign it over to the tribe. But then what would I do for a replacement home?"

"That's a tough one."

They pulled into the main yard. Ruby whistled as she caught sight of the house. It looked like some of the showplaces she had seen on Mt. Hood years ago, a big log lodge with a tall A-frame roofline in the center that pointed west, with two long low wings extending from each side.

Gabe snorted. "It is impressive-looking, isn't it?"

"It's—not at all what I expected." And even though they'd repainted the big ranch house five years ago, her own place looked shabby in comparison to this.

"The charger is over by the machine shed, under the carport."

Ruby nodded. She parked her rig next to Gabe's. As she got out to plug it in, a couple of border collies charged out of the building next to it, barking. One slammed against the wire fence.

"Jed! Tawny!" Gabe snapped as he hobbled out of the truck. The collies barked once more, then settled, returning to the building. "They don't do well with company. Tim or Kathleen probably locked them up before your men got here."

"I see." She helped Gabe get his roller bag out of her rig. He didn't unholster his cane, using the roller bag as support.

"Want me to take that?" she asked.

He shook his head. "Gotta keep doing this stuff myself. It's the only way I'm going to get stronger. Thanks anyway."

As they reached the door a short woman with long dark braids opened it. "We were getting worried," she said. "Everyone's in the living room."

"Kathleen, this is Ruby. Ruby, Kathleen," Gabe said. He gestured inside. "Come on in, Ruby."

She took three steps in then halted, catching her breath at the great windows and open space. A big chandelier made of antlers hung from the highest point of the ceiling. But unlike many other places of this design, she didn't see trophy heads. Gabe had never been one of that ilk of hunter and she was grateful for that. Instead, two huge brightly colored quilts with space and star themes lined the rise of the ceiling on each side. Large spaceship models from several video series hung higher than the chandelier, two of the five glowing faint green in the shaded peak of the roof.

"This is not at all what I expected," she said.

"Rachel liked science fiction and fantasy," Gabe said. He rested his hand on a large carving of a dragon sitting on its haunches. The smooth polished wood rippled with different shades of brown. "It was an interesting theme. A different kind of life. We went to a few conventions."

"That surprises me." Brandon had mentioned going to science fiction conventions with Gabe and Rachel, but Ruby hadn't realized how much they were into it.

Gabe shrugged. "It was different. And it made her happy."

"You doing okay, Ruby?" Charlie rose from the couch. Martin joined him, along with Tim. "Thought you two would be here a half an hour ago."

Ruby shrugged. "Just some traffic getting out of Portland."

"Let's take a quick tour," Gabe said, suddenly sounding nervous. "Come on." He popped his cane out of its holster, secured it, then headed for a staircase that Ruby hadn't noticed until now.

As they descended into the next level, the theme changed to Western notes with Pendleton blankets, bits, spurs, and hats dominating the decorations. At the bottom they were clearly in a working office, but Gabe didn't stop there. He marched through a door and led them down a hallway, until he opened a plain gray door and led them into what was clearly the furnace room.

"This is a safe place to talk," he said, turning around to face them. "Ruby, you want to do the honors or shall I?"

"I'll start," she said. As she repeated what Sheriff Wilhite had told them, Charlie scowled.

"What the hell does this mean?" he said finally.

"Your guess is as good as ours," Gabe said.

Charlie shook his head. "There's a creepy feeling about some of these AgI people coming onto the place. Not Maggie and her film crew. But some of the inspectors."

"I've noticed that as well," Kathleen said quietly.

Ruby and Gabe exchanged looks.

"Yeeaah," Gabe said slowly, dragging out the word. "Ruby and I have observed this during filming. Plus, Brandon has said and done a couple of things that don't match up with what we remember of AgI in the past. He can't talk freely but from what he *has* said—there's something going on."

"And they have a lot of indentured staff," Ruby added. "More than I had ever seen there before. It's creepy once you start noticing."

"We don't have adequate evidence to make any connections that go beyond speculation," Martin said thoughtfully. "But the way the lab inspectors have been behaving hasn't felt right to me. Nothing I can call them on. Nothing specific. Just little niggling things that could just be hypersensitivity on my part."

"Same here," Tim said.

"That's why I asked Charlie and Martin to come here and why we're all talking now," Ruby said. "I don't think any of us should be traveling alone until we're done with the Superhero

—and maybe even beyond then. Not even on our own places. No one goes out alone, even to check fields."

"That's going to be a challenge," Tim said.

"My sister and her husband can come stay with us for a while," Kathleen said.

"That'll be a help," Gabe said. "But this is our big news and I wanted to talk about it someplace that AgI isn't taping."

"They'll probably notice," Charlie growled.

"What are they going to do about it? We do have privacy clauses and concerns," Ruby said.

"For what it's worth."

"That's not all we wanted to talk about where we're not being recorded," Gabe said. "Ruby and I are going to be ramping up our role play for the romance storyline. Various reasons. AgI wants it, and the numbers respond well when we smooch. I'm going to meet up with Ruby and Vickie tomorrow to do some further planning about how we implement the storyline, and stay at the Double R tomorrow night."

"And I'll be here the night after, unless we decide on something different," Ruby added.

"That's—pretty much all I had to say," Gabe added.

They chatted a bit longer, until the remote timer dinged to tell Ruby the truck was fully charged.

"Guess we'd better get going," she said.

Tim and Kathleen stayed inside but Gabe went to the truck with them. As Charlie unplugged the truck and Martin took his rifle out of Gabe's rig, Ruby paused, turning to Gabe.

"I guess we'll see each other tomorrow, then," she said.

"Yeah. Until tomorrow." To her surprise, Gabe took her into his arms and held her tight for a moment. "You be careful, Rubes. I—yeah. Be careful." He kissed her forehead and stepped back.

"You be careful too," she said. Then she climbed in.

When she looked back in the mirror, Gabe stood in the middle of the driveway, watching them leave. The two border collies sat next to him.

Ruby's lips tightened. This was getting deeper than she had anticipated. What had Gabe meant to say back there?

CHAPTER 13

"THIS IS GETTING TO BE REALLY COMPLICATED," VICKIE said after Ruby had told her about the events of the last Innovator recording. "And not a word of this is showing up in any of their social media." She scowled. "Plus it sure sounds to me like things are heating up between you and Gabe, and it's not all role play."

"There's still a lot of stuff that hasn't been said between us that has to be dealt with for Gabe and me to go beyond friendship, Vickie, and I don't think it's going to be brought up," Ruby said. "I don't think he's told me everything about twenty-one years ago." She hadn't told Vickie *everything* herself—some things, especially sexual, needed to stay private.

"If you say so. But be careful. Sharing rooms?" Vickie shook her head.

"I *am* being careful. He sleeps in a recliner these days, not in a bed. What he said before he woke up that last time, though, makes me wonder."

"That dream could be just a dream," Vickie said. "This other stuff with AgI that you mentioned, though. Now that worries the crap out of me."

"Just two more weeks," Ruby said. "I keep telling myself that. Just two more weeks and we're done with it, for better or for worse." She tightened her hands around the coffee mug. The warmth felt good. Last night had been clear and cold, and even though the sun had been shining all day, it still wasn't that warm outside. But the reports from the RubyBots in the field were flowing in as they should, albeit with a few glitches from the Homestead field.

"How soon before Gabe gets here?" Vickie got up from the table. "I'd better put the kettle on."

"Should be pretty soon," Ruby said. "He had texted me that the water meeting was running late, but I came over anyway so we could talk first."

Her comm buzzed with a text.

I can't find Gabe. He's disappeared. Tim.

"What the...!" Ruby clicked to call back. "Tim? What do you mean you can't find Gabe?"

"He ducked out to use the restroom just before the meeting wound up," Tim said. "I mean—Ruby, this is a safe place. Or it should be, damn it, here on the Rez. But he didn't come back, he didn't come back. I went to check and...nothing. I've got security looking at their cams. He went in the restroom and didn't come out. There's no windows. They're checking the air ducts now as it looks like there's been a fight in there. He's just —disappeared."

"Shit. Shit, shit, shit! Keep me posted."

"I will."

Ruby hesitated after disconnecting. Then she called Brandon.

"Brandon Ramirez's comm. I'm not available right now. Please leave a message."

"Your father is missing from his meeting," she said. "Call me as soon as you can."

She looked at Vickie after she hung up. Vickie's mouth dropped, staring at Ruby in shock. Her comm buzzed again. Sheriff Wilhite. Ruby put this one on speaker.

"Ruby, where are you?"

"I'm at Vickie Chandler's."

"Do not leave. I'm sending a deputy over right now."

"You know about Gabe's disappearance?"

"Huh? What? No. Charlie called in a threat. Someone called his comm and said *Ruby's next. Burn, baby, burn.* Gabe has disappeared?"

"His ranch manager just texted me. He went into a bathroom at the Rez during one of his meetings—and didn't come out. They're looking at videos and checking ducts right now."

"I guess I'd better get in touch with those authorities too," Wilhite sighed. "Already talking to Metro."

"Is it time to call out the Home Guard?" Vickie asked.

"That's—not my call," Wilhite said slowly. "I'm not a Guard officer."

"But I am. I'll get back to you." Vickie turned away, speaking into her own comm.

"Stay where you are, Ruby," Wilhite repeated. "I'm texting you a confirmation code for the officers I'm sending. They'll go back to your place with you and run comms."

"A confirmation code? Why? I know all your deputies."

Wilhite hesitated. "There's body-modded fakes out there right now on the corporate circuit. One of my sources got me the information just before Charlie called the threat in."

"Interesting timing."

"Isn't it? Anyway. Texting you the code now."

"Brandon Ramirez," her comm announced.

"All right. I'll check them," Ruby said. "I've got an incoming call I need to take."

"All right. Be careful!"

She switched channels.

"Mom, I hate to keep saying this, but what the hell is going on?" Brandon said.

"Tim just called me. Your father has disappeared—and I just got off the phone with Sheriff Wilhite. I've been threatened and Wilhite has just learned that the corporate ties to the other day's shooting may be using body mods. I have to verify the deputies when they get here."

"What the hell—oh shit," Brandon groaned. "All right. Be careful."

"We're not going to be able to shove this one under the rug, Bran. You need to be careful, too. And keep in mind that Mariah threatened both of us at the last show."

"What? That little fight was in the script. Georgy's idea."

"Was it Georgy's idea for her to threaten us just before we started arguing?"

Brandon was silent for a few moments. "I thought that was just a script embellishment," he said finally. "You two were supposed to have an argument, but it was over something else, not her telling you to watch your back."

"Some embellishment." Her comm beeped again. "I've got to go, but Bran. For god's sake be careful! Who knows who is really the target?"

Tim again. "Kathleen just called. The house and lab are on fire."

"Wh-what—is she okay? Hopefully Gabe's not there!"

"She got out with the dogs, and there's not enough time for him to have been taken there. But not a word on what's happening with Gabe."

"And I've been threatened too. County sheriff just called. Do you have a safe place to go to?"

"For now, yes. I'll keep you posted."

Ruby placed both hands on the table after disconnecting

from that call, waiting for her comm to buzz again. When it didn't, she took a long, slow breath, distantly noticing how her hands were starting to tremble now that she had a couple of moments to think.

Don't lose it, Ruby. You can't lose it now, she told herself. *Gabe and Brandon will need you to be level-headed. It is not time for you to react.*

She pressed her lips tightly together and exhaled, repeating those phrases to herself until her hands were steady.

Vickie sat back down at the table. "Home Guard's been activated. I called Wilhite. She told me about the body modders. We've got verification codes set up. Ruby, any news about Gabe?"

"No. But Tim called to say that Gabe's place is on fire."

"What the hell?" Vickie reached across the table and took Ruby's hands. "You okay?"

"Not really. It's just—Vickie, *why?* The RubyBot? Something else?"

"I don't know. But it pisses me off that someone is hurting people I know and care about for no logical reason," Vickie said. "So now what?"

Ruby rubbed her face. "I guess I go back to the ranch once the deputies are here to pick me up—and wait to see what happens next. Hopefully there's a ransom demand at some point."

"Mike's gathering the Guard to protect your place, give the deputies a break. I'll go over with you."

Ruby exhaled. "All right. I guess until we know more, we just wait."

"It's the hardest thing to do," Vickie said. She patted Ruby's hand and got up. "I'm going to stay at your place until we know what's what."

"You sure? What about here?"

"Deedee's got Dave. The two of them can run the place—are running the place more than me and Mike these days anyway. We're just the old fart parents who haven't bothered to retire yet. I think you need a backup more than they need me here to run things."

"Thanks, Vickie." She sat and stared at her cup while Vickie gathered up her things for an overnight stay.

Why did they take Gabe?

It had to be Mariah. Didn't it? But what would she get out of this? It wasn't WLAN's pattern to kidnap people, so it couldn't be them, could it? And AgI had bought out Gabe and Brandon's gambling debts, so it couldn't be an angry mob boss seeking to break Gabe—could it?

None of this made any sense based on what she knew. Which meant she didn't know something important.

BECK HUGGED RUBY AS SHE CAME IN THE KITCHEN. "You all right?" she asked.

Ruby nodded. "You?"

"So far. I heard the call with Charlie when it came in." Beck's face hardened. "It's a familiar voice. Matches some of the threat calls that we got before the firebombing."

"Did you tell the sheriff?"

Of course she did, that's why Wilhite said something about Metro authorities.

Beck snorted. "I may be paranoid about cops, but I'm not stupid."

Ruby sighed. "I didn't think you were. Dumb statement on my part."

"Hey. I know how it is when you get shook up by something like this," Beck said, rubbing Ruby's shoulder. "Going to the lab now, got an algorithm I'm wrestling with. Let me know if you need anything."

"I will."

Vickie looked around the kitchen. "Where do you want to settle in, Ruby? Here?"

"I should probably work in my office for a while. Still paperwork to get done. Maybe you and the deputies should take over the dining room—the big oak table has six leaves so you can spread out."

"Okay. We'll try not to trash things too badly."

"It doesn't matter. Has to be done." Ruby hesitated. "Can you check with Beck about getting a recliner set up for Gabe in the room next to mine upstairs? Thinking positive."

"I'll do that."

Ruby wandered down the hallway to her office. Once there, instead of looking at her feed from the RubyBot, she pulled up the news. Nothing about Gabe on the Innovator page—but two of the local news pages had brief reports on his disappearance. The second site had shots of the fire. Ruby winced at the short video clip. It looked as if the entire center section of the house was wrapped in flame. The lab and barn didn't look much better.

She leaned her head on her hand, shaking it. This fire would put Gabe out of the Superhero. Even if he was all right. Even if whoever it was didn't physically harm him—she didn't quite see how he could come back from *this*.

At least not on his own. God. A niggling tendril of doubt pulled at her. He wanted out. Didn't appear to have many prospects for selling Moondance other than a showplace. Would he do this to himself?

She buried her head in her hands. Was Gabe really capable

of doing this kind of fraud? After all, it had been twenty-one years since she had been close to him. He still held secrets. Could one of those secrets be a man so desperate to move on that he'd stage a kidnapping and burn his home for the insurance money?

It didn't match the Gabe she knew. But did she really know him any more?

"*Mariah Meyers*," her comm announced.

Ruby lifted her head. She wouldn't dare. She hadn't dared. She didn't dare. Would she? Red-hot rage boiled up in her. If Mariah had anything to do with this...no. Why would she call herself to make a ransom demand? She was smarter than that. No, this was probably a fake sympathy call. At best she might be trying to make another offer.

She'd put an end to that notion right away. She was in no mood to spend much time sparring with Mariah, but this was a damn good reason to rip into her.

"What do you want, *bitch?*" she snarled as Mariah's form appeared in front of her desk.

"Wha—what the hell is this all about, Ruby?" Mariah raised her hands.

"You know damn good and well what's going on!" Ruby yelled. A part of her was secretly pleased at the confusion spreading across Mariah's face. "So where have your minions taken Gabe?"

"What?" Mariah stared at Ruby, still looking confused.

"I said," Ruby repeated slowly. "Where have your minions taken Gabe?"

Mariah shook her head slowly. "Ruby, I don't know what the hell you're talking about. What do you mean, *taken Gabe?*"

"Oh. I forgot. Your corporate bosses won't publicize it and the news is only out on the local nets. Someone's kidnapped

Gabe and his ranch is on fire. I don't have time to play your games right now because someone might call me with a ransom demand."

She hung up before she said anything more, but not before she saw the shocked expression on Mariah's face.

Her comm buzzed again. Mariah. Ruby rejected the call.

She didn't call again, nor did she leave a message.

With a sigh, Ruby banished the news reports and began studying the first field profiles from the RubyBots. Slowly, following the data sucked her in.

"Ruby?" Vickie stuck her head into the room. "We got a call on the ranch line. Deputies recorded it and they want you to see it. Looks familiar but we can't place it."

"I'm coming." She followed Vickie to the living room.

"It's not much, Ruby," Paul said. "But it might mean something to you."

She watched tensely as the clip fed through. Two androgynous figures in gray, snug-fitting jumpsuits that included full head masks glowered at the camera.

Body-modded former indentured, she thought.

"This is for nature abuser Ruby Barkley," one sneered in a flat, emotionless voice.

Nature abuser—WLAN for sure. But they've never gone this far before—have they? Or have they and it's just been hushed up?

Ruby looked beyond them to try to make sense of the background. Trees. Light. Late afternoon, when it was still light. A draw somewhere, but it could be anyplace in Thunder County —or Umatilla County, or anywhere in the Blues. So this was a recording and not live. The background looked familiar but it was too blurred for her to make it out clearly.

"Remove your bots from your land. Stop abusing nature.

And turn over your payments from AgI to an address we'll send in the next clip if you want to see your precious Gabe again." They stepped apart to show Gabe on his knees, hands and feet bound together, no sign of the sling his arm had been in. A bruise marked his face.

One of the body-modded activists marched over to Gabe and tried to grab his short hair to wrench his head back. Gabe pulled away and spat at it. The activist smacked him across the face.

"Beg for your life from nature abuser Ruby Barkley," it yelled.

"Never," Gabe gasped. "*Ladyslipper*, Ruby."

Ruby gasped as she suddenly realized where this was.

Another smack, and the clip ended.

"I know where they are," Ruby said. "Gabe just told me."

"Ladyslipper?" Paul asked.

"Yes. I'm betting they're here. On my land. The draw north of the Homestead field, the one that runs all the way onto Forest Service land and divides my place from Reed's."

"They accessed your land on the flat before," Paul mused. "But you're sure of this?"

Ruby nodded. "That's where Gabe and I rode to talk." She paced the room. "They can't transmit from that location; it's always been out of reach. Gabe said *ladyslipper*. We saw ladyslipper orchids there the other day. He saw them first and pointed them out to me. Haven't seen them for years."

"On it." Paul got up and strode away, speaking into his com. "We'll get a search party out there right now."

"I'd better get my things together so I can join the search party," Ruby said.

"No," Vickie and Tina, the other deputy, said simultaneously.

"I know exactly where it is," Ruby protested.

"You're also a target," Tina said. "I want you here, under guard. One kidnap victim and ranch burned is enough."

"But I—"

"No." Vickie took Ruby by the arm and led her into the kitchen. Paul finished speaking to his comm.

"Okay. Calling out the full SWAT team," he said. "Been on reserve and ready to roll."

"Maybe I'd better talk to Tim," Ruby said.

"Tim?" Vickie asked.

"Gabe's ranch manager. He'll want to know."

"Wait until we get Gabe back," Paul said from the doorway. "Tina will monitor the ranch line. Don't take any other calls until she approves them. Don't call anyone. Full silence. Who knows how closely monitored your comms are? Tina's running a blocker but let's be cautious."

Ruby sat down hard at the kitchen table after Paul left, and buried her head in her hands again. Vickie patted her back.

"Beck," she called. "Do you know where the good booze is?"

Beck thumped into the kitchen. "No but Charlie does. I'll go ask."

"I shouldn't be drinking," Ruby said into her hands. "I should be riding out there with them."

"No," Vickie repeated. "This isn't the Old West and the Home Guard is here to protect you and the ranch. Let the pros do their job."

Ruby raised her head, staring at her fingers, dread cinching her stomach tighter than ever. Beck returned with a bottle filled with amber liquid.

"Charlie says this is the special stash Ruby told him to put out of the way for a special occasion."

"This isn't a special occasion," Ruby said dully.

"No, but it's good booze and I say you need a shot of it right now." Vickie deftly fished a square shot glass out of the cupboard and filled it nearly to the brim. She set it in front of Ruby. She stared at it for a moment, then tossed it back in one gulp.

"Whew," Ruby gasped as smoothness switched to a fiery burn.

"And now we wait," Vickie said, gesturing to Beck to join them. She took one of Ruby's hands and Beck the other.

Waiting. God, I hate waiting.

But she couldn't move a muscle to do anything other than stare straight ahead.

AFTER A WHILE, THEY RELOCATED TO THE LIVING ROOM, where Tina was monitoring communications.

"Team's moving into place," she said as they came in. "They've identified at least four people in the draw."

"Good," Ruby croaked. She collapsed on the couch. Beck curled up next to her. Vickie sat next to Tina. She turned on the video to an ancient black and white Western movie. Ruby watched it without following the story line, focusing on the galloping horses and the shootouts, hands tightly wrapped around each other.

The movie ended in a fanfare of dramatic music and a couple riding off into the sunset. Ruby tucked her knees to her chest and hid her face. There was no chance at all that things would turn out this well for her. They never had before. Why would something good happen to her now?

But even as she thought that, she knew it wasn't true.

Could almost hear Granma grumble about her never seeing the positive side of things.

Just as easy to see the half-empty side as it is the half-full side of things, kiddo, she'd told Ruby many times over. *It's your choice to make about which side you choose. Doesn't matter what the issue is. Half-empty, or half-full? It's up to you. Yeah, you've been through a lot, more than a girl your age should have. But what you do to overcome it is what matters.*

"They've got Gabe!" Tina called.

Ruby sat up. "Is he all right? Where are they taking him?"

"They're bringing him here," Tina answered. "He's ambulatory. They'll be here in ten."

"I bet he's going to be hungry." Ruby shot to her feet. "I know we've got soup."

"Let's wait and see what's what," Vickie said softly, resting a hand on Ruby's shoulder. "It won't take that long to get things together, okay, Ruby?"

"Okay."

But she paced the kitchen floor until she saw lights in the driveway. She hurried to the front door and would have opened it but Tina stopped her.

"Wait. Let's confirm that this is who we think it is."

Ruby fidgeted impatiently as footsteps clomped up on the porch, and Tina stepped out to speak to them. At last the door swung open. Two deputies guided Gabe inside. A bandage wrapped the back of his head and a makeshift sling held his arm. He looked around the room, eyes dull and glassy until he focused on Ruby. Then his face brightened.

"Rubes. They say you knew where I was."

"You said the right thing. *Ladyslipper.*"

He wobbled a little. She opened her arms and he staggered to her, wrapping his good arm around Ruby and slumping against her. She braced herself to take his full weight.

"You hungry?" she asked.

He shook his head. "Tired. They drugged me, and I've had painkillers. I want a shower and a recliner, if I can get it." His voice slurred a little, as if he'd been drinking, but she couldn't smell any alcohol.

The drugs.

She looked past him at the deputies. "Is there anything else he needs to do?"

"We debriefed him in the rig, and the doc's done what she can for him right now," Paul said.

"Thank you," she said to him. "Can you walk upstairs or do I need to get help?" she asked Gabe.

"You should be plenty," he murmured. "Just you, Rubes, if you can swing it. Please. I've had enough of people right now."

Tina tossed an evidence bag to Ruby. "His clothing's been swabbed already. Still, once he's changed, bag what he's wearing and bring it downstairs."

Ruby nodded. "Okay," she said skeptically to Gabe. "Let's see if we can make it without help." She turned sideways and wrapped her arm around his back. Gabe shifted his left arm to rest on her shoulder. She tentatively moved forward. He shuffled along, leaning on her, but at least he wasn't staggering.

"At least this isn't as bad as when you'd get shit-faced after a go-round during the rodeo days," she muttered once they were out of earshot of the others.

"Only because the painkillers haven't fully kicked in," he mumbled. "But damn, I feel like the worst parts of losing a Saturday night final go-round without having had the fun beforehand."

"You mean you didn't end up hitting the dirt enough?" At least he felt like joking a little.

"Augh, I hit the dirt plenty this time. It wasn't fun. Not like riding a bronc." They stopped at the stairs.

"I knew I shouldn't have taken out Granma's elevator," Ruby said.

Gabe huffed. "I should be able to do this." He raised his right leg slowly and leaned on Ruby. She stepped up with him. It was easier than she thought, certainly less complicated than steering a drunken Gabe around.

Did plenty of that in the old days.

She guided him into the room he'd used the other night. Someone had brought one of the recliners up from the living room and set it down next to the bed.

Gabe pulled away from her and hobbled over to the chair. He collapsed into it and bent to undo his muddy shoes with his good hand. "Good thing I wore my trainers, I guess." He flexed his fingers and struggled with his shoelaces. "Damn it. I can't move them right. Shit, I don't *want* to have to go to slip-ons!"

"Let me do that. It'll probably be better in the morning." She undid his shoes and slid them off, dropping them into the bag. Gabe sank back into the chair.

"I don't have any clothes here," he groaned. "And they're gonna want these for evidence."

"There's some old sweats of Brandon's around," she said. Did he even know what had happened to his house? She didn't want to be the one to tell him. "Would that work?"

"Better than nothing," he said.

Ruby pushed herself up. "Think he has some old slippers around here, too. I'll grab them."

"Thanks so much." He leaned forward, wincing as he undid the sling. "Where can I drop these clothes? They're a mess. Mud. Blood. I probably shouldn't have sat down in this chair, but then again, maybe I left all the chunks on the van seats."

Ruby frowned at him and shook the evidence bag. "Drop them in here. You going to be okay while I round up the sweats?" Not a good sign that he missed Tina throwing her the evidence bag. Then again, he could just be overwhelmed.

"Should be. Might be in the shower when you get back." He shook his head. "I really want to get cleaned up."

She eyed him. "Maybe you should wait for me to be around to go into the shower. What if you fall?"

"You didn't take the handrails out of the shower," he said. "I noticed that the other day. I'll be *fine.*"

"All right." She conceded to the irritation in his voice. At least that was part of the Gabe she had known, unhappy at appearing vulnerable.

When she returned, the evidence bag sat by the bathroom door. Ruby opened the door and dropped the sweats on the floor. "Sweats, slippers, and robe," she called through the crack.

"Thanks!"

She checked the chair—nothing on that—and dropped a blanket on it, then looked in the bag. Mud, blood, and torn fabric. Gabe would need fresh clothes and she wasn't sure how close in size he was to Brandon.

Deal with that tomorrow.

Gabe was in the chair when she returned from taking the evidence bag to Tina. Somehow, he'd managed to get the sling back on by himself. His eyes were closed but snapped back open when she came in.

"Ruby?"

"Yeah." She stood by the chair, looking down at him. God, he looked awful. Pale, bruised, bones standing out in his face, a little bit of mud and blood still in his hair—they must have told him not to wash it. It made sense with the bandage on his head. "You could have washed your hair. I'd rebandage it," she said awkwardly.

"They told me not to do it for twenty-four hours."

"I see. You gonna be okay?"

"Could you—stay? Not just when I fall asleep, but all night." He grimaced. "I know. I'm being a baby. But every time I close my eyes I'm going through that fight in the bathroom. I thought they were going to kill me."

"Give me a few minutes and I'll be back. Want me to call Beck to sit with you until then?"

"Oh God no. No one new." He pushed himself more upright. "I can last that long. I'll turn on a movie."

"The Western channel's running old black and whites tonight. Vickie had that running while we waited."

He half-smiled. "Maybe I'll do that."

When she came back from showering and getting into her pajamas, carrying her book, Gabe was glaring at an old '70s-era sitcom. He snapped it off.

"I couldn't handle the Westerns," he said grumpily. "God, I'm being such a wuss. But it's just...." His voice trailed off.

Ruby pulled back the covers and crawled into the bed next to Gabe's chair, fluffing the pillows to support her sitting up while she read. She noticed that he had managed to shove the recliner hard against the bed.

As she settled in, he tentatively extended his left hand. "I'm sorry. I'm being a wuss," he repeated. "But I just—I need contact. If you don't mind."

"I don't mind." She rested her hand on his. He sighed and relaxed, leaning his head back and closing his eyes. She took that as a signal that he was going to sleep and opened her book.

After a few minutes of silence, he sighed again, fingers tightening on her hand. She looked up from her book to see him looking at her, and slipped her bookmark into place.

"I talked to Tim on the way over here," he said flatly.

"So you know about your place."

He nodded. "That pretty much wipes me out. He won't know what the damage to the lab means yet. But—" he exhaled through his teeth. "I'd say I'm the next one cut from the Super-hero. Tim's talking to insurance, but you know what a bitch that can be."

"Yeah. But it might be something." She shook her head. "Gabe, this doesn't make sense. None of this. WLAN hasn't had a history of kidnapping people or even attacking people, not like we've just experienced."

"That's because it's not WLAN but someone using them as a cover," he said. He raised their twined hands to his forehead for a moment, then kissed her hand before lowering it.

"How do you know this?" A chill tightened her gut.

Gabe's face sagged even more into a defeated expression. "Because I finally figured out what was going on." He shook his head. "They meant to break me. It's taken them thirty years, but they finally managed to do it."

"Thirty—Gabe, what is going on?"

Oh God. What he was saying the other night wasn't just a bad dream, then.

He closed his eyes for a moment and shook his head. Then he opened them and sighed. "Ever wonder how it was that I ended up on the rodeo circuit? After graduating college with a *very specific* ag robotics and microbial design degree that should have gotten me some of the best damn jobs available at the time? That should have kept me too busy to be chasing rodeo titles?"

"At the time you just said you wanted to have fun."

"Well, there was that element, too. But. I was running, and not from the indentured bounty hunters I told you were after me. The witness protection program blew up on me. I had hoped that running would keep me out of his grasp. I hoped he would leave you and Brandon alone. Damn him."

"What? Who are you talking about?"

Gabe squeezed her hand. "I lied to you about not having

any family years ago. My name wasn't really Ramirez. Well, it was my mother's name, not my father's. My family name is Martiniere. I used to prefer the Spanish naming. I am Gabriel Marcus Martiniere Ramirez, not just Gabe Ramirez."

"Wait. Philip Martiniere is one of Georgy Batineau's backers—you're from *that* family? The Martiniere Group?"

And why the hell didn't you draw on that money years ago if you're one of them?

But at least it explained why Philip and Gabe had reacted to each other like that at the Superhero. And why he had been tracing the Martiniere trefoil into her palm.

"Philip Martiniere is my uncle." Gabe grimaced. "He got custody of me when my parents died, back when I was twelve."

"Uncle? Oh shit. That explains why he was glaring at us during the last recording."

Gabe nodded. "I was worried that he might decide to confront us."

"But Gabe, why?"

"I was *supposed* to go into the family business and work on body mods. Integrating artificial parts into indentureds. Ostensibly to improve workplace safety and security, but the real purpose was something totally different. Very, very different. I couldn't do it. That's why I went to the Feds. Why I testified. Why Philip—" He swallowed hard. "Human trafficking is what's going on, Ruby, and it's tied to indentureds and body mods. And Philip is after the RubyBot."

"But why the RubyBot?" she asked in a very small voice. "There's nothing human about it. Never has been."

Oh God.

Even on the rodeo circuit Gabe had been touchy about human trafficking. She knew of at least three cases where he'd intervened—it had been one thing that had attracted her to him. He'd been a flirt but respectful at the same time.

"Even from the beginning it has had one of the best biobot interfaces out there," Gabe said. "That's what Philip wanted. That interface we designed that's still at the foundation of the Ruby. I—Philip used Mariah to break us up, Ruby, gave her my mind control words. And then Philip demanded that I divorce you or else. And *or else* in his world meant he would kill you. I knew I had to get away from you and do it in the biggest, most dramatic means possible. When you both got sick at the same time I was terrified that Philip had found a means to hurt you— and me." Bitterness edged his voice. "Easy enough to do considering it was the family business, after all. You don't have to believe me about this. It's far too late, anyway. I hoped that losing the Superstar and leaving you would get you out of Philip's sights."

"I don't know what to say. " Ruby exhaled. It did make a sickening sort of sense. "Why didn't you tell me then, Gabe?"

"I just—I couldn't, Ruby. Somehow, Mariah managed to use mind control structures to lock me down so I couldn't even say my own name. Not without seizures. I tried writing it down. I broke every pencil or pen I tried to use. I tried to write it on the computer. I had seizures. I tried to reach out to the Family for help—and my most likely sources didn't respond. Damn it, I should have told you before Mariah happened to lock me down. But I was afraid. If you didn't know, then if necessary, I could run and you could tell Philip you didn't know a damn thing—I hoped that would protect you and Branny. I left a packet with Remy Trask with everything you would need if I died." He flinched. "He warned me then that he would break me when the time was right if I didn't come back into the Group. I refused and—he set it up so the divorce happened. When Bran told me what was going on with him and AgI, I knew that Philip had pulled the strings to get Georgy to play along."

He fumbled and brought up his comp, biting his lip. "You don't have to believe me," he repeated. "But here's my *whatthehell* file. I'll send it to you."

"I'm not going to look at it just yet," she said. "I want to hear it from you. I—I just—oh, I don't know. What are you going to do now, Gabe?"

He released her hand. "I don't know. There's not much I can do, frankly. From what Tim said, I might have some salvageable microbial lines. But I suspect that the house is close to a total loss, and even with insurance that's going to delay my plans to pay everything off and retire. The Superhero is gone. I'm not going to have that means to restructure."

"AgI will probably give you some sort of compensation." Ruby pressed her lips together, thinking. Could she take in another stray?

If she didn't help Gabe, Brandon would. She liked that option even less than her being the one to take Gabe in.

"It'll be something. But I'm just afraid that AgI would use that to dig their claws into Brandon deeper. There's a link between them and Philip's organization—all those indentureds we saw at the taping. Far too many compared to their past numbers. And Brandon's done too much to try to help me already. Philip would just love to suck him into the Group as a means of striking back at me."

"Or you could come here," Ruby said.

"Ruby, you're already at risk. Philip doesn't fool around."

"So you're just going to let him beat the crap out of you? Gabriel Ramirez—Martiniere, whatever the hell you are, that's not the man I knew for you to give up so damn easily."

Gabe swallowed hard. "I've already put both of you at risk. I just can't—Ruby, it was bad enough learning about Bran's gamble with the Superhero. If I have to, I'll sell myself to my uncle to save you two."

"And I'd sell the Double R if I thought that would save Bran. No, Gabe. You're not going to do this. If Philip Martiniere thinks the RubyBot is going to help this sick business of his, then he's not going to back off from me just because I let him kick you into the gutter," Ruby retorted. "We're going to do better fighting this as a team, Gabe. And you are *not* out of the Superhero yet. Not if you move your base to the Double R and we combine our operations. Instead of a separate Ramirez and Barkley entry into the Superhero, we'll combine forces." She smirked. "Maybe we should see about bringing Jeff Swait into the mix. His bots are different from mine, but if the three of us join forces, now wouldn't that be a coup to pull off?"

"You're crazy, Ruby." But a faint smile twitched Gabe's lips. "You think Swait would play the game?"

"Let's talk to him at the next recording." Ruby chewed her lip. "There was something—oh yeah. There's a cooperation clause. We can terminate the Superhero early if at least three contestants sign a cooperation contract."

Gabe frowned. "I'd have to look at the contract again."

"Let me pull up Remy's notes." She called up her comp with her free hand and scanned Remy's notes on the Superhero contract. "Yeah. I need to talk to Remy about the details, but she notes the possibility."

"It does sound promising."

"I'm betting that they'll cut you, so that it's me and Swait at the end. Wouldn't it be an interesting twist if the three of us joined forces at the next show so that they had to split the prize three ways? Now I bet *that* would jump their numbers up."

"Do we tell Brandon?"

"No," she said firmly. "For his own sake. Not until we have signed agreements and coordinated choreography with Swait. You and I can combine forces. But the two of us alone don't shut down the competition. I think the magic number is three."

Gabe sighed. "It is tempting. But God, Ruby. It's a huge risk, especially if Swait doesn't come on board. And the Group...it's going to make you a target."

"If I don't do something to give you a hand, then Brandon will do something drastic. That's why we're in this pickle in the first place. And I'm probably already a target."

"That's true," Gabe conceded.

Ruby took a deep breath. *Remy and Vickie are so going to yell at me about this. Maybe. But it's the only option.* "I'm in a better position to help you than he is. So you're moving your operations here whether you like it or not. Brandon can't afford to get in any deeper. Not with the Martiniere Group as a behind-the-scenes player."

"Unless things are better than I think they are at Moondance."

"Okay. I'll grant you that." Before she could say more her comm buzzed.

"Brandon Ramirez."

"We'd better let him see that you're okay," Ruby said. She brought up video on both sides.

"Dad. Mom." Brandon exhaled, sagging back in his chair. "God, Dad, that was scary."

"It wasn't exactly a piece of cake being the star of that particular performance," Gabe said wryly.

"What are you going to do now?"

"For tonight I'm at the Double R. Tomorrow I go to Moondance and reassess things, see what can be salvaged from the fire. Your mom's going with me." He raised his brows questioningly at Ruby.

"Yes," she said.

"So you're doing the reunion storyline."

"I would be an idiot not to do it," she said. "It'll pull the clicks. Plus it's the right thing to do. Your father needs my support right now."

Gabe's fingers tightened even more on hers and he raised her hand to kiss it again.

"But it's been a long day for both of us, so I don't want to talk too much longer," he said. "I'm safe, Bran. I'm all right. I'm not withdrawing from the Superhero, so I will be there at the next recording. And I am going to do my best to be competitive."

Brandon nodded. "Keep AgI posted about the losses. We're putting together a compensation package right now." He winced. "It won't be much, certainly not enough, but it should help a little bit."

"Thanks. Even a little bit counts. And good night."

Ruby disconnected them.

"Thanks," Gabe said. "I didn't want a long conversation. And thank you for saying yes to coming with me tomorrow."

"Martin needs to assess what we can handle here," she said. "Plus, I know how I'd feel if the situation was reversed. No one should go through something like this alone."

"Thanks, Ruby," Gabe repeated. "I don't know—God, I owe you. A lot."

"At least now I know why things happened the way they did when we split," she said softly. "Doesn't make things any better. I wish you'd trusted me then."

"I was a dumbass. But I just couldn't see any other way out. And in the long run, it didn't make any difference. Philip managed to corner Bran, in spite of what I did to try and prevent it."

She sighed. "Well, it's done."

"Yeah." Gabe shook his head. "Yeah. I'd talk longer but I'm feeling the meds finally. Just—stay here tonight, okay?"

"I will."

He squeezed her hand and closed his eyes. Ruby picked up her book and read for a while. When she was ready to sleep, she had to ease her hand out of Gabe's in order to get comfortable. He stirred restlessly until she put her other hand on his. This time he didn't fumble to grab for her hand but settled deeper into the chair.

CHAPTER 14

Oh God Oh God Oh God.

Ruby stared at the images her comp projected from Gabe's *whatthehell* file, hands covering her mouth. She went through the sequence again, swallowing hard, a sour taste rising from her gut.

Full face. A teenaged Gabe who looked *so much* like Brandon, his chest a mass of bruises and cuts. Back picture of a bigger and taller Gabe. Open cuts, like he'd been beaten hard with a whip.

Those scars on his back. That's where they came from.

She *knew* those scars. And the others. Gabe had claimed they came from a car wreck. Now she knew better. More bruises. More cuts. Her gorge rose about halfway through the set of pictures and she stumbled out of bed to the bathroom, doing her best to stifle her sobs and keep from throwing up until she was safely over the toilet.

Matching memories. *Running from Daddy as he chased her around the room with a lunge whip. Mama slapping her hard, knocking her off her feet. Pain in her ribs and being hit as she cried out in agony. Tire iron to her leg. Blacking out after being hit in the head by a full beer can. Watching Daddy beat Mama to death, hiding the .38 underneath her, knowing that if she didn't use it on Daddy he'd kill her too. Oh God Oh God Oh God.*

Her stomach was empty but her gut kept tightening in dry heaves as she sobbed, unable to move except to flush, her own memories of abuse mixing with the images she'd just seen.

She couldn't look up as the light switched on and she heard water running. Gabe knelt beside her with a washcloth, gently wiping her face. Ruby collapsed into him, unable to stop the tears. His good arm tightened around Ruby and he rocked her back and forth, trembling. Was he crying too? She didn't know but God, she couldn't blame him one damn bit.

"Rubes." His voice trembled. "I turned it off."

She lifted her head. His face was tight and hard, eyes dark, lips narrowed, brows scrunched together. Angry. Not at her, she was certain. Not after what she'd seen.

"How," she croaked. "Who. Oh Gabe, damn it." She shuddered. "How the fucking hell did you keep from killing him?" There was no doubt in her mind that Philip had done this to him. Had to be Philip.

Gabe sighed. He scooted them across the room until he leaned against the bathroom cabinet for support and she was in his lap.

"I had no power, Rubes," he said finally, his voice quavering. "If I dared raise my hand back to him, he would have killed my cousin Justine in one of his rages. *His own fucking daughter*. I took some of her beatings. I had no one to turn to besides Justine. No one. He was the Martiniere and had money and power. I tried to tell someone once. That was when he used the cat o' nine tails on my back." He shivered. "The happiest day of my life back then was when Justine married Donald Atwood at seventeen and got the hell out of Philip's control. That meant I didn't have to worry about her safety any more. It was just me."

He gulped. "When I realized that he knew who Gabe Ramirez really was, and that I had a family he could threaten...I was back in those days again. Oh Rubes. I am so, very very sorry. I wanted to spare you and Branny. I just delayed the day of reckoning. I should have told you before I couldn't say anything because you would understand. God only knows, you went through it too. Worse because you were a little kid." He exhaled a deep, shaky breath.

"The God damned motherfucking son-of-a-bitch," she snarled. "I hate him. I hate what he did to you. I will make him pay for it if it's the last damned thing I do."

A weary smile touched his lips. "I hope I live to see you do just that, Rubes."

They huddled together, Ruby wrapping her arms around Gabe. He began to stroke her upper arm, tracing the Martiniere trefoil on it.

I mean it when I say he'll pay, Gabe.

"WHAT A MESS." GABE'S HAND TIGHTENED ON RUBY'S THE following afternoon as they looked at what remained of the Moondance house. Smoldering ruins dominated the middle and the southern wing. Part of the northern wing remained. But it was all taped off.

"We were able to recover some of your things from the office and your bedroom once the insurance people did their inspection," Kathleen said from Gabe's other side. "And my sister is loaning us a trailer so that we can stay here to manage things—if you approve of that."

"Someone's got to watch the fields," Gabe said. "I appreciate it, Kathleen. This probably means I'm going to transfer the lands over to the tribe sooner rather than later, but for now...." His voice trailed off. "Business-wise, I've been maintaining off-site backups for years. What can't be replaced in the office is personal stuff. Memories."

"We were able to save some of the things we knew meant something," Kathleen said.

"Thank you." Gabe kept staring at the wreck of the house. Ruby shivered next to him as a cold gust of wind blew up ashes, remembering what else had been in Gabe's *whatthehell* files before the pictures of abuse.

She'd done a quick search on *Gabriel Martiniere* and *Gabriel Marcus Martiniere Ramirez* before looking in the file, just to see what, if anything, was findable. Gabe hadn't been joking about his playboy past. And then, suddenly, Gabriel Martiniere disappeared from all coverage, shortly after testifying against the Martiniere Group. A few months later, *Gabe Ramirez* started showing up on the lower-level rodeo circuits.

She'd compared the last known picture of Gabriel Martiniere to Gabe Ramirez's early pictures. Gabe Ramirez had a scar down the left side of his face that Gabriel Martiniere lacked, raw and red instead of the faint white line it now was. Part of cosmetic surgery or something else that had happened before he'd gone into witness protection, that wasn't included in those damned pictures? *Her* Gabe had more sculpted cheekbones than Gabriel Martiniere and a haunted, craggy look that didn't appear in his youthful pictures.

He hadn't lied to her all those years ago about not having close family. Parents and his sister had been killed in a plane crash when Gabe was twelve. Philip, his now-dead wife Renate, and their children Joseph and Justine had been Gabe's closest living relatives, so he went to them. The pictures of the young Gabriel Martiniere after his family's death could almost have been Brandon at that age. The only reason Gabe hadn't been in the plane with his family was due to him being in a military boarding school due to his past antics. He'd been a wild kid.

She still didn't know what to think about the long-term, post-Superhero future with Gabe. Pick up a deeper romance with Gabe now that she knew what was going on? While the prospect was tempting, she didn't know if she wanted to take what they had past the friendship that was tentatively reforming now.

Twenty-one years. And while he had reasons, he had still been a damn ass about the whole thing.

And Ruby didn't know just what to think about *that*. Still. Though Philip's past treatment of Gabe explained a lot. Especially when she considered what might have happened to her if her parents hadn't died that awful night. If she hadn't had Gramps and Granma to take custody of her, and had gone to Aunt Grace and been raised by the Barkleys instead of the Ryders.

Gabe coughed. "Well, let's go check the labs."

She matched her steps to his. Rick, Martin, and Tim had pulled several freezer storage canisters from the partially-burned building. Ruby couldn't see the temperature printout numbers on the sides of the two canisters close to them but she could see the green color. Green was good. It meant the temp controls hadn't been breached.

"Looks like some of your canisters made it," she said to Gabe.

"Three so far out of twenty-one," he grumbled.

"Three is better than nothing."

He slipped his good hand out of hers and ran his fingers through his hair. "I'm going to need more than that to stay afloat in the Superhero."

"My offer still stands," she said quietly, conscious of the cams floating around them.

He shook his head slowly. "I may not have any other options." His hand closed on hers again. "Thank you for believing in me. For trusting me."

Tim joined them. He gave Ruby a wary glance. "I think we've got some idea of what's left."

"Go ahead," Gabe said, eyes flicking to the cams. "We're being recorded, so I don't think any of this is going to remain secret."

Tim sighed. "Martin thinks we can recover about half our canisters. He's a lot more optimistic than I am about it."

"What does Rick say?" Ruby asked.

"He says a third."

"His estimate is probably the correct one," Ruby said. "Martin tends to run to the optimistic side. Then again, he's also recovered some borderline stem seeds and biobots that I know others would have given up on. But Rick—that's probably your most accurate baseline measure. At least it won't be a smaller amount than that."

"A third. That means six or seven canisters. Still not enough," Gabe said. "But if Martin can push one or two more over the top, then that might leave me as a viable Superhero candidate. *Maybe.* We won't know more until we start working with them."

"The plan is to move operations to the Double R?" Tim asked.

"Lab, at the minimum. I'll be coming over from Ruby's every other day to check on operations with the fields we already have in production. I just—I'll be in your way in a trailer."

Tim nodded. "Kathleen's sister and her husband have offered their help."

Gabe exhaled. "I'll pay them double their usual rate. Need to talk to the water management people as well."

Ruby stepped aside and let them talk about Moondance plans. Not her place. She walked back over to the house, trying and failing to visualize the same thing happening to her house. The Home Guard was still there, at least.

Kathleen joined her. "It's hard to see this. He and Rachel put so much effort into making Moondance what it was. Losing those quilts—she had made those."

"Yeah," Ruby said.

"At least you're here to help. Thank you."

Ruby faced her. "He's the father of our son. I can't just walk away from this. And it was a horrible thing to have happen. It's not right."

Along with a lot of other shit.

Kathleen's eyes darted sideways as Ruby became aware of a cam recording them.

"Thank you," Kathleen said. "I hope it works out."

Ruby shrugged. "I have a big house and it's been empty for several years. Now it's filling up again. I'm glad to see the space being used."

Gabe joined them. "Kathleen, Tim said you had things I should be looking at to take to the Double R?"

"Yeah. Over here." Kathleen led them to a pile of suitcases and boxes in the machine shed. "The clothes will need washing—I tried to get the ones with the least amount of smoke smell in the top suitcase. And the rest—do you want me to put it in storage or will you take it with you?"

"I'll take all the clothing," Gabe said. "Let me sort through the boxes." He hobbled back into the machine shed. "Ruby, can you help me set up a table of sorts? I'd just as soon not be bending over. My back is killing me."

She helped find several two-by-fours and a couple of sawhorses to rig up a temporary table. After lugging the boxes over for Gabe to go through, she and Kathleen loaded the suitcases into her truck. Rick and Martin were carefully packing the salvaged canisters and other materials from Gabe's lab into the truck bed as well.

It didn't take Gabe long to sort through the four boxes, putting a few things in one box and setting the others aside.

"Ruby," he said finally. "Got a question." He was looking at a double silver frame.

"What?" She looked at the pictures. On one side she recognized the horseback picture of the two of them taken at their wedding. On the other, Gabe stood with a lovely dark-haired woman wearing a pale blue dress and holding a bouquet. "Is that you and Rachel?"

Gabe nodded. "Would you have a problem if I had this around while staying with you? I can pack it away if not."

"That looks like the old wedding set we had."

"Yeah. I found it when I was going through things after Rachel died. I decided to replace your individual picture with that of me and Rachel—somehow it just seemed right to have both of you on my desk at that point."

"Gabe." She rested a hand on his. "It's all right. I guess I'm flattered that you wanted to remember our relationship as well as the one you had with Rachel."

"Okay. Thanks." He gave her a small smile and put the frame into a box. "It's also a reminder to me of how I can screw things up. Kathleen," he said as she joined them. "These three boxes can go into storage." He pointed to them. "This box will go with me." He picked up the small box that he'd put the frame into. "And thank you. For everything."

They walked back over to Ruby's truck. She eyed the load. A couple of office chairs and desks—yes, they'd need more of those. Eight canisters with green readouts, and what looked like two more with amber readouts—perhaps Martin's more optimistic forecast would prevail. Assorted bits and pieces of lab equipment including tables, dividers, and packages of biosuits.

Stripping all the usable supplies from Gabe's lab, she thought.

On the one hand, it made her sad. On the other...it was what had to be done if they were going to pull this one off.

THE NEXT MORNING RUBY LEFT GABE AND THE OTHERS TO do the lab organization. One of the county guards went with her as she drove to Remy's office in town, a small manufactured home on the hillside overlooking Lakeside with the office in front and the living quarters Remy and Shannon shared in the back.

"Go ahead, she's waiting," Shannon said as Ruby and Sam came in the office section. Sam sat and pulled up his comp. Ruby went into Remy's office.

"Girl, you know I love seeing you, but what's this all about?" Remy said, spinning away from the comp display over her side desk.

"Things I can't talk about over the comm."

"Figured as much. So what's going on?"

Ruby drew a deep breath. "I need you to draw up a professional agreement between me and Gabe. It needs to fit the format of the cooperation agreement in the Superhero contract. But it needs to last for an indefinite period, not just for the duration of the Superhero."

"What. The. Hell. Ruby, is this really a good idea? I know he's had a major setback and you like to take in strays, but why is it that *you* have to be the one to rescue him?"

"There's a lot at stake that I can't talk about and it involves Brandon and AgI." Ruby took another deep breath—she'd been doing a lot of that lately, she realized. "Gabe came clean to me about what happened twenty-one years ago, Remy. I can't tell you everything for your own protection, but for Bran's sake—for our own sakes—this has to happen."

"Shit, that's got to be bad if you're taking these kinds of steps. What have you gotten yourself into?"

Ruby studied her hands for a moment, thinking about what to say and how much to say. At last she sighed and looked up.

"*Gabriel Ramirez* is an assumed identity from thirty years ago," she said. "He comes from a very problematic family. The situation is a witness protection program gone bad."

"What, he's related to Georgy Batineau?"

"If only that were the case. Remy, he's a Martiniere."

"He's a Martiniere?" Remy leaned back in her chair. "One of *the* Martinieres?"

Ruby nodded.

"Oh, *fuck*. So you need something strong enough to hold off the Martiniere Group. Dare I ask how closely related he is to Philip and Joseph? Must be a close relative if you're taking these measures."

"He had plastic surgery done. Do a web search and you'll find out, though—look back about thirty-some years. Same first name. Spanish naming protocol. Gabriel Marcus Martiniere Ramirez."

Remy's jaw dropped. "Oh God. I don't need to look him up. *That* Gabriel Martiniere. I was working prosecution in that era. I saw transcripts of some of his testimony before the Marshals whisked him off to the protection program. The stuff he revealed stuck in my brain. Wild, speculative stuff. Oh, shit. Shit, shit, shit."

"Yes. And I'm not going to say any more. You don't want to know."

"Okay." Remy tapped her fingers on her desk. "So that's

you and Gabe specifically. You want a second cooperative contract for you two and a third. You need a third participant to shut down Superhero competition according to this cooperation language. Are you bringing Mariah in?"

"Hell no. She's in this mess up to her neck already. No, we're going to approach Jeff Swait. His line of research will—also be of interest to certain parties. If you could also draw up a separate collaboration contract for the Superhero involving all three of us, that would be great."

"And you want it as soon as possible, of course."

"That would be helpful."

"All right. I'll get on it."

Should she ask about the envelope that Gabe had mentioned?

No. That's for him to bring up.

They chatted for a few minutes more, and then Ruby left.

One thing done, she thought as she got back into the truck with Sam. *One step at a time.*

She just wished she knew where they were going to end up.

GABE SETTLED BACK INTO THE ROOM THAT HAD SERVED AS his office before their divorce, just down the hallway from Ruby's office on the first floor. He split his time between the Double R and Moondance, and when he was at the Double R most of his waking hours were in the lab, working with Martin, Julie, and Rick to coax what he could out of his microbials.

Ruby, Julie, and Charlie spent time in the fields checking the RubyBot's work. After a second run of glitches from the Homestead field, they shut it down, releasing another round of counterbots to ensure no active biobots remained. After three days they reseeded it using Gabe's microbials for support, from a batch with a low survival rate. It was entirely possible that the nutrients from the breakdown of the RubyBots and counterbots might energize the performance of the microbials and overcome whatever it was that was causing the glitches in Homestead. At least that was the theory. Ruby hoped to have some data from Homestead by the time they went to the next cut show. The other fields were performing well—just the Homestead was problematic, and who knew what had been going on close to it?

Worth a try, Gabe had muttered when she went to his office to propose the Homestead subproject.

The numbers for his recovery from the fire still looked stark. He had a high sympathy rating on social media. But the performance numbers were slow on Moondance's fields, reflecting the need for further microbial doses that just weren't going to be ready to release on time as a result of the fire. Ruby kept the stats separate on the Homestead field. She hadn't mentioned it to Gabe yet, but she planned to turn them in on behalf of the combined Barkley-Ramirez project once they announced it at the next cut show. Ironically, those numbers looked a lot better than Gabe's own fields, if not as good as those of her RubyBot releases.

She ended up spending her nights in the bed next to Gabe's chair. Besides struggling to fall asleep, he had nightmares that led to yelling and screaming if she didn't wake him in time. Then they ended up talking, and neither of them slept well as a result. Philip and other Martinieres haunted Gabe's dreams. She learned a lot more about Gabe's secret past, especially the period after his family's deaths and then again when he was on the run creating a new identity, before she had met him.

But at least things were quiet.

Too quiet, Ruby mused, as she hung out with the horse herd at the gate in the afternoon before their next trip to LA. No sign of any further WLAN threats. No whisper of any further involvement from the Martiniere Group. The kidnappers sat sullenly in the Thunder County jail until a labor pool attorney came to collect them for an undisclosed indenture management company.

Hired guns, was all Wilhite could say. *Charges filed, but the lawyer made bail. We'll see if they show up for trial.*

"So here's where you are," Gabe said from behind her. He slipped through the gate and joined Ruby in scratching Sunshine's itchy places. "Any luck getting in touch with Swait?"

"We're going to meet Jeff for dinner tomorrow night, before recording," she said. "We'll pick him up." She arched a brow at Gabe. "It seems that Mariah has intensified her pressure on him to sell. She's particularly interested in the Swaitbot."

"From what I've been able to see of his work, it's a different pathway from what you and I chose with the Ruby," Gabe said. "But it's still something the Group could use for their own purposes."

Ruby nodded. "Different stem sources and slightly different algorithms. He said he's getting a lot of weird stuff happening around his place, but he got security ramped up high after I had my first incident."

"It's a good thing he's being cautious. That's another tech that the Martiniere Group will want to play with."

Ruby turned to Legacy and started scratching her neck. "I'm wondering if we can create an alliance of independent biobot producers to stand up to the Group once the Superhero is done. Something that will last longer than the Superhero collaboration agreement. It just can't be us who are affected by what AgI and the Group are doing."

"I think this thing is much bigger than we realize, Ruby." Gabe patted Sunshine and moved on to Casey. "I'd be satisfied if we all got out of the Superhero without losing anything more than we have already."

"I want more than that. Philip put you through hell. He needs to pay for it."

Gabe snorted. "I admire your boldness and your loyalty, Rubes. But you don't know how tough Philip is."

I have a pretty damned good idea after looking at what he did to you as a teen.

"He's an old man now, Gabe. How tough can he be?"

"Pretty damn tough. And if he's failing, then it'll be my cousin Joseph we're facing. Joey is as bad as his dad if not worse. He's sure a hell of a lot more crude and violent than Philip." Gabe scowled. "I had time to wonder during my kidnapping if some of what we've been going through isn't Joey's doing and not Philip's. Philip has always had a certain style. What we've been going through is cruder than what Philip has done in the past. Either that or he's desperate."

"Both are possible. After what he did to you as a kid...." Her voice trailed off.

"True." Gabe was quiet for a few minutes. "Whatever happens from here on, this past week has been nice, all things considered."

"It has been, hasn't it?" Ruby sighed. "We'd better go in and get ready for tomorrow."

"Yeah."

After the gate was closed and latched, they walked hand-in-hand back to the main house. He hadn't been this affectionate since their early days of marriage.

And it made her wonder about what was going to happen after the Superhero. She still was not inclined to move beyond friendship with Gabe again. Sooner or later she'd go back to sleeping in her own room. But the professional collaboration brought back fond memories. Gabe had ideas for side expansions that combined the RubyBot with his microbial work, and he might have finally figured out how to effectively combine the two.

Sometimes she thought that the drive to push them apart had been propelled by the fear of others about what they might have been able to devise together.

We'll never know the answer to that now, will we? Fucking Martinieres.

CHAPTER 15

Gabe worked his shadowy connections to find a safe place to take Jeff Swait to talk about their plans. They went for a late afternoon meal catered at a private residence to give themselves plenty of time to talk and then get back to the studio.

"Kind of interesting how this is playing out," Swait commented from the back seat of their rental car as Gabe read directions to their secretive meeting place to Ruby and a second car full of hired security followed them. "All cloak-and-dagger-ish. What's going on besides discussing a collaboration agreement?"

Gabe read the last direction to Ruby. "We're going to be parking soon."

"There's complicating factors," Ruby said as she turned into the driveway. It led to a mid-20th century modern-style house overlooking the ocean, set apart from the others around it. "We want to keep this hush-hush until recording tonight."

"Complicating factors beyond your place being burned down, Gabe?"

"Yes," Gabe said sharply. "That's actually the simplest piece."

"Figured as much," Jeff said. "WLAN doesn't normally mess with people like they allegedly did with you. They're not that organized. The story doesn't hold water. Someone else has to be using them as a front."

"I'm glad you could see it."

Jeff shook his head. "I'm a Black man from the South. I recognize when weird shit comes down. Do I really want to know the specifics?"

"The fewer details you're aware of, the better," Gabe said as he opened the green door framed on each side by foot-wide wire reinforced glass panels. "We'll tell you what you need to know, but—oh." He stopped dead in the foyer.

"Well hello there," a lanky brunette woman wearing tan slacks and a red, low-cut t-shirt said from the living room. She sidled up to Gabe. "It's been one hell of a long time, cuz."

"What the hell are you doing here, Justine?" Gabe moved a step away from her. "This is Serg's place, not yours."

Justine shook her head. "Gabie, Gabie, Gabie. You don't think I'm not keeping track of Joey's little games now, do you? You're a particular favorite of his right now."

Ruby swallowed hard.

Justine Martiniere.

That was who this had to be. Oh, she somewhat recognized the woman from when she was taking lessons at the stable where Ruby had worked during her college years. What role was Justine playing now? Gabe hadn't talked much about Justine except to say he'd protected her. But how much like her brother Joseph had she become? She was Philip's daughter, after all.

"I'm out of the game. I've been out for years. You know that."

Justine laughed. "Dear cousin, are you this unsophisticated? I don't think so, especially since your son's working for

Georgy. You know damn good and well that Daddy-damned-dearest and my dear brother don't think along those lines." Her voice sharpened. "How much information has your boy been feeding you?"

"I had nothing to do with Brandon's choice of employer," Gabe snapped. "If anything, I discouraged it. And he doesn't tell me stuff about his job."

Justine shook her head. "Typical headstrong Martiniere boy." She turned her gaze to Ruby. "And this must be the famous rodeo queen I've heard so much about." She frowned. "You look familiar—wait. That's right. You were Lora's barn manager. Now I remember."

Gabe inclined his head. "Ruby Barkley, Justine Martiniere. So why the hell are you here, Tine? Serg was supposed to keep this meeting quiet from the Family. Has he sold out to Philip and Joseph?"

Justine laughed. "Oh, no, not at all. Serg and I have an alliance of sorts, shall we say? I heard things within the family after your ranch burned, and gambled that Serg was still somewhat in touch with you. I wanted to say hi. It's been years, after all, and it's entertaining to see you back in the game."

"I am *not* back in the game," Gabe said firmly. "I walked away from the business. Blew it up. You know that. And your father is unlikely to welcome any notions of my return with open arms."

"Alas, that's true. Daddy-damned-dearest is *so* unreasonable at times." Justine's face turned solemn and the playful tone left her voice. "Look, Gabie. You're not the only one with issues about the Family business. Especially since my divorce. I wanted to let you know this, and that's why I leaned on Serg to set up a contact. If you step up to taking control, you might be surprised."

"That's an option I hope to avoid," Gabe said. "I walked

away from the Martiniere Group years ago. Did my best to burn those bridges."

"Keep thinking about rebuilding those bridges, Gabie. Now that you're back on the Family's radar, let me give you this piece of advice. The Group is not what it used to be. Daddy-shithead-dearest was bad enough, but big brother is even worse. There are a lot of cousins who think that the way we've done business needs to change, because Joey attracts too much attention from the wrong people. But until it all gets worked out, watch your backs, all of you. The family is no longer united. You're a tempting target because no one believes you're staying out of the mess. All the same, you have allies in places you don't suspect." Justine walked past them, then paused in the doorway. "And I hope you will think of me as one of them, Gabriel. Joseph has to be stopped, and soon." She met Ruby's eyes, raising one brow questioningly. Her hands moved in an odd manner. Then she left.

Jeff whistled. "Holy shit. Okay, I get the picture now, big time. I had no freaking idea."

"Still want to talk?" Gabe asked, raising one eyebrow in unconscious mimicry of Justine.

"Now more than ever," Jeff said. "I know better than to put myself in a position where I'm going to be out in the cold with shit like this coming down. And if you're who I think you are—yeah. I want to be on your side, *Gabriel Martiniere*. Okay. Let's talk contracts. How are we going to handle this?"

Ruby caught a glimpse of red outside one of the windows by the door. Justine stood by their rental car. She paused before following Jeff and Gabe further inside. "I'm going to talk to Justine," she called back.

"You sure you need to do this?" Concern flitted across Gabe's face.

Ruby exhaled. "Yeah. I need a little bit of fresh air, anyway."

Gabe joined her. His lips tightened as he looked through the window. "You be careful, Ruby." His good hand clasped her shoulder. "You sure? I could handle it."

"She looked at me. I think I'm the one she wants to talk to."

"You be careful," Gabe repeated. "She may be on our side but she's still a *Martiniere*. Watch out."

"I intend to be careful. And besides. Since you're a Martiniere, that makes Brandon one, and me the mother of a Martiniere. I should know how to handle Martinieres."

Gabe sighed. "That is true. But don't count on it getting you very far." He pulled her in front of the window and kissed her. Then he raised his head and glared outside. "Remind her that I still remember Walter."

"Oookay," Ruby said slowly. "And that's supposed to mean?"

"She still owes me a favor. And I will protect you like I did her."

"All right."

Gabe squeezed her shoulder. "Justine isn't that bad to deal with. Just be careful. She's still part of the Family, and, well...I didn't think things through with Serg." He grimaced. "I'm going to have to get past that and fast if things are really as messed up with the Family as she says." He kissed her head and rejoined Jeff.

Ruby opened the door.

"About time," Justine said, leaning against their car.

"Gabe says that I'm supposed to remind you of Walter," Ruby said as she joined Justine.

"Yeah, well, tell him go to hell too," she growled. "I got his message loud and clear when he kissed you. He wasn't exactly subtle. Don't worry. You're not one of my targets." She examined her nails.

"I saw the pictures you took of Gabe."

Justine's face tightened. "Which ones?"

"All of them." Ruby swallowed. "Including the ones that left scars."

Justine flinched and closed her eyes for a moment. Her face set hard in an angry expression uncannily like Gabe's. "Do you have any idea at all about what the hell you've gotten yourself into?"

"Not everything, not until the last few days. Gabe told me after the fire—well, at least about the Martiniere Group and what happened to his family." Ruby pressed her lips together and shook her head. "And then I saw the pictures."

"Gabie's father was the Martiniere."

"The Martiniere?"

"The head of the Group and the Family. Gabie was supposed to be his successor," Justine said, unsmiling. "He told you that?"

"Mmm—no. Just that Philip was his uncle. He's been sharing bits and pieces."

And he walked away from that? Testified against...that kind of opportunity? Wow.

"But did he say that Uncle Saul—his father—was going to change the focus of the Group before he was killed?"

Ruby shook her head. "He's not said much about his father's role in the Group."

"Can't say as I blame him." Justine sighed. "He needs to tell you more, though, given what's coming down. Listen. Gabie's still a pig-headed stubborn Martiniere man, no matter what he calls himself these days. I don't know what role you're going to be playing in his life and how much of that stuff popping up on the AgI is real. For his sake, I hope you are the real thing and are on his side. He needs someone tough like you backing him up."

"We've got a kid together. That counts for something."

"Well, that's good. I was really worried when he was with that Rachel woman. She was nice, from all reports. But the Family's been working up to doing something about Gabie for the past few years, and…" she raised her hands, then dropped them to her side. "Nice does not go very far with the Martinieres. She could have proven to be a liability for him and —if he's forced into a choice, he needs to have someone strong backing him up." She eyed Ruby. "Are you strong?"

Ruby bared her teeth in a grin. "How much do you know about my past? Besides when we were both at Lora's stable."

Justine shrugged. "Rodeo queen, so a bit of a prima donna and privilege. That worried me, even though I knew you were working while going to college. Apparently damn good at creating short-life biobots designed to increase plant resilience in the face of rapid climate change. Rancher. And not afraid to duke it out with Gabie in public. That's the piece that impresses me the most."

Ruby snorted. "Prima donna and privilege? Like hell." She glowered at Justine. "Here's my reality. My parents were child-abusing meth-heads. They were killed in front of me when I was six."

Until I know her better, I'm not giving her the real details.

"Shit. I'm sorry."

"Luckily my grandparents were able to take me in. But life on a ranch just barely big enough to pay for itself wasn't easy. My time as a rodeo queen? I worked my ass off to do it. I struggled to put together enough cash to buy a decent string of horses, trained them myself and sold tickets like crazy. Prima donna and privilege? More like dedication, focus, and hard work."

"So you're not the prima donna I thought. That's a relief. I'd say that I'm sorry for misjudging you but that's not how I roll. You've got a bite. Good." Justine faced Ruby. "Here's the deal that I want you to pass on to Gabriel. He's going to be hearing from a certain set of Family interests—the side I'm on—very soon now. Gabie-boy has to take a side. He can't sit this one out. He needs to remember who he is. He has more allies than he thinks. And you need to keep reminding him of this."

"And if I don't?"

Justine frowned. "There's—military ties going on. Political."

"Military?"

"Both government and private research." Her face tightened. "I don't know everything that is going on—yet. But the body mods may even be moving into cyborg development. Maybe even clones. Gabie knows all of this stuff, even if he wants to forget about it."

"God."

"Yeah." Justine sighed. "I suspect that if you pull off what I think you're planning with Swait and shut down the Superhero tonight, you're gonna hear from the Family once you walk off that sound stage. Just that fast. I've heard whispers but nothing definite. I know Joey is in town. So is Daddy-fucking-dearest. Are you armed? I'm pretty sure Gabie is."

"We flew commercial."

"Then no, *you* aren't even if he is. That's got to end soon for your own safety." Justine dug into her purse. "I don't have one for Gabie, in case he's slipping. But you carry, from what I've seen of you, and you've got the outfit to wear it."

She handed Ruby a holstered snub-nosed .38, similar to Ruby's own. Ruby slipped it out of the holster and popped open the cylinder. Loaded. She checked the bullets. And the weapon looked clean. Ruby nodded, replaced the cylinder, and holstered the pistol. She slipped it into her jacket pocket.

"Thank you."

"Get that where you can easily reach it," Justine said. "Ask Gabie for help if you need it. He knows what to do. It's been treated so it won't show up on a scan. Won't work for a patdown search, more's the pity, but here's hoping that Daddy and Joey continue to think that you're nothing more than a pretty redheaded hayseed hick beauty queen. That *is* what they call you, by the way." She smirked at Ruby's flinch. "Don't take it personally. Gabie always took me seriously, but then he didn't pick up on the family machismo." Her face softened. "Auntie Angelica—his mama—made sure of that. Before she was killed."

"After the show's recorded, then we need to expect trouble."

Justine nodded. "I'd be prepared for anything. And something else. Hold out your hand."

Ruby complied. Justine dropped two data chips into it.

"What are those?"

"One's the true account of what happened to his parents and sister. Serg and I have been digging for that info for a few years now, figuring that something was wrong about the plane crash reports. The other—my ex wasn't good for much, but there are advantages to being married to a banker. Gabie had a trust fund that was supposed to be absorbed back into the Group's accounts. It wasn't. Donald isolated it in a batch of my accounts, and it's been drawing interest for a long time. That chip's the key that will give it back to Gabie. You two will need those funds even if you win the Superhero, to avoid the wrath of the Group if nothing else. And you'll really need it if you lose."

"How much?" Ruby breathed.

"Twenty million right now, give or take a few hundred thousand. He can't access it all right away, but when he activates it, his share of the Family income comes rolling right on in. That will double it, at least." A chime sounded and Justine startled. "Damn. I have to get out of here, *now*. Joey's sending out trackers for me. Look, you'll see me tonight. Don't be surprised at anything that comes down." She turned and marched down the driveway. A white sports car pulled up at the turnoff, and Justine got into it.

Ruby stared at the chips in her hand. Then she went back inside.

"Gabe. Gotta talk. Private."

Gabe looked up from where he and Jeff were reviewing the collaboration contract. "What's up?"

"I've got something for you."

His brows shot up. "Let's go on the balcony."

She followed him out the slider.

"What did Justine give you?"

She dropped the chips in his hand. "She says one chip is the true record of what happened to your family. The other— it's the accesses to your trust fund. She said her ex-husband hid it in her accounts."

Gabe poked at the chips in his hand. The first one lit up. His lips tightened and he closed it. The second one lit up and he took longer, calling up a secondary comp skin to enter accesses. Then he stared at it, whistling finally.

"Did she give you any idea of what the trust fund was worth?"

"Twenty million, give or take a few hundred thousand, is what she said."

"Yeah," he said slowly. "That matches."

"She says to expect that we will hear from the Family— Gabe, is it really with a capital F, like I keep hearing?—immediately after the recording. That Philip and Joseph are in town. That you can't sit on the sidelines any more, and that her side is going to be in touch real soon now. Gabe—does this mean what I think it does?"

Gabe shut off his comp and tucked the chips into a pocket. "If you're thinking I'm going to be approached about leading the Martiniere Group—yes. And yes to the other. Capital F in Family. *The* Family."

"Do you know what you're going to do?"

"God, Ruby, I don't know yet. I've been thinking about it. This changes things big time. You're still game to follow through on this, Rubes? I wouldn't blame you if you just took the Superhero and went back to the Double R."

"And what about you and Brandon? I'm supposed to walk away from you two? Gabe, I'm not stupid. The Group is going to try to suck both of you in. Not just you but him as well. You're both going to need me to watch your back...and keep you two on the straight and narrow."

"This," Gabe tapped his pocket, "means that Brandon is safe. But there's a catch to all this. I'm going to have to become Gabriel Martiniere again, much as I've hoped to avoid that fate. And where that road leads—Ruby, are you sure you want to be a part of this?"

"For you and Bran—yes." She met his eyes as she pulled out the gun Justine had given her and examined the holster setup. Yes. One of those holsters with an apparatus that could go under her shirt, right under her bra. "And because I personally want to make Philip Martiniere pay."

Gabe chuckled as she put it back in her pocket. And then he pulled her close, first for a kiss, and then to hold her for a moment. "Oh Ruby, Ruby, Ruby. I should have trusted you years ago. But I was just so afraid for you and Bran."

She straightened up and looked him in the eyes. "You know

when I told you that shooting my father when he was beating the crap out of my mother was an accident?"

Gabe nodded.

"It wasn't. But—" her voice trembled. "I didn't have the nerve to do it until he killed my mother and had turned to me."

"Oh, Rubes. Self-defense."

"I wanted them both gone." Her voice broke. "It wasn't just nerve. It was a choice. That's what I hid." Her hand went up to her locket. "Gramps and Granma somehow knew what really happened. They knew and they didn't judge me because they knew what I had gone through. I screamed and fought the last time my parents stole me from Gramps and Granma. And even though I was only six, I *knew* what I was doing."

"Oh Rubes."

She pulled away from him. "I won't delay with shooting if I have to, Gabe. If it comes to that."

He studied her, then nodded. "All right. Here we go on the roller coaster ride."

CHAPTER 16

"You doing okay?" Gabe asked Ruby as they waited with Jeff to walk onto the stage.

She nodded. "Feels like the run-in for the Pendleton Round-Up and wondering if Sunshine was gonna take the fence down instead of jumping it. Or run away with me and beat the queen around the track."

Gabe laughed. He squeezed her hand. "At least you don't have to worry about the fence."

"Yeah."

He had helped her secure the holster harness under her shirt when they returned to their hotel room and—as Justine had predicted—revealed his own hidden weapon in a shoulder holster obscured by his sling. *Welcome to the world of the Martinieres,* he'd said wryly. Then they packed up and stashed their minimal luggage in the rental car. Gabe had switched their tickets to the last shuttle heading to Portland that night. Jeff already had plans to leave immediately after the recording. It sounded like a *really* good idea to leave once they were done.

"And now, who will survive this week's Superhero cuts?" Georgy announced their cue.

They marched on stage, Ruby and Gabe hand-in-hand, Jeff behind them, Mariah behind Jeff.

"So it's been a rough week for our contestants," Georgy continued. "Ruby Barkley is still in the lead, followed by Jeff Swait and Mariah Meyers. But Gabe Ramirez got hit with a huge chunk of bad, bad luck. Besides getting kidnapped by animal rights activists and experiencing a heroic rescue by the Thunder County sheriff, his house and lab were burned down by persons unknown."

The audience moaned.

"So while we have a lot of sympathy for Gabe, especially as he and Ruby have gotten back together—and Ruby has gone the extra mile to provide Gabe's surviving microbials with a lab where he can work—his stats are such that we have to cut Gabe from the Superhero at this time."

"No," Ruby said, stepping forward, just as they'd rehearsed with Jeff. "Gabriel Ramirez is *not* cut from the Superhero. In fact, I want to announce a collaboration agreement that Gabriel Ramirez, Jeff Swait, and I have signed. Our combined scores are sufficiently high that we can invoke the collaboration clause. Together, we *win* the Superhero."

Jeff stepped up on her left side and Gabe on her right. They clasped hands and raised them high as the crowd first inhaled in shock, then broke out in loud cheers, the ranks slowly standing to applaud.

They dropped their arms as Georgy stood there, a stunned expression on his face, exchanging worried looks with Mariah. As the applause died down, Gabe stepped forward, still holding on to Ruby's hand.

"Actually, there's one modification," he said. Ruby shot a worried look at him.

"What?" she whispered. "We didn't rehearse anything else."

He shook his head.

"The agreement is not with Gabriel Ramirez," he said slowly and firmly to the audience.

Chills ran down Ruby's spine.

No. No. He wouldn't.

On the other hand...this might be the best thing. Get it out and public. Make it harder for Joseph or Philip to do something in secret.

"*Gabriel Ramirez* is an identity I assumed thirty years ago, after going through cosmetic surgery and a short stint in a witness protection program. I've concealed who I really am for all these years. The agreement is with—" he paused, eying Georgy and Mariah. "A person who disappeared thirty years ago. My real name is Gabriel Martiniere, and my father was Philip Martiniere's brother Saul, late president of the Martiniere Group. So, the collaboration of Barkley, Martiniere, and Swait invokes the collaboration clause to win the Superhero."

Surprise flitted across Mariah's face and Georgy frowned, seemingly unsurprised. Stunned silence from the audience. Then whoops and cheers, louder than before.

Gabe raised a brow at Ruby. Then he swept her into an embrace, knocking off her hat as he kissed her thoroughly while the applause ratcheted upwards. When they broke apart, she recovered her hat and took Jeff's hand again, along with Gabe's good one, and the three of them took their bows.

"Well," Georgy said finally. "Isn't *this* an interesting little twist? Folks, this is the first time in the history of the Innovator that our finalists have invoked the collaboration clause, and it's in the Superhero, no less."

Ruby tuned out the rest of Georgy's patter. Out of the corner of her eye she spotted Brandon at the edge of the set, Markey next to him, the two whispering frantically. She caught a glimpse of a blue-green mark on Markey's hand, shining bright against her dark skin in the studio lights.

No. Branny. No. Not if that's what I think it is. Oh God. Straight out of romance bestsellers.

Georgy concluded. "And stay tuned! Even though the Superhero is resolved, we've still got a hot competition in the Superstar! And that's it from the AgInnovator this week!"

As they retreated Brandon intercepted them in the exit hallway.

"Dad. That's for real? You're a Martiniere?"

"It's very real," Gabe snapped. "*We* are Martinieres. That includes you and your mother. Now we've got to go. You too, Bran. Come on. We have to get the hell out of here before it's too late."

"Gabriel," a deep bass voice rumbled from behind them. "Father wants to talk to you."

Gabe stiffened. He squeezed Ruby's hand before releasing it and facing the speaker. Ruby turned with him to see a dark-haired, stocky man who resembled Brandon, pointing a pistol at them.

Joseph. It must be.

"Brandon. Ruby. *Go,*" Gabe growled, not looking away from Joseph.

"We've had this discussion already," Ruby said. "Bran, get the hell out of here." She took Gabe's hand.

Brandon stepped up next to her, Markey at his side. "No. We stay together."

Joseph laughed. "How touching. My father's business isn't with the rest of you."

"Oh, but I think Daddy dearest *especially* should meet with Gabie's whole family, Joey." Justine walked past Joseph, accompanied by another man with features similar to Brandon's and Joseph's. She deftly plucked the gun from Joseph's hand with surprisingly no resistance. "Better to do it sooner rather than later. Come on."

Joseph scowled at his sister. "Give it back."

"Not unless you promise to put it away. Or shall I sic Serg on you?"

"*Shit,*" Gabe breathed as Joseph paled slightly and the other man—Serg—took the pistol from Justine.

Joseph and Serg glared at each other.

"All right," Joseph huffed finally. Serg removed the clip from the pistol and handed the pistol to Joseph. He waggled the clip between his fingers until Joseph tucked the pistol away. Then Serg handed the clip to him.

"Daddy's holding court in Georgy's office?" Justine asked.

Joseph growled something that Ruby couldn't hear.

Justice waved at them. "Well, come on, everyone. I'll lead the way." She and Serg swept past Joseph. Gabe and Ruby followed, with Brandon and Markey after them as Joseph brought up the rear. Ruby heard a faint click and realized that Joseph had reloaded his pistol. She didn't look to see if he had put it away but thought about her own weapon.

Reach under my shirt and release it. Easy-peasy if I need to pull it.

Justine led them up a stairwell and down a different hallway with better carpeting and nicer paint. Two men flanked Mariah in a doorway, one with the same shade of white-blond hair as hers. She scowled at them.

"What are you doing here, Justine?"

"Family business," Justine said loftily. "And none of yours, Mariah. Now move over, along with Eric and Alexander, and let us through." She and Serg stepped aside next to Mariah.

Mariah glared at Ruby as she and Gabe passed. And then they were inside a plush office very similar to the one where she and Mariah had met at the after party—it seemed ages ago, even though it had been only three weeks.

"Hello, Daddy dearest," Justine said, sweeping past Ruby and Gabe to cross the room and kiss his cheek. "Guess what. I found the prodigal cousin."

"We already knew where he was," Philip Martiniere growled at his daughter.

She snickered at him and rolled her eyes. "That's not what I was hearing a few days ago."

Gabe halted ten paces away from Philip, drawing himself up straight as he released Ruby's hand. The two men exchanged glares.

"If there was any justice, you'd be in your grave now," Philip finally growled. "Boy, do you realize how much harm you did to the Group with your bullshit thirty years ago?"

Gabe raised an eyebrow. "Maybe the Group shouldn't be engaging in human trafficking. Or mind control experiments on unwilling indentureds."

"And just what do you think put food in your mouth and clothes on your back when you were growing up?" Philip stood up and stalked toward Gabe, stopping an arm's length away from him.

Gabe laughed. "Oh please, Philip. You and I both know better than that. There's a lot of legitimate tech and agtech work out there that carries the Martiniere Group label. Data management systems. Pharmaceuticals. Recreational body mods. Shall I go on?"

"I know what our core businesses are." Philip moved in front of Ruby.

"Then you know that the Group has never needed to stoop to human trafficking to make money, not even to condition indentureds."

"You're an idealist." Philip reached for Ruby's chin. "But

you've got good taste in women, at least." She grabbed his wrist, easily pushing it away.

"Don't do that," she said harshly. "I'm not a broodmare to have my mouth inspected."

His other hand swung up to slap at her face. Brandon shoved him away but not before she landed a slap of her own on Philip.

"You!" Philip snarled. She wasn't clear whether he was speaking to her or Brandon.

"Don't touch her," Gabe said icily.

Philip pointed at Ruby. "You threw your lot in with Gabriel. A good Martiniere woman knows her place!"

"Then it's a damned good thing that I'm not a *good Martiniere woman*," Ruby said.

Someone grabbed her arms. "You will learn how to be a good Martiniere woman unless you renounce Gabriel," Joseph sneered. "And I will enjoy teaching you that."

"*Let her go.*" Gabe's voice was low, steady, and even colder than it had been.

Ruby stomped on Joseph's instep as his arms loosened. She pulled away to see that Gabe held his pistol to Joseph's head. She reached under her shirt and pulled hers, whirling to aim at Philip—to see Brandon already pointing a small semiautomatic at Philip. She distantly noted that his hand was steady.

Good boy. Remembers the shooting lessons.

"Well now isn't this a lovely state of affairs," Justine drawled. "Daddy, I don't think Gabie's family appreciates you throwing your weight around."

"Shut. Up." Philip glared at Brandon. "You're pretty damned bold for someone facing lifetime indenture."

"I'm not under indenture contract any more," Brandon said. "Someone paid it off. Though I'm willing to bet that this week's Innovator scored the highest points ever, so I made my target without that help. Thanks for the announcement, Dad. And both of you for the collaboration contract."

"It's nothing. You set it up, so we took advantage of it." Gabe's voice was back to his normal tenor. "So, Philip. What's this going to be about? You and Joey going to behave or not?"

"One yell and my bodyguards will be in here—" Philip began.

"Actually not," Justine said, frowning at her nails. "Oh bother. I've chipped my polish."

"What do you mean?"

Justine smiled innocently at Philip. "Well, Serg had a few concerns for your bodyguards with regard to some things in Mariah's office that shouldn't be there. Something about a bomb, I think? He assured them that you were perfectly safe with me and Joey here, and took Eric and Alexander, along with Mariah, to search her office."

"You dare," Philip growled.

Justine shrugged. "We're all armed. It's a stand off. And this is private family business. Hey, as far as I'm concerned, things are proceeding normally for a Martiniere family gathering. It's looking good so far. After all, Gabie's never had a violent reputation. Unlike the three of us. I can't speak for his family, but for people who haven't been raised around the Martinieres, they seem to adapt to our reality quite quickly."

"Jus-*tine*."

She waved one hand. "Oh, Daddy-poo. *Really*. If you and Joey would just *settle down* and drop the intimidation game, maybe we could all talk like adults. You think? It's pretty clear that Gabie and his family came prepared for one of *those* little Family meetings." She strolled over to Philip and took his arm. "I think you can put that weapon back now, new-to-me cousin Brandon." She led Philip back to his chair as Brandon tucked his small pistol into a wrist holster.

Ruby half-turned to face Joseph and Gabe.

"Gabie, you're going to let Joey ooze away from you, take the long way around Ruby, and come over here by Daddy-poo," Justine continued, also now holding a pistol.

Joseph glared at Gabe and then Ruby before obeying.

"And now we're all going to put our weapons away and talk like adults, right?" Justine said brightly.

Ruby reluctantly holstered her pistol. Gabe moved to her side while Brandon moved back to his assistant Markey—who, Ruby noticed, was tucking away a weapon of her own. Ah. Brandon put an arm around Markey and she turned her face away from Philip, leaning into Brandon. Ruby found herself staring at the blue-green tattoo on the webbing between Markey's right-hand thumb and index finger.

Bran's involved with an AgI indentured. Shit. This is straight out of the boss/indentured soap opera clichés. What is this kid going to do next?

"Hurry up," Gabe said. "We've got shuttle reservations."

"You'll leave when I'm ready to let you leave!"

Gabe laughed. "Philip, I don't owe you a damn thing. But I'll give you five minutes. What the hell do you want from us?"

"We need you back in the Group. We've got to fix this mess you made."

"Not happening." Gabe took Ruby's hand. "I've got my own thing going now."

"The Family needs you. Needed you years ago. We're breaking apart."

"No, Philip. I'm not going to work with you. My answer was no thirty years ago and it's still no."

"All right, all right." Philip threw his hands up. "But don't complain about future events. You've been given your chance to cooperate with us. Let me warn you, though." His voice sharpened. "I am going to assume that this attitude is going to hold even when you're approached by dissident factions within the Group. Otherwise...."

"Otherwise what? You'll kill me and my family just like you had my parents and sister killed?"

"A regrettable but necessary action. Just like the deaths of those you hold dear will be if you step out of line."

Gabe's nostrils flared. "You admit that you were responsible for their deaths? Just like that?"

Philip bared his teeth in a humorless grin. "I'm not soft, and I suspect that *someone*—" he glared at Justine. "—leaked information to you about what happened. I should have had an accident happen to you the first time you came home from boarding school. I regret that now. I was soft when I shouldn't have been, and thought that I could influence Saul's kid. I was wrong."

"Now, now, Daddy-poo," Justine said reproachfully. "Do we really need to go there?"

Philip glowered at her. "And I have to wonder just what your loyalties are, *darling*."

"I'm not interested in a boring life," Justine said. "And, besides, Daddy dearest, don't forget about Donald's Little Divorce Present. I find Gabie's reappearance to be quite amusing at the moment."

"We do need to be going," Gabe said.

"It's taken care of," Justine said. "So, Daddy dear. Do you have anything else to say to Gabie?"

A soft chime sounded in Ruby's ear. "*AgBank notification.*" She quickly blinked up the message.

AgI deposit of three million dollars confirmed.

"Keep out of our business," Philip growled. "If you meddle, there'll be a price to pay."

Gabe pointed at him. "And you keep the *hell* out of our business. That includes the biobots. No more sabotage."

"What, you're going to compete against us?" The humorless grin returned.

Gabe bared his teeth in a matching snarl. "Wait and see." He jerked his head toward the door. "Come on. We'll just barely make our shuttle."

"I've *got it*," Justine said. "Go on."

They exited the office, Gabe hobbling as fast as he could. "God damn it, I'm going to slow us down," he muttered, stopping at the head of the stairs. "Brandon. I bought out your contract this afternoon. Resign from AgI *now* because you're no longer safe. Come with us to the Double R so we can decide what to do next."

"It's not just me," Brandon said. "I've got to get Markey free."

"*Kris*," Markey said firmly. "My name is *Kris*. Not my indenture name."

Ruby and Gabe exchanged glances. Then Gabe sighed. "I'll transfer funds once we're on the shuttle. We just got our AgI payments."

"Gabe, *no*," Ruby said. "I'll do it. You don't need to draw down your funds any more than you have already. We need operating capital."

"And I say you *don't* need to worry about any of this," Justine said as she joined them. "Now come on. My jet is warming up. I'll take you back to Portland and we can talk on the way."

Gabe eyed her. "I'm not so sure that's safe. My family has a bad record with airplanes."

Justine laughed. "Gabie, Daddy dearest doesn't dare touch me right now, and my trusted security has had eyes on the plane at all time. But let's get the hell out of here as soon as possible anyway. Your money's back in your account and Brandon and Markey—excuse me, *Kris*—are freed from their obligations. Consider it my welcome back to the family present."

Gabe stared at Justine. "What's in it for you?"

"Let's get out of here and we'll talk. You've done me a favor by popping up now."

"We should probably get our things," Brandon said.

Justine shook her head. "Too late. There'll be Martiniere security waiting for you at your apartment. You pulled a gun on Daddy-poo, and you're Gabriel's son and heir. My damned father and brother won't forget or forgive that. I'm not joking. Let's get moving, *now*."

"Your cousin's right," Gabe sighed. "Tine, our things are in our rental car."

"Already taken care of."

"Damn."

"I gambled that you'd accept my offer. It's not like you had a lot of options, and one of them would be that you all ended up dead." Justine led them toward a bigger van with obscured windows. Two men and a woman stood guard.

"Ready to go, Justine," the woman said. "We had to get a little—assertive—with some of Joseph's people. Serg is at the wheel."

"Thanks, Shanice."

They clambered into the van. Justine took the front seat while Gabe and Ruby took the next row. Gabe's good hand held Ruby's tight, his breath coming short and quick.

"You all right?" she asked softly.

"I'm going to need a med soon," he whispered. "That's all."

Justine turned back to face them. "What was your original plan for getting home from Portland?"

"Two of my people are driving one of my trucks down to meet us," Ruby said.

"Can we divert them to a closer airport? How close can we

fly to your ranch? You wouldn't happen to have an airstrip, would you?"

"No money to dedicate land to an airstrip, but the Thunder County airport in Lakeside can handle small jets."

Justine grinned. "That's wonderful news. Please divert your people there—and let's talk about remedying this situation with the airstrip. Serg, what do we need to do to get this change set up?"

"Contacting Patrick now," Serg said. "Thunder County Airport, you said?"

"Yes," Ruby confirmed. She sent a message to Charlie and Martin. *Turn around. Not coming into PDX. Plans changed. Will arrive at Thunder County Airport at—*"How long will it take us to get to Thunder County, so I can tell my people?"

"Two hours to PDX," Serg said. "Maybe a half hour more to Thunder. Give me a minute." He paused. "Right. Patrick says two and a half hours."

We'll be there around midnight, Ruby sent.

What the hell is going on? Charlie sent back. *We saw the show.*

Martiniere shit coming down, Ruby replied. *Explain later. Coming in by private jet to Thunder.*

Understood.

Silence reigned as they arrived at a small private airfield. Ruby grabbed their bags, but Brandon and Kris took them from her.

"Focus on helping Dad," Brandon whispered. "He's not looking good. We can handle this part."

"Thanks. Keep his bag close. He's going to need his meds once we're in the air." She took Gabe's arm, noticing a slight tremor. They loaded into the jet, five more security joining them, and settled into the comfortable seats. A couple of minutes, and they were racing down the runway, then in the air.

"I need my bag," Gabe said once they leveled off. "Meds."

Brandon shoved it over to Ruby. She helped Gabe open it. He grabbed his pill dispenser and took two pills, dry-swallowing them. Then he leaned back, eyes half-closed.

"How bad are your health problems?" Justine asked, the playful, mocking tone of her voice gone.

Gabe's eyes flickered open. "Bad enough," he said flatly. "I was hoping to use the Superhero to cash out and retire. Not get sucked into the Family schisms." He sighed. "Clearly that's not going to happen. Okay, Tine. Spill it. It's pretty damn clear from what just went down that you are, in fact, the leader of one of those dissident factions that Philip referred to. Though I am curious about your reference to Donald's Little Divorce Present and why that would restrain Philip—or Joey."

"Oh, *that*." Justine giggled. "Donald protects me. He controls a worm in the Martiniere Group databases. If I don't check in with it at specific but irregular intervals, it trashes all the data. *Everything*. Donald and I have a much better relationship than Daddy-poo realizes. We just don't live together."

"Then why haven't you taken Philip and Joseph out?"

"They've got—their own versions targeting me. And the Family will not unite around me. I'm Philip's daughter, after all, and the Family is sexist as fuck, even now. *You*, however, are the one who was supposed to replace Philip. You are most definitely not connected with him after thirty years away."

"A standoff, in other words, but I'm the outsider they can't control." Gabe shook his head.

"Especially now since your son and his girlfriend are free." Serg joined them. "Gabe, one of the big issues has been that there's no one to pull the different groups together within the Family. Tine and I lead one faction. There are three others."

"I've been able to cover for us until now," Justine said. "I suspect that tonight's activities have shown my hand. But it's worth it. Gabie, we need you. We really need you. Not just you but your son." She was silent for a moment, her lips tightening. "Daddy dearest and Joey are using the Family's mind control techniques to condition indentureds against their will. I have reason to believe that they are engaging in controlled and interdicted research. Possibly even cyborg techniques. Weaponizing them."

"You've got details?"

"When you can focus for a few hours, yes."

"Tomorrow morning, then." Gabe rubbed his face with his good hand. "I hear you. But I don't know. I have to think about this. It's going to take careful planning to stop Philip and Joseph, and I have partners that I need to be working with as well. And then there's my health. I can't say yes or no at this moment." He drew a ragged breath. "I have to think about this very carefully, and I want to know more details. Just not tonight. It has been one hell of a hard day and I don't trust my judgment right now."

"Understood. Then we'll drop you off and come back, now that we know we can fly into Thunder."

Ruby and Gabe exchanged glances. "Or you can stay with us tonight. There is room on the second floor," Ruby said. "Let me comm Charlie. We're going to need to move things around for Brandon and Mar-*Kris*, anyway. Gabe, I'll have your recliner and other things moved into my room."

"Um—recliner is okay for them to move but I have to be there for the rest of it," Gabe said. "Security protocols and all. Ruby, are you sure about doing this?"

She squeezed his hand, carefully thinking about how to phrase what she wanted to say. "Yes," she said finally. "Not just for reasons of space. We need to watch each other's backs."

He half-smiled at her and raised her hand to his lips. "I'm sorry. I really had no intentions of getting you sucked into my family's business."

"Don't apologize for something you can't control."

"Thank you." He leaned his head back. "The meds are kicking in, and I *have* to nap. Tine, Serg, let's talk in the morning. Brandon, we need to get rid of those AgI cams at the Double R ASAP. Can you do that tonight?"

"Yes."

"Good." Gabe closed his eyes.

Ruby commed Charlie, then followed Gabe's example.

What a roller coaster ride. This certainly wasn't what she had expected when she signed up for the Superhero.

"I NEED TO GET OUTSIDE." GABE APPEARED AT THE doorway of Ruby's office mid-afternoon of the following day. "Can we go visit the horses or something? I have to talk to you, too, but I'd just as soon do it outside."

"Sure." She closed her spreadsheets. "I'm ready for a break."

They walked arm-in-arm to the horse pasture, one of Justine's guards following them.

Our new life, I guess.

She wondered how many of the guards knew how to ride horses. Well, perhaps Charlie could start up a lesson program.

Gabe didn't talk for a few minutes, but focused on scratching the neck of Casey's yearling colt, Dancer. Finally, he looked up at Ruby, busy scratching Legacy.

"Justine and Serg told me everything. Showed me everything. Rubes, what's going to happen is bad. Really bad. I ended up bringing Bran in to hear the details because, well—for better or worse, he's in this up to his neck now. Then he and Kris started talking about the situation at AgI. They're sharing indentureds with the Group, and it's not just about body mods. It's rewiring brains. Introducing biobot controllers into indentureds. Kris was scheduled for one of those treatments once the Superhero was over. What she said—" he shuddered.

"God." Ruby shook her head, wanting to bury it in Legacy's neck. "What are you going to do?"

"I don't see that I have a fucking choice but to get involved with the Family again." He exhaled. "I just—don't. I don't want to do this, but my conscience won't let me walk away after seeing what Joseph has planned. But." He paused, clearly fumbling for words. "I don't know if it's fair to bring you into this. I treated you like shit years ago. It's one thing for you to bail out *Gabe Ramirez*, your ex-husband. But asking you to be at Gabriel Martiniere's side as we plunge into an all-out war between Martiniere Group factions? Because that is where this will go. I don't know if it's right to ask this of you."

"Gabe. Our son is a part of this. And for better or worse, I think it's too late for me to walk away. I—" now she was the one fumbling for words. "What I've heard already is enough for me to say yes. I want to support you and Brandon. I spent the morning working out plans to expand those pre-release counterbots just based on the little I know. From what you just said, I'm going to be on the front lines of this fight anyway. There's no way I can condone this whole indentured thing—it's wrong."

"And us?"

"We're friends. Colleagues. Parents. Business partners. I've got your back and you've got mine. For heaven's sake, we're sharing a bedroom if not a bed. Does there need to be more, at least for now?"

"When you put it that way—I guess not." He half-smiled. "Thanks, Ruby." He stretched. "Okay. I'd better go talk to

Justine and Serg and give them an answer." He hesitated. "Would you come with me? Bran's going to be there but you— you're my partner. It would be very helpful for you to be there."

"Yes," she said, fully aware of what he was asking.

Commitment to my role as a Martiniere woman.

But by God, she'd show Philip and Joseph Martiniere what it meant when Ruby Barkley took on that role. And she suspected that Justine and Kris would be right beside her as well.

THE END

OUTTAKE: GABE

Timeline: Conclusion of INHERITANCE, *between the last two scenes*

He couldn't sleep. Too much was happening, far too quickly, sands shifting under his feet even faster than he had anticipated. Gabe carefully lowered the footrest of the recliner that served as his bed these days, eying the still form on the platform mattress next to his chair. For once, Ruby was sleeping soundly. She usually roused at the slightest noise, had on the rodeo circuit even when they tied on a hard drunk—one manifestation of *her* past ghosts. Tonight, he'd encouraged her to take the sleeping pill Justine offered, despite turning one down for himself.

He'd learned the hard way that they didn't work well with his post-G9 syndrome medications.

Gabe glided softly across the floor to the bathroom. Washing his hands afterwards, he caught a glimpse of himself in the mirror and paused. Seeing his uncle Philip up close, confronting him, had been almost been like looking at his reflection. How could that be? The cosmetic surgery years ago in that aborted witness protection program had meant to reduce that likeness. But as he aged, especially after he'd contracted the G9 virus last year, his face had slipped back toward its old self.

The man that looked back at him from the mirror was clearly a Martiniere. A Martiniere with a faint, surgically-created, scar down the side of his face. A bumpy and slightly crooked nose, gift from one of the saddle broncs he'd ridden years ago. A Martiniere with darker brown skin, a legacy from his Hispanic mother.

A Martiniere, none the less. But was it the face of *the* Martiniere, the Family head? The man who controlled the great Martiniere Group, the consolidated family companies? Justine and Serg wanted him to replace Philip as the Martiniere. Could he do it?

Gabriel Marcus Martiniere Ramirez, you've got to stop running someday, he told himself.

Running had cost him that beautiful woman sleeping in the bed next to his chair and the early years with their son Brandon. Their reunion—even if it was just on the professional level—was a gift that he couldn't believe was real. Could there be more to it? Could he and Ruby ever be other than business partners again?

He'd have to beg one fuck of a lot of forgiveness for the crap he'd given her during their divorce twenty-one years ago to make it happen. Apologize like hell for running. Ruby didn't forgive easily. She'd make him fight for her absolution.

But she's well worth the battle.

He sighed and eased his way out of the bathroom, soft-footing it to the door, not feeling much like fighting too many more battles tonight. As restless as he felt after the adrenaline of successfully pulling off that Superhero competition hack, then telling Philip to go to hell afterward, and everything else wrapped up in that, he wasn't going back to sleep any fucking time soon.

Too many sleepless nights after Rachel's death had taught him that. He might as well see if he could find some alcohol in the kitchen. Too cold tonight for his favorite spot here at Ruby's Double R, the front porch, sitting in a rocker and gazing at those gorgeous, gorgeous Thunder Mountains in the moonlight. Ruby understood his need to sit outside on rough nights, unlike Rachel.

Rachel. The gnawing ache in his soul after her death was finally fading, especially now that he and Ruby were—friends again.

Rachel could never have been the Martiniere's wife. And while he'd loved Rachel, she was still a pale second to Ruby. Rachel put him back together after what he'd done to Ruby in the divorce.

But Rachel wasn't the rodeo queen he'd wooed. Ruby had held his heart. Still held his heart after all these years.

He could do it again. It might take a while, but he could win her back. After all, he'd won Ruby over once before, even if Ron Ryder had never quite completely yielded. She'd had to face the tough old fart down just like she had Philip—

A quick memory flash of Ruby slapping Philip before Philip could hit her made him grin. God damn, he loved that woman. Pulled a gun on the head of the Martiniere Group without hesitation, in spite of his uncle's vindictive reputation. Stood up to him.

Why had he ever thought that running to keep her and Brandon safe was the smart thing to do?

No answer for that.

Light spilled from the kitchen as he walked down the hallway, reminiscent of those nights with Ron Ryder when the old man couldn't sleep, along. Those nights they'd shared beers. He wondered who was in the kitchen. Maybe Brandon?

He pushed the swinging door open. Justine sat at the old green Formica and chrome kitchen table, a bottle of whisky next to her as she studied her screens.

"Don't you know only the lower classes drink straight from the bottle?" he said, just like Philip would say when he caught them doing something that he considered to be *déclassé,* and not worthy of the high status of a Martiniere.

Justine startled. "Fuck, Gabie. I forgot how quiet you can move." She shuddered. "And the way you look now, with that voice...*fuck.* For a minute I thought you were Daddy-poo."

Gabe snorted. He plopped in a chair across from her and swiped the bottle. "So you have those nightmares too."

He took a long swig, cowboy-style, coughing a little and wiping his mouth. *Good* whisky. He checked the label. The real thing.

Probably shouldn't be chugging it like this.

Then again, why the fuck not? If it hadn't been for Justine, things could have easily ended up with all three of them—him, Ruby, and Brandon—dead.

And there it was in a nutshell. Why he'd urged Ruby to take that pill, and why he couldn't sleep. Probably the same for Tine. She could have easily ended up dead too. His old pet name for her came back smoothly.

"And more." Justine grimaced and dismissed her screens. "Thirty more years of it since we last saw each other." She reached out a hand. "Gimme. Don't bogart the fucking Highland Park. That's the last bottle I have. Will ever have, thanks to fucking global warming."

Gabe took another long guzzle before passing it back. "Maybe we need to get soused on something less rare. Ruby's got home brew around here somewhere. Distilled by her lab manager from grains grown on site. It's got a kick."

"Eh, fuck, your return to the Family is worth the good stuff, Gabie. And watching your Ruby and your son in action is priceless."

"She's not my Ruby again, Tine. At least not yet." He took the bottle back from Justine, sipping this time. Such good booze should be savored.

Justine arched a brow at him—oh God, how he had missed this cousin, one of the few Family members he had been able to trust. But it hadn't been safe to depend on her at the end. Not for her sake.

"You haven't noticed the way she looks at you."

"Pish." Gabe exhaled through his teeth. "I've a lot to make up for. I treated her like shit during the divorce."

"Yeah. Been reading about it." Justine took the bottle back. "You were a complete *cochon*. A total *connard*."

The language came back to him easily. "But I'm not the son of that son of a bitch," he said to her in French.

She flinched at that. "Still doesn't justify what you did to her." Still in French.

He sighed. "And I probably deserve every fucking epithet you can think of in both English and French for the way I treated Ruby back then," he said in English. He took another big gulp of the whisky and pushed it back across the table to Justine. "I could spend the rest of my life doing what I could to make it all up to her and it wouldn't be enough."

Justine sighed. "Eh, Gabie. The past is past. What's ahead of us?"

"I don't know." He examined his hands. "I honestly don't know how long I can keep ahead of the post-G9 syndrome."

"I have access to Dr. Chan."

That brought him up with a jolt. "Dr. Chan? Of the Chan Protocol?"

"The very same."

Now that was a twist on things. "I couldn't qualify for it before. My condition wasn't severe enough."

"There are other things that can be done. Medications."

He shook his head. "Cost...." He stopped. He had access to the twenty million dollars from his trust fund now. And now that he'd activated the account, income was flowing into that fund. He'd checked it again before going to bed. After thirty years away from the Family, living hard, living tight, to suddenly realize that financial strictures no longer existed was a shock.

Justine gave him a measured look. "You *have* been away, haven't you?"

He took another sip and exhaled even more deeply. He was a Martiniere again. Martinieres didn't think about the cost of things. They didn't have to. "It's been a long time on the run from who I am, Tine."

"Can't say as I blame you."

"I still have the scars."

She flinched again. Philip had beaten him multiple times for slight infractions, but the biggest had been when Gabe had helped Justine evade Walter Braun, the man Philip had wanted her to marry. He could have filed assault charges against his uncle. But all of them knew better.

It had been one of the brightest days of his life when Tine married Donald Atwood and escaped Philip's clutches. Almost as good as the night he first saw Ruby.

"So what is going to happen?" Justine asked. "Are you going to challenge Daddy-poo?"

"I need data," he said. "The information that you and Brandon and Kris have to tell me. And I don't want to think about it tonight, or else I could drain that fucking bottle and still not sleep. Tonight was so fucking close. I heard the Grim Reaper whispering my name. If you and Serg hadn't been there—"

"Yeah." Justine sighed. "So. Ruby."

"Ruby," he sighed in echo. "Tine, I really fucked things up when I ran from her. And I don't know if I can make it better. I want to make it better. But Ruby isn't just someone you can buy. Or steamroll."

A smile pulled Justine's lips slowly upward. "God. She is a prize, Gabie. I *loved* it when she slapped Daddy dearest. That look on his face was priceless. You'd be a fool to let her get away from you."

"I'm gonna try to get her back if it's the last thing I do."

And even as he said it, he realized it was a promise to whatever future he had left.

Like what you've read? Want to follow Joyce either through her monthly newsletter or through an email feed of her irregular blog posts?

Sign up for Joyce's newsletter here:

https://tinyletter.com/JoyceReynolds-Ward

Sign up for blog posts through Substack here:

https://joycereynoldsward.substack.com/welcome

Interested in further serial stories in the Martiniere Multiverse? Check out Martiniere Stories on Substack.

https://joycef1d.substack.com/p/an-introduction-to-martiniere-stories

Acknowledgments

First of all, I want to thank my friend, mentor, and marvelous editor, Phyllis Irene Radford. Phyl helped brainstorm some tough sections of the world of *The Martiniere Legacy*, and brought a sharp eye to the edits.

Roslyn McFarland did a wonderful job on the cover, as always.

Vixen Radford-Wecks for late-night advice via Facebook Messenger about the pickup ride scene—but any mistakes are mine, not hers!

My dear husband Lew for putting up with my obsessive writing behavior and providing the necessary feed and care for the focused writer.

My opinionated but still energetic Quarter Horse mare in her 20th year, Miss Olena Chic (Mocha), for the good mind-clearing rides and reality checks.

Erl McLoughlin for a long chat about wheat farming and agricultural technology at one of the local Christmas bazaars, when I was still figuring out what this story was going to be about.

Afternotes, Influences, and Music

I started this book in January, 2020, just before Covid-19 struck. At first it was going to be nothing more than a stand-alone submission project to break into traditional publishing. However, as I wrote, Covid-19 became more of a reality.

I didn't incorporate a lot of C-19 into this book, simply because even as I write this now, in late August of 2020, we just don't know what the long-term impacts will be. I did add small touches. I will say that Gabe's G9 illness was influenced more by polio than C-19. I knew several people who were impacted by polio long-term aftereffects when I was younger.

At the same time, Gabe resisted the easy pigeonhole that slotted him into being That Sleazy Bad Cheating Ex. He started yelling at me that *he had damned good reasons to act the way he did,* and I needed to figure them out because he wasn't going to tell me why just right away. In the process of figuring it out, I realized that this story was bigger than a single book could cover.

"Martiniere" comes from a Victoria Holt book about Marie Antoinette, and refers to the name of one of her doctors. I always wanted to use that last name, and, well...here it is.

Other influences—regular reading of the email newsletter AgFunderNews. Following several farming groups online. Initial reports of "right to repair" issues involving farming equipment. Marital connections to the Tillamook Cheese Co-op. Life in a rodeo town. A fondness for Western riding disciplines, which includes years of reading the *Western Horseman* magazine. In recent years *Western Horseman* has featured interviews with tough ranchwomen like Ruby, and I drew upon my memories of those interviews in creating her.

Musical influences:

"Last Plane Out," as performed by Toy Matinee.

"Delicate Sound of Thunder" concert, performed by Pink Floyd.

"Wolf Totem," by The Hu.

Assorted songs by Hanggai.

Assorted songs by Hassak.

Willie Nelson.

The Martiniere Legacy

First Meetings: A Martiniere Legacy Short Story
Inheritance: The Martiniere Legacy Book One
Ascendant: The Martiniere Legacy Book Two
Realization: The Martiniere Legacy Book Three
A Belated Christmas Honeymoon: A Martiniere Legacy Short Story
The Enduring Legacy: The Martiniere Legacy Book Four

The People of the Martiniere Legacy

The Heritage of Michael Martiniere: A Martiniere Legacy Novel
Broken Angel: The Lost Years of Gabriel Martiniere: A Martiniere Legacy Novel
Justine Fixes Everything: Reflections on Mortality

The Martiniere Multiverse Books

A Different Life—What If?
A Different Life—Now. Always. Forever.
Dreamwalker: Gabriel (to be determined)
The Cost of Power (to be determined)

Goddess's Honor titles currently available (chronological order):

The Goddess's Choice: A Goddess's Honor Short Story
Beyond Honor: A Goddess's Honor Novella
Exile's Honor: A Goddess's Honor Novelette
Birth of Sorrow: A Goddess's Honor Short Story
Pledges of Honor: Goddess's Honor Book One
Return to Wickmasa: A Goddess's Honor Short Story
Crown Anniversary: A Goddess's Honor Short Story
Challenges of Honor: Goddess's Honor Book Two
Cleaning House: A Goddess's Honor Outtake Story
Unexpected Alliances: A Goddess's Honor Rough Draft Outtake Story
Choices of Honor: Goddess's Honor Book Three
Judgment of Honor: Goddess's Honor Book Four

Netwalk Sequence Author Preferred 2022 Editions

Life in the Shadows: Book One
Netwalk: Book Two
Netwalker Uprising: Book Three
Netwalk's Children: Book Four
Learning in Space: Book Five
Netwalking Space: Book Six
The Netwalk Sequence Box Set

Bright Star Fair Witches

Becoming Solo: A Bright Star Fair Witches Novella

Non-Series Titles currently available:

Alien Savvy: A Western SF Novella
Klone's Stronghold

Beating the Apocalypse

Vella Titles:
Falcon of the Martinieres (part of *Justine Fixes Everything*)
Bearing Witness
Beating the Apocalypse
A Different Life—What If? An Alternative Martiniere Legacy Novel
Becoming Solo: A Bright Star Fair Witches Novella
A Different Life—Linda's Story: An Alternative Martiniere Legacy Novel

Audiobooks Available:
Alien Savvy: A Western SF Novella

Released from other publishers:
"Queen of the Snows," in *Once Upon A Winter: A Folk and Fairy Tale Anthology*, edited by H. L. Macfarlane
"My Man Left Me, My Dog Hates Me, and There Goes My Truck," in *Black-Eyed Peas on New Year's Day: An Anthology of Hope*, edited by Shannon Page
"Lost Loves," in *All Worlds Wayfarer*
"The Wisdom of Robins," in *Whimsical Beasts: A Campcon Anthology*, edited by Joyce Reynolds-Ward
"The Cow at the End of the World," in *Well...It's Your Cow*, edited by Frog Jones
"To Plant or Pull Up Stakes," in *Pulling Up Stakes: A Campcon Anthology*, edited by Joyce Reynolds-Ward
"The Notice," in *Children of a Different Sky*, edited by Alma Alexander

ABOUT THE AUTHOR

Joyce Reynolds-Ward has been called "the best writer I've never heard of" by one reviewer. Her work includes themes of high-stakes family and political conflict, digital sentience, personal agency and control, realistic strong women, and (whenever possible) horses. She is the author of *The Netwalk Sequence* series, the *Goddess's Honor* series, and the recently released *The Martiniere Legacy* series as well as standalones *Klone's Stronghold, Alien Savvy,* and *Beating the Apocalypse.* Samples of her Martiniere short stories/novel in progress and her nonfiction can be found on Substack at either Speculations from the Wide Open Spaces (general, writing) or Martiniere Stories (fiction). Joyce is a Self-Published Fantasy BlogOff Semifinalist, a Writers of the Future SemiFinalist, and an Anthology Builder Finalist. She is the Secretary of the Northwest Independent Writers Association, a member of the Science Fiction and Fantasy Writers Association, and a member of Soroptimists International.

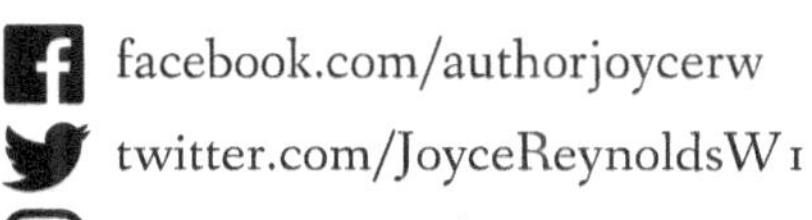

facebook.com/authorjoycerw

twitter.com/JoyceReynoldsW1

instagram.com/Instagram.com,jreynoldsward